Praise for

A Heart Set Free

"Wow! Rhine's novels are difficult to put down and *A Heart Set Free* was no exception. We suffered along with Ruth Anne as she held on to the hope for better days—we experienced her fear as the abuse escalated—and we rejoiced with both of them as the Word of God brought about change. I love the way Donna brought the story's message and scripture together."

Becky & Stan Shadbolt

"*A Heart Set Free* takes a hard look at how abuse of any kind destroys the soul of both the abuser and the victim and challenges those who know God's redeeming love to be active in the ministry of reconciliation. What a reminder of God's redeeming love and grace ... only He can take two broken lives and blend them into one in Him. Rhine reminds us that the truth spoken in love can bring healing and wholeness. II Corinthians, 5: 18-19 (NIV) '*All this is from God, who reconciled us to himself through Christ and gave us the ministry of reconciliation: that God was reconciling the world to himself in Christ, not counting people's sins against them. And he has committed to us the message of reconciliation.*'"

Betty McDonald

A Heart Set Free

Donna Rhine

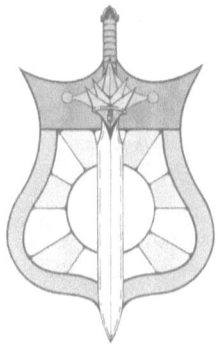

© 2014 Donna Rhine

Published by:
Armoury House Publishing
P.O. Box 60
Carleton, MI 48117 USA

http://www.ahpsite.com

ISBN-10: 0-692-021906
ISBN-13: 978-0-692-02190-3

Library of Congress Control Number:

All scripture quotations, unless otherwise indicated, are taken from The King James Version of the Bible.

Author: Donna Rhine
Cover: Stephen Rhine, James Dunayski, Chamira Jones
Editor: Rebecca Hayward, Kathryn MacDonald, Stephen Rhine
First U.S. Edition 2014

Cataloging Data

Rhine, Donna, 1958-
  A heart set free / by Donna Rhine. -- 1st U.S. ed.
    p. cm.
  ISBN-13: 978-0-692-02190-3 (pbk. : alk. paper)
  ISBN-10: 0-692-021906 (pbk. : alk. paper)
  1. Marriage--Fiction. 2. Runaway--Fiction. 3. Frontier and
pioneer life--Michigan--Fiction. 4. Step Family--Fiction. 5. Domestic
fiction. I. Title.

For current information about releases by Donna Rhine or other releases from Armoury House Publishing, visit the author's Web site: http://www.daisytales.com or http://www.ahpsite.com

Printed in the United States of America
tv5 05JUN20
cv2 05JUN15

Dedicated to …

My Lord and Savior Jesus Christ, the innocent Son of God.
Who suffered unto death for the sins of mankind!

And to the victims of abuse.

Jesus came to heal the broken hearted.
He alone can set captives free.
Let me assure you,
when the Son of God sets you free,
you are free indeed!

In our weakness,
He is made strong ....

Words from Donna Rhine

The message woven through this novel came to me in a dream so vivid it shook me from my slumber. As hard as I tried to lay it aside, I could not slough off the impact it had on me.

Lo and behold, the next night I awoke after the same dream. I wondered if God was telling me to write, but I convinced myself I had to be hearing Him wrong. Sound familiar? Why would He ask me, a woman blessed with a kind and loving husband to write a novel about abuse? Perhaps my exposure to various forms of abuse down through the years would help to guide me, but I didn't think for a quick second that qualified me. Still, I did nothing with it.

However, when I had the same dream for the third night, I did not go back to sleep. I crawled out of bed in the wee hours of the morning and went to my laptop. There was no doubt in my mind what must be done. How was still a bit fuzzy, but who could sleep at a time like this?

Often the warning signs of abuse are present early on in a relationship, but for one reason or another warning signs are ignored or excused. As a result, many are in the throes of abusive relationships or marriages, feeling trapped or alone with nowhere to turn. Please! I beg you! Don't believe that lie. You are not trapped or alone, but you must take the first step and seek help.

It is for those who are hurting that I take this leap of faith. My prayer is that you will turn to God for comfort. His love is constant and freely given without conditions.

Is there hope for restoration? Yes, with God all things are possible. If change were not possible, God never would have said to: "Let all bitterness, and wrath, and anger, and clamour, and evil speaking, be put away from you, with all malice" —Ephsians 4:31. However, we are wise to remember that God will not work against our will. Change can occur, but only if the abusers, and his or her victims, are willing to take the steps necessary toward healing and restoration.

I challenge you as I have been challenged to look beneath the surface when dealing with the human heart ... there is more than meets the eye. Never forget that many abusers were once victims themselves. While we know that love overcomes a multitude of sins, the ability to love all men as Christ commands is not easy— even so, our inability does not alter God's call ....

The trials of life often take us by storm.
  Without warning we are thrust in their midst.
To curse or praise in times like these.
  The response is up to us.

Will your trials make you bitter or better?
  Will they bind you or set you free?
The choice is yours, but choose wisely, Friend,
  Middle ground is a raging sea.

by:
    Rebecca Hayward,
    Donna, and Joshua Rhine

Acknowledgments

Writing this novel has taken me down many paths. If given the choice, I would have avoided some of them, but I am richer for having walked them.

It was during the writing of this novel that I lost my precious mother. Although my loss was heaven's gain, experiencing grief on such a personal level has given me a greater understanding of the way God works. I could not change the circumstances surrounding her death—they were out of my control—but walking through this fire has taught me more of the nature of man and the things that God allows so that His Grace may abound.

Lord, thank you for using Your Word, the experiences, deep hurts, and trials in this life to draw me closer to you—thus fanning the flames of the gifts You have given. My heart is overwhelmed by Your goodness.

It is no coincidence that God has brought many along on this journey who enrich, encourage, and strengthen my faith. What a joy!

Stephen, my cherished husband, through the many trials and victories, the depth of love and oneness we share has deepened further still. I am so blessed.

I am very thankful for the amazing love shed abroad in my heart through His children! I have been and continue to be touched immensely by your expressions of love—the greatest gift any of us can offer.

For everyone who has been there, supporting and praying for me along the way, I am truly thankful.

Pastor Rocky Barra, thank you for allowing me to weave your life-giving messages throughout this novel.

Without the teachings of the A.A.C.C., June Hunt, Roy Thomas Sr., Jennifer Schmatz, Shari Cornell, and many others in the counseling ministry who have contributed throughout my life's journey, this novel would not have been possible. Thank you for allowing His Spirit to flow freely through you.

Linda Smith, thank you for your help in building Samuel's character. Your counsel was invaluable.

James Dunayski, thank you for sharing your illustration gifts, I continue to be blessed by your efforts. Chamira Jones, your finishing touches are amazing.

To my editor, Rebecca Hayward, and copy editors, Kathy MacDonald, Sue Andrews, and Stephen Rhine, thank you! Your input and hours of hard work is so appreciated.

Blessings and much love,

Donna Rhine

A Heart Set Free

Contents

THE Michigan Chronicles

The Michigan Chronicles are a collection of stories from the days of yesteryear. The adventures begin in the nineteenth century, with two families farming in a small pioneer community nestled along the Huron River. The site, now known as Ypsilanti, is where the old Indian trail crossed over the Huron River. Come travel to a place in time where life was simpler ....

He Loves Me!

Chapter One

Somewhat Unscathed
Detroit, Michigan
Summer of 1792

"'BOUT TIME you crawled out of bed!" Florence Schmidt chided, as her daughter meandered into the kitchen looking all disheveled.

Ruth Anne yawned and after a nice long stretch admitted, "You and Papa wore me out with that silly game we played last night."

Smiling, her mother's glistening eyes met hers. "We did have fun, didn't we?"

"Umm hmm ..." Ruth, giggled in remembrance as she poured herself a cup of tea, savoring a few sips while her mama proceeded to fill a basket with baked goods. "Where are you off to so early this morning?"

Placing the last of the muffins in the basket, she looked up at her daughter. "Paul came by an hour ago. Meg's in labor."

Excitement danced in Ruth's eyes. "That is good news!"

"Sure is. Listen, Honey, there's no telling how long I'll be away, so I'm counting on you to help Papa in my absence."

Ruth, hearing strain in her mama's voice, asked, "Help him with what?"

Florence snatched her cream shawl off the hook, slipped it around her shoulders, and said, "Mr. White and his son Samuel will be coming by this afternoon to look at the team Papa's hoping to sell."

Thoughtful, Ruth reached for one of her mama's yummy, cinnamon-apple fritters, took a seat at the table, bowed her head and offered up thanks. As she took her first bite, her mind went to the young man her mama spoke of. The rumors she had heard were enough to give her pause. Even so, mentioning them would not be wise. Her mama had no tolerance for tall tales, even if they were true. "I've heard of the Whites from some of my friends, but I don't recall meeting them."

"I don't believe you have, but that's neither here nor there. Papa will expect you to serve refreshments. You could make a nice big batch of those tasty sugar cookies. They always go over well."

Ruth nodded in agreement; however, she was all too aware, her mother was not telling all. "Mama ..."

Florence's hand came up to forestall her questions. "I really should be on my way, Ruth. Meg needs me. Papa mentioned that he has business to discuss with Mr. White, so don't give him a hard time about entertaining young Samuel on the porch."

"Oh, Mama ..." she grumbled, "do I have to?"

The scowl that erupted on Florence's face exclaimed her displeasure. "Ruth Anne Schmidt! What has gotten into you?"

Her eyes lowered and then rose to meet her mama's uncompromising glare. "Sorry ... woke up on the wrong side of the bed, I suppose. Don't worry about Papa's guests. I'll see to them. You just take good care of Meg, and give my little buddy Brent a big squeeze from me."

"Thanks, Honey, I will." Florence picked up the basket of food, secured it on her arm, and glanced back at Ruth. "I have lemons in the pantry, so make a pitcher of lemonade to serve with the cookies."

"Sounds wonderful ... If Papa's guests leave before it gets too late, I'll ride over to see how Meg's coming along."

Florence's smile was tender. Ruth's spunk could chafe at times, but her heart was as big as the moon and Florence cherished her. Though she still had a bit of growing up to do, Florence clung to the few threads not yet severed from Ruth's childhood. "That's fine, but keep in mind, supper will be your responsibility. Delivering babies is no easy task. I'll have to rest when I return home."

Ruth's head had no more dipped in acquiescence when Florence walked out the door.

The morning passed in a whirl of hard work and preparation. The house was tidy, the porch swept, and the cookies were neatly arranged on two of Grandma's fancy plates from the china cabinet. Ruth's stomach ached from overindulging in the tasty confections as they came out of the oven, but she would have to make the best of it. Her papa was depending on her. A quick glance around their humble home told her he would be pleased with her efforts.

If her mama's predictions were right, she'd be stuck entertaining young Samuel while their fathers discussed business. Although she didn't care for the idea, her anguish would end in a few short hours. Even she could survive that.

As Ruth climbed the creaky steps to wash up and put on a dress her papa would deem acceptable, she mulled over the rumors she had heard about the young man she was about to meet. Could they be true? Perhaps her overactive mind added to her surmise, but one could not be too careful these days. Detroit's unwillingness to surrender to the Americans continued to weaken the confidence the settlers had in one other. She had heard the whispered accounts of those who would gladly send the British packing, but few were brave enough to voice their treasonous thoughts. Even laying political unrest aside, this young man's actions raised her hackles.

Constance, one of her dearest friends, had mentioned meeting Samuel in town a few weeks back. Although dreamy-eyed when describing his handsome features, she did not hesitate to elaborate on his less desirable qualities as well. In truth, her animated description had given Ruth something to giggle about for days.

Her mama had told her often enough not to believe everything she hears. *"Talebearers,"* she would insist, *"rarely speak the truth. They often embellish stories to make them sound more interesting."* It was her mama's final assessment whenever they had this discussion that gave Ruth pause, *"Those who listen to such tales are just as sinful as those who tell them."*

Well, I guess I'm a sinner, 'cause I couldn't help listening when Constance went on and on about young Samuel. I paid close attention 'cause I was sure her words had merit. Besides, if only a portion of the things she said were true, I'd be wise to take heed—especially now that I'm about to meet him.

"Ruth Anne!" her papa called from the base of the stairs, jolting her out of her *sinful* musings. "Quit dawdling, Girl ... get yourself down here. Our guests have arrived."

"Coming, Papa." Although a patient man, when he spoke in that tone Ruth knew better than to keep him waiting. Fastening her black boots, she took a quick peek at her reflection in the mirror and flounced down the narrow flight of stairs.

After catching her papa's eye, she spun around expecting him to comment on her appearance. When he did not, she could only assume his mind was otherwise occupied.

Gerald held out his hand and urged, "Come on, Ruth Anne! They're standing in the yard waiting to meet you."

"Me, Papa ..?" *I thought they were coming to see horses?* Ruth's thoughts were suddenly all in a dither, and her papa's silence as he led her out the door did nothing to ease her disquieted mind.

The humid breeze swirled her silky curls as they stepped off the porch and into the yard. Although the stifling heat was almost unbearable, the gray clouds moving in held the promise of rain. After a week of sweltering temperatures, a downpour would be a welcome relief.

"Hello!" Gerald said as he and Ruth approached their guests. Wrapping his arm around Ruth's shoulder, he drew her close. "I don't believe either of you have met my lovely daughter, Ruth Anne."

The elderly gentleman offered Ruth a cursory nod before he glanced at his son and said, "I'm Mr. White, and this here is my son, Samuel."

"Nice to meet you," Ruth murmured, barely noticing

the younger man because her thoughts were held captive the moment Mr. White spoke. *Never in all my days have I heard a voice so deep—so raspy.* Allowing her mind to wander could get her into trouble, but this time she couldn't help it. The thought of this man raising his voice in song at Sunday meeting' tickled her right down to her toes. *Why he'd frighten every child within range.* Her fingers came up to cover her mouth. Considering the circumstances, she deemed it wise to restrain the giggles bubbling up. Good thing she did, 'cause her pa sent her the evil eye. He must not have been pleased with the way she was gawking.

"Ruth Anne!" he admonished, "what has gotten in to you?"

She flushed and eyes filled with uncertainty met his. "Nothing worth mentioning, Papa ...."

"Then pay attention! Your guest is speaking to you."

"Oh!" *He's your guest, not mine,* her thoughts amended as her eyes swept over her papa's guest. Although speaking her thoughts out loud would be untoward, she did wonder if her papa believed she would have anything to do with this ignoble, albeit handsome young buck if he and his father were not guests and potential buyers for the team. Perhaps her mother was right. She should not judge him too hastily.

"Ruth Anne," Gerald said, "Mr. White and I have business to discuss. Will you be a dear and show Samuel the team?"

"Sure ..." she agreed, with much reluctance. However, she was unprepared for the butterflies that took flight in her stomach as she stole another peek at the young man standing so near. His tall masculine build was a sight to behold, and those deep brown eyes, so probing, set her on edge. As if her insides were not unsteady enough, the beat of her heart increased tenfold when he claimed her hand and bowed to kiss the back of it—as if he were a lord, and she a lady of the realm. It was all done so quick and sheepish-like she wasn't given the chance to deny him the pleasure.

"I've been looking forward to meeting you for some time, Ruth Anne."

"You have?" Staggered by his admission, she could not look away.

In Samuel's reluctance to release her, he enclosed her hand in his and gave it a gentle squeeze, marveling at its softness. "Your father does nothing with haste, Ruth Anne, but now that we've met I can see why."

Her face snarled quizzically.

The radiant sun slid out from behind a cloud, obstructing Samuel's vision. After readjusting his stance to gain a better view of his lovely companion, he offered an endearing smile. "I didn't think it was possible, but you're even prettier close up."

"What?" His straightforward appraisal caught her off guard. Try as she did to slough off the odd feelings stirring inside, the way he ogled her made that impossible. If only the warmth trailing up her neck would ease. Her hope of being rescued from this audacious man dissipated swiftly—as her papa and Mr. White walked away.

Ruth chanced another peek at Samuel's unreadable features and knew she had never laid eyes on him before, of that she was sure. "You must be mistaken. I've never met you before."

"Not face to face."

Her eyes rolled and her head swayed. "What other way is there, Mr. White?" For ten bold seconds, she glared at her papa's overzealous guest. Although attractive, his amiable façade did not fool her. Not in the least. Being a fairly good judge of character, she found him arrogant, an attribute she could not abide. Since it was possible the rumors she had heard added to her surmise, she attempted to give him the benefit of overwhelming doubt.

However, Samuel confirmed her first suspicions when he took a firm hold on her arm and led her toward the barn. Annoyed and somewhat frightened by his forcefulness, she tried to break free, but the pompous toad would not release her. She considered giving him a piece of her mind, but her papa heard their tussle and sent her another chiding look. At first she didn't understand. He must not be aware of the way his guest had been manhandling her. Since allowing her sharp tongue to ruin this deal would not be in her family's best interest, she swallowed her pride and attempted to be more congenial. The way Samuel strolled alongside her, one would have thought they had been courting for years and his closeness was something she should welcome.

She did not.

When he warmly met her tentative gaze, he felt her trembling and that gave him pause. Knowing so little about the fairer gender had him at a disadvantage. Had he given her cause to fear him? He thought not, but her father did say that she had never entertained gentlemen callers. Samuel smiled, thinking this was a good thing. Treading in unfamiliar waters himself, he could only hope his awkwardness would go undetected. Though propriety demanded it, he could not look away from the woman at his side. She was full of life and strikingly beautiful—all that he remembered and more.

Unable to hold his intense look, Ruth's eyelids slid shut. She even tried to pull away, but he would not release her.

The clearing of his throat brought her eyes back to his. "Ruth Anne, if you'd like me to finalize the contract with your father, you could be a bit more agreeable."

"Agreeable!" Inwardly she groaned in frustration as her hands fisted around the fabric of her dress. When he only stared, she saucily stated, "I'm not sure what you're getting at, Mr. White? You came to look at horses, not visit with me."

The negative sway of his head puzzled her all the more. The rippling of her brow while hinting at annoyance, he couldn't help but smile when her frown deepened and her upper lip came up on one side in the cutest way. If he wasn't mistaken, it took every ounce of restraint she could muster to contain her temper. "That's not entirely true. And please, call me Samuel. When I spoke to your father in town, I mentioned that I'd like us to become better acquainted. I'm hoping we might form a friendship of sorts. After all, we are neighbors."

There seemed to be a hidden meaning behind every word that came out of his mouth. If they were neighbors, she had no prior knowledge of it. She could only hope the White farm was on the other side of town. On second thought, Chicago in her estimation would be too close.

Brushing a fleck off his shirt, his deep eyes met hers. His calloused finger ran down her warm cheek. "Surely you can't expect me to make an offer without a clearer picture of what I would be gaining?"

Her lack of response must have encouraged him because his arm slid around her waist. The intensity of his look as he drew her close chilled her insides. She turned to locate her papa, but he and Mr. White were already moving into the house. Yelling seemed like a proper response, but then how would she explain Samuel's closeness? Seconds ticked awkwardly by as uncertainty plucked at her runaway heart.

Samuel, sensing her unease, attempted to reassure her, "Our fathers have details to iron out before the contracts can be signed, Ruth Anne. We'll join them as soon as you show me the team."

"If you'd be so kind as to release me, I will gladly show you to their stalls!"

But instead of releasing her, his thick finger pointed to a row of pines. "Tell me who that gawking lad is and I will."

"James!" Ruth squealed in elation. Feeling suddenly rescued, she had every intention of asking him to join them. However, when she squirmed and tried to break free, Samuel would not release her. "What are you doing?" she snarled. "Let me go!"

By the time he did, James was nowhere to be found. "Thanks a bunch!" she berated, as she gave him a sturdy shove. "You had no right to do that! James is one of my dearest friends."

Samuel harrumphed. "The way he was glaring, one would think he's your beau."

Scowling, she said, "Whether he is, or not, is no concern of yours!" Her anger at the fore, Ruth strode into the barn toward the stalls at the far end, with Samuel trailing close behind. "Zeek is on the left and Zeb is on the right. They're twins—a perfectly matched set."

Samuel opened Zeek's stall and patted his thick neck as he stepped in. The horse had a passive nature, making Samuel question his stamina, but a quick inspection of Zeek's muscular build told him otherwise. "He's a fine piece of horse flesh."

"So is Zeb."

"Would you mind if I take a look?"

She nodded tersely. "Go right ahead. Take all the time you need." Ruth moved away, stopping to inform him as she neared the barn door, "I'm heading back to the house."

Samuel chuckled softly as he watched her flee. It was obvious this porcelain beauty was not at ease in his presence, but given time ...

After looking the team over and observing the extreme difference between his own barn and this inferior one, Samuel made his way back to the house—his mind resolute. He would sign the necessary documents to proceed.

Ruth stirred sugar into a pitcher of cool water, added fresh squeezed lemon juice, and filled four tankards, leaving two on the tray for Samuel and her. Although the thought of spending more time with him did not bode well, what choice did she have? She was serving her papa and Mr. White when Samuel came in the front door and wiped his feet on the braided rug. As she added a plate of cookies to the tray, he strutted towards her with an air of familiarity. Though she refused to look up, she flinched when he slapped his leather gloves against his hand. What was it about him that put her on edge—that caused her blood to run so hot and cold?

Samuel's eyes were stayed on the beautiful young woman before him. Not even her timid look dissuaded him when the desire to touch her prevailed. Slowly, running his knuckles along her jaw, he leaned close, whispering, "Your skin is so soft, My Dear."

My Dear? Her cheeks flamed on his audacious declaration. Try as she did to put his endearing words aside, they taunted her. She had never met anyone like him. As if the way he gawked was not irritating enough, he had some kind of nerve touching her—in front of their fathers, no less. Although she ached to give him the sharp side of her tongue, her papa was watching her, closely. He would not be pleased if she gave in to that urge.

"What's the verdict, Son?"

The Verdict? Ruth's anxious mind stumbled over Mr. White's inquiry. The way Samuel's gaze held fast to hers, made her fidget something awful. *Why are you staring at me?* she silently queried, as her heart did a jig in her chest. It was the strangest moment of her life. She could not look away from this bold uncompromising man. His deviant look, combined with the suggestive wink he sent her way, did nothing to ease her disquieted mind. Her stomach churned. When her blood ran wild she was ready to bolt, but she fought against that insatiable desire. How could she leave now? Curiosity had gotten the best of her. So ... she simply busied herself with trivial things, effectively shielding her eyes from his flirtatious glances.

"I will proceed," he fervently stated.

Proceed ... with what? Ruth's thoughts whirled, as her eyelids flipped up. Unfortunately, her papa's overconfident guest gave nothing away. *His aggressive manor has me all in a twirl—for what? For nothing!* At least she hoped it was for nothing.

Samuel turned to her papa, awaiting his response.

Gerald nodded in acquiescence, saying, "Consider it done."

"Consider what done, Papa?" Timidity reigned as Ruth inquired, but her words had fallen on deaf ears. Her papa did not so much at glance her way.

Samuel went to the table, his brow furrowed as he looked down at the scattered documents. "Where do I sign?"

She never would have thought the sale of a team could be so involved. Samuel put his signature in several places before her papa and Mr. White got to talking again, leaving her in the lurch. Needing to allay the thunderous beat of her heart, she assured herself; *they must be referring to the horses.* Giggling nervously, her thoughts confirming, *that is why they are here, is it not?*

Gerald looked up when young Samuel offered to carry the refreshments to the porch for his daughter. While the gesture pleased Gerald, Ruth was exasperated. The display this rogue put on for her papa made her ill. Samuel, though he hid behind the mask of a well-bred gentleman, did not fool her—not in the least. Despite the fact that spending time with him was the last thing she wanted to do, Ruth swallowed her pride yet again and followed him out the door.

Samuel put the tray down on the small table and waited for her to take a seat. When she opted for the double swing, he came toward her, so she moved to the rocker instead. That she had to visit with him was one thing, sitting close for the next hour would put her stomach in more knots than it was already in.

Samuel, all too aware of her evasive move, grinned shamelessly when she skillfully avoided his watchful eyes. In truth, he didn't mind. He saw her timidity as a good thing.

While they sipped lemonade and nibbled on cookies, he carried the conversation for the most part, going on and on about his farm and the new house he had built. The way he talked, it sounded more like a castle than a home. Why he found it necessary to tell her about every detail was beyond her. Before long, Ruth was bored senseless. And, it didn't take long to come to the conclusion that her friend's description of Samuel had been *much* too kind.

The afternoon dragged on as their fathers took what seemed like an excessive amount of time conducting business. Although her relief was great when Samuel and his father finally bid them good day, they left without taking the horses.

"Papa, I thought they were buying the team?"

He wrapped his arm around her, squeezed her tight, and held the door so she could precede him. "The Whites and I have entered into an agreement that has put my mind at ease. No need to concern yourself, Ruth Anne, just leave everything to me."

"But, Papa ..?"

"Not now, Honey."

She would have grilled him further, but his extended meeting had put him behind in his chores. While he would never admit it, he seemed a bit under the weather of late. Instead of pressing him, Ruth went to the kitchen and began preparations for their evening meal. She was weary. Entertaining her papa's guest had not been without challenges, but there was much to do in her mama's absence. As she secured her apron, she whispered a prayer of thanks that she had survived the afternoon somewhat unscathed—and that she would never have to endure Samuel White again.

Chapter Two

Promises

*R*UTH'S HEART FILLED WITH JOY as she leapt off the porch and headed for the barn. The day was near perfect. A few gray clouds dappled the pale blue sky, but she was hopeful the warm sun kissing her face would chase them away. It just had to. Her plans would not welcome a single drop.

After saddling Thunder, she rode away from home at a respectable gait. Racing off would have appeased her spirited nature, but knowing her papa could be watching kept her from giving in to that insatiable yearning. He wouldn't be pleased if she did. *"A proper lady,"* he kept reminding her, *"is never rowdy."*

Never?

Never was a long time, and besides, being proper was rarely much fun. In some ways her papa was just too old-fashioned. As much as she loved him, she refused to act all skeery and bashful just to appease his conscience. That wasn't who she was. Even so, he teased her something fierce—said she'd never catch a

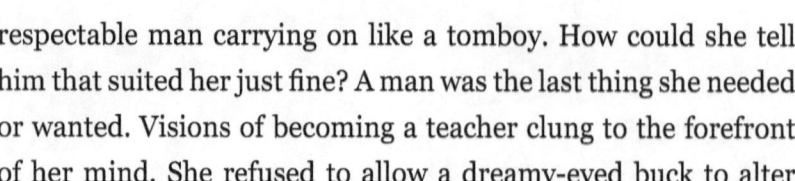

respectable man carrying on like a tomboy. How could she tell him that suited her just fine? A man was the last thing she needed or wanted. Visions of becoming a teacher clung to the forefront of her mind. She refused to allow a dreamy-eyed buck to alter her plans.

With no wish to irritate her papa, she waited till clearing her parents' farm before nudging Thunder into a canter and heading up the back trail toward town.

Today, of all days, she could not be late to school. Not only was this her last day, Constance had said that James might show up to help them move the supplies into the new schoolroom for Mr. Burns. Oh, how she prayed it would be so. After that fiasco the day when Samuel White was at her house, she had much explaining to do. She could only hope James would understand her predicament. His friendship meant too much to allow a rogue like Samuel to clog up the works.

Nearing the turn off, she was slowing Thunder to take the sharp curve when someone came around the turn at a fast clip. Thunder reared up and she was thrown. Stunned, but otherwise unharmed, she stood to her feet, shook the dust off her worn frock and stomped a few times in frustration. Reaching for her horse's reins to gentle him, large hands grasped her shoulders, but she was not frightened.

"Sor-ry, Ruthie! Wa-sn't payin tension, I sup ..." he hiccupped, "I suppose."

Rolling her eyes she bellowed! "Snaggle Tooth! I swain! If I wasn't so forgiving, I'd report you to the sheriff for drunk and disorderly conduct!" Feeling a twinge of conscience, she helped the inebriated man get back on his horse. Ruth, thinking he could use the nourishment more than she, snatched the sandwich out of her saddle bag and tucked it into his hand before sending him on his way.

Snaggle Tooth had always been an odd sort. For the most part he was harmless. Unfortunately, his drinking binges had gotten out of hand after his wife died of the influenza. Ruth's heart ached for him. The man was wasting away to nothing. When she asked her papa if he was ill, he said, "No, just heart sick. Loneliness is a terrible force to reckon with."

Ruth watched the frail man nibble on her sandwich as he moved down the path. Suddenly she was thankful for the encounter. It had given her the chance to show him a kindness.

The rest of her morning, though fairly uneventful, was hardly dull. It didn't seem to matter what she and Constance were doing, just being together brought them inexplicable joy. Their teacher was pleased with their joint efforts. The new schoolroom was clean, organized, and even the donated curtains had been hung.

After collecting their horses from the livery, Ruth and Constance headed west toward the Rouge. If their efforts in fishing were fruitful, a relaxing swim in the river would be their reward. Although her papa had predicted rain later in the day, the blazing sun seemed to mock him. In truth, Ruth hoped that he was wrong.

As Ruth and Constance rode out of town they remained on their guard. Though Indian attacks on settlers were rare, there were others who could wish them harm. Even so, they weren't about to let fear of the unknown spoil their day. Settling into an easy gate, they chattered away, allowing their horses to lead the way.

Ruth slid off Thunder when they reached the river and busied herself digging up worms while Constance hobbled the horses. The flourishing grass would keep the horses content while she and Constance whiled away the hours.

"Ruth," Constance asked as she came toward her with the poles, "did you see your friend watching you as we came out of the livery?"

Ruth's face snarled up. "My Friend?"

"You know ... the tall handsome one you can hardly wait to see again."

Aghast, Ruth's muddy hand came up to rest on her throat. "Samuel?"

Constance nodded. "He couldn't take his eyes off you. If you ask me, he's ..."

Ruth stomped her foot. "Don't say it, Connie! Don't you dare say it! I never want to hear another thing about him."

"All right," she agreed, a little stunned by her adamancy.

Meeting her friend's odd look, she begged, "Please, Connie, promise you won't bring him up again."

"I won't ... didn't mean to upset you."

Her mouth curved up in a feeble attempt to smile. "I'm not upset ... Perhaps a bit annoyed, but I'd rather put him out of my mind."

"That's fine. So tell me, are you disappointed James didn't come by this morning to help?"

Ruth wiped her sweaty brow with the back of her hand. "A little .... I was hoping I'd have the chance to explain what really happened the day Samuel was at my house."

"Are you sure you can?"

With her heart all a flutter, Ruth turned to find James standing a ways behind her. "I can try."

"From where I stood, the man appeared to be staking his claim."

The color in Ruth's cheeks went from a rosy pink to a deep cherry. "His arrogance astounds me!" Walking over to where James stood, she reached for his hand and squeezed tightly. "You must know I would never encourage someone like *him*."

With a tilt of his head, James admitted, "He did a good job making me jealous."

"There's no need. Samuel and his father were only there to look at the team Papa's hoping to sell."

"Are you sure?"

She was dripping with sweat from digging for worms, but her skin warmed even more. "Samuel was hoping we could be friends, but I don't see that happening ... not in this lifetime anyway." Ruth tucked his wavy blonde hair behind his ear and smiled. "My affections lean toward the gentler sort ... if you know what I mean."

"I think I do." The playful wink James sent her way put her mind at ease.

"Good!" Holding out her hand, she asked, "Are we still friends?"

Instead of shaking the offered hand, his arms wrapped around her and he hugged her tight. "For life!"

Although being in his arms was a rare delight, Ruth had no wish to give him false hope. She cared for James. Even so, she was not ready to settle down with anyone. "So ..." she asked him, and then glanced back at Constance, "are you here to help us catch supper, or did you just come to watch?"

He shrugged, "Be glad to help, but I didn't bring a pole."

"That's a lame excuse!" Constance put in.

"Did you bring two?"

"Well, no, but I have an extra hook and string."

"That'll work, now all I need is a ..." his words suddenly trailed off when he noticed the mud smears on Ruth's slender neck and forehead. "A little early in the day to be covering yourself with mud to keep the bugs off, don't you think?"

Constance said, "Ahh, but she'll make a fine sod-buster's wife, someday ...."

He nodded. "As long as her husband doesn't mind a dirty bride."

Constance countered, "Nothing a nice swim in the river won't wash away."

"Then," he announced, "we'd best get to fishing. We wouldn't want to chase dinner away when we throw her in."

"James!" Ruth berated.

Constance retorted, "Ain't no we about it, James! I learned the hard way to steer clear of your shenanigans."

He grinned. "Then perhaps I should throw you in first, Miss Prim-and-Proper!"

"Well, I never!" Her eyes filled with mischief as she glanced Ruth's way. "Maybe the two of us should gang up on him!"

He shuddered in mock fear. "Oooo! I'm really scared!"

The playful bantering made Ruth smile as she began scouring the area for a suitable pole for James.

The three of them, having known each other for years, were the best of friends. James no longer attended school, but he made it a point to seek them out when time allowed. No matter how hot the sun or deep the snow, the adventures they embarked on were memorable.

Sadness crept into Ruth's heart as she thought of all that would change over the next few years. Would the three of them be able to keep their promise not to let anything get in the way of their friendship? Her excitement over her last day of school and then going on to become a teacher diminished in the light of their friendship. Why did growing up have to come with so many drawbacks? Like she, her friends would be moving forward in their own endeavors. For all Ruth knew, she could end up teaching in another town. More than likely she would. As much as she longed to pursue her dream, doing so would come at a cost. Her parents and those she loved would have to be left behind. Could she just walk away?

For today she prayed that time would stand still—or at least slow down to a snail's pace. The dinner hour would be here before she knew it and there was yet a world of fun to unfold.

"Will this do?" Ruth asked as she came towards Constance and James. The way Constance jumped when Ruth spoke made her a tad uncomfortable. "Are you two telling tall tales about me?"

James, noting her uncertainty, said, "Connie was just mentioning the way Samuel stalks you. Should I talk to your father?"

"No! That would only make matters worse. Besides, there's no harm in looking, is there?"

"Suppose not, as long as he keeps his distance."

Ruth tried to slough off the odd sensations swirling inside her, but it wasn't easy. "He's probably afraid to approach me. I didn't exactly cave in to his overbearing manner the day he came for a visit." As if needing to convince herself, she added, "I'll have you know, I stood my ground quite fearlessly!" Ruth's outrageous scowl made James and Constance laugh out loud.

"Enough, you two! We came to have fun, not talk about *him*. Besides," she said, as she held her frayed skirt out and swayed from side to side, "If I don't catch enough fish for supper, Papa will never forgive me for wearing this lovely frock to school."

James, relishing her capricious spirit, grinned. "We can't have that!"

The three of them reached for their supplies, and had been fishing on the banks of the Rouge for some time before Constance caught the first of many victims. As it turned out, they would all be going home with enough fish to fill their families' hearty appetites.

After indulging in a cool swim, they went their separate ways. Chores would have to be tended and time had gotten away from them.

Ruth, though careful not to lose her catch, rode home at a fast clip. Her papa was stepping down off the porch when she neared the house, his expression stern. "Where have you been, Young Lady?"

She held up the string of fish and his irritation melted away. "Didn't Mama tell you I was going fishing after school?"

"Must have slipped her mind."

When Ruth nodded, he asked, "So tell me, am I seeing to Thunder or cleaning the catch?"

She smiled as she slid off her faithful horse. "Your choice!"

"In that case, I'll clean the fish. Make sure you walk him out and brush him good before bedding him down."

"I will, Papa." She could have told him there was no need to remind her—that he had taught her well—and that she was a grown woman now, but for some reason she held her thoughts. He was aware, she suspected, but wondered if watching his little girl blossom into womanhood was a difficult transition for him.

Letting go of the past was not easy for her either. Change was inevitable.

As Ruth headed into the barn, she smiled recalling the promise James had whispered in her ear, *"I'm coming by on Saturday for afternoon tea. There are a few things I should be discussing with your father."* The way he winked before riding away left her wondering about her future. If her papa decided against her becoming a teacher, her heart would be broken, but perhaps settling down with James wouldn't be so bad. After all, she did care for him. Perhaps in time love would follow.

As she brushed Thunder, the sky rumbled causing him to side step. Thankfully he only caught the edge of her boot, missing her toes entirely. After giving him a thorough brushing, she bedded him down with fresh water and hay.

Ruth had no more stepped out of the barn when rain began to fall from the sunny expanse in great abandon. Her heart leapt in anticipation of what was sure to follow. Lifting her gaze to the heavens, brilliant shards of lemon light danced in the sky as she turned slowly around until it appeared in all its glory—a rainbow. Lingering longer than she should have, Ruth found it difficult to look away from this colorful display.

The story of Noah's Ark had been one of her childhood favorites. Memories of her parents' retellings came flooding back, and once again she was caught up in the wonder of it all. As she grew older, their renditions changed. Details became more vivid and her assortment of questions would always follow. The thought of all those animals living together on the ark intrigued her. What child wouldn't be curious about such things? She viewed the great *I Am* with awe, but more than that with fear and trembling. And Noah's unshakable faith, to this day, it remained a mystery to her. Although she understood that he had to be strong or he never would have endured mans' criticism, what made his faith so strong that he would be obedient to accomplish such a task? It frightened her to learn that everyone except those on the ark had drowned because of their transgressions. Even so, she was relieved to learn that the rainbow was God's promise not to flood the earth again.

Whether true or not, she did not know, but she'd heard from a friend that if you make a wish when a rainbow appears, your wish will come true. For a long moment she closed her eyes and did just that. Perhaps it was frivolous and childish, but she couldn't resist. Her hopeful heart raced with excitement, that is, until she opened her eyes and the rainbow was gone—and with it the sun. Alarmed by the sudden darkness, she ran up the back steps and into the house. Her papa was standing at the worktable peeling potatoes and the aroma of frying fish permeated the room.

"Ruth Anne!" he gently chided, "when are you going to quit acting like a child? Look at you all dripping wet, and in that rag no less!"

"Can't go fishing in a good dress, Papa."

"True, but don't you think you're getting too old to be dancing in the rain?"

She grinned unremorsefully. "I'll never be too old to dance,

Papa! You told me so."

He stomped on the wood floor, pretending he was coming after her. Though startled, she giggled out loud. She so loved his playful heart.

"Get yourself upstairs and into dry things before you catch your death."

With caution, Ruth drew near and kissed his cheek. "I love you, Papa."

"That goes both ways .... Now, get a move on. I've got a hankering for berry pie, and I'm counting on you to put one in the oven before supper."

She, stopping at the base of the stairs and glancing back at him, admitted, "Does sound good, but aren't you forgetting one small detail?"

His head swayed from side to side. "Nope! I picked the patch behind the barn while you were off to the fishing hole."

She beamed. "You and that sweet tooth!"

His wagging finger was aimed at her. "You, Little Missy, have no room to talk."

"I suppose ... I'll have to add extra sugar. First harvest is rather tart."

"And how! You know I can't resist sampling berries while I'm picking. They sure made me pucker."

"I promise ... the pie I make won't have that effect."

He nodded. "I'll hold you to that promise."

Ruth, while changing into dry clothes, smiled as her thoughts drifted from her papa to a tall blonde gentleman who had promised to visit on Saturday for afternoon tea.

He Loves Me!

Chapter Three

Desperate for Clarity

FLORENCE SCHMIDT SLIPPED QUIETLY into her daughter's bedroom, drew back the ruffled curtains covering the narrow window and tenderly coaxed, "Ruth Anne, it's time to wake up."

"Oh, Mama," she whined, as she pulled the quilt over her head, "that dreadful sun is hurting my eyes, and besides, I'm still sleepy."

Florence patted Ruth's bare foot that was poking out of the covers. "Enough complaining! Papa has guests coming by this morning. Important ones! He expects you to have your bath out of the way before he comes in from morning chores."

Ruth frowned as she peered over the edge of her quilt. "Who is it now? Can't I just stay up here and sleep the morning away? I'll be as quite as a mouse. Promise! Your guests will never even know I'm here."

Thoughtful, Florence folded Ruth's colorful afghan and draped it over the quilt rack at the foot of the bed. Running her fingers over her own mother's handwork, she looked back at her daughter and sighed. How had time passed so quickly? Her mother had given her this afghan the day she married, and now ... "The way I hear it, they're coming to see you."

Curious, Ruth propped herself up on one elbow. "Me?"

"Us too, I suppose, but Papa has a wonderful surprise planned for you."

This news completely altered her mood. She loved surprises—good ones anyway. "Do you know what it is? Do you?"

Florence's eyes sparkled with glee. "I do ...."

"You do? Oh, tell me, Mama. Please! I'll act surprised so Papa doesn't know you told me. Promise!"

Although sorely tempted, Florence's head swayed in the negative. "Sorry, Darlin', Papa went to great lengths to plan this day. If I were to spoil his surprise, he'd skin me for sure."

Ruth's eyes rolled at her outlandish remark. "Mama you know Papa would never raise a hand to you."

Scowling, Florence scolded, "That's 'cause I do what I'm told. Now, get out of that bed and see to your bath."

Grimacing, Ruth sat up. "Oh, all right, but the minute they leave I'm heading over to Meg's. Truth is, Papa's plans are putting a crimp in mine. I promised Brent I'd help him with the garden, and I'm itching to hold that baby again. She's so sweet."

"And growing fast! Time passes too quickly when you're raising a family. Seems like yesterday I was snuggling you close in the rocker. Look at you now, you're all grown up." Florence, needing a moment to sure up her wavering emotions, gathered Ruth's dirty laundry and placed it in the corner basket. "This day will be full, Ruth Anne. You'll have to plan a visit with Meg and the children at another time."

Hearing hesitance in her mama's voice, she glanced her way, though she skillfully avoided Ruth's intuitive gaze. Something was amiss, but what she did not know. If only Ruth could read her thoughts.

"Papa would like you to wear the new dress he bought you last week. You'll find it hanging from the hook in the kitchen."

Ruth's face snarled up. "I'd never want to hurt Papa's feelings, but I tried that dress on the other day. Truth is, I felt like a peacock fanning my feathers. The puffy sleeves and ruffles with all those colors, it's too much! I was really hoping we could exchange it for a different one."

Florence's scowl was so fierce, Ruth's eyes lowered. She had gone too far. "I'm sorry. I'll do as you ask. Anyway, James might be coming by. If he does, I suppose I should look my best." *Even if I don't like that dress!*

A line of worry crossed Florence's brow. "Did James say when?"

"For afternoon tea ... I can't be sure, but I think he's sweet on me. He mentioned needing to talk to Papa about a thing or two," she shrugged, "not sure what though."

While her daughter's dreamy expression only confirmed what she had suspected all along, Florence could not allow her mind to take it in. "You need to get moving, Ruth. We mustn't keep our guests waiting."

"Just give me a minute to collect my unmentionables."

Shaking her head, Florence said, "No need. I bought you new ones. They're in the kitchen with the dress you abhor."

Regret washed over Ruth as she scooted off the bed. Would

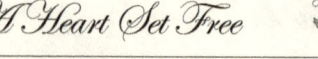

she ever learn to think before opening her mouth? "This must be some occasion for you to have gone to all this trouble."

"It is. I'm sorry we had words, Ruth Anne. I so wanted every part of this day to be special for you and ..."

Ruth was leaning over to pick up her boots when she stopped suddenly and looked up. Curious, her brow furrowed. "And who, Mama?"

Florence stammered, "Papa ... ahh, Papa will do the telling."

Her mama was acting strange and although the tears pooling in her eyes confused Ruth, she couldn't bear to think that she had caused them. "I wish I knew what has you so troubled, but if you don't want to tell me, I won't press you."

"I'll be fine, Honey. I'm just a little emotional is all."

Oh, how she wanted to ask why, but something in her mama's voice kept her from doing so. "What time will our guests arrive?"

"Right after breakfast." With tenderness, Florence reached out and touched her daughter's cheek. "I love you. I hope you know that."

Ruth's heart squeezed. "Oh, Mama, don't go getting all sentimental on me. You'll have both of us crying, and you know how Papa hates tears."

"I do." Florence pulled a hanky out of her sleeve and dabbed at the drops trailing down her face. "Go ahead and see to your bath, while I tidy up your room."

"Thanks ..."

When Ruth just stood there staring, Florence turned her away, playfully swatting her backside. "Go! Quick like!"

Ruth turned back long enough to plant a noisy kiss on her mama's cheek before flouncing down the stairs. She hoped her inflection would lighten her mama's dark mood. Whatever the day would hold, her mama was both happy and sad about it, and the knowledge of it was dreadfully unsettling.

Florence had just put the finishing touches on Ruth's ebony hair when Gerald came down the stairs all dressed up in his tan trousers and matching coatee.

"I do declare, both my girls look stunning today."

Ruth's features brightened. His opinion meant the world to her. "You look handsome yourself, Papa. Who are these guests that we must put on airs?"

Gerald glanced at his wife. "They'll be arriving any minute, Flo. Perhaps we should tell her."

"Tell me what?" Ruth's innocent inquiry made him smile as he joined her on the settee. She couldn't fathom what he was about to say, but when her mama sat down on her other side and patted her hand, signals went off in her head. Eyes, filled with uncertainty, swung from one parent to the other. "Papa, you and Mama are making me nervous."

"There's no need, Honey. It's just that you've blossomed into such a beautiful young woman. Little wonder you've captured a young man's special attention."

Her brow knit together. "A young man's what?"

Gerald swatted at the air, dismissing her question. "Mama and I have wonderful news, Ruth Anne. A fine young man has asked for your hand in marriage."

Her face snarled up. "So ..."

"So! Is that all you have to say after everything we've done to arrange this union?"

Ruth, convinced that he had to be jesting, took a moment

to really look at him. His staunch features were anything but soothing. "Papa, the only man I'm even remotely interested in is James, and he wouldn't ask for my hand—not yet anyway. He knows I intend to earn my teaching certificate before ..." Her words trailed off. He was shaking his head and his placating look set her on edge.

"Now, Ruth ... I understand that James has been a good friend, but what kind of a father would I be if I allowed you to marry someone so young—so unstable? The man I've chosen for my girl is not only financially secure, he owns a running farm with a home all ready for you to move in to."

Staggered by his admission, she could hardly breathe, never mind respond. Moments ticked awkwardly by before she managed to ask, "You chose someone without my knowledge?"

"Of course. As your father, it is my place to arrange a suitable match."

She lifted her troubled gaze to the man who had been more than a father—a confidant as well. How could he turn on her like this? "But ... but I assumed ..."

Gerald tenderly tucked a few of her soft curls behind her ears. "What did you assume?"

Still in a clouded haze, her mind took a moment to clear. "I assumed that you would allow me to choose a husband when the time was right."

His head swayed from side to side. "Oh, Honey, what would make you think that?"

"I don't know ...." She wanted to cry, scream, yell—something! Perhaps her pride was involved, but she couldn't help it. Her desire to become a teacher was supposed to shelter her from this antiquated coming of age practice. Something had gone terribly wrong.

Gerald, sensing her struggle, reached for her chin and gently brought her gaze back to his. "Ruth, your betrothed is a good man. He cares a great deal about you."

"That may be, but I'm not ready for marriage. Did you even consider how I would feel about your little *surprise*?"

Nothing was said as he scanned her delicate face. His love for his only child ran deep. Although he'd like to shelter her from the harsh realities of life, this time he could not. "You knew the answer before you asked, Ruth Anne."

A wave of guilt washed over her. He was right. As much as she loathed the idea of being any man's wife, she adored her papa. He had never given her a reason to doubt that he had her best interest at heart. She needed to hear him out. "If not James, then who?"

Ruth's inquiry made him smile. In her own way she was trying to accept his decision and the knowledge of it warmed his heart. "In truth, I've never known anyone more persistent than your betrothed." Chuckling, he admitted, "I haven't made this easy for him. Surely you know that. It took me months to even consider his offer and several more before I agreed to his terms."

Her nose snarled up. "But you could have told him no."

"Oh, Honey, how could I do that?" Caressing her cheek, he added, "He has so much to offer you—so much more than Mama and I had starting out. And, he adores you."

An uneasy hush lingered as she fought to tamp down her fears.

When Gerald could stand the silence no more, he reached for

her quivering hand and enfolded it in his. "Perhaps it was selfish to keep this from you until now, but look at you. If we would have told you sooner, you'd have been fretting until this day arrived. Mama and I wanted to enjoy our last days with you living under our roof, without anything getting in the way."

"I suppose I can understand that." She was still trying to take it all in when the words he had just spoken came to rest. "Will he come courting today? Is that why we're all dressed up?"

Gerald glanced at his wife before meeting Ruth's tentative look. "The summer months are upon us. Your betrothed has a farm to run. He doesn't have time to come courting, Ruth Anne. That's one of the reasons arranged marriages are a necessity here in Detroit. You'll have plenty of time to get to know each other after you are wed."

Wide eyes, filled with apprehension, met his. "What are you saying, Papa?"

"Today is your wedding day. He and his parents will arrive with the circuit preacher at any moment." When her features tensed, she looked ready to bolt. He tightened his grip on her hand.

"Oh, Papa! Why so soon?"

"This is how it is done. You know that. The papers have been signed. Today is the day we agreed on."

"But, I didn't agree to anything!" Her mind reeled as she thought of friends whose marriages had been arranged. Is this how they felt? At the time it all seemed so romantic, but then it wasn't her being married off to a complete stranger. No wonder they looked so nervous—so scared. "Oh, Papa, please! I can't. I just can't! When he arrives, you must tell him that you've changed your mind." Hoping her statement would put an end this twaddle, she tried to get up, but he detained her.

"Now, Ruth, I cannot, nor will I change my mind. We've surprised you is all."

"Surprised! Of course I'm surprised. I want to be a teacher. You know that. Why? Why did you even consider his offer?"

When Gerald reached to caress her cheek, she pulled away. He owed her an explanation. How could he tell her all without upsetting her further. "I did what I thought was best."

She stared at her papa, her mind a mull of confusion.

"Your desire to become a teacher is commendable, Ruth Anne, but life has a way of altering our plans. I'm afraid your needs took precedence when I made my decision."

Barely holding her emotions in check, she pressed him, "This isn't like you, Papa. What aren't you telling me?"

Gerald rubbed at his freshly shaven chin. Her insight astounded him. "This is a bit of a sticky wicket, but your betrothed has done everything I've asked of him. I cannot keep him waiting any longer."

He was skirting her question. There had to be more to this. "Papa, we've never attended church regular like, with us being so far out of town, but I remember the preacher saying that marriage is a covenant—one that's not to be entered into lightly. How can I do that if I don't know him?"

The tension in his jaw softened. "That's just it: you do know him. More than your mama and I knew each other before we were married."

"I do?" *I know him?* As her head lowered, her brow furrowed in contemplation. When it suddenly dawned on her who he could

55

be alluding to, her heart stopped and then sped out of control. With breathless anticipation, she pleaded, "Please, Papa! Tell me the man you offered my hand to is not *Samuel White* ...."

Gerald glared at Florence, who shrugged saying, "I didn't tell her. Her friends at school have been talking. Apparently her head has been filled with lies about him."

Ruth stood to face her parents, her temper scarcely contained. "That's not entirely true. I have heard rumors, but I also spent the longest afternoon of my life with *him*! Every moment we were together tried my patience. I even prayed that I'd never have to see him again, but apparently God only answers the prayers of those who talk to Him on a regular basis." She burst into tears.

When Gerald stood to gather her in his arms, she came willingly. "You've misjudged Samuel. I should know. We've met on several occasions. He's everything I could ask for in a son-in-law. Given time you'll agree."

Frantic, Ruth distanced herself, swished away her tears with the back of her hands and said, "Papa, please don't ask me to spend my life with a man I despise."

"Ruth Anne!" he admonished, "that will be enough. Things are at stake here that you know nothing about."

"What things? Tell me. Make me understand."

His features stiffened. "Not on your wedding day. You're going to have to trust me. Samuel will afford you the stability you'll need in the days ahead."

Ruth looked away in agitation. "Stability is nothing without love!"

Florence's heart ached for her daughter, but their hands really were tied. "Honey, our marriage was arranged the same way. I struggled at first, but your papa and I were committed to making a life together. The love we've shared has been rich and full. You know how happy we've been. The choice is yours—you can choose to love Samuel."

"But I don't even *like* him ...."

"Ruth Anne!" Gerald cautioned, "you mustn't talk like that." He should tell her all, but how could he without upsetting her further?

"I won't marry him!" she ardently stated.

Gerald's head tilted on her bold inflection—his eyes narrowing as he informed his defiant daughter, "I'm afraid you'll have to! You know I've always been a man of my word, and I've given it. You were standing right there when I did. The way you and Samuel were exchanging glances, I could only assume you were taken with him."

Tears filled her eyes and spilled down her face. "But he frightens me, Papa!" She would have said more, but a buggy was pulling into the yard.

All eyes turned to the door.

Their guests had arrived.

"Nooo ..!" Ruth wailed, as she ran up the steps to her room and slammed the door. Emotions transfused her on levels she never knew existed. Not only was she disheartened by her parents' news, she was petrified as well—of Samuel!

Anxiously, her thoughts questioned, *what am I going to do? A woman needs time to prepare for this step in her life .... On second thought, a lifetime wouldn't be enough to convince me to marry that, that, pompous toad! Oh, Papa, why him?* She fought against the tears threatening to choke her. There was no time for hysterics. Not now! That *horrible man* was here, in her house!

Ruth needed to think.

She had to get away.

Strange voices floating up the stairwell set her in motion. She reached for her small bag. As she shoved a few things in, a plan was formulating in her head. Opening the window, she tossed the bag out.

It landed with a thud.

Although she wondered if she would break a leg when she jumped, considering the alternative, she deemed it a worthy risk. As if the voices were not enough to throw her into a tailspin, she heard footsteps.

Someone is coming.

In a progressive panic, Ruth stuck her leg over the window ledge. She was attempting to curl the other one up enough to squeeze through the small opening when someone knocked. Startled, she slipped, but recovered quickly. In fact, she was hanging from the window frame, trying to convince herself to let go when she heard the latch on the door lift.

The floorboards creaked.

Her heart raced.

It was now or never.

She let go of the frame, but her body suddenly jerked. *Oh, no!* she exclaimed, though only in her brain. Her arm was caught in a vice-like grip ....

Chapter Four

Vulnerable and Out of Control

*For our light affliction, which is but for a moment,
worketh for us a far more exceeding and eternal weight
of glory;*

- II Corinthians 4:17

SECONDS TICKED BY before Ruth summoned
the fortitude to look up. When she did she was staring
into the pointed glower of the man she was slated to wed. She
opened her mouth to speak, but Samuel beat her to it.

"Now where would you be going in such a big hurry, My
Daring Porcelain Beauty? Our wedding is today. It would never
do to have my bride running off, now would it?"

Ruth was still dangling from one arm, struggling to loosen
his grasp with her free hand when he captured that one as
well. No holds barred, her mouth opened wide and words that
surprised even her flew out, "I'm *not* your daring anything, and
I'm definitely not your *bride*! You let me go you—you, Yellow
Bellied Two Faced Snake!"

"Ruth Anne," he countered, his words dripping with
sarcasm, "so nice of you to go out of your way to welcome me this
fine morning."

As if her anger were not already at the fore, his raised brow and mocking grin infuriated her all the more. "You may have honey-fuggled my papa, *Samuel White*, but you don't fool me. I know what you're like. You're crazier than a loon if you think I'd marry the likes of you!"

While it was not without effort, Samuel managed to pull his disinclined fiancée back in through the small window. However, her feet had no more touched the floor when the toe of her shiny black boot connected with his shin. Pain shot through his leg. When he lost his hold, she darted for the door, but his recovery was swift. He snagged her arm before she made her escape and was anything but tranquil when he drew her near.

"Ruth Anne," he berated when she continued to squirm, "you need to settle down so we can discuss this like adults."

Her heart beat wildly as she glared up at her *betrothed*. "Nothing you have to say would make me change my mind!"

"About what?" he inquired, with casual indifference.

She shot him a fiery glare. "As if you don't know!"

With a slight shrug and a tilt of his head, he met her heated stare. "I'm sorry you're disappointed with your father's choice of a husband, but he did offer your hand, Ruth Anne. Within the hour you will be my wife."

Samuel's self-assurance rankled her. His words and then the possessive eyes that scanned her feminine frame triggered something inside.

Her foot came up to stomp on his, but this time he was ready for her. He spun her around so fast her head had barely stopped whirling when she caught a glimpse of his big brown eyes—just as they were narrowing in on her. A thread of fear slithered up her spine.

"You know, Ruth Anne, I'd hate to have to spank you on our wedding day, but I will if you keep this up!"

Tears filled her eyes, and her shoulders slumped. "As if your threats are going to win my heart ...."

Samuel, regretting his blunder and longing to do something that might ease her disquieted mind, sat on her bed. He captured her hand and with little effort pulled her down next to him. She did not shy away when his arm slid around her waist. The warm embrace he offered had the effect he was hoping for. She calmed, but was she ready to be reasonable? "This is more like it. Don't you agree?"

"No ... you have to let me go."

"I'm afraid I can't do that, Ruth." He drew her closer as if to make his point.

❀ ❀ ❀

Gerald, hearing a commotion going on in his daughter's bedroom, pulled his wife aside and asked, "Do you think I should go and see what's keeping them? He won't hurt our Ruth, will he?"

"I would hope not, but think this through. You offered her hand without her consent. I understand why, Gerald, but she does not."

"I can't tell her now, Flo. It wouldn't be fair to her or Samuel. This day should be special, one that holds fond memories."

Florence wasn't sure that was possible. "As hard as this is, we'll have to accept Samuel's ways and so will she. Give them a few minutes. The papers have been signed. He is her husband in the eyes of the law, but their vows of commitment need to be spoken before God and those who love them. If they don't come down soon, then by all means go and check on her."

Gerald nodded. On their way to the kitchen to join their guests, he whispered a prayer that Samuel and Ruth would come to an understanding, quickly.

※ ※ ※

"You see ..." Samuel explained, as he slowly ran his finger along her pale soft cheek, "convincing your father to offer your hand has been one of my greatest challenges. Now that he has, I'm not about to let you go." The tenseness in her face eased when he added, "It was not my intent to threaten you, but you must admit, you haven't exactly been agreeable."

Her head lowered. "Why should I be?"

"I'm going to be your husband. Don't you think that should be reason enough?"

The negative sway of her head was her only response.

"Your parents were pleased. Apparently my offer has eased their minds considerably. I was hoping you would share their sentiments."

Eased their minds? Although she wondered what he alluded to, she refused to ask. The only thing she wanted from *Samuel White* was for him to walk out of her house and never come back. Apparently, her wants were irrelevant.

"Ruth, I'm sorry you were kept in the dark about our marriage, but surely you know that was not my doing. Your father insisted on my silence."

"I'm not surprised. Papa didn't want you to tell me because he knew ..." When still she had not looked up, Samuel's long fingers slid down the trim line of her jaw, and lifted her chin. Of their own volition her timid blue eyes met his.

"Tell me, Ruth Anne, what did he know?"

"That I'd never ..." clear thought evaded her as his thumb ran softly across her mouth. Although she resented the power his touch had over her, she could not pull away.

"Never what?" he asked, desperately needing a distraction. Now, he assumed, was not a good time to give into his insatiable desire to kiss her rosy lips for the first time.

Not even the lowering of her eyes helped. The man's very presence unsettled her. "He knew I'd never agree to court you, never mind marry you."

"But we are going to be married. You know that, don't you?" He tucked her wayward curls behind her ears, admitting, "You're a bit mussed from your daring attempt to flee, but you look lovely otherwise. The dress you chose for our special day is real pretty."

Pretty? Her face snarled up. His comment about her horrible dress bolstered her weakening stance. "There's nothing special about this day, Samuel. So far it has been the worst day of my life. And, if you'd really like to know, I despise this dress almost as much as I do you."

While her open hostility surprised him, his mind was not swayed. "Ruth Anne ..." he said, and then waited. When she finally peered up, he leaned close before adding, "That's not a very nice way to speak to your fiancé."

All too close to tears, she murmured, "Hiding the truth will not change the way I feel."

"Nor will exposing the truth alter our contract of marriage."

He was right, but knowing did not make this easier to accept. She had barely looked away when she felt his warm lips on the corner of her mouth. Startled, her cheeks flamed, along with her ire. With a hearty shove, she informed him, "You have no right to be taking liberties with me!"

Even in her prickly mood he found her wonderfully irresistible. "You're about to become my wife, Ruth Anne. That gives me the right to kiss you anytime I want."

Well, I wouldn't recommend trying it again! She ogled him for the space of several heartbeats—she knew this to be true because hers was thudding quite loudly. "Samuel, can't you see that this would never work? I don't even like you!"

"So you've said," he acknowledged, but thought, *I beg to differ with you. Even our fathers have witnessed our attraction for one another.* Samuel saw her reluctance as nothing more than a minor setback. He had been working, planning, and dreaming of this day for so long, he could no longer imagine life without her. She, on the other hand had been given no warning. When he spoke to her father, he offered to court her, but his silence was her father's only addendum to the contract. No wonder Ruth was uncertain. Although he would prefer she came to this union willingly, her parents had their reasons for not telling her. Samuel would marry Ruth regardless. Letting go of his dream was not an option. Not now. Not ever. She would come around. She just had to.

Ruth, misinterpreting the silence that lingered, a thread of hope seeped into her anxious mind. "I'm sure if you tell Papa you've changed your mind he'll release you from the contract."

For someone so young, her tenacity amazed him. "I'm not about to change my mind. I want nothing more than to make you my wife."

But you don't even know me! "What about what I want?"

He, thinking the time had come to put an end to her valiant attempts to discourage him, caressed her cheek. "Have you forgotten that you're only fifteen?"

"No! But my age has nothing to do with this!"

His brow lifted on her plucky inflection. "It has more to do with it than you know. Because you're only fifteen, your father had to sign the legal documents for you. He did that when I was here a month ago. I couldn't run the risk him backing out, so I met with the preacher on our way home that day. He signed his part and dated the contract for today. The documents have already been filed at the courthouse."

Flustered, her dander rose. "Legal documents or not, I still have to say I do, and I won't!"

His head swayed from side to side. "Not true. The contract alone is legal and binding, but I'm sure you would agree that saying vows to each other before God and man is important. Our parents believe the ceremony will give us a good place to begin."

Her hands fidgeted with the ruffles on her dress. "But I don't want to be your wife."

"I can see that. If nothing else, you're honest to a fault, a quality I find most reassuring. If that's all you have to offer, along with your exquisite beauty, I'll take it. Who knows, given time, you might even decide to like me."

"I won't!"

His arms slid around her and he kissed her brow. "Forgive me, Ruth, if I aim to prove you wrong."

When he released her, she stood and went to the open window. A warm breeze taunted her, but not even the morning sun in all its brilliance could ease the storm brewing inside her. She glared back at her betrothed. This was not how she had envisioned her wedding day. This was supposed to be the happiest day of her life. Instead it was the worst. If things went as he said, she would be his wife within the hour.

His wife!

How dreadful!

As if she were not humbled enough, unbidden tears filled her eyes and trailed slowly down her cheeks.

Noticing her tears, Samuel removed the hanky from his pocket and went to her, tucking the clean cloth into her small hand. He longed to say something, anything that would ease her fretful mind, but what? He knew so little about her, about women for that matter. Perhaps a bit of tenderness could help—couldn't hurt. Rubbing her back, he waited, hoping that at any moment she would turn and allow him to enfold her in his arms. He had been so pleased to finally gain her hand. Ruth's disapproval had him baffled. Most men in Detroit were poor farmers who had little to offer her. He, on the other hand was financially secure, and he cared deeply for her. What more could she ask for in a husband?

As he stood there staring at the woman before him, he could not look away. She was beautiful. Her womanly curves were more than evident, but they did not make her a woman. *After all,* he thought, *she is young, perhaps a bit spoiled and used to having her own way. Maybe her father should have told her sooner. That would have given her time to adjust, but it is too late for regrets now. The preacher is here. The papers are signed, dated, and filed. And besides, I've already waited longer than I intended to take her to wife.*

He, thinking she had carried on long enough, squeezed her hand. "Come on, Ruth Anne. Dry your tears and blow your nose. We need to head downstairs. The preacher has other appointments, and we have chores at home to attend."

Hearing a soft knock, Samuel went to the door, relieved to see her father standing on the other side.

Gerald patted Samuel's arm in a reassuring manner. "Let me talk to her."

Samuel gladly moved aside so he could enter.

Gerald slipped his arm around his daughter and drew her close. "I'm sorry you're struggling, Ruth Anne, but you've put this off long enough. All the tears in the world won't change the fact that you are going to be Samuel's wife."

"But, Papa ..."

"Hush now. It's time for you to marry and raise a family of your own. Samuel has worked hard to build you a nice home. He has promised to take good care of you. We'll have to trust that he too is a man of his word."

Drawing in a shuddering breath, she admitted, "He frightens me, Papa .... What kind of man threatens his bride on their wedding day?"

"With the way you've been carrying on, I can't say as I blame him. Your mother and I had such high hopes of this being a happy union. You're struggling and I only have myself to blame. I should have told you sooner, but you need to hear me, Ruth Anne, this union is no longer about what I believe or want. The contracts have been signed. Things are at stake that you don't understand."

Eyes filled with anguish met his. "Then make me understand, Papa. Don't shut me out."

For a brief moment Gerald weakened, but a quick glance at her betrothed fortified his wavering emotions. His head swayed from side to side. "Not on your wedding day, Ruth Anne."

She allowed her papa to walk her down the stairs, but she told him in no uncertain terms, "I won't promise *him* anything? I don't even like *him*."

"Give yourself time—time has a way of changing the way we look at everything."

Samuel was right behind them and heard every word. He did not react. While this puzzled Gerald, he did not question him. The young man's desire to take his daughter to wife despite her disapproval was more than apparent. As hard as it was to see Ruth this distraught, he led her into the parlor. After placing her hand in Samuel's, Gerald reassured her, "Ruth Anne ... you are going to be fine."

As her papa turned away, she pleaded, "Please don't do this ...."

Meeting her desperate look, his heart ached for her, but he had to be honest. "It's already done. Just you wait and see. In time you'll be glad I accepted Samuel's offer."

"I'll never be glad! I want to marry ..."

Though Gerald's hand covered her mouth, the words she had already spoken were not without effect. An uncomfortable hush blanketed the room. He leaned close and spoke for her ears alone, "Samuel is the man I have chosen."

To defy him could bring her more grief, but compared to a lifetime with *Samuel White* ...

Having watched her papa take his place beside her mama, she peered up at her betrothed. She could not hold his gaze.

Every rumor she had ever heard about him ran precariously though her mind.

How can I spend a lifetime with him?

Ruth stood her ground as the pastor came to stand before them. However, when his beady gray eyes narrowed in on her, an overwhelming sense of doom swept over her. She turned to flee and ran straight into Samuel's broad chest. Her heart thudded so she could hardly breathe. How could she have forgotten he was so near?

Samuel's strong arms encircled his bride. Overwhelmed by the essence of her femininity—her vulnerability, he sighed. "Your father is right, you have nothing to fear, Ruth Anne. I only want to love you." With tenderness he ran his knuckles down her tense cheek, bringing her stone cold eyes to his.

If only she could believe him.

A quick glance around the room told Samuel everyone, including the preacher was waiting to proceed. He rotated Ruth and held her gently in his arms, fully convinced that she was right where she belonged.

If only his bride would agree.

If only her trembling would ease.

In an attempt to shut everything out, Ruth closed her eyes. Unfortunately, her lack of sight did not shut out the words being spoken, in fact, they resounded in her ears.

The pastor asked for the second time, "Ruth Anne Schmidt, do you take Samuel White to be your lawfully wedded husband?" It wasn't until her papa nudged her from behind that her head dipped slightly. Her gesture must have been enough because Samuel slid a ring on her finger and they were pronounced husband and wife just the same as if she had spoken the words out loud. Her hand felt unnaturally weighted, like her heart now sinking deeper within.

When the pastor told Samuel he could kiss his bride, his lips brushed softly against hers. On impulse, she wiped it off with the back of her hand. If anyone noticed, she was unaware.

The ceremony had no more ended when Samuel's father announced that they should be on their way.

Alarm sliced through Ruth, knowing she would be expected to leave as well. Her eyes skittered about the room. Several excuses came to mind, but knowing they would only delay her departure kept her from mentioning them.

Samuel, aware of his wife's desperation, stayed close, allowing her to say her goodbyes. He hated to rush off, but like his parents, he too had chores to be tended.

While Gerald and Florence tried to put on a brave front, inside their hearts were wrenching. Ruth's constant flow of tears was almost their undoing. No doubt, this was difficult for all of them. If they had it to do over again, they would have done things differently. They could only hope that given time their daughter would find joy in her union.

Samuel picked up the bag Florence had packed and was nudging Ruth out the door when he turned back to look at Gerald. "We'll be by to pick up Ruth's other belongings after she has time to get settled."

"That'll be fine, Samuel. We'll have them ready."

"You might want to retrieve the small bag she dropped out her bedroom window." Ruth glared over her shoulder at him.

Gerald glanced at Florence before meeting Ruth's tearful

gaze. *Had Samuel thwarted her plan to escape?* Since now was not the time to ask, he merely said, "We'll see to it." Gerald, knowing how hard it would be to watch their daughter leave, reached for his wife's hand and closed the door.

Samuel and Ruth were almost to the carriage when Ruth managed to break free from her husband's grasp. She ran for all she was worth. Ignoring his stern bellow, she darted around the side of the barn, ducked into the woodshed, stooped down near the entrance, and just listened.

Taking a moment to catch her breath, she pulled the hanky out of her sleeve, dried her tears, and just happened to look up. A large brown spider hovered precariously overhead. A bad case of the chills struck her, but she remained perfectly still. The thought of Samuel finding her frightened her more than the eight-legged creature.

Moments passed before she chanced opening the door—a crack. Hearing nothing out of the ordinary, she poked her head through the opening and scanned the area. No one was lurking, so she snuck out. As she neared the tree line, a dry branch snapped beneath her feet.

Her heart faltered.

Craning her neck around, she caught movement out of the corner of her eye. She held a breath that she quickly released. It was only a fawn. Still she pressed on. A few more feet and the forest would shroud her. She did not as much as pause moving into the wooded haven. Letting down her guard was not an option. Not yet! Distancing herself was her only thought.

Minutes slipped by. Sensing her immediate danger over, her steps slowed, but her determination to flee did not wane. Only one question transfused her frazzled mind. *Where can I go?* She couldn't go to James. He wouldn't understand. Besides, she couldn't face him. Not as Samuel's wife.

Then it came to her. *Meg's house! I need time to think and Meg's is close. She'll be understanding. Won't she? Surely she won't take my parents' side in this! I've been wrong before, but no ... in this I am fairly confident she will understand my reasons for fleeing.*

Realizing that she should pay attention or she'd be lost in the woods for hours, Ruth stood perfectly still while she took in her surroundings.

Hearing something, her mind reeled.

Is someone coming? Unwilling to stick around and find out, she took off running in the opposite direction. Glancing back, no one came into view, but her stride quickened. She could hear footsteps. They were getting closer. Too close. Her heart raced faster and faster. Chancing a peek over her shoulder, she saw him.

Oh, no!!!

The beat of her heart increased with every step.

Refusing to give up, she rushed through the dense trees, weaving as often as she could. A limb caught her dress, it tore, and still she kept on, gasping for every breath. Weary, her legs were close to giving out when her feet suddenly left the ground.

"No ..." she bemoaned as she was swept up into her husband's burly arms.

Her heart pounded so, it hurt to breathe. Moments passed. In fact, they were heading out of the woods before she managed to say, "Samuel, please! You have to put me down. I can't be your wife. I won't ..."

He did not wait for her to finish. "You are my wife!" he declared. His nostrils flared. The veins in his neck twitched, but he offered no further response. One was not necessary. There was no mistaking the fury in his eyes as he bore her to the buggy, stepped up into the back seat, and secured her on his lap.

Samuel's narrowed glare met his fathers. "Go!"

The team had been moving for some time before her breathing evened out. Humbly she implored, "Samuel, please let me sit beside you. I'm not a child."

"Could have fooled me!" Instead of releasing her, he drew her closer still. "Having you in my arms feels wonderful. You'll just have to get used to it."

"Never!" she squirmed, but his hold only tightened. "I hate you!"

"That may be, but you're staying right where you are." He pulled her head against his chest and firmly kissed her brow.

Wiping it off, she tried to pull away, even started to cry, but it was no use. He offered not so much as a sputter of compassion.

Samuel did not care about her.

That much was clear, if only to her.

Like it or not, she was no longer under the covering of her papa's household.

How this oversized tyrant had ensnared her was still a mystery. Although she didn't have answers to the many questions racing through her head, she aimed to find them out.

Never in all her life had she felt more vulnerable and out of control. With so many unfamiliar sentiments swirling inside her, there was nothing rational or serene about Ruth Anne—*White*.

He Loves Me!

Chapter Five

His Home

*T*HE RADIANT LIGHT OF DAY sparkled brilliantly in a cloudless sky, but not so much as a flicker of hope pierced Ruth's wary soul. She was still in Samuel's arms when his father turned down a narrow path and pulled the team to a halt in front of a whitewashed farmhouse, no larger than her parent's home. *So much for the castle Samuel told me about.* The sound of rippling water came to Ruth's ears, telling her the river had to be near. A deep covered porch wrapped around the quaint home, possibly leading to a back entrance. She hated to admit it even to herself, but it did have an inviting appeal.

When the elder Mr. and Mrs. White stepped out of the buggy, Ruth was confused. Could this be his parent's home? Or did Samuel lie about having his own place?

Would she be expected to live with them?

The thought alone sent her blood to racing through her veins. There was no question in Ruth's mind: Mr. White did not like her. His evil glare when Samuel lifted her into the buggy was frightful.

Perhaps her antics added to his surmise, but she harbored no doubt, living with them would be disastrous. Besides, these people weren't exactly the happy sort. Then again, neither was their son. Although she wanted answers to her questions, she refused to speak to Samuel—about anything!

The second he loosened his grasp, Ruth leapt off his lap and then out of the buggy. She shuddered as she moved away, trying to dispel the feeling of being in *his* arms—on *his* lap.

If she'd been paying attention instead of stewing the whole way, this would have been a perfect time to escape. Her father had mentioned that Samuel's place was about five miles from home. She could walk that with little effort. Even so, she deemed it prudent to get her bearings before another brazen attempt. Tamping down her desperate need to flee, she meandered toward a nearby tree.

Samuel, watching his bride closely, warned, "Ruth Anne, that's far enough!"

In her estimation, England would not be far enough. Since igniting his ire would serve no purpose, she obeyed but did not as much as glance his way. Ruth simply leaned against the tree and waited while Samuel conversed with his parents, trying for the life of her to understand what her papa saw in *him*.

Thoughtlessly, she tugged at the torn fabric of her dress, rendering it beyond repair. In truth, she didn't care. She hated this dress and all that it would serve to remind her of—the worst day of her life.

After a time, she glared over at the three of them. She didn't even know these people. They were strangers. The things she had heard about Samuel continued to plague her mind. It was obvious that her papa had been sucked in by Samuel's lies. *You're usually such a good judge of character, Papa. There has to be something I'm missing here, something I don't understand. Arranged marriages are common enough, but this, this was different— underhanded almost. Papa, you wouldn't have offered my hand to someone like him unless you were desperate, unless ...* She refused to allow her mind to contemplate such thoughts.

Feeling defiant, she moved around the backside of the tree, slid to the ground, and buried her face in her knees. *Regardless of what has brought me here, by law I'm bound to Samuel for life ... for life ... for life ....* The words resounding in her head only served to steel her will against them. Ruth would find a way to break free. She just had to. Tears pooled in her eyes, but she refused to let them fall. Pride kept her from exposing the extent of her vulnerable state. She was alone, so very alone she could hardly bear the weight of it. Like a misfit wandering in a foreign land, she was lost and feeling so out of place.

"Ruth ..." the woman called in a husky voice as she came toward her.

Ruth pulled herself together as best she could and stood. The men were still knee deep in conversation in front of the house, so the woman spoke freely. "I'm sorry we weren't properly introduced earlier. I'm Samuel's mother, Naomi."

Ruth had no way of knowing if Naomi could be trusted. Even so, she nodded in greeting. She had no wish to come across as disrespectful.

A Bible story her mama had told her about a young girl on the brink of womanhood came to mind. Her name was Tamar. Like Ruth, Tamar was married off to Judah's evil son Er without time to come to terms with her plight. Er, not at all pleased with his father's choice of a bride, treated Tamar with disdain. Ruth suspected her situation wasn't all that different. Samuel was obviously attracted to her. After all, he pursued her hand, but he knew nothing of her true nature. She on the other hand knew much about him—too much. If she remembered correctly, Tamar's mother-in-law wasn't much better than her son. Perhaps her mama had embellished the story to make it more interesting, but Ruth intended to stay on guard where this family was concerned—for now anyway.

"You're welcome to call me, Mom. I cannot tell you how pleased I am to have another woman in the family after all these years."

"Thank you." Ruth's heart warmed considerably on her kind welcome. She also realized that it wasn't Naomi's fault she was in this predicament, so she attempted to be cordial. "You look very nice. Your dress is lovely."

Naomi glanced down at the deep red organdy fabric and smiled. Her daughter-in-law's gentle manor took her by surprise. The poor girl had been so emotional during the time they were in her parent's home that Naomi had no way of knowing her true nature. She suspected Ruth was only frightened. Little wonder, with the way her father had kept her marriage from her until just before their arrival. "I appreciate your saying so, Ruth Anne. Sewing is the one task I find pleasure in. Even serviceable cotton can be special if the design is unique."

Her talent truly was amazing. "Perhaps you'd be willing to share your gift with me. I do enjoy sewing, but Mama never did. I'm afraid she only taught me the basics. As you can see, this frilly frock was store bought."

The reserve in Ruth's voice tore at Naomi's heart. In many ways she understood Ruth's uncertainties. Although Naomi knew her husband prior to their wedding day, hers too had been an arranged marriage. Her years with Samuel Senior had brought her little more than pain and misery. "I'd be glad to teach you what I know. I can see that you're not happy about becoming my son's wife, but I'm hopeful time will change all that. Try to be patient with him. His father has not been the best example in matters of the heart."

Ruth's eyes, filled with suspicion, met Naomi's.

"I'm always available if you need to talk. I've been married to the same kind of man for years. I would hate for you to have to learn the way I did."

Innocently, Ruth asked, "How is that?"

"The hard way ...."

As Naomi's words came to rest, prickly shivers ran up Ruth's spine. *What are you saying?* she wondered, but couldn't bring herself to ask. She suspected Naomi would have said more if the men were not heading their way. Ruth grimaced when Samuel's large hand enveloped hers. Although she tried to pull away, his determination and strength won out—for now anyway.

When he spoke, her stormy blue eyes met his. "Come on, wife. It's time for us to be on our way. I'm looking forward to showing you around our home and getting better acquainted."

Would she ever not cringe at the sound of his voice? For reasons of self-preservation, she offered no resistance when he led her away from his parents, swung her up into the front seat of the buggy, joined her, and took up the reins. They were about to pull away when Naomi called out, "Samuel, would you like to come by for dinner?"

Ruth held her breath, hoping he would say *yes*. In truth, she liked Naomi and would enjoy getting to know her. Besides, anything would be better than spending time alone with *him*.

When Samuel glared at Ruth, as if she had been the one to solicit the invitation, she could not hold his fiery look. Needing to distance herself, she moved to the far side of the buggy, and stared blankly at the distant field. She didn't know how or when, but she would get away from this horrible man.

"I appreciate the offer. We'll take you up on it in a week or two. Ruth and I need some time to settle in to our new life together."

Naomi nodded. "You know best, Samuel. Come by if you need anything."

"I will." With a snap of the whip, the team moved forward. His wife looked ready to bolt, but Samuel didn't think she would try anything at the speed they were traveling.

Ruth scanned the area for landmarks she might recognize. If she was ever going to find her way back home, she would need to get her bearings. They'd only been moving a short distance when her spirit quickened. Several familiar landmarks appeared before her vigilant eyes. No doubt, they were heading back towards her parents' house. This was definitely a plus. By the time they veered off the main trail, she had a good handle on her location.

Samuel drove the team around a grove of trees and through a natural arbor before entering a large clearing. When his home came into view, as difficult as it was, Ruth steeled her reaction. The house was everything he had described and more. The covered porch looked so inviting and the huge barn that sat back amongst the trees was built to last. Samuel did not lie about this. He had much to be thankful for. Even so, she refused to give him false hope. The things he had to offer would come at a huge price—a price she was unwilling to pay.

In a way she felt sorry for him. If he had married for love, his wife might be thrilled to live in such a place, but that was not the case for her. Ruth wanted nothing more than to flee his side.

Samuel jumped down, came around to her side and alighted her from the carriage. He would love to know what she thought of the farm he'd put so much time and effort into preparing for her, but he refused to ask. She hadn't spoken a word to him since he insisted on holding her in the carriage. More than likely she wouldn't answer him anyway. He harbored no misgivings; her silence was her way of getting back at him for pursuing her hand. His wife still had a desperate look in her eyes which meant it could be a long day—week—life if she didn't come to accept her plight.

"Ruth, I don't know about you, but I'm hungry. I'll show you around the house. Then you can prepare our dinner while I see to the team."

Samuel reached for her hand, but this time she was ready for him and pulled away before he could get a good hold. Since she was moving toward the house, he let her go.

From the moment they entered *his* spacious home; she was awestruck. Even so, she gave nothing away. Ruth refused to give this atrocious man the slightest inkling that she would ever come to accept the life he was offering. When he insisted, she followed him to the right, down a narrow hall with two doors.

He pointed to the first one they came to, saying as they passed, "That's a nursery. I thought you might prefer having our children close while they're small."

There won't be any children. I'm not staying!

"I put four bedrooms upstairs. They'll need some work before they're livable, but all in due time." He opened the door at the end of the hall and led her in. "This is our room."

Your room!

"You can put your things in the armoire to your right. Mine are in the one to your left. Around the corner there's a bathing chamber with a small stove for heating water. The outhouse is around the back of the house. There's a chamber pot under the commode if you need to use it during the night."

I won't be here!

"We're close to the woods."

You're close to the woods!

"I've had a few problems with bears and cougars, so don't strike out on your own after dark."

Not to worry, I have no intentions of being here!

When they entered the kitchen and still Ruth had not so much as looked his way, Samuel wanted to shake her. Even a negative reaction would be better than this dreadful silence. Knowing he would frighten her more if he did anything rash, he swallowed his bruised pride and moved into the pantry.

Samuel lit the lantern, reclaimed her hand, and pulled her around the corner, stopping in front of a set of access doors that were angled up from the floor. Leaning down, he lifted one of the doors and laid it against the wall. "This is our cold cellar." He pointed to a smaller door cut out of the floor. "At times I keep the milk, eggs and butter in there for easy access. The pantry is well stocked, but you'll need to keep a running list, so I can fetch supplies when I ride into town."

Ruth didn't care for dark places, but when he insisted on her following him down the narrow steps, she obeyed. He draped a string of wax beans over her arm, handed her several potatoes, and a large onion. Then he reached for a chunk of ham, cheese, butter, and a covered pitcher of milk before following her back into the kitchen.

"Extra wood is just outside the door if your basket runs low."

Your basket, Samuel, yours! Can't you see that I want no part of what you're offering? Though her thoughts rambled unapologetically, Samuel was oblivious to her inward rebellion—or was he? In truth, she didn't know or care.

"I'll fire up the stove so you can prepare our meal. Look around, Ruth. The kitchen is fairly well stocked. You should be able to find everything you need. The water barrel outside the back door is full if there's not enough in the pitcher on the washstand. Tomorrow, I'll show you around the place. The Rouge is close, but it's hidden." When still she refused to look at him, or speak, he swallowed his pride, yet again, and went to collect a stack of firewood.

Samuel smiled when he came back in and found his wife at the counter with her sleeves rolled up and the apron his mother had quilted for her looped around her neck. So many times he had tried to envision what it would be like to finally have her here. Oh, he saw her in town from time to time, but didn't have the chance to meet her properly until the day he and his father were invited to the farm. Finally, she was here. Only one question remained unanswered: would she ever be truly his?

When Samuel went back outside, he stayed longer than

necessary. Convinced that Ruth would take off the minute he was out of sight, he was pleased to see that she was making herself to home upon his return. From the looks of things, she gave up on him lighting the stove and saw to the task herself. Initiative was a good thing. Even if he had the time to do so, he would not coddle her.

A sliced onion was simmering in a skillet smattered with bacon grease. As Ruth peeled and sliced several potatoes, she added them as well. The aroma made his stomach churn. The morning's activities had served to give him a powerful appetite.

Did he dare hold onto the hope that she would accept her new life with more grace than she had thus far? Unsure, he was not ready to let down his guard. The day was young and he had an inkling his silent beauty was *almost* as strong willed as he. She would not easily tear down the wall she was erecting between them.

"Smells good in here. Did you have any trouble finding what you needed?" She offered no response, so he answered for her, "I'll take that as a no. I have to put the team away. I'll be back in a few minutes. Can I count on dinner being ready when I return?"

She continued to ignore him and his irritation peaked. In three great steps he reached her side, grabbed a hold of her arm, and swung her around so fast the knife in her hand put a gash in his arm.

The room had barely righted itself when Ruth saw blood dripping from Samuel's shirt. Eyes filled with fear met her husbands, who looked just as stunned as she.

Feeling guilty for no reason, Ruth reached for the towel, wrapped it around his arm and went for the pitcher and basin. She did not mean to cut him. Actually, she had been so absorbed—so lost in her own mull of despair she never heard his approach.

"I'm sorry," she said as she rolled up his sleeve and poured cool water over the wound on his thickly muscled arm. "I didn't ... why did you?" She burst into tears.

"Don't cry, Ruth. It's not your fault. I shouldn't have come at you the way I did." When he lifted her chin, damp eyes met his. Sure that he had her undivided attention, he said, "But the silent treatment has come to an end. Do I make myself clear?"

Her head dipped before she turned and moved away. Though all in a muddle, her heart ached something fierce, but she had to find something for ...

"Ruth Anne!" he bellowed, his stern tone stopping her in her tracks. "Don't walk away when I'm speaking to you!"

She craned her neck around. "Would you rather I let you stand there and bleed to death? I have to find something to use for a bandage."

His eyes rolled up as he shook his head. "You could have said that!"

She nodded, thinking, *what I want to say is goodbye— forever* ....

In a better mood, he suggested, "You'll find what you're looking for on the top shelf of the tall cabinet in our bathing chamber."

You mean your bathing chamber, don't you? Ruth hated the thought of being back in *his* room, but she found herself there nonetheless. Without Samuel stalking her every move she allowed her eyes to take in her elaborate surroundings. Her mouth dropped open when she rounded the corner to *his* bathing chamber. The room was much larger than she anticipated, and the tub that sat in the far corner ... why, it was long enough for a grown man to stretch his legs all the way out. She tried to imagine what it would be like to relax in such splendor after a long arduous day, but she caught herself. No amount of pleasure would be worth putting up with *him*! Clearly, Samuel did not skimp on anything in this house. Even so, it was not for her. She wanted no part of anything he had to offer. Thinking she had best quit daydreaming and get back to the bleeding man in the kitchen, she found what she had come for and was on her way.

After bandaging Samuel's arm, she returned to her meal preparations while he took his time sipping at a glass of water. Ruth could feel the heat of his eyes on her back. She wondered why he was sticking around when he had horses to tend. Since it was not her place to question him, she kept her thoughts to herself. When he finally stood and moved out the back door, she slid the food off the hot stove and practically ran toward *his* bedroom.

Chapter Six

Brokenness

$\mathcal{R}$UTH HAD TO GET OUT of her colorful frilly frock or she'd never be able to make her escape. She would stand out like a beacon amidst the trees in the woods. The tiny buttons down her back made it almost impossible to manage alone, but she undid most of them and then wiggled out. Pulling her dark skirt over her hips, Ruth secured the clasp. Having just poked her hand down the first sleeve of her blouse, she heard heavy footsteps.

The door flew open.

Squealing, she turned away, making haste to get her bare arm in the other sleeve. The last button was fastened when her husband grabbed her arm and swung her around to face him—yet again. Why he insisted on doing this was beyond her. Did it make him feel more powerful to handle her in such a way?

"What are you doing in here?" he insisted on knowing.

This man is ridiculous! "What does it look like I'm doing?"

His fierce scowl stilled the beat of her heart. "Ruth Anne,

that smart mouth is going to get you slapped."

Her eyes lowered. She did not doubt that he meant every word and since she was not in an agreeable mood, she simply offered, "I'd rather not talk to you at all, but you said I had to."

Samuel took a deep breath, willing himself to calm before he did something he'd regret. He had not anticipated his young wife being quite so obstinate. His father recommended a firm hand from the start. Even so, he would prefer not to take such drastic measures. Be that as it may, Ruth would have to mend her ways. He would not put up with her impertinence for long. Her inward struggle could not be denied. She needed time to come to terms with the new life that had been thrust upon her. Besides, this was their wedding day—a day that should hold fond memories. For that reason alone, he would swallow his pride and go against what he knew to be right.

Samuel's hands slid around her slender waist and he drew her close. Fingering the top button on her blouse, he unbuttoned it and then another, warmly suggesting, "We could always forego dinner."

Her wide eyes met his. Horrified, she dipped under his arm and ran from the room.

Chuckling tersely, Samuel watched her leave. Her uncertainties were more than evident, but he so ached to hold her, kiss her, snuggle her close. Good things, he reminded himself, come to those who wait. For now he settled for plucking her colorful dress off the floor, bringing the fabric to his face, and reveling in her sweet floral scent. He'd waited so long for this day to arrive. She was now his wife. Even so, he could not help wondering, *will she ever be at ease in my arms?*

After hanging her dress from a hook, he found Ruth in the kitchen working fast and furiously on their meal. He couldn't resist wrapping his arms around her and kissing behind her small soft ear. "No hurry, My Porcelain Beauty, we have the rest of the day ... and night."

Not if I can help it!

Ruth trembled nearly out of control when Samuel turned her to face him. His large hands captured her face, and he planted a kiss on her mouth. His kiss was brief, but one that brought with it very different emotions for each of them. His heart surged with bridled passion, while every inch of her skin crawled with revulsion.

Ruth shivered as she watched her husband walk out the back door. Although she'd love to take her leave at this very moment, filling her rumbling stomach did have merit. If she were to get lost it could be a long night. She could not face it hungry.

The food was simmering on the back of the stove when she decided to make a batch of cookies. Perhaps the sweet confections would soothe Samuel's foul disposition when he found her missing.

Smiling at her own ingenuity, she went to the pantry and collected the ingredients she would need. The butter was running low, but she would have enough to make the cookies and get through their meal. Come evening Samuel would be on his own again. *Poor boy!*

She giggled, trying to imagine him churning butter. No doubt, he would not have the patience to accomplish the mind-numbing task. She could only assume his mother had kept him supplied up till now.

Sooner than expected, Samuel came in the back door, removed his boots, washed his hands in the basin, and took a seat at the table.

Did he expect her to serve him? Testing the waters, she asked, "Samuel, will you pour the coffee while I put the food on the table?"

"I'm in no hurry. Pour the coffee. Then serve the food."

"Fine!" she shot out. *Keep thinking you're the biggest toad in the puddle. For supper you can fend for yourself!*

"You keep that up, you'll get more than you bargained for."

Where have you been? I already got more than I bargained for when Papa offered you my hand! Thinking she had better not open her mouth or it would surely get her into more trouble, she poured the coffee, put the food on the table, and sat down across from *him*. When he stared at her as if she had taken leave of her senses, her irritation soared. "What now?"

"You forgot the cream and sugar for the coffee, the salt and pepper, and the bread. Surely you know how to set a table proper-like by now!"

She leapt out of her chair, nearly knocking it over, mumbling as she strode toward the pantry, "When it comes to being irksome, Samuel, you go the whole hog!"

Though seething, he waited for her to set the items he requested on the table before grabbing her arm and yanking her close. In fact, they were practically nose to nose when he said, "Apparently you're not hungry enough to be civil. Go to our room and get settled in. I'll join you as soon as I finish my meal."

It's barely three o'clock!

She tried not to panic, but it wasn't easy. "Samuel, please.

I'm hungry. I'll be good. Promise!"

"Too late for apologies!" He turned her toward their room. With a firm swat to her backside, he said, "Obey me!"

After a few agonizing steps, she turned back to face him with tears pooling in her eyes. "I need to use the outhouse."

He hesitated for the space of several seconds. "Go ahead, but be quick about it."

Samuel's back was to her, so she snatched a stack of cookies off the counter and swiped her sweater from the hook before hurrying out the back door. Not knowing if he was watching from the window, she went into the outhouse. After counting to twenty, she snuck out and pulled foot toward home. For a time she stayed on the beaten path, but there was no doubt in her mind, Samuel would realize she was missing and come after her. If he were to find her—well, she just couldn't allow that to happen. She had to speak to her parents before doing something rash.

Ever watchful, Ruth did the unthinkable and moved into the trees. As much as she feared the creatures that lingered in the forest, she saw no other way. A good fifteen to twenty minutes had passed before she heard a horse galloping her way. She hid behind a thick trunk and stood perfectly still, unwilling to chance anyone capturing a glimpse of her. When the rider passed, she took a cautious peek. Sure enough, it was Samuel and he was heading towards her parents' farm. She could only hope he would be gone when she arrived. If not, she could always wait it out in the barn. Although doing so would not be her first choice, anything would be better than going back with *him*.

The orange-golden sun was sinking in the western skies by the time she neared her parents' farm. Like a cat on the prowl, she padded in. Thankfully Samuel's black stallion was nowhere in sight. Perhaps he had already been there and gone.

Please, Papa, her mind implored as she moved up the back steps, *don't let me down. You're the only one who can free me from that horrible man.*

When Ruth finally summoned the gumption to slip in the back door, she found her mama lying on her arm at the table, crying.

Florence didn't hear Ruth come in and started when she asked, "Mama, why are you so upset?"

Florence stood, gathered Ruth in her arms and held on tight. "Oh, Honey, where have you been? Samuel was just here. He's worried sick. You can't run away from your husband. It's not right."

Ruth scowled and took a step back. Apparently her papa was not the only one believing his lies. "That man doesn't give two hoots about me. I'm nothing more than a possession to him. I won't go back there. I can't. Mama, please! You have to help me convince Papa to have this marriage annulled." Ruth flinched when Gerald's voice suddenly filled the room.

"I won't do it, Ruth Anne!"

When she turned to face him, his stern look met hers. "I told you before and nothing has changed. You're Samuel's wife. You should be thankful he chose you. He has so much to offer."

Incensed by his uncharacteristic coldness, she grew defensive. "Things can't buy happiness. You've drummed that into my head from the time I was little. Oh, he has temporal things to offer all right, but they come at a cost."

"Give yourself time to get to know him. He's a good man."

Ruth harrumphed. "You're wrong, Papa! I'm not sure what

that scoundrel has over you, but he obviously came to you as an angel of light. You bought his lies, and now I'm expected to live with him. He doesn't even like me." She started to cry.

"You're mistaken, Ruth Anne. The man adores you."

"You're the one who is wrong, Papa! Besides, the thought of him touching me makes my skin crawl."

Gerald's heart ached for her, but his hands really were tied. "These things take time."

She swallowed hard passed the lump in her throat. "I never want to see him again!"

His eyes widened. "I'm afraid you'll have to. He's your husband. You live under his roof now."

The turmoil in his eyes was unmistakable. Surely there was more to this then he was saying. There just had to be. Something had happened to her tower of strength? Before her stood a weak, defenseless man.

Did Samuel have something on him?

Her papa wasn't being totally honest, that much was obvious.

"I'm not sure what you're getting out of this contract, but I'm the one getting the raw end of it."

His hands came up to accentuate his words. "Your future is secure. You could show a little gratitude. Give Samuel a chance to prove himself."

She shook her head in disbelief. "Thanks, but no thanks! He's proven himself quite thoroughly already! The man doesn't know the first thing about love. He's mean and self-centered. So tell me, Papa, what more could a girl possibly want in a husband? If you wanted to get rid of me so badly, why didn't you say so? I would have married James. At least then I could have been happy!" Her sarcasm, though well-noted, altered nothing.

"Forget James! Samuel will come around. You need to get to know each other is all."

Her scowl grew fierce. "I know *him* well enough to know I could never be happy with *him*. Since you won't help me, my choices are limited to two. I can leave this area and never come back or stay and be doomed to a life with that atrocious man. Fine choices, wouldn't you say? Thanks for nothing!"

He scowled right back. "Don't put this on me. Your pride is getting in the way."

Tears flooded Ruth's eyes. "You're the one who arranged this union. You go live with the brute if you like him so much!"

Surprised by her contempt, Gerald took an uncompromising step toward her. "Ruth Anne, that's enough! I promised Samuel I would bring you home the minute you arrived."

"And because you're a man of your word, you will do as promised." Ruth stood, took a tankard off the shelf, walked to the pitcher and had a long drink of cool water. As she did, the clock on the mantel struck five times. Darkness would be settling in.

Turning back to face her parents, she said, "Don't worry about me. I'll find my own way. I love you two, but today I lost a huge portion of the respect I've always had for you." On that note, she stormed out the door.

Not knowing if she would ever see her parents again tore at her heart. Being disrespectful to them went against all she knew to be right, but their actions had cost her dearly! How could they just give away their own flesh and blood? As if her feelings were of no significance, they had remained silent, keeping this sham from her. Some surprise her marriage had turned out to be—

more like her worst nightmare!

"I don't even like him!" she bellowed to the open air, needing to vent. That offered no respite, so she raised her eyes to the heavenly expanse. "What have I done to deserve *him*?" When no answer came, she wandered aimlessly, kicking at the tall grass that framed the trail and swayed in the swirling breeze. She was alone, deserted by the only family she had ever known, and the weight of her aching heart made it difficult to press on. Knowing her papa would return her to Samuel if she didn't leave, kept her moving down the beaten path one agonizing step at a time.

Ruth had been walking for some time before she came to the conclusion that she was going to have to make some hard decisions, and soon. If only she could think clearly. She needed time, but time was not on her side. Soon the creatures of the night would be on the prowl. And Samuel ... he would be looking for her.

Exhausted and hungry, her spirit quickened as she headed toward Meg's. Her friend's husband was still away and Ruth was fairly certain Meg would allow her to stay with her until she could make other arrangements.

One thing I know for certain, I am not going back to my husband.

Not now!

Not ever!

If only it was as simple as all that. She had other things to consider. Could she really walk away from her parents and never come back?

She had every right to be angry! The two people she trusted more than anyone in the world had turned on her. They married her off without so much as a by your leave. Just like that, their lives were being ripped apart.

This has to be Samuel's fault!

Maybe my frustrations are getting out of hand, but little wonder. No one would like being in my shoes—married off to the worst catch in the territory. The rumors I've heard about him must be true. Only a tyrant would treat a woman so!

Desperate to find a sense of peace, her eyes slid shut against the weight of her circumstances. *Papa you said that with every why I ask, remember to ask the what. What do I need to learn through my struggle that I couldn't have learned any other way?*

If only she knew!

Perhaps in time she would. For now she had a decision to make. What should she do?

Was the phrase her grandmother stitched on her bed pillow true? *"Though troubles and sufferings will come in this life, despair not, they often lead to God's richest blessings."*

Oh, Grammy ... do they? I wish you were here so we could talk. My parents don't know what this man is like, but I do. Perhaps I shouldn't despise him so, but I do.

The late afternoon sun slipped behind a cloud, casting gloominess along the trail, as if a foreboding evil haunted her every step. The birds had ceased their merriment. Although an owl would not cease his hooting, she whispered thanks that the other creatures of the forest remained hidden from view. Did they sense her unrest, her despair? Or was her spirit so numb she no longer heard or saw them?

She had always been such an agreeable child. Even as a young adult she did her best to honor her parents. She didn't always understand their beliefs, but in some ways they were beginning to make sense.

Why were you in such a big hurry to marry me off?

Did I do something wrong—disappoint you in some way?

If only she knew.

This whole experience has definitely brought out the worst in me.

Ruth's damp eyes rose again to the heavens. For a time she just stood there, wondering, *God, are you really watching over me? Do You care? Mama told me that You're waiting with open arms to catch me when I fall. That You love me, and have since before I was formed in her womb—before the foundation of the earth. I can hardly fathom this, never mind all that she has taught me about Jesus, Your Son. Did You really send Him to earth to pay the price for my sins? Today my sins have been many, Lord. Can You ever forgive me?*

I don't know You as well as I should, but I need someone to talk to—someone who cares. I hope Mama was right, that You really are listening. I'm in a desperate place, Lord. This has been the worst day of my life. Papa made me marry Samuel White. Do you know how cruel and unfeeling he is? I'm really not sure why I'm telling You all this. More than likely You know him better than I do. I'm no peach, but then I'm sure You know that too. Forgive me, God. I know he's my husband now, but I can't go back to him.

I suppose it's wrong to hate him so.

How can I not?

Tonight I said some hurtful things to my parents. I've always thought of myself as a good person. Even so, the way I feel about that man cannot be right. I don't like what's going on inside of me.

Please help me!

I don't know how to make this right.

Ruth's decision to go to Meg's forgotten, she had barely reached the outskirts of her parent's land when the crushing weight of her burden became too much for her. As she tumbled to the ground in a torrent of brokenness and tears, she continued to cry out to God, hoping He cared—hoping He would hear.

How can I be his wife?

Did You hear the way he talks to me?

What good can possibly come from our union?

For what seemed like an eternity, she lay there sobbing—grieving—exposing her disparaging heart to God. Desperate for a resolution, she pleaded again on her own behalf.

Help me, Lord, Jesus! I can't do this by myself. I need You in my life. Forgive me for the many times I've sinned against You. Mama said that You paid the ultimate price for my sins on the cross.

Will You come into my heart and make me new?

For a time she remained still, as if waiting in expectation, for what she did not know. And then, like a gentle wave covering a sandy shore, a sense of peace washed over her. It was like nothing she had ever experienced before. The weight of her burden lifted and Joy filled her body and soul.

Chapter Seven

Gentle as a Lamb

*H*OW LONG RUTH LAY ON THE GROUND, she did not know, but warm hands gently wiping away her tears drew her from her prayerful trance. Her eyes fluttered open as she was being lifted into her husband's strong arms. Perhaps she should have been frightened, but for some strange reason she was not. As her conversation with God played over in her mind, she beamed in contented bliss.

Is this Your answer, Lord?

Am I supposed to be with him?

Ruth had no way of knowing for sure, but her spirit, though fragile, was peaceful. At the moment that was all the reassurance she needed.

Samuel did not expect this. He anticipated resentment, uncertainty, or trepidation at the very least, but her serene glow puzzled him. He had been furious when she didn't return to the house. However, his anger dissipated when he found her in this vulnerable state. Hopeful, he asked, "Does that smile mean you're glad to see me?"

Tears still mingled in her swollen eyes as she looked up at him. For a time she could only stare. This man, who both terrified and confounded her, seemed to need and want her in his life. He pursued her, and attained her hand without her consent, but she could not lay the blame for that entirely at his feet. Her papa had insisted on his silence. Why, she did not know.

Would she ever be at ease in Samuel's arms? Could she ever come to love this intolerant man, her husband?

Desirous of knowing where she stood with him, she answered his question with one of her own, "That depends, are you going to be nice to me?"

A single eyebrow lifted. "If you want me to be nice, you're going to have to make a few changes yourself." His manner went from kind to unwavering, "First off, you won't be leaving the farm again without my say so. You're my wife now. I have expectations. I've given you some leeway today, but I have every intention of holding you accountable from here on out. You have responsibilities that need tending. I like my meals on time, and you'll not be leaving the kitchen in such a shambles. As for your other chores ..."

Samuel, noting her sour expression was silenced.

Several moments passed before he softly intoned, "I suppose we can go over them in the morning."

She wanted to scream. "Samuel, why must you talk down to me the way you do? Papa and Mama are the best of friends. Don't you want that for us?" Here she was trying to find a sputter of light, anything that would give her hope, and he had the audacity to wink.

Wink!

As if playfulness after all his harshness would alter anything.

"It's just the way I am, Ruth Anne. You'll get used to me."

Her scowl, so fierce, reminded him of a snarling feline. Although she made no attempt to escape his arms, his hold tightened. He would not chance losing her again.

"That's an excuse and you know it!" she boldly stated.

Before responding to Ruth's accusation Samuel set her sideways on the front of his saddle, mounted behind her, and settled her close.

Too close. For the second time that day, she found herself on his lap.

Noting her uncertainty, he said, "I'd like a clear view of your face in the moonlight. Your expressions speak volumes, and I have much to learn about you. In answer to your comment, I would like us to be friends, but you're in for a rude awakening if you keep carrying on the way you do!" His long finger reinforced his words as he tapped on the tip of her nose. "I won't put up with your impertinence, Ruth Anne. As long as you do what you're told, without all the lip, we'll get along fine."

Her irritation rose with every word he spoke. She'd like to tell him a thing or two! Even so, she was not born yesterday. Ruth was in Samuel's arms and his tone did not encourage insolence. Although her husband was just as crude now as he was before, and she could not see how anything good could come from being with him, something told her she had to try looking beneath his rough countenance. There had to be something good about him or her papa never would have agreed to their union. As hard as it was to admit, even to herself, her papa was right, Samuel was her husband for better or worse.

When the silence lengthened, Samuel offered his lame excuse yet again, "You'll get used to me and maybe even come to tolerate me."

"That's just it. I'm hoping we can share more."

"More?"

"Yes ..." her voice faltered.

"Don't get yourself all tied up in knots, Ruth Anne. We'll find a way to make this work."

I hope so! Her chance to run was obviously gone. This man would not be letting her out of his sight any time soon. Of this she was certain. Although her flesh still balked at his closeness, she fought against it. She even managed to let down her guard and relax against him when he snuggled her close. Her husband may never be all that she had hoped for, but she suspected that went both ways. Perhaps, given time, she might come to like him. For now tolerance was a good place to start. Ruth closed her sore eyes and rode the rest of the way to her new home, meditating on all that had transpired.

Samuel was heading for the barn when he nudged her and said, "Ruth Anne, we're home."

Opening her eyes, she looked around. "Samuel, I know it's late, but I'm starving. If you drop me off at the house, I'll start supper."

His sudden burst of laugher not only startled her, it mocked her. "I'm not about to fall for your tricks again. Your home is with me. The sooner you accept that the better."

Running off the way she had, she deserved his sarcasm, but ... "I won't leave, I promise." She peered up at him, eyes pleading. "All I've had are cookies since breakfast. It must be nearly eight."

"If I remember correctly your impertinence kept you from dinner. Amend your ways. See that our meals are on the table proper like and I won't be sending you off to bed hungry."

The peace she had known earlier was dissipating—quickly! Every time this man opened his mouth, her resolve to give their marriage a chance waned. He thought of her as a child, no doubt. A child who would toe the line or else. What he expected was impossible.

When Samuel rode into the barn and dismounted, she leapt to the ground. Although she was not surprised by the possessive hand that slid around her arm before she had a chance to wander, the act annoyed her. Setting her irritation aside, she attempted to soothe his obvious suspicion as she allowed her eyes to roam, "You really went all out, Samuel, this barn is as nice as the house."

His features softened. "Are you saying you're pleased with the home I built for us?"

"For us?" Confusion swept over her. It wasn't as if a place this big could go up in a month. Although she'd like to ask him just how long he had been planning to make her his wife, she wasn't sure she was ready to hear how long her papa had been keeping Samuel's pursuit a secret.

"Yes, for us! Who else? When we arrived this morning I wanted to ask what you thought, but I just couldn't."

Recalling her anger over their arranged marriage, her head lowered. Nothing had changed. Not really. She wasn't happy about being this man's wife, but her heart was softening. Why mystified her. "I'm sorry, Samuel. I know I wasn't very agreeable."

Her eyes flipped up when Samuel's long fingers weaved through the hair at the base of her neck. Although she wanted to pull away, she swallowed an enormous portion of pride and surrendered to his tenderness. His kiss wasn't what she'd call pleasurable, but she did survive. Although the longing in his eyes frightened her more than a tad, she had promised to stay, and a promise from her was as good as gold.

Thinking his timid wife could use a distraction, he lit several lanterns, illuminating the inside of the barn. Unlike their tour through the house, she held nothing back as she took in her surroundings. Samuel reveled in her fascination. How could he not? The change in her was astounding.

"I've never seen a barn like this." Allowing her eyes to roam, she admitted, "A body could eat in here, it's so neat and clean." Everything was tucked in its own special place. The stalls had been mucked and layered with fresh straw for bedding. There was no question about it: Samuel's horses liked him. Every one greeted him as he passed by. Perhaps he was more at ease with animals than her.

Ruth found the ladder to the loft and climbed up. She was only planning to take a quick peek, thinking it would be dark, but the lanterns offered ample light. Curiosity got the best of her. It was so much larger than she had anticipated. Throwing her leg over the edge, she pulled herself the rest of the way up. Drinking in the scent of hay and leather, she stood on her toes to get a closer look at the upper beams. Although she couldn't see them clearly, she noticed several bird nests. She would have to keep a close eye on them. For a time she stood at the edge, looking down at her husband. *He really is a handsome man. Too bad his disposition leaves a bit to be desired.*

She was heading toward an old rocking chair that sat off in the corner when Samuel called up to her, "Ruth, be careful you don't fall through the hay drop."

"Where is it?" she asked and then squealed when her foot took a sudden plunge, but she caught herself before her body followed. "Never mind!"

Samuel snickered, but she ignored him. The carvings on the rocker had captured her attention. When she brushed the hay off, she took a closer look. A mountain man's face had been carved into the back. His mouth was gaping open and his scruffy beard made him appear a bit scary—too scary for her liking. Shuddering, she covered it over again with hay and was thankful her husband had the sense to hide it away. She did not think she would sleep a wink if the gruesome man were ogling her in the night. Imagining how the chair would appear sitting in a corner of their room at dusk brought forth an exaggerated quiver.

Ruth descended the ladder and continued her investigation while Samuel worked. "You must spend hours in here every day to keep it like this." His big black stallion nudged her arm, so she turned and rubbed his thick neck. She wondered when or if she would be allowed to ride him alone, but didn't ask.

Samuel chuckled softly as he hung his saddle. "I had to do something to keep my mind occupied over the winter months. It wasn't easy convincing your father to offer your hand, Ruth Anne."

Shaken by his admission, she spun around to face him. "What do you mean? We met a month ago for the first time."

"True, but I saw you in town on several occasions over the last year."

She nodded, her expression revealing her desire to know more. "When I was riding to and from school?"

"That, and from time to time I'd see you shopping with your parents. From the moment I laid eyes on you ... well, let's just say

I decided then and there I would do everything in my power to make you my wife."

Perplexed, she fingered his stallion's long flowing mane. Odd as it was, knowing she was more than a passing fancy pleased her. "The day you and your father came by to look at the team, was that just a front, or did you really want the horses?"

"An acquaintance of mine on the east side of Detroit bought the team."

"I see ...."

He opened a stall door, threw hay in the corner and filled the mare's water bucket. After patting the horse's long neck, he slid the door shut. "I told your father I'd like to meet you face to face before we came to terms."

"Terms ..?"

Noting her irritation, Samuel continued, but he did so with care, "The marriage contract ... I wanted to meet you before I signed it."

"That's understandable, but I'm confused. Why do you suppose Papa didn't tell me?"

Samuel finished wiping off his horse's bridle and hung it from a hook. "He made it clear that if you were aware of how soon I wanted to marry you, you'd never consent, so he asked me not to tell you. He said something about you wanting to earn your teaching certificate. I couldn't wait, Ruth. Surely you can understand. When a man builds his wife a home, he wants her with him. Besides, no wife of mine will ever work outside of our home. Not while I have breath left in me."

This did not surprise her. For many men this was a matter of pride and Samuel was among the proudest she had ever known.

She could only hope his pride would not get in the way of their happiness. "My desire to teach has little to do with work, Samuel. I love teaching."

"Just put it out of your head. Our little ones will come along soon enough. You'll be so busy caring for and teaching them, you'll forget all about your schoolgirl dreams."

Ruth, mulling over his confession, spoke her thoughts out loud, "So Papa lied to me the day you came?" The realization hit her hard and fast. She turned away, crushed.

So much for you being a man of your word. Her voice crackled as she pressed Samuel further, "What were these terms you and Papa agreed upon?" When the silence lingered, she clarified, "My hand for what?"

"There's no need for you to know that, Ruth."

She faced him, with tears streaming down her exquisite features, hands clamped on her narrow hips. "Tell me, or I'll leave and neither you nor my parents will ever see me again."

Ruth looked angry enough to try, and in truth, he was tired of her antics. Sooner or later she would find out anyway. Perhaps he should be the one to tell her. After all, he was her husband. "Your father is ill."

Her brow furrowed. "He has had a few maladies, but when I've asked, he slough's it off as nothing serious."

Samuel's head dipped in acquiescence. "That was true until a few months back. Apparently, Doc's latest findings have not been favorable."

So she hadn't been imaging his failing health. "Doc hasn't said anything to me … does he know what's wrong with Papa?"

"Some sort of blood sickness. Doc made it clear that …"

When Samuel hesitated, she pressed him, "Tell me!"

"Your father is dying, Ruth Anne."

The lowering of her eyes did nothing to hide the effect of his words. She would have fallen had the stall door not been there to catch her. *This can't be.* Needing confirmation, she asked, "He's dying?"

Samuel's reticent nod said it all. "For your sake, I wish it wasn't true. I had to approach your father several times before he was willing to give me the time of day. His desire to secure your future eventually softened him."

Is that why you chose him, Papa? "If there's more, I'd rather hear it from you, Samuel."

"My willingness to pay off his debts and support your mother in the event of his untimely death swayed him."

Her slender hands covered her face as she burst into tears. *Oh, Papa, why couldn't you tell me?* Her aching heart was nearly in shreds when she peered up. "So you bought me instead of the horses?"

"It wasn't like that."

"But I wouldn't be your wife if Papa didn't agree to your terms," she stated flatly.

One of the lanterns flickered, distracting him for a brief second. He glanced back to see her moving away. "I would have worn him down sooner or later."

Turning back to face him, she shook her head. "No, you wouldn't have. Not if Papa knew how I really feel about you!"

Samuel did nothing to stop her when she bolted past him and ran toward the house. Her words, like a knife in his gut, penetrated deeply.

Opening the door, she made a beeline for *his* bedroom. She hated the thought of being anywhere near *his* room, but she had to lie down or surely she would collapse. The day had been too much. Sleep would claim her, it just had to. Although sleep would help her to escape what her husband had revealed, unfortunately, it was only a temporary fix. She would never escape this man— she was bound to *him* for life.

A sea of misery engulfed her as she surrendered her weary bones to *his* bed. She tried, but could not move past the horrible ache inside her. Nothing helped. She cried thinking about her papa. Her mama loved him so. How would she find the strength to go on without him? Ruth, unable to make sense of anything, gave in to the tears threatening to choke her, grieving her past and contemplating the future. She did not know how much time had lapsed when sweet mercy claimed her, and she drifted into a fitful sleep.

Ruth awoke slowly, fully cognizant of the arms surrounding her. She did not doubt that it was Samuel. His musky scent was unmistakable. For a while she just lay there combating the uncertainties assailing her. Although disquieted by his closeness, the unfathomable emotions swirling inside, they made her wonder if she knew her own mind. Could she give herself to a man she hardly knew?

Did she have a choice?

While his arrogance astounded her, there were other things about him that troubled her—meanness being the most troubling. He was self-centered to a fault, but to what end? His offer of marriage had eased her papa's mind. Samuel had done so much to prepare for her arrival. He was still the same man, everything she despised and then some, but now he was also her husband.

Nothing would change that.

Nonsensically, her mind swung like a pendulum back and forth between shutting him out and surrendering all. If only she could find middle ground, a place where vulnerability did not reign. Deep down she knew, such a place did not exist.

Samuel was not one to take things in stride.

Her anxieties and fears might not be considered. Could she move forward in this new life that had been thrust upon her?

She despised this man. Didn't she? Or was her flesh merely balking because the choice had been taken out of her hands?

She had a choice to make.

She could not do this halfway.

It had to be all or nothing.

True, she did not choose to be his wife, but she was his wife nonetheless. How she would respond to that reality lay perilously before her.

His wife!

Could she take the good with the bad, cleave only to him, remain faithful as long as she lived?

If it came down to a battle of wills, Samuel would win, and that would only erect more walls they would find difficult to break down. She didn't want that.

Why she did not know, but as the minutes passed, she grew more at ease with his closeness. He had every right to be near, but she did wonder, would it always hurt this much to remember Samuel's confession—to remember what had brought her to his house—to his bed?

Her parents would be counting on her. They would need

to know they were forgiven. But could she forgive her papa for arranging their union?

She would have to. God's Word was clear on that. If she did not forgive others, she would not be forgiven. Ruth knew so few passages. Why did the ones she could recall have to be so demanding? If she had to forgive to be forgiven, that meant she would also have to forgive *Samuel*. Could she? Forgiving him would not be an easy thing. But what choice did she have?

She thought it wise to try.

At least that was true at the moment.

Slowly she opened her eyes to find her husband's gaze riveted on her. She tried to move, but he was lying on her skirt.

Perhaps it was unintentional.

Either way, she suddenly felt like a snared rabbit. She wanted nothing more than to break free, but she fought against the urge. Instead, she only stared at the man who held her captive.

With his palms, Samuel dried her damp cheeks. He rubbed her silky curls between his thumb and forefinger, saying, "I never should have told you, Ruth. I'm sorry. It was heartless of me."

His tender words had a soothing effect on her anxious mind. "Papa was wrong to keep this from me. He should have trusted me."

Samuel caressed her delicate face. When that was not enough, his large hand slid slowly down her slender neck, across her shoulder, around the slight curve of her arm, before gathering her hand in his, lifting it to his mouth, and kissing her palm. The aroma of sweet blossoms tantalized his senses. And her skin, it was so soft—softer than anything he had ever touched before. As much as he wanted to press her further, the uncertainty in her eyes kept him from doing so. "You're his little girl. In his mind you'll always need his protection. Now you have me. I'll see to your needs. I'll take good care of you, you'll see."

"If only ..."

His fingers came to her lips to stop the flow of words. "No regrets, Ruth Anne. I'm not sure I agree with your father, but he is convinced that nothing happens by chance. He said that God must have His hand on our union. We can't go back. We can only go forward. You heard what the preacher said, you're my wife until death do us part."

Defeat washed over her. Samuel had paid an awful price to attain her hand. Perhaps she should feel honored that he chose her, but instead she felt obligated. "More like master and slave."

"No, Ruth."

"You bought me, Samuel."

He shook his head. "Men have been paying a bride price for centuries. I wanted you for my wife. In truth, I was determined to have you no matter the cost."

"But you don't even like me."

Running his thick fingers down the side of her lovely face, he grinned as he said, "Trust me, Ruth, I like you plenty. You're comparing me to your father. He and I are as different as night and day. You need time to get to know me is all."

I'm not convinced, but what choice do I have? For a moment her thoughts trailed off. In fact, she was contemplating what life would be like with this man when she suddenly realized, "I need to see my parents, Samuel."

"Not now."

"But I said some horrible things. I have to ... I have to tell them I didn't mean them."

"Tomorrow ... tomorrow is another day ... tomorrow will be soon enough."

There was something in his voice that gave her pause, and then his eyes, they were entranced with her hair—her face—her mouth. He must have sensed her apprehensions and drew her closer still. In fact, he was so close she could feel the warmth of his body against hers. Samuel's knuckles ran ever-so-slowly along her jaw, trailing down her slender neck before he undid the top button on her blouse.

"For now, Ruth Anne, I'd like to indulge in several of your sweet kisses—and then, when you're more at ease with my closeness, I will make you mine."

"But, shouldn't we ..?"

He kissed the tip of her nose, his tenderly spoken words stroking her every concern. "Shouldn't we what?"

"Wait ..."

"You are mine ... I am yours ...."

Frozen in place, she could only stare, stunned by his words, vividly aware of his every caress. When she offered no further objection, Samuel's kisses came softly, tenderly, and then again with such passion. No longer distasteful, each one grew sweeter and brought with it a swell of emotions she could hardly define.

While at first he suspected that she had merely resigned herself to the unavoidable, her response to his affection said otherwise. Eventually her trembling eased and his bride relaxed in the warmth of his tenderness.

Although her husband's unyielding nature still annoyed her to no end, when it came to making Ruth Anne his own, Samuel White was as gentle as a lamb.

He Loves Me!

Chapter Eight

Compliance

"*I*'M STARVING, PLEASE LET ME GO ...."

Unaccustomed to being woken from his slumber, Samuel informed the squirming woman in his arms, "It's the middle of the night, Ruth Anne. You can eat in the morning."

She groaned in frustration. "But you snore like a moose! If I don't fill my empty belly, I won't be able to sleep."

He chuckled softly.

Annoyed, she snarled, "You're laughing at me!"

"You just said that I snore like a moose. How would you know what a moose snores like?"

She giggled. "I don't. Mama says the same thing about Papa. After listening to you snore for over an hour, I just found it appropriate."

"So what are you making us to eat?"

"My stomach's gnawing on my backbone. I'm not about to be picky. What are you going to help me make?"

"Surprise me."

She elbowed him in the stomach.

"Hey! What was that for?"

She craned her neck around to glare at him. "You lazy sponge! It's the middle of the night. If you want something to eat you can help me fix it!"

When he swatted her backside, she scowled. "What was that for?"

"You were warned about that smart mouth."

She had a retort. Boy did she have a retort, but she swallowed it, moved off the bed, reached for her robe and was putting it on when she asked, "Are you telling me not to expect help from you in the kitchen—ever?"

"Ahh, but you are wise for your fifteen years."

"I'll be sixteen in a few weeks!" *In a few weeks …. No wonder Papa rushed this marriage. The choice would have been mine after my sixteenth birthday. Papa, you knew I'd never agree to be Samuel's wife if you waited.*

Unaware of her incisive thoughts, Samuel said, "I have no intentions of lifting a finger in the house, and I won't ask you to help in the barn. Deal?"

"No!" she declared as she scurried out the door.

"Ruth Anne," he bellowed as he ran after his wife.

She'd had a good head start and ducked out of sight before he could see where she was heading.

Samuel lit the lantern and scanned the room, but she was nowhere to be seen. "When I find you, and I will find you, My Daring Beauty, you're in big trouble."

Hearing his soft chuckle, she prayed that he was only teasing, but really didn't know. Considering his ignitable ire, she thought it best not to taunt him overly much.

Ruth, still in hiding, sagged with relief when Samuel gave up the chase, pulled a chair away from the table and sat down. Thinking the danger over, she snuck up behind him, tapped his shoulder and shouted, "Boo!"

He swung her around and she landed in his lap. "Boo, yourself! Now what are you going to do, Creep Mouse?"

Frightened by his dark tone, she begged, "Samuel, please. I was only toying with you."

A single brow lifted. "And I'm not?"

Would she ever understand him? She had never seen his lighthearted side. In truth, she didn't know he had one. When he wrapped his arms around her and tickled her sides, he confused her all the more. "Samuel!" she squealed as she laughed in delight. "Stop!"

"Are you ready to make us something to eat?"

Saucily she turned to face him, her head tilting as she boldly informed him, "I'm ready to make myself something to eat."

His look narrowed. "Ruth Anne, you're tempting fate."

"Oh, all right!" she conceded. "I may never agree with your way of thinking, but I suppose I'll have to adjust."

Righting his testy wife he drew her close for a kiss. "That's my good girl," he had the gall to say and then add, "now get to work!"

You're such a crude man, Samuel White. Why must you irritate me so? She had a verbal response she could have offered, in fact, she had several. Fortunately, she was wise enough to keep them to herself. If she didn't learn to hold her tongue, she had a feeling Samuel would make her life miserable. Though he had proven himself to be a kind and gentle lover, his level of patience in all else thus far was close to zero.

Ruth found a loaf of bread in the breadbox on the counter and decided ham sandwiches would be simple and filling. Unfortunately, the thought of going into the cold cellar at night gave her a bad case of the chills. Her pleading eyes fell back on Samuel.

"What?"

The depth of his voice startled her. Worry furrowed her brow. "Any chance you'd go to the cold cellar for the ham?"

He shook his head in the negative. "What did I tell you?"

Her gaze lowered as she softly intoned, "I know, Samuel, but dark places scare me enough during the day."

For a long moment, he stared at her profile. "Giving in to your fears won't help you move past them, Ruth."

"That's what Papa tells me, but I can't convince myself that it's true. If you won't go, I'll settle for a slice of bread and a tankard of water."

Sighing, he stood, reached for the lantern, grabbed her arm and brought her along with him. As they neared the back of the pantry he felt her trembling—fiercely! She really was frightened. With a flicker of compassion for his young wife, he pulled her close. "Ruth, until you're more comfortable with your new surroundings, I'll come with you. Truth is, I thought you were bluffing."

"You told me this morning that I'm honest to a fault. I won't lie to you without good cause."

His brow lifted. "So lying about having to use the outhouse earlier was a good cause?"

"It was either that or climb out the bedroom window. You

have a tendency to catch me when I leap out windows, so I figured it was my only means of escape."

He chuckled as he moved down the cellar steps and reached for the ham. Peering up, he asked, "Do you want the cheese?"

"If you'll be kind enough to put them both away when we're finished?"

Her coy look made him grin.

"I will," he conceded, "but only when we eat in the middle of the night."

Nibbling on her lower lip, she said, "I suppose I can live with that."

With the mound of cheese secure in her arms, she dashed around the corner to begin preparations. Filling the tall wooden tankards with cool water, she placed her husband's plate in front of him before claiming the seat across from him. She waited, hoping he would lead in prayer. When it did not happen, she closed her eyes and whispered a silent one for both of them.

"Having trouble staying awake?" Samuel probed, the moment she opened her eyes.

"No, I was thanking the Lord for His provision."

I'm the one providing for this household ... his thoughts corrected. "Waste of time if you ask me."

I didn't ask you. "You have a right to your beliefs, but so do I. God's Word reminds us to give thanks with a grateful heart, so if you don't mind, I will continue to do so."

The wicked look he sent her way made her wince. "Watch your tone with me, Ruth Anne."

Afraid he'd send her back to bed without her meal, she complied. Her burning stomach, demanding satisfaction, began to rumble as she lifted her sandwich to her mouth and took a big bite. She couldn't remember the last time a sandwich had tasted so good. For a while the silence lengthened, but she welcomed the reprieve.

Samuel finished eating and leaned back in his chair, his eyes watching her every move. "With all your shenanigans today, I've gotten behind on my chores. So have you for that matter."

"Me ..?"

"Yes, you!"

"But I just got here!"

"We both had chores that were ignored when you took off. I'll be heading out to the fields right after breakfast and be back before the sun gets too hot. See that you have our dinner ready on time. I'll need to eat and head back out."

Her brow furrowed in thought. "Okay ... I think I can make it to my parents and be home before then." She took another bite of her sandwich and almost choked when she caught a glimpse of his evil glare. Nearly a minute passed before she managed to swallow and ask, "Did I say something wrong?"

"You won't be running off without my say so, Ruth Anne."

She scowled. "I would hardly call going to see my parents running off, and besides, you're the one who said I could speak with them today."

"We'll fit in a visit if we finish our chores before the day is spent."

"But, I have to see them," she entreated. "I said hurtful things. I need to make them right."

"And you will, when I can take you. Not a moment before."

Her head lowered. "But I'd prefer to do it alone."

"That is not an option. You will wait until I can take you."

The way Samuel talked that could take days, weeks, even months. Did the man not have a heart? Her papa was dying. She had no way of knowing how long he had. Could the massive bruises she had questioned him about be a side effect of his illness? And what about his spells of lightheadedness? He often sloughed them off as nothing more than a minor annoyance. They had to be a part of the sickness eating away at him.

With a sense of renewed urgency and even a touch of boldness, she sat up straight and met her husband's stern glare. "You know, Samuel. I did have a life before you plucked me out of it. I have friends and family that I'm going to want to see. Please tell me I'm not a prisoner in this house."

Inside he was stewing, but he let her go on. Perhaps it was best to know up front what he'd be up against.

"If you have a horse in that big barn you wouldn't mind me riding, I could saddle it myself. Then I could come and go when I have extra time. I wouldn't have to bother you at all." When he offered no response she added, "I'd be real quick about it. You'd hardly know I was gone." As the silence trailed on, her hopeful heart plunged in despair.

Her appetite was gone.

Ruth had been such a fool to think his gentleness with her earlier meant he would no longer be cold and heartless. He had never hidden his true nature—not from her anyway. His silent response sent a clear message. Well, she had a message of her own to send, and she would send it loud and clear. After all, she was an adult. She had a right to be treated with kindness, didn't she?

Her marriage was a farce.

Samuel didn't give a lick about her. He only wanted to use and control her. *Well, good luck trying, Samuel. I no longer care.*

Ruth stood, wrapped her sandwich in a towel, picked up the small lantern, and walked out the back door into the moonlit night. Her husband would be angry with her for not waiting for him, but right now she needed to distance herself or surely she would lash out.

Was it wrong to welcome a confrontation with a bear? Perhaps a wild cat would take her life with less suffering. Her reasons for living were being ripped away. Freedom from this world would be a welcome relief. But thoughts of her mama made her look beyond her own anguish. How would her mama find the strength to go on if she and her papa were both gone? No doubt, her desire to escape this life was not only selfish, it was wrong.

Fraught with desperate emotions, a sliver of fear raced up Ruth's spine as she opened the creaky door to the outhouse and stepped in. The smell along with her turmoil left her feeling queasy, but she refused to give in to her body's revulsion. She needed the nourishment her sandwich would offer.

As she contemplated her situation, she began to wonder if seeing her parents so soon was such a good idea. How could she apologize when they were the ones who put her in this mess? She needed time to sort this out, but she could not do it now. If she continued in this state, she would never sleep tonight. Her head hurt from thinking too much and her eyes were sore and swollen from crying. Perhaps the heaviness in her heart would ease. She just had to find a way to go on.

Ruth, thinking again that this had been the worst day of her life, opened the door and found her husband waiting for her. Fury oozed from his narrowed eyes. She had a dreadful feeling her day was about to get worse.

"You don't think it's necessary to heed my warning?"

Her mood darkened and her arms spread wide, accenting her disgruntled words. "Unfortunately, there were no bears willing to free me from my gilded cage."

He caught her meaning. It angered him all the more.

When he took an uncompromising step toward her, she took two back. He was still close—too close for her liking. She considered running. Only knowing he would catch her within seconds kept her from doing so.

"You saw me leave, Samuel, if it bothered you that much you could have followed."

Her brazen retort earned her a painful slap. Stunned, her hand came up to cover her stinging flesh. Warnings went off in her head, but no ... did she listen? She allowed her anger to rule. "I don't know what Papa ever saw in you!" She turned away from his heated glower, adding in an outraged snarl, "I despise the very ground you walk on. I have since the moment we met!"

His oversized hand wrapped around her frail arm as they moved swiftly toward the house. Although she tripped in her attempt to keep up, he did not let her fall.

"I was hoping you wouldn't push me to this, but my father was apparently right! The only wife worth having is one who knows her place." They were back in the kitchen before Samuel noticed the red welts across her pale face. They gave him pause.

"I was angry, Samuel ... I said things I shouldn't have. I'm sorry ..." she humbly entreated as tears flooded her eyes. "There's so little that is good between us. Please don't destroy that by hurting me more." Her plea must have hit a nerve in his icy heart because he calmed and she breathed a little easier.

"You have much to learn about compliance."

"I'm far from perfect. I'm bound to make mistakes." *And so are you.* "This day has been ..." she paused. How could she say *horrible* when he was so close to lashing out? She settled for, "... difficult. Please be patient with me."

"Don't press me like this again, Ruth Anne *White*."

The emphasis he put on her new last name hit its mark. She nodded, hoping she could comply.

"Clean up this mess while I put the food away. We need to get back to bed."

Ruth did as she was told; however, she no longer wondered to what extreme Samuel would go to control her, she knew.

Chapter Nine

A Hard Road Ahead

*S*AMUEL'S SILENCE AT BREAKFAST grated on Ruth's nerves, but soon he would be off to the fields and out of her hair. Oh, how she relished the thought of having the morning to herself, time to settle in, to do as she pleased without him stalking her every move.

She finished her meal, cleared the table, and filled the basin with sudsy water. After scraping the leftovers into the slop bucket, she was rolling up her sleeves to wash the dishes when Samuel came out of the back room.

"I'm heading out, Ruth. I'll be back around noon."

She nodded, but it wasn't until he came up behind her that she forced herself to turn and face him. Instead of kissing her as she had assumed he would, he handed her a piece of paper.

"What's this?" she innocently inquired as her eyes fell on a long list of his expectations. Without thought for her welfare, she wadded it up and threw it at him, declaring, "If you don't want me telling you how to manage the barn, then don't tell me how to clean the house!" She would have turned away, but he now had a firm hold on her upper arms.

He drew her close. Too close. The heated look that met hers raised the hair at the base of her neck. "I don't recall asking your opinion!" Releasing her, he picked up the list, stuck it in her sweater pocket, and informed her, "Half of the things on that list had better be done when I return, along with my noon meal being ready."

Ruth couldn't summon the fortitude to respond. If she chose to defy him, Samuel would show no mercy, she could see it in his eyes. So much for her dauntless plan to stand up to him from now on. *For you, Mama, I will swallow my pride and yield to this atrocious man.*

She waited until he walked out the door before taking the paper out of her pocket. Pouring herself another cup of coffee, she slumped down into one of the kitchen chairs and began reading. As she did, Samuel's aim became crystal clear. He intended to keep her so busy she wouldn't have time to breathe, let alone gather a moment to herself. Maybe if she hurried she could salvage a little time at the end of her day to escape these prison walls and pretend that she was Ruth Anne Schmidt again, carefree and loved, if only for a while.

After dusting, she salt scrubbed the kitchen floor, and then quenched her thirst with a tall tankard of cool water before heading out to the tool shed. As was becoming the norm, she was in awe when she opened the door and stepped inside. Not only was everything in its place, Samuel had more tools than she had ever seen. Finding them in immaculate condition did not surprise her. Not even the shovels held a trace of the soil they were made to cultivate. Reaching for the hoe, she was heading out of the small structure when she noticed a slim pair of leather gloves on a bench by the door. There was a note attached.

> Ruth,
>
> We had a rough start to our morning, but I'm hopeful our evening will be more enjoyable. Thoughts of my lovely bride will no doubt make my workday pass quickly.
>
> I ordered these gloves for you several months back. They should protect your tender skin. I'm sure I don't need to remind you to wear your straw hat while tending your garden. Be sure you clean and return the tools to their rightful place.
>
> See you at noon.
>
> Samuel

Ruth snarled up her nose. *How did I end up with someone like him, Lord? Will he always irritate me so?* She knew all too well that her attitude going into this could alter the outcome, so she did her best to face it with a willing heart. In truth, she actually enjoyed being out on such a glorious day. That is, until she started yanking on a deep-rooted weed that wouldn't budge. Several attempts proved unsuccessful. Taking a moment to regain her strength, she gave it all she had and finally the stubborn weed came out. Unfortunately, she lost her balance and landed hard on her backside. Although thankful no one had witnessed her happenstance, the budding tomato plant she landed on was in dire straits. Not even the three sticks she found to try and support the prickly stem offered it much hope. In the end, she pulled it out, smoothed the ground and stuck the limp plant in the weed bucket. Samuel might not be pleased when he found it missing, but it wasn't as if she did it on purpose.

She had to keep moving or she'd never finish her chores before the evil lord returned to his castle and found it wanting. Giggling, her thoughts trailed on. She so loved spinning yarns in her head, but this one hit a bit too close to home. In truth, it wasn't funny.

Ruth was working her way down the second row of beans when her father-in-law's gruff voice shattered her tranquility.

"Where is your bonnet, Girl?"

Her racing heart took a moment to ease. Regaining her composure, she peered up. "Hello, Mr. White." Although her voice trembled when she spoke, she couldn't help it. The man had just scared the wits out of her.

"Answer me?"

She couldn't believe the audacity of this man. "I ... I forgot it when I left the house." Her excuse was lame, but she had to say something. His eyes had narrowed, irritating her profusely. *Who does he think he is bossing me?*

"I see you found the gloves Samuel left you, so I know you read the note."

"Did you need something in particular?" *Or did you just come over here to chastise me?* The White men sure did have a knack for making her squirm.

"If you don't mind I'll keep working. As you can see, I have a ways to go."

He moved toward her with more agility than she knew he possessed. His thick hand wrapped around her arm and he flung her none-too-gently toward the house. She wanted to shout in protest, but thought better of it.

"Your husband wants that fair skin of yours protected. Get the bonnet before you go any further!"

Hmm! Guess I know where your son gets his manners. She scowled at the man and while she did go back to the house, she busied herself with other things on the list instead of going back out. Putting up with her husband's abuse was one thing; she wasn't about to take it from her father-in-law as well.

Ruth had been working so diligently at her chores, she forgot about making Samuel's meal. When she heard him come in the front door, her heart faltered. Glancing his way, she wondered if all she had accomplished would appease him.

Samuel's eyes fell on the mantel clock. Realizing he was early, he asked as he moved toward his wife and softly touched her warm pink face. "Did you have a productive morning, Ruth?"

Sticking out her tongue seemed an appropriate response, but then his anger would flare and where would she be? Instead, she avoided his question, and turned to leave, saying, "I should start dinner."

"You have time. I'm early." When she craned her neck around to see if he was serious, he was moving toward her again. He captured her hand while eyeballing her skin. "Didn't wear your hat, did you?"

"There were more weeds in the garden than I expected."

He nodded in understanding. "See that you wear it from now on. The tools were left out. Care to tell me why?"

Her head lowered, contemplating what she should say. "Your father ... he stopped by."

"I see ...."

She looked up at him. "Samuel, could you please tell your father ..."

His brow furrowed as he waited for words that did not come. "Tell him what, Ruth."

That he'd best not touch me again! If only she could have summoned the nerve to let the words tumble out. "Never mind ..."

"All right, then come. Show me what you've done."

Her dander rose. Kicking him in the shin might make her feel better, but she was wiser now than the day they were married. As humiliating as it was, Ruth did show him. She even tried to listen as he critiqued her work. When it became obvious he would accept nothing less than perfection, she escaped his grasp and ran out the back door.

Samuel followed fast in her footsteps, stopping abruptly when she lost her breakfast before reaching the outhouse. Confused, he went back into the house, dampened a clean towel, returned to where his wife stood and demanded to know, "Why are you ill?"

After wiping her mouth, she glanced up at his puzzled face. *I'm not used to being treated like a dimwitted servant! It turned my stomach.* "I'm not sure ...." This seemed to be her day for lame answers, but the truth would get her slapped and her burnt skin was already hurting enough.

For the longest moment, he only stared. "Would you like me to haul water so you can soak in a warm bath?"

Taken aback by his generous offer, she admitted, "That would be wonderful, but a bath in the middle of the day might make me sleepy." Her gaze lowered. "If I fall asleep I won't have time to finish my chores."

"You let me worry about that. Your health is more important. Besides, you made some good headway. Perhaps I was too hard on you. Give yourself time. When you understand what I expect, you'll do better."

Every once in a while you show the slightest flicker of human kindness, Samuel. Regrettably, my hopes barely begin to peak when you open your mouth and remind me of your true nature. I might as well resign myself to the fact that I will never live up to your expectations. Only God is capable of perfection.

As frustrating as her morning had been, Ruth was pleased when Samuel hauled in the last of the promised water. She thanked him repeatedly and truly meant it. After a relaxing bath and a long afternoon nap, Ruth awoke feeling a bit more like her old self. Her husband might still be lurking, expecting too much, but she felt better equipped to face the remainder of her day.

Chilled, she pulled a sweater over her blouse, made the bed, and left the room. As she headed toward the kitchen, the mantel clock struck three times. Supper! If she didn't get it started they'd be having ham again. As she entered the kitchen, a note on the counter caught her eye. She stopped to read it.

> Ruth Anne,
>
> I butchered a chicken. I'm hoping a calm meal will ease your ailing stomach. You will find it in the large pot on the back of the stove. If you have supper ready early, we might be able to fit a quick visit in with my parents. Don't push yourself if you're not feeling up to it.
> See you soon, My Love.
> Samuel

Hmm, she thought, *he was kind this time. Wonder how long it will last?*

As soon as supper was in the oven, Ruth poured herself into her chores. Staying busy kept her mind off her woes. The smell of chicken baking tantalized her senses. Even so, she kept working until it was roasted to perfection—a nice golden brown. She could hardly wait to bite into the succulent meat. The potatoes were mashed and the tender carrots buttered before she took the meat out of the oven. After putting the chicken on a large platter, she set it on the table. She was stirring the gravy when she heard Samuel come in the back door.

He removed his boots, stuck his feet into his house shoes and stopped to wash his hands in the basin before joining her in the kitchen. His eyes met hers as he reached to caress her cheek. "You look better. Are you?"

"Yes. Thanks for asking."

"How long before supper is ready?"

"Five minutes."

He glanced at the steaming platter on the table. "Won't the chicken need time to cool a bit before you pick the meat off the bones and add it to the gravy?"

Scowling, her gaze met his. "Why would I do that? I prefer it plain."

"Then leave yours plain and put mine in the gravy."

She turned away in an attempt to calm her rising irritation.

"So ... when will supper be ready?"

"All I had left to do is finish the gravy, now ..." she shrugged, "hard to say." *I'm thinking, three, maybe four hours!*

Ignoring her obvious annoyance, he leaned down to kiss her

warm cheek. "Do the best you can. I'll get changed."

The moment he turned to leave, she wiped her cheek and snarled up her nose. *Why must you grate on my nerves so?*

Ruth retrieved the chicken and pulled the skin off so it would cool. After thickening the gravy, she numbly picked the meat off the bones and threw it into the pot. She was angry enough to douse it with cayenne, but she restrained herself.

Her appetite was gone, but needing to appease her husband, she put a few dry pieces of meat on her plate. When the meal was on the table, she sat down, said grace, and added a small amount of potatoes and a carrot to her plate. Samuel might be angry with her for starting without him, but she proceeded anyway. She had just swallowed her last bite and stood when Samuel walked into the room. Dutifully, she poured his coffee.

"Samuel, if it's all right with you, I'm going out to sit on the porch. I enjoy watching the sun set."

He frowned. "You need to eat, Ruth."

Sullen eyes met his. "I did eat some. I'm not very hungry."

Her lack of appetite sent a message of its own. "I'll allow it this time, but from now on I'll expect you to take your meals with me."

In no mood to fight, her head dipped in acquiescence as she turned to leave.

Ruth stepped out the back door and strolled around the side of the house, finding solace in the familiar sounds, smells, and movements that reminded her of home. If she were to close her eyes, she could pretend she was there, but then she might trip and fall. Instead, she listened intently, allowing her gaze to roam, attempting to take it all in. Crickets chirped from their hidden coves, horses pranced playfully in the field, and frogs croaked in a nearby pond. The hoot of an owl resonated from the edge of the forest alerting the inhabitants that he was near. A colorful butterfly graced her with its presence. For a while Ruth was content to follow its progress. When the winged insect landed on a budding flower and then took flight again, she trailed closely behind. Allowing herself a frivolous moment, she cupped her hands and captured its feathery softness. Nary had a second passed before it kissed her palms. She opened her hands and watched it flutter away. If only she could do the same.

Ruth sank into the chair on the porch and drank in the gleaming shades the setting sun exuded as it slowly immersed itself in the clouded expanse. Words could not begin to describe its beauty. God's creative design held such a fascination for her.

As if all that she had partaken of was not enough, her attention was drawn to the leaves on the narrow tree limbs. She, intrigued by the way they rustled as the gentle breeze carried them along, always in motion—always bound by the limb's constraints. Although she wanted nothing more than to forget her existence with Samuel for a time, she couldn't help wondering, *Is this what my life is to be like from now on, never knowing what will happen next? Tossed to and fro, ever controlled by Samuel's whims.*

Why, God? What purpose could You have in bringing us together? Am I missing something? Marriage is supposed to be for a lifetime, but I'm struggling. I sure could use some encouragement here.

Her peaceful time came to an abrupt end when the front door open and Samuel called out, "Ruth, you need to see to the mess in the kitchen, so we can be on our way."

"You go ahead without me. To be honest, Samuel, I'm not up to visiting."

He stepped out onto the porch and caught her eye. "We're going together. Get in the house!"

Always the gentleman! she thought. Swallowing her pride yet again, she forced herself to stand. When she turned to go back the way she had come his stern bellow stopped her.

"Ruth Anne, now!"

Though her defenses heightened, she was wiser and held her tongue as she turned to face him. "I need to use the outhouse. You're welcome to come along if you'd like." Her hand came out in a welcoming gesture, but he did not take it. "If you're busy, I'll finish my chores and then look for you."

"Go ahead! I'll be in the parlor. I have reading to catch up on."

Ruth took her time with clean up, hoping Samuel would say it was too late for them to go. In truth, she wasn't feeling well. She threw the dirty water off the back porch and hung her apron from the hook. As she turned to seek out her husband, her heart suddenly took flight. He was standing directly behind her. Squealing, she shoved him and said, "Don't do that to me!"

"If you weren't feeling guilty for taking your sweet time, you'd have heard my approach."

She couldn't deny it.

Tucking her stray wisps behind her ears, he said, "We should go or we won't have time to visit."

His tender gesture did nothing to soothe her turbulent mood. She dreaded going to see his folks and spoke without thought, "Your mother can barely breathe, never mind converse when you're father is around. The man doesn't like me, so tell me,

Samuel, how will my going to see them be considered visiting?"

You and that smart mouth! He was ready to explode.

Noting his bristly look and red face, she added, "Don't misunderstand me. I would love to visit with your mother. I just think it would be more productive if you were to send her over here. Then we could talk while you spend time with your father."

"Get your sweater on," Samuel demanded.

Knowing she was treading on thin ice did nothing to alter her strained mood. She grabbed her sweater off the hook, stormed out the door, and headed back to the outhouse. Her stomach was in knots, again. This time she knew why.

At the peak of his endurance, Samuel sat on the back step and waited. He should give his wife a sound thrashing. She certainly deserved it. Even so, there was a principle involved. She didn't want to go with him and he was determined to take her. Their relationship, he was finding, held more challenges than he had anticipated. No doubt about it, his porcelain beauty would need to mend her ways, and soon.

Samuel stood when the door to the necessary room creaked open. Ruth, pale as a ghost, staggered toward him, her arms wrapped around her stomach.

"Ruth, what is it?"

"Something's wrong, Samuel. I lost my supper."

If her complexion were not so pasty, he would have thought she was lying to get out of going. "Let's get you into bed. A good night's rest will do you some good."

She said not a word when he swept her up into his arms and carried her back to the house, helped her with her nightclothes, and tucked her in before walking over to his parent's house to tell them they would have to visit another night.

Ruth was ill throughout the night and by morning her weakened state, combined with her lack of sleep, left her teary. "Samuel, you have to take me home."

"You are home."

She tried snuggling into her pillow, but it offered no comfort. "You know what I mean."

"You're too weak to travel, and, besides, you wouldn't want to expose your father to a stomach ailment in his condition."

"But Mama's chicken soup is the only thing that will make me better."

He tucked her stray curls behind her ears. "You'll be fine. I'll ask my mom to make you some tomorrow."

When tears flooded Ruth's eyes she turned away. "You don't understand! Only Mamas will make me better."

"Nonsense! You're too dependent on your parents for your own good. I'll take care of you. You'll see." He leaned down and kissed her forehead. Though she didn't feel feverish, she was shivering, so he added an extra blanket to the bed. "Close your eyes and try to rest. I'll be back to check on you after I feed and water the livestock.

She did close her eyes as he suggested, but not because she was tired, she was frustrated, distraught, and she had the worst headache. Although Samuel's concern seemed genuine enough, she strongly suspected he would not give her what she wanted more than anything: to be back in her parent's home, sleeping till noon in her own bed, awaiting the healing ingredients hidden within her mama's chicken soup.

Ruth cried herself to sleep, knowing that while her husband did have a few redeeming qualities, she still had a hard road ahead.

He Loves Me!

Chapter Ten

A Meal to Remember

I KNOW YOU'RE TIRED OF ME ASKING, Samuel, but it's been four days. I have to check on my parents."

He stopped eating long enough to look up, his invasive eyes making her squirm. "I've asked you to make a list for when I go into town. Is it complete?"

"Yes. I put it on the secretary in *your* room."

"*Our* room," he corrected, as he scanned the kitchen. "Are your chores caught up?"

"Look around, Samuel. Your house is always clean, is it not?" *It's our relationship that needs work.* Her words, though humbly spoken, were not without effect.

His eyes narrowed in on her. "Watch yourself! You know what I mean. The list of chores I gave you, are they done?"

Fortunately, her husband had not mastered the art of reading her mind. "I still have a few things to finish. If you'll take me, I promise to catch up tomorrow."

Several second staggered by. "That's fine for today, but you'll not be making a habit of it."

Her chest swelled with pent up anger. This was not the time to lash out, but shutting out her wayward thoughts took great effort. When her hopeful gaze fell on him her calm astounded her. "When would you like to leave?"

"Put the kitchen back in order. I'll come for you as soon as I finish up in the barn. Be quick about it, Ruth Anne. I won't be long."

Without giving her a chance to respond, Samuel strode toward their room, stuck the list in his shirt pocket, retrieved the funds he would need, and then went to the barn to saddle Pride. In truth, he didn't care if Ruth ever saw her family and friends again, but he refused to allow her parents to think he was completely heartless. He had to live in Detroit, and bad rumors had a way of spreading like wildfire. Keeping Ruth from her dying father would not be well received. His wife was right. Her mother would need her support in the coming days. A visit here and there wouldn't hurt as long as Ruth kept her head about her.

Ruth carefully wrapped the extra cinnamon rolls she had made that morning and placed them in a small basket to take to her parents. She knew them to be her papa's favorite. They would make a fine peace offering. Her callous choice of words the last time they were together still plagued her. Unfortunately, she couldn't take them back.

The second she heard Samuel ride up to the house, she snatched her shawl off the hook and hurried out to meet him. In the mood he was in he wouldn't think twice about leaving her if she kept him waiting. She wasn't about to let that happen.

"Hand me the basket, Ruth."

She complied, thankful he did not question her about the contents. The man was insufferable. She had made an extra plate of cookies yesterday and asked if she could take them over to his parents. He informed her that his mother was capable of making cookies. She didn't need to be cooking for them. The man had no concept of what it meant to be neighborly. As far as she could tell, he didn't do anything out of the kindness of his heart. He did for others, including her, only if it meant he had something to gain. Love and friendships were foreign to him, something he had learned to live without. Did he expected her to do the same.

"Ruth Anne! Quit your day dreaming and listen."

Startled, her eyelids flipped up. "Sorry!"

"Put your foot in the stirrup and give me your hand. I'll pull you up."

"All right ...." She did as she was told, but again her mind strayed. *There are other horses in the barn I could ride if you were feeling generous.* More than likely he had ulterior motives for wanting her near. Ruth did not share his sentiment. Needing to stifle her annoyance, she made a conscious effort to change the direction of her thoughts. "Thank you for doing this, Samuel. Spending time with my parents is important to me."

He pulled her close and kissed her cheek. "I know it is. I'll drop you off and be back to pick you up after I see to a few things in town."

She peered up at him and chanced asking, "Would you mind if we stayed for supper?" When the silence lingered, she was sure he would say no, but she didn't press him. Experience had taught her that it would do no good. Samuel did only what he wanted to, no matter how much she pleaded.

"I suppose we can as long as we make it an early meal. The animals will still need tending, so we can't stay late."

She craned her neck around. "I'd be glad to help you, Samuel."

His brow lifted. "And the next thing I know you'll be looking for help in the house. No thanks! I'll manage."

Her head lowered, her spirit suffering yet another blow. "I'm not sure I'll ever understand the way you think. We're supposed to be a family. We should find joy in working side by side."

"Enough! If I want your opinion I'll ask for it." His oppressive manner had its effect. They rode the rest of the way in silence.

No doubt, Samuel would never see her as an equal—a helpmate. While he demanded obedience and respect from her, he returned the sentiment, only if it served his purpose. She often wondered what his father was really like. Tyranny, was it a curse handed down from generation to generation? If it was, she prayed that they would never have children. Oh, her heart would ache for little ones, but at the same time it would tear her apart to raise a son who ended up treating his wife like Samuel did her.

Please, God, help me to concentrate on the positive things about my husband. Forgive me for judging him so harshly. He is a good provider and a gentle lover. Ruth was trying to think of more of his finer attributes when she saw the turnoff for her parents' farm. The heaviness in her heart began to lift. As they rode into the yard, her parents came out of the house to greet them. The second she met her mama's gaze, she fell completely apart. In fact, she cried so hard, when she slid off Pride, her mama wrapped her arms around her and led her into the house. Ruth never looked back. The security she found in her mama's arms was such a welcome reprieve.

Gerald, noting the strange expression on Samuel's face,

tried to make light of his daughter's emotional state. "Other than Ruth's time away at school, or fishing, they've never really been separated. Looks like their glad to see each other."

Imagining all sorts of things, Samuel considered taking her back home. Only knowing how hurtful his actions would appear kept him from doing so. Instead, he nodded and said, "I have a few things to see to in town, Mr. Schmidt. I'll be back to reclaim my wife in a short while."

"Florence and I would love to have you and Ruth stay for supper."

Samuel stared at him for several seconds, surprised that his request so mimicked his wife's. Nodding, he said, "That's fine, as long as we can make it an early meal. The cows will have to be milked and the stock fed before I can call it a night."

"Not a problem." Gerald waited until Samuel rode out of sight before joining his wife and daughter in the house. His heart ached for Ruth. Something was dreadfully wrong. While he wanted to question her on the matter, he needed to use caution. He had no wish to make things harder on her than they already were.

Gerald smiled when he walked into the room. "Well, you got her to quit crying, Flo. I hope that's a good sign?" Gerald immediately went to embrace his daughter. "It's good to see you, Honey."

"You too, Papa. I'm sorry I said such horrible things the last time we were together. Can you forgive me?"

"Already done. Tell me, Ruth Anne, how are you and Samuel getting along? Are you settled in your new home?"

"I brought you a surprise, Papa. I know how much you enjoy them."

Gerald took the basket she held out to him and peeked inside.

"Oh, my! Florence, did you see what's in here?"

Her mama's eyes sparkled. "No, but I can smell them. I hope you're planning to share."

He hemmed and hawed before offering, "If you'll make us some tea, maybe I will."

"I'll fix it if you'd like, Mama."

Florence stood and moved toward the pantry. "I'll see to it. Papa asked you a few questions. I think he's waiting for answers."

Ruth's head lowered hoping to hide the fresh tears pooling in her eyes, but her papa reached for her chin and brought her sodden gaze to his. "You really don't want to know, Papa. Besides, I want this to be a pleasant visit."

"That may be, but I have a feeling your burdens are too heavy for you to bear alone. Sometimes when we share them with others they seem lighter."

Ruth reached for the hanky she had tucked in her sleeve and blew her nose. "Samuel's house is very nice. You were right, he has worked very hard to be sure I'd know every convenience."

Gerald's brow furrowed. "Samuel's house? But it's your home too."

Her head swayed in the negative. "Home ... no, Papa, my home is here with you and Mama. I might live with Samuel now, but my heart is here with the two of you."

His heart squeezed so tightly he found it difficult to breathe. "You just need time to get to know your husband. He's a good man. Perhaps a bit stern, but I'm hopeful time will change all that."

"Only a miracle could change him. He needs me, but only to clean his house, make his meals, and fill his carnal needs. I wish it wasn't so, but it is."

"But those things are all part of being a good wife. Surely he brings you some pleasure."

She offered a halfhearted smile. "The first night we were married, we shared a few happy moments, and he brought me here today."

"Yes, he did." Gerald confirmed.

"Papa, I'm not asking you to understand, but Samuel is the last person I want to think about right now. Do you mind? It took me four days to convince him to bring me home. Wasting precious time talking about things I have no control over won't change a thing. Please, just let me have this time with my two favorite people in the whole world."

The kettle was boiling, so Florence asked, "In that case, tell me, Ruth, what kind of tea you would like? And supper? Does anything sound especially good?"

Her mama had a way of making her feel so special. "My choice in everything?"

"Absolutely!"

Ruth jumped up, twirled around and giggled out loud. "It feels so good to be myself and laugh again!"

Gerald and Florence shared a knowing glance while Ruth went to pick out her favorite tea. Their regrets were many. If they had it to do over again they never would have accepted Samuel's offer, but they couldn't go back.

For Gerald, the thought of leaving his wife and daughter with financial burdens hanging over their heads had pushed him to make this decision. He could only hope that in time God would change Samuel's heart. Unfortunately, sharing his regrets would not help their daughter. Ruth was right. If Samuel really was an ogre, she needed a time of refreshing.

Ruth poured the water into her mama's pot, added the spearmint tealeaves and smiled as she turned to face her parents. "Tell me. What did you have yesterday for supper?"

"Ham," Florence said as she snarled up her nose.

"So did we." Ruth poured tea into their cups and Gerald stole a cinnamon roll out of the basket. Ruth was not surprised when he took the one with the most icing.

"Mmm!" he said after taking a nice big bite. "These are delicious, Honey."

"I'm glad you like them."

"Ruth," her papa asked, "I could butcher a few chickens?"

Her mouth watered. "Oh, Mama, I can almost taste your fried chicken, creamy mashed potatoes, and sweet buttery corn bread."

"I made a pecan pie this morning. Will that do for dessert?"

Her eyes sparkled with delight. "Will it do? Don't tease me, Mama. You know pecan is my favorite."

"If Samuel doesn't like it I'd be glad to make something else."

Ruth grinned mischievously. "I really don't know, but if he doesn't that's all the more for us."

Gerald, thinking someone should defend Samuel in his absence, spoke up, "Now, you girls. You'd better be nice. Samuel will never understand how to love if we don't set a good example."

Stomping her foot, Ruth pouted. "I've had to be nice for four days and still got myself into a world of trouble. It hasn't been easy, Papa, so please don't scold me."

"Oh, all right. You and Mama enjoy your visit. I'll head out to the coop and pick out two plump birds."

Gerald had no more walked out the door, when Ruth reached

for her mama's hands and sat down next to her at the table. "Samuel told me all about Papa's illness. How is he really?"

"He has his good and bad days. For several months now he has been struggling. Unfortunately, Doc is just as baffled as we are. He wrote to some of his colleagues, I'm afraid the response has not been favorable. The other doctors haven't found a successful treatment for his disorder either."

"Mama, Samuel won't allow me to leave the farm without him. Will you and Papa come and visit. Please don't stay away. I'm so lonesome. Besides, I need to spend time with Papa before ..."

Florence patted her hand. "I'm not sure Papa will remember where Samuel's place is. He was only there once, and you know what his memory has been like."

Ruth went to retrieve paper and pen. "I'll draw you a map. It's hidden from the main trail, but it's not far." She wrote out explicit directions and then took the map and put it on her parents' dresser. How long her papa had, she did not know, but she was determined to enjoy every moment they could scrape together.

"I've been thinking. Samuel won't give me one of his horses to ride, but maybe if you and Papa were to give me Thunder ...."

Her mama's head swayed in the negative. "If I'm not mistaken, Samuel sold the riding horses to a rancher on the other side of town. The team is going to someone else."

Ruth didn't understand. "Why should he have any say over Papa's livestock?"

Florence reached out and caressed her cheek. "It was all part of the marriage contract, Honey. Without Samuel's generosity, we would have lost our farm to the bank last month. "

"Oh ..." she didn't realize things were so bad. Knowing didn't make her feel more secure in her marriage, but it did shed some light on why her papa might have overlooked some of Samuel's less desirable qualities.

The afternoon flew by in a whirl of laughter and excitement as Gerald, Florence, and Ruth joined in their efforts to make a meal to remember. In fact, they were having so much fun they didn't hear Samuel come in the front door. One moment they were laughing and carrying on, and in the next total silence blanketed the kitchen.

"Don't let me spoil your fun," Samuel stated, as his eyes remained firmly planted on his wife. He had never witnessed her real nature and in truth, he was taken aback.

Gerald was the first to find his tongue. "Welcome back, Samuel. Any news from town?"

He nodded tersely. "Doc sent his regards." Samuel took a small bottle out of his shirt pocket and handed it to Gerald. "He asked me to bring this to you."

"Thanks. That'll save me a trip."

Ruth, sensing her husband's unease, asked, "Would you like a cup of coffee, Samuel?"

"I would, thank you."

Gerald watched his daughter with her husband. There was nothing heartfelt about the way they interacted with one another. In fact, Ruth's fear of angering him prevailed. It saddened him to see her like this—unable to relax and be herself.

What have I done, Lord? He, knowing God alone could change her circumstances, determined to pray for them more often. Gerald took the time to help Ruth set the table while Florence finished frying the chicken. As soon as the cornbread came out of the oven, they sat down to share their first meal together.

Out of habit, Gerald reached for Florence and Ruth's hands

to pray over the meal. When Ruth held her hand open for her husband to take it, Samuel simply shook his head.

"You go ahead and pray with your parents if you want to. You know how I feel about such things. Waste of time!"

Gerald bowed his head, unwilling to allow Samuel's comment to sway him. Gerald may not be as serious about his faith as he should be, but he was appalled by his son-in-law's response to his daughter's simple request. No doubt, Samuel White had misled him to gain Ruth's hand. He could not undo what he had done, but he could certainly pray for his daughter and new son. If Samuel could be this crude in front of them, what must his dear sweet Ruth be dealing with behind closed doors?

The food was being passed when Samuel asked, "Have you had any offers on the farm, Mr. Schmidt?"

"Samuel, you're our son now. You're welcome to call us Dad and Mom."

Samuel nodded.

"We've had a few nibbles, but no solid offers."

Confused, Ruth asked, "When did you decide to sell, Papa?"

"Samuel and I discussed this a while back. I'd like to see your mama settled in town before ... we'll, you know."

Samuel said, "I did some checking today. The banker is planning to sell his place before long. I think you'd like it, Mom. He fixed it up real nice."

Florence, trying to sound interested, asked, "Is he leaving Detroit?"

"No. He's in the process of building a larger home on the outskirts of town."

Ruth put her hand on her husband's arm and calmly suggested, "Samuel, I'm hoping Papa will be with us for a long time, but if not, I'd like Mama to move in with us."

Gerald looked up at Samuel, who was shaking his head in the negative. Samuel's true feelings on the matter were no mystery and in some ways he supported them. "Honey, you're going to be raising a family of your own soon. You'll need your privacy. Besides, you can visit Mama in town as often as you'd like."

"But ..." Ruth protested. Her words, however, were cut off when her husband took a firm hold on her leg under the table.

"Your father and I will handle this."

Annoyed, she winced and pushed his hand away. Samuel wouldn't let her leave the farm alone now. Papa's death would not make a difference. When she regained her composure, her wary eyes lifted to her papa's, but his head swayed ever so slightly, so she let the subject drop. This was not what she wanted, not in the least, but the choice was apparently not hers or Mama's to make.

"Do I need to speak with the banker, Samuel?"

"He's in no hurry. I did tell him we were interested, so he'll contact us when he's ready to sell."

"Good."

"Ruth," Samuel informed her when everyone had laid their forks aside. Help your mother clean up, so we can be on our way."

Gerald was quick to put in, "No need for that, Ruth Anne. Mama and I enjoy doing the dishes together. You're welcome to dish us up a nice piece of that pecan pie."

Ruth glanced at her husband who said, "We've had plenty, but thanks for the offer. You're a wonderful cook, Mom. You'd be proud of your daughter, she's learning."

Offended by his demeaning remark, Ruth looked straight at him and sneered. "Pecan is my favorite. I'm not leaving before I have some."

Florence, catching the frightful look Samuel sent Ruth's way, stood, playing peacekeeper. "I can pack a nice big piece for you to take home, Ruth."

A quick peek at her husband altered her original plan. "That would be nice. Thanks, Mama!"

"You're welcome." Florence turned to Samuel, saying, "I'll only be a minute."

He nodded and headed for the door, stopping long enough to say, "Meet me outside, Ruth Anne."

Gerald followed his son-in-law. As awkward as the moment was, he offered, "It was good to see you again, Samuel."

Accepting the hand Gerald offered, he shook it and said, "Likewise."

Ruth trembled in her papa's arms when he hugged her and said goodbye. "Are you cold, Honey?"

Her hand came up to caress his face. "I'll be fine. We only have a few miles to go. Ruth stood on her toes and whispered in his ear, "I love you, Papa. Come see me soon."

Gerald kissed her brow and whispered in return, "I love you too. You're in our prayers."

She thanked him for their special time together, stuck her foot in the stirrup and took the hand-up Samuel offered. Unfortunately, he would not allow her sit behind him as she had hoped. Encountering his fiery glare, she lowered her eyes and quit fighting the inevitable.

The piece of pecan pie her mama had made was secure within the basket she held on her lap; however, Ruth felt anything but secure in her husband's arms. She made no attempt to stem the flow of tears as they rode away from the only security she had ever known, her parents' love.

Daisytales

He Loves Me!

Chapter Eleven

The Cost of Friendship

Wherein ye greatly rejoice, though now for a season, if need be, ye are in heaviness through manifold temptations: That the trial of your faith, being much more precious than of gold that perisheth, though it be tried with fire, might be found unto praise and honour and glory at the appearing of Jesus Christ:

—I Peter 1:6-7

RUTH'S NEW LIFE, though laborious and dull, had settled into somewhat of a routine. While she harbored only the smallest measure of fondness for the man who dominated her life, she was trying to take her papa's advice and concentrate on his finer points.

Her parents had stopped by the other day and Ruth was overjoyed. Thankfully her husband was working in the fields when they arrived. The three of them were able to have a nice long visit without interruption.

Ruth tried not to laugh at her mama's annoyance when she found the list of chores Samuel expected her to accomplish that day.

"Gerald," she had said, *"look at this. What's wrong with our son-in-law? Doesn't he know our daughter is capable of running a household without his strict guidance?"*

"We know different, Flo, but we should encourage Ruth to honor him. From the looks of things she has enough on her plate without us challenging her husband's oddities."

"I'm sorry, Ruth. Papa is right. Promise me you'll never forget that joy comes from within—it's a choice that is not affected by your circumstances."

Although Ruth could agree with her mama when Samuel was not around, the moment he reappeared all would change. There was little about living with him that made her joyful. *"I'm not sure I understand what you're trying to say, Mama."*

Florence's brow furrowed. *"I'm sure Samuel does things for you that make you happy. Am I right?"*

Ruth nodded. *"Then there are those things he does that frustrate me to no end."*

The strained look on her daughter's face brought a smile to hers. *"You're not very happy when that happens, are you?"*

Ruth rolled her eyes. *"No!"*

"Whether we like it or not, our happiness is affected by our circumstances, but, as I said, joy comes from within. It comes from God and no one can take that from us unless we allow them to."

Her mama's words made so much sense. Just because her husband could be a grump, didn't mean she had to be one too. Imbedding this in her heart and mind would no doubt be a help to her throughout her life. She meditated on her mother's words long after their wagon pulled away, thanking God not only for the love they shared, but for the joy abiding in her heart.

Samuel, though he was angry when he came in for supper and realized that her chores were barely started, accepted her excuses after seeing what she had been up to. In truth, he was pleased. Her mother had taken the time to teach her how to make a French baguette to have with one of Ruth's favorite dishes: chicken with noodles and red sauce.

Her mama had mentioned before she left that Meg was ill and wondered if Ruth would take the time to stop by her place to check on her and the little ones. Meg's husband was still away on business and wouldn't be expected for two more weeks.

Three days had gone by. She pleaded with Samuel to let her go, but he would not hear of it. On the fourth day, she did some extra baking and put it aside for Meg and her son. When she confronted Samuel that evening and again he denied her, she had reached the end of her endurance. She was sick of his refusals. Inwardly, a plan was developing.

The following morning when Samuel went out to the fields, she filled a basket with food and went to the barn to saddle a horse. Pride would have her there and back in no time. Even so, Samuel was meticulous about his stallion. He would know if Pride had been out. She assumed that Samuel didn't need the workhorse or he would have taken him, so she settled on Fred. Although old, Fred would have to do. She didn't like deceiving Samuel, but he left her no choice. As long as she could make it to Meg's and back before he came in for dinner, he'd be none the wiser.

It didn't take long to find out that old Fred was unaccustomed to being ridden. Although he danced and pranced when she threw a saddle on his back, she was more determined than he and eventually won the battle.

The stubborn horse refused to canter, about jarred her insides apart with the fast trot she settled on.

As she approached Meg's farm, her son, Brent, came running out of the house, yelling, "Miss Ruthie! Miss Ruthie!"

She slid off old Fred, tied him to a post and hunkered down to greet her small friend with a great big hug. "How's the sweetest little man in the whole world doing this fine day?"

His chin lowered. He was such a bashful thing. "Mama's sick, Miss Ruthie."

"So I've heard. Is she doing any better?"

He shook his bushy head. "No, she's missin' Papa."

"I'll bet she is." Ruth tucked his small hand inside hers and said, "Come on, Brent. We'll see if we can cheer her up."

He smiled, more than willing to comply.

Ruth let herself in the front door and found her friend in the kitchen, rocking her tiny infant daughter who was nursing contentedly. How's our Cynthia doing, Meg?"

"She's growing so fast her papa might not recognize her when he returns, but her mama's still under the weather."

Ruth set the basket on the table. "I brought along some baked goods and cheese. Are you hungry?"

"Starving, but I try not to think about it."

Ruth went to her friend and hugged her, careful not to disturb the little dolly in her arms. "You could be feeling ill from lack of nourishment."

"I know. I thought about butchering a chicken for soup, but I'm too weak to do the deed. I've been feeding Brent the things your mother left us. He had the last of the bread for breakfast, so your coming is a real answer to prayer."

Ruth's eyes filled with tears as Meg handed her the baby. Awed by Cynthia's small features, Ruth kissed the infant's soft cheek and snuggled her close. "Brent and I can handle the chicken. How's your supply of water and wood holding out?"

"Fine. Your papa made sure the barrels were full the day he was here. While you see to the chicken, I'll put water over to boil."

Within an hour they were sitting around the table chatting and nibbling on the muffins and cheese Ruth had brought. "Are you happy with your papa's choice for a husband?"

"He had his reasons for accepting Samuel's offer, but if I had been given the choice, I never would have married him." When Meg seemed at a loss for words, Ruth admitted, "I suppose my greatest disappointment is that I'll never be able to teach."

Meg suspected she would have said more if Brent were not hanging on her every word. "Ruth, I'm not sure if you're interested, but before Paul left, he mentioned that a group of believers are holding Sunday meetings in the Somers' barn. We'll be attending as soon as he returns."

Ruth looked up at her friend and asked, "I'm not sure, do I know the Somers?"

"He's the dark haired gentleman your father introduced you to the last time we were in town together."

"His wife's name is Jayne, right?"

Meg nodded. "They're newlyweds, here recently from New York. Apparently, they started the fellowship out of their own desire to meet with other believers on a regular basis."

Ruth's head lowered. She'd been hearing about small gatherings like this, but never had the desire to venture out to one before. "I'd love to, but Samuel's not the most agreeable man." She leaned forward and spoke for Meg's ears alone, "He'd skin me for sure if he knew I was here."

Concern etched Meg's face. "Then why did you come?"

"You're my friend. You'd risk life and limb to help if I was the one ill."

Meg's downcast expression lifted, if only slightly. "I would at that .... Listen, Ruth, you've done all you can for now. Go home."

Ruth giggled at the worried look on her friend's face, but she did stand to leave. "Tell me, Meg, in case I can get away. Where is the Somers' farm?"

"Do you know the trail that forks off near the Weber farm?"

"The one with a small cabin on it?"

"Yes. Take the path to the right. You can't miss it."

"I won't promise you anything, but I'll try. Take care of yourself, Meg."

"I will. Thanks for coming." They shared a warm hug and Meg said with tears glistening in her eyes, "Have a Happy Birthday."

"Thanks! I'll give it my all."

"We love you."

Ruth's eyes glassed over. "I love all of you, too."

"Brent," his mother said, "give Miss Ruthie a big birthday hug. It might have to hold her for a while."

"Why?"

This seemed to be his favorite question of late, so Ruth wrapped her arms around him, tickled his sides, and said in a deep craggy voice, "Because, my handsome little prince, the dreaded lord who holds me captive will not grant me permission to leave—I must sneak out!"

His small face scrunched up. "You funny, Miss Ruthie!"

"So are you!" They giggled, but the knowing glance she and Meg shared as Ruth walked out the door told Meg that it was no tale, she meant every word.

The sun in all its radiance splattered shimmering shards of yellow light across the trail as Ruth journeyed home. She smiled, drinking in the scent of lilacs as she passed several patches in full bloom. Apple trees were also blossoming at every turn and she could hardly wait to see what kinds of apples they would produce. God willing, there would be an abundance of succulent fruit come fall.

Hurrying old Fred along became an impossible task, so she gave up, plodding along at a pace better suited to turtles or snails. If she had it to do over again, she would have walked. It certainly would have been faster.

She stayed at Meg's longer than she had intended, but her resolve to enjoy her last moments of freedom overshadowed all else.

Ruth giggled when a chipmunk scampered across her path, paused, stood on his hindquarters and peered around before taking off in the opposite direction. Cattle were bawling off in the distance, but she never did see them. She wondered if they belonged to Samuel, his father, or possibly a nearby farmer. One of these days she would have to ask. A wide array of her feathered friends fluttered from tree to tree, twittering away, as if discussing her invasion of their world. What she wouldn't give to trade lives with one of them, if only for a day.

Shading her eyes against the sun's bright rays, Ruth glanced up at the house and wondered how much time she would have before Samuel came in from the fields for dinner. The pleasure she was finding in this splendid day came to a screeching halt when Samuel came into view. He was sitting in a chair on the porch—and he was staring right at her. The beat of her heart thudded to an unfamiliar drum. *Why did I go?* she asked herself, but knowing she would do it again gave her a smidgen of courage. From the looks of things, she would need it. She dreaded the confrontation that was sure to come. As she neared the porch, a thread of fear raced through her veins. What was it about him that terrified her so?

Although she considered fleeing, old Fred's lack of gumption obliterated that thought. Samuel would catch her before she made it out of the yard. She'd best hold her ground and get this over. There was no doubt in her mind, Samuel was mad. She recognized the look. It was the same one he housed the day they were wed as he carried her out of the woods. He told her not to leave. Even so, she could not in good conscience ignore her friend's need any longer. Besides, she was tired of being confined to his house. Like he, she was an adult. She had every right to come and go as she pleased.

Didn't she?

Ruth was naive enough to believe that Samuel would listen, possibly even understand why she had gone. At least that was true before she slid off old Fred and saw a leather strap wrapped around his hand. The second her feet hit the ground he lunged toward her. She dropped the empty basket draped over her arm and turned to flee, but not soon enough.

He captured her arm with his oversized hand and led her none-to-gently into the house.

"Samuel ..." she pleaded, "you're hurting me."

"Not nearly as much as I'm going to!" he spat, as he shoved her down the hall and into their room.

In a frantic state, she tried to explain, but there was no reasoning with him.

"I told you not to leave this house!" he reminded, tightly.

"You have no right to treat me like this! I'm not a child. I'll come and go as I please!" she informed him.

His penetrating gaze hit its mark.

Defeat washed over her. "My friend needed me, Samuel. I had to go ...."

"No, you did not!"

The anger oozing from his icy glare, sent irrepressible shivers up her spine. *Self-righteous*, was the only word that came to mind. If only his smug intolerance could be ignored.

Oh, Papa, why him?

In the moments that followed, her worst fears were realized. And then, as if the pain he had inflicted was not enough, he glared in contempt as he strode from the room.

Ruth's inflamed flesh continued to burn as uncontainable tears spilled down her face. Her desperate need to be anywhere but in his room gave her the strength to look beyond her suffering—her shame and humiliation. Pulling herself together as best she could, and wrapping a blanket around her shoulders, she moved cautiously up the steps to the second floor.

Samuel could hear her soft sobs as he prepared his meal. His harshness plucked at a nerve in his cynical heart, but he was convinced he was in the right. His young wife may be a sweet thing to cuddle, but she would have to mend her ways. She'd think twice before defying him again. His father must be right. A bit of fear was a good thing.

Ruth couldn't believe he would stoop to such measures. He could be so tender and loving when it suited him. How could he turn on her like this? As justifiable as her anger was, shame washed over her, turning the tide of her turbulent thoughts. Doubt overshadowed all else. Maybe she was partly to blame. Even so, she sensed something deeper going on. There were things about him she was coming to love, but hatred was fast becoming her only weapon against him in his battle for control, binding her wounded heart and building a protective wall.

When Samuel called to Ruth from the base of the stairs, she ignored him. Her enflamed skin was a reminder of what he had just done and she would not be quick to forgive him. Feigning sleep, she curled tighter inside the blanket when she heard him coming, preferring the hard floor to being anywhere near him. Unfortunately, hoping he would go away did not make it happen. The thought of him touching her in any way made her feel ill, but touch her he did. She groaned in anguish when he lifted her off the floor—she even begged him to leave.

He refused.

Ruth ached to tell him just how much she despised him for his cruelty. She wanted to leave and never come back, but her mama's face came to her, silencing her every thought. Her spirit was weak. Her new-found faith was almost non-existent. Her heart was crushed, quite possibly beyond repair.

Samuel laid her on her pillow, tucking a stray curl behind her ear. When she refused to look at him, he said, "This was all your fault, Ruth Anne. You brought this on yourself."

As ludicrous as his words were, they did not surprise her. When he climbed into bed beside her, she turned the other way. She wanted nothing to do with the snake whose arms slithered around her and drew her near. As he snuggled into her neck, passion transfused her on levels she never knew existed. Love and hate were powerful enemies, warring inside her.

She, needing to feel something besides revulsion for this man, began to pray. Since the night they married, her conversations with God had become her refuge. She yearned to know Him more, but did not understand where the yearning came from.

You were there for me the day we married when I cried out to You, Lord. I was sure You wanted me here, so I came willingly. Is this what You had in mind? Am I to live my life being hurt and controlled by this man? What good can possibly come from our union? As she stared at the blank wall, a single word ran through her mind.

"LOVE!"

Baffled, she wondered why this word, of all words, came to her. What did *love* have to do with *their* union? While contemplating that very thing, Samuel spoke.

"Ruth ..."

She feigned sleep, again.

"I know you're awake."

Ignoring him would do no good. He wouldn't think twice about hurting her. He had proven that quite thoroughly. "Hmm?"

"Why did you go?"

"Just leave me alone! You can't undo what you've done, Samuel."

He waited. A minute, two, then a third crept by.

She could feel herself slipping—slipping deeper into a pit—a pit of despair. If her mama's face had not come to the fore, she could have slid right in and never emerged. Ruth couldn't give up. Her mama needed her. She couldn't let Samuel destroy her spirit. Besides, if she did, he'd win, and she wouldn't give him the satisfaction.

When Ruth offered no further response, he pressed her, "Have you forgotten so soon, the cost of defiance?"

Her temper flared. "Brutality! Is that your answer for everything, Samuel?"

"Ruth Anne," he gently berated.

She burst into another onslaught of tears. "How can I forget?"

His tone softened. "Make me understand why you would go after the discussion we had last night?"

"Just leave me alone!"

"No! Make me understand." Again, the silence dragged on ... and on ... and on.

"My friend needed me. I told you that, but you don't listen to a word I say. You don't care about the people who are important to me."

He couldn't deny her accusations. "Was it worth it?"

"A friend's worth cannot be measured, Samuel. I couldn't ignore her need any longer."

"You're my wife. You know what I expect. Why do you press me?"

He was still angry; she could hear it in his voice. She couldn't change him, but that didn't mean she had to fall into the trap with him. As much as she loathed the thought of being anywhere near him, she swallowed a large slice of pride and turned toward him. Seconds passed before she summoned the courage to open her eyes.

"Today I had to choose whom to obey, you or the voice inside me that said my friend needed me. She's ill with a nursing baby and a small boy. If I didn't go to her, Meg and her son would have gone without food. So you tell me, was facing your wrath worth it?"

"I don't think so."

"I'm not surprised ... but I couldn't disagree with you more."

His eyes narrowed in on her. "Then you're a fool."

All too aware that a soft word could turn away wrath, she murmured more to herself than him, "Only if I allow resentment to fill me."

For a time he appeared thoughtful. Then, as if nothing had happened between them, he lifted her chin, dried her tears with the back of his hand and tenderly kissed her—confounding her all the more.

If only his kisses weren't so sweet. She might have summoned the courage to deny him. Betrayed by her own flesh, by her desperate yearning to be loved, she melted into the arms of the man who beat her.

"You missed your dinner, Ruth. You should eat something."

"I will." Where his sudden concern for her welfare came from, or how long it would last, she did not know—perhaps until she crossed him again.

When Samuel went to his armoire and pulled out a clean set of work clothes, she scooted cautiously off the bed. She watched as he stuck his long legs in a pair of jeans, added his shirt and then came to stand in front of her. Wrapping his arms around her, he drew her close, kissing the tip of her nose. "Go and make yourself something to tide you over."

She forced herself to ask, "Are you hungry?"

Shaking his head, he admitted, "No, I ate while you were upstairs. I'm thinking Fred must be worn out from his adventure. I'll see to him before I finish my chores. I won't be long, so put the roast in the oven and get ready to go."

Damp lashes flipped up. "Samuel, I don't want to see anyone with my face this red. Look at me, my eyes are swollen and how ..." His fingers came gently to her mouth, effectively silencing her frantic plea.

"You won't be seeing anyone and we can walk instead of ride."

"Are you going to tell me where we're going?"

"No, Ruth. Just be ready."

As much as she wanted to refuse him, her curiosity peaked. The moment Samuel took his leave, she blew her nose, washed her face, and threw on a tolerable frock before heading for the kitchen.

While nibbling on a sandwich, Ruth collected the ingredients she would need to begin preparations for their evening meal. Standing at the counter she added miscellaneous items to the supply list. Feeling bold at the moment, she also added something she wanted and believed she needed more than anything else—a Bible. Although she had never longed for one before, something happened the day they were married that sparked her yearning. She had an inkling that a Bible would have answers for some of her questions. Although she may never get one, it couldn't hurt to ask.

Chapter Twelve

Forgiveness – A Process

$\mathscr{S}$ AMUEL REACHED FOR HIS WIFE'S HAND as they walked along the perimeter of their land. Her ability to put their earlier confrontation aside puzzled him. Although her gentle smile as she met his gaze warmed his heart, his insecurities plagued him. Did he dare hope that her smile meant his touch was welcome, that she cared, if only in the smallest measure? Ruth did seem to be enjoying their time together. While this encouraged him, he was at loose ends where she was concerned. He simply didn't understand her. Perhaps if she could begin to see how much he had planned for her arrival, how much he cared, she wouldn't fight him so. He had failed to give her a proper welcome to her new home, but he intended to rectify that starting now.

Ruth listened as Samuel shared his thoughts, and even asked her opinion from time to time. As much as she would like to believe her opinion mattered, their previous conversations told her otherwise. Besides, how could he treat her the way he did and then go on as if nothing had happened? Her tender flesh and aching heart were a constant reminder of his tyranny. Right now she wanted nothing more than to shut this man out of her heart and mind. Could she? Should she? If she did, who would really be losing out?

Her parents would tell her to concentrate on the positive. *Samuel is a good provider. And from time to time he shows me that he cares.* Unfortunately, he would often leave her wondering about his motives.

Why God? Why can't he just love me like Papa and Mama love each other? Their love is given so freely—without expectations.

Is that where I go wrong, Lord? Perhaps comparing our relationships are wrong? Samuel and I are not my parents, nor will we ever be. I want to love him as I should, but right now my flesh is screaming out for revenge. Help me to move past this, Lord. I can't do it on my own.

Although pressing forward would mean going against the turmoil swirling inside her, she could see no other way. Her mama's words were a gentle reminder that she must do her part. *"When things get bad, they can get worse or better, the choice is partly yours and partly Samuel's. The rest is up to God."*

"A penny for your thoughts!" Samuel offered.

Drawn from her musings, she grinned halfheartedly. If only her thoughts would be well received. Suspecting they would not, she changed the subject. "You said you'd show me the path that leads to the river. Do we have time? I'd love to go swimming, Samuel."

He squeezed her hand. "You can't be serious!"

Looking up at him, she asked, "Why wouldn't I be? I love to

swim. The cool water would feel so ..."

He was shaking his head, effectively stemming her unspoken words. "If you need a bath, Ruth, I'll haul water. I won't have my wife running around half-dressed in public."

As was often the case, his words disturbed her. Could she tell him? Hesitant, her steps slowed. Taking a breath for courage, she murmured her disgruntled response, "I'd hardly call the woods public domain." For a time she just walked along side of him, frustrated, but weary of fighting him. If only her overactive mind would remain quiet. *If this marriage is ever going to work, if he is ever going to know me, the woman he insisted on marrying, I am going to have to get beyond this dreadful fear of upsetting him! Does he not understand how much swimming means to me?* "You've taken me from all that I know and love, Samuel. Surely you won't deny me this simple pleasure." When the silence trailed on, she suspected he was thinking. Pushing him would not help, so she waited.

"Since it's only us, I suppose we could swim for a while."

His tone, so reserved, forced her to ask, "I'm curious, Samuel. Have your parents never encouraged you to do something frivolous, just for the fun of it?"

His brow furrowed. "Not that I can recall."

Annoyance etched her face. "That's terrible!" How could she not feel sorry for him? *No wonder this man is so regimented about everything.* "Your childhood must have been awfully boring."

He shrugged. "I didn't see it that way."

Well, she did! Acting on impulse might get her into a heap of trouble, but what else was new? She had to help him see that life didn't need to be so cut and dry. "I can hear the river, are

169

we close?"

He pointed up the way. "See the path leading into the woods?"

"Yes!" she said, then took off running. Samuel called to her, telling her to slow down, but she kept on until she reached the ever flowing waters. The view was spectacular. Branches from trees and shrubs lined the bank, leaning toward the river as if awaiting a sip of the life giving fluid. Although the rippling stream clipped along at a faster pace than she had anticipated, she refused to let that discourage her. Shedding her outer clothes, she padded down the muddy bank in her bare feet. Cautiously, she waded in.

Samuel's heart faltered. Just as he reached the river's edge his wife slid under the water. When she didn't readily reappear, he shed his own attire and moved swiftly into the murky water.

"Ruth!" he bellowed, as he searched the area.

Resurfacing, she met his anxious glare. "Samuel, what is it now?"

Although ready to ring her scrawny neck, he held his anger in check. How could he lash out at her twice in one day?

She, hoping to lighten his turbulent mood, grinned mischievously. "I'm glad you decided to join me."

"I didn't have much choice. The way this current's moving, a skinny little thing like you could be carried away."

"I'm fine, Samuel. I've been swimming in stronger currents than this for years." She giggled when he reached out and pulled her close.

"That may be, but I won't risk losing you."

But you'll whip me and then carry on as if nothing happened! Although she may never understand her husband's controlling nature, or his motives, little by little she was learning to read between the lines. Usually, he had reasons for reacting the way he did. "If it makes you feel better, I'll stay close, but you might regret it." She doused him good, informing him, "I can splash you better from here!"

Her actions surprised him. Lightheartedness, though it made his wife alight with pleasure, was an unfamiliar reaction to him. Responding to her playfulness felt awkward at first, but plunging into the unfamiliar did have a euphoric effect. "You're *playing* with fire! You know that, don't you?"

"I'm not too worried. Fire can't burn me in this cool water." She cupped her hands and flung water into the air. "Doesn't it feel wonderful, Samuel?"

When he only nodded, she tried to swim away but he captured her ankles and pulled her back. "What did I tell you?" he asked when she came up sputtering.

"I wasn't going anywhere."

"Ruth Anne!"

"Samuel ... whatever your middle name is! Why must you always be such a crank?"

He wrapped his arms around her and slid under the water with her. As they came up, he asked, "Better?"

Her features brightened. Where the sudden urge came from she wasn't sure, but she leaned over and sweetly kissed his thick lips. "Much better!"

Hearing movement on the opposite side of the river, Ruth threw herself into her husband's arms and then chanced a quick peek over her shoulder. She flushed, feeling a bit foolish, it was only a deer. Fortunately, Samuel didn't seem to mind. As he held her tenderly against his chest the sound of his beating heart brought her gaze to his.

"Grady ..." Samuel said, seemingly out of the blue.

"What?"

"My middle name is Grady."

Her brow lifted. "Hmm ... I like it."

"Good, 'cause I plan to name our second son Grady."

Her thoughts took a sudden dive. *I'm not so sure I want to have children with you, Samuel Grady. I couldn't bear to watch you hurt them the way you do me.* Since she couldn't bring herself to expose her true feelings on the matter, she asked, "And the first?"

"Kaleb ... Kaleb Samuel White."

Ruth wasn't so sure about the Samuel part, but Kaleb she liked. Kaleb had always been one of her favorite names. Even so, the notion of having this man's child gave her pause. Surely, the burden of bringing a child into their fragile marriage would be too much.

After swishing her hair back in the water, she climbed up the bank, picked up her stray clothes and started walking back toward the house in her shift.

"Ruth Anne!" Samuel yelled at her fleeing back.

She craned her neck around. "What?"

"You need to put your dress on."

She shook her head. "Can't ... in a bit of a hurry ... need to use the outhouse something fierce."

He laughed out loud when she took off running and didn't look back.

❀ ❀ ❀

Ruth stood in front of the small mirror in her room and noticed the ugly dark bruise forming around her arm where Samuel had grabbed her and hauled her into the house. Although the day was sticky and hot, some things were better kept from curious eyes. Perhaps hiding Samuel's cruelty would not help her. Even so, she had heard enough comments about men who abused their wives to know that most people believed a woman deserved whatever she got. Although Ruth didn't agree, the thought of exposing their union to ridicule did not sit well.

Slipping her arms into her long-sleeve yellow calico blouse, she tucked it into her skirt before securing the clasp. As she brushed through her damp tangles, she thought about her earlier confrontation with her husband. His anger was understandable. She had gone when he told her not to, but his reaction was wrong. Wasn't it? His gentleness with her afterwards was a complete contradiction, but she was glad for it. She so longed to find joy in their union. Their adventure had given her the thread of hope she so needed to press on.

Ruth was hanging her damp clothes from the hooks when she heard a soft knock at the front door. Samuel had just gone out the back, so it couldn't be him. The timing was rather odd. When she opened the door and saw Constance and James standing on the porch, her mouth dropped open in shock.

"Who told you? How ... how did you find me?" Ruth, leery of inviting them in, stepped out on the porch. She could only imagine what Samuel would say if he found James anywhere near their home.

Constance wrapped her arms around Ruth and held her tight. "I saw your papa in town. He told me he had arranged your marriage to Samuel. Oh, Ruth ... I've been sick with worry. How are you holding up?"

James didn't wait for her to answer. "I thought we had an understanding? How could you keep this from me? You never said a word, even knowing how much I love you."

Ruth, unable to bear the pain in his eyes, practically fell into his arms. "I didn't know, James. Papa didn't tell me until a few minutes before Samuel and his parents showed up with the preacher."

"If only I understood."

Tears filled Ruth's eyes. "Papa is dying, James. Samuel's generous offer for my hand was an answer to his prayers. Papa didn't know about us. By the time he did, it was too late. He had already signed the marriage contract." Ruth could have stayed in James' arms forever, but it wasn't right. She was Samuel's wife.

When she pulled away, James tenderly caressed her cheek. "Is he treating you right? I could bear it if I thought you were happy, Ruth."

James was hurting. Telling him the truth would only hurt him more and she refused to do that. Nothing good would come from his knowing. "I'll be fine. Promise me you won't waste your life dreaming of what might have been. You will find someone else. You're the kind of man a woman dreams of sharing her life with." *At least this one did anyway!*

He nodded. "We should go. We don't want to cause you problems. It's just ... well, I had to see for myself that you were all right and wish you a Happy Birthday!"

Ruth forced a smile. "Thanks! I'm so glad you came. I miss our times together."

Constance brushed her tears away with her sleeve, cleared her throat, and asked, "Do you think Samuel would mind if I stop by from time to time?"

"I don't care if he does. I'd come and see you, but he frowns upon me leaving the farm without him."

"Overprotective?" James asked.

Her impish grin altered his mood. "Either that or he's afraid I'll leave."

"Would you?" He simply had to know.

"With Papa so sick, Mama and I need the financial security Samuel offered." She shrugged. "Besides, he is my husband. We're bound to each other for life."

Constance and James nodded. Though hard to accept, they understood her position and would do nothing to interfere.

"If you ever need anything, get word to me, Ruth. No matter who has come between us, we're friends for life."

"Thanks, James. That goes both ways."

Ruth, hearing the door creak, looked back and saw Samuel coming towards her. She didn't know how much he had heard, but she ignored her own trepidation, reached for his hand and introduced him to her friends.

Samuel's first question was directed at James, "Aren't you the young man I saw ..?"

James nodded in the affirmative, so there was no need for Samuel to continue. He looked to Ruth for answers.

"James is my friend, Samuel. I told you that."

Samuel glanced at Constance, somewhat confused. "So, is he your beau? Husband?"

Constance looked at Ruth, wondering what she should say

when James spoke for her.

"We're too young to be making a commitment as huge as marriage."

The boy was alluding to Ruth's age, but Samuel saw no reason to defend his actions. "I see. Ruth, is there a reason you haven't asked your guests to come in?"

She wondered where his sudden need to be hospitable came from. It wasn't like Samuel to be cordial. Truth be told she didn't trust him. "Constance and James just stopped by to say hello. They have somewhere else they need to be."

James looked up, offering a sideways grin. Ruth was lying through her teeth, but something in her expression kept him from calling her on it. "We'd best be on our way. It was nice to meet you, Samuel. Ruth, stop by the farm when you're in town. My parents would love to hear all about your marriage and your new home."

She would have pinched him if Samuel wasn't watching her every move. "As soon as I convince Samuel to give me back my freedom, I will. Constance, promise you'll come back when you can stay for tea?"

"I will soon ...."

Had Samuel not been so close, Ruth might have allowed the tears burning at the back of her eyes to fall. Instead, she walked back into the house, wondering as she did what the man following her would have to say about her guests. She was pleasantly surprised.

"James seems to be accepting our union?"

Ruth swung around to face him. "Why wouldn't he be?"

His gaze narrowed. "I'm not dense, Ruth Anne. It's as plain

as the nose on his face, the lad has feelings for you."

Her head lowered as she contemplated her next words, "I never said you were. I've always thought James was sweet on me, and even wondered if we would marry, but we're friends, Samuel, nothing more. I told him a while back that I didn't want more than friendship until after I earned my teaching certificate. How was I supposed to know you would steal me away before he had the chance to speak to Papa?"

"And?"

"And what?"

"Are you glad we married?"

His question caught her off guard, but she opted for honesty. "I'm not sure you want to hear my answer."

He paused, his hands running leisurely through her soft curls. "Try me."

She stared up at him, questioning the wisdom of being so bold. "Most of the time I wish we had never met. Then there are those times I enjoy being with you."

His eyebrows knit together. "Like this afternoon?"

"Yes ... you were trying. Your effort meant the world to me."

He reached out and caressed the flawless skin of her cheek. "I love you, Ruth ...."

"Just so you understand that no matter how hard you try, you can't make amends for what you've done. You can only change the way you respond to me in the future. Trust is sadly lacking in our relationship. Trust is something that can only be earned."

His long finger touched the tip of her upturned nose. "Just so you understand that goes both ways!"

She lowered her eyes and then slowly peered up. "That's

true, Samuel, but how would you feel if our roles were reversed?"

For a moment he appeared to be considering her words. Then he leaned over, kissed her tenderly, and said as he walked away, "They're not, and never will be, so don't try me again, Ruth Anne White!"

Ruth's heart raced with excitement when she heard a wagon coming into the yard. Sure that it was her parents, she ran out the back door in her bare feet.

Samuel came out of the barn just as his wife reached her parents. Like the last time she saw them, she burst into tears. What was it about them that stirred her so?

"You remembered!" Ruth exclaimed, drawing Samuel's attention.

Gerald hugged his daughter and asked, "How could we forget your sixteenth birthday, Ruth Anne?"

"Oh, I don't know." Ruth said, glancing over her papa's shoulder and meeting her husband's stunned look.

Florence, unaware of her son-in-law's oversight, asked, "So, Samuel, what have you and Ruth been doing to celebrate her special day?"

Ruth could see that Samuel was fumbling for the right words, and not wanting him to look bad in the eyes of her parents, she answered for him, "Samuel took me for a long walk and we ended up at the river."

"Oh!" Gerald said, sure that she had more to add.

Her husband, vividly aware of her rescue, winked when she

announced, "Samuel took me swimming, Papa. I made him a little nervous, but we had so much fun!"

Gerald grinned as his eyes met Samuel's. "Swimming has always been a summer favorite of Ruth's. I'm glad the two of you have that in common."

"So am I" Samuel admitted, still feeling awkward, but trying not to let it show. He only had himself to blame. How could he have forgotten something as important as his wife's birthday?

Ruth, thinking her husband could use a reprieve, reached for her parents' hands and said, "I put a big roast in the oven earlier. Can you stay for supper?"

Florence smiled. "We would love to, as long as we're not imposing."

"Oh! Mama, how could you ever think that?"

Florence held out the basket she had in her arms. "I brought a little something for dessert."

Ruth licked her lips in anticipation. "What is it?"

When Gerald lifted the lid, Ruth took a quick peek. "Yum! Samuel, it's lemon cake."

"Sounds good! Ruth, go ahead and take your parents inside. I have a few things to finish up, but I won't be long."

As Ruth and her parents sat around the table sipping sweet tea, she wondered if Samuel forgetting her birthday was an oversight at all. His expression revealed his shock, but she wouldn't be surprised if his family didn't celebrate birthdays, or any other holiday.

However, when Samuel came in the back door holding a package tied with a yellow bow, and his mother and father following close behind, her previous thoughts were dashed away.

Apparently he had planned ahead. He'd just forgotten that her birthday was today. She could hardly wipe the smile from her face when Samuel came near, kissed her sweetly, and handed her the gift.

Her eyes twinkled as she glanced over at her parents, and then at her mother-in-law, before meeting her husband's gaze. "Can I open it now?

With a slight tilt of his head, he teased, "Or you could just set it on the table and look at it for a while."

When she bumped into him and turned a light shade of cherry, he led her to the table, took a seat and pulled her into his lap. His parents joined them as well.

Loosening the bow, Ruth looked inside. Although her hopes of finding a Bible were not realized, her heart was overturned by his thoughtful gift. She now had embroidery supplies of her own and several dress lengths of fabric.

Naomi reached across the table and handed Ruth a sewing box she had put together for her. She also promised to help with her endeavors. Ruth couldn't have been more pleased.

Although touched by their generosity, Ruth almost burst into tears when she started going through the chest of treasures her parents had brought her from home. She loved knowing she would now have these items that held so many memories from her past. Her mama cherished them and that made them all the more special.

After setting her gifts on the sill, she took a moment to gaze out the window. The bright shades of golden light which had saturated the day with warmth, were settling into a husky gray with varying shades of vibrant color exuding from the setting sun.

Her parents would need to be on their way before too long, so the women set the table. They had no more finished their meal, when Ruth looked at her guests and asked, eagerness resonating in her smile, "Are you ready for cake?"

Florence, noting her daughter's excitement to sample the sweet delight, smiled and helped her serve it up.

Without delay, Ruth took the last plate of cake from the tray, reclaimed her seat next to Samuel, and although she hoped no one detected her childish glee, she could not wait a moment more. She pick up her fork and took a big bite. "Oh, Mama, this is delicious!" Her smile was contagious and everyone except her father-in-law sampled the cake and then offered their praise.

"I'm glad you all like it." Florence admitted, pleased to know that she had played a part in her daughter's present happiness.

As Ruth glanced around the table at her family she thought about her sixteenth birthday and the extreme mix of emotions that had come with it. *Although being there for Meg meant the world to me, facing Samuel's rage has challenged me in ways nothing else ever has. I don't understand what made him think he can treat me that way? Perhaps I never will. He confuses me, Lord. Sometimes I am so sure he loves me, but then he hurts me and I'm confused all over again. I choose to forgive him, even if he never sees the error of his way, but I do wonder if we will ever share a relationship built on mutual trust? Papa says that nothing is impossible if we believe. Help me to put my trust in You. Help me to press on, not just for Mama's sake, but for my own. I do want to love him, Lord.*

Ruth smiled inside, listening to her papa, mama, Naomi, and even her husband conversing. They were enjoying each other immensely. Her father-in-law, on the other hand, was a different story. Being a crank came so naturally to him. He made no effort to join in their merriment and while his stern intolerance saddened her, when he tasted her mama's yummy lemon cake, she could have sworn she saw him smile.

Ruth, convinced that happiness was a choice, reached for her husband's hand under the table. Leaning close, his evening shadow brushed coarsely against her silky lips when she kissed him. "Thank you for doing this, Samuel!"

Puzzled, he leaned close and whispered back, his deep, yet hopeful eyes holding hers, "For doing what? I forgot today was your birthday. Can you ever forgive me?"

With a raised brow, a tilt of her head, and a slight shrug, she said, "Have to! If I don't, God won't forgive me."

Samuel didn't offer a verbal response. One was not necessary when he snuggled her closer and kissed the corner of her mouth. For the remainder of their parents' visit she stayed in the crook of her husband's arm, sampling delectable bites of her mama's sweet confection, while listening intently to her papa's retellings. He was telling secret tales—well, not really tales, they were semi-embarrassing stories of things she had done as a child. Ruth scowled at him often, but how could she stop him when everyone except her father-in-law was laughing? Sweet laughter was such a rarity in their home that she relished it and was thankful for whatever brought it.

Chapter Thirteen

A Love That's Sweet

"YOU'VE PUT THIS OFF LONG ENOUGH! No more excuses, Ruth Anne. We are going to see my parents after dinner."

"Fine!" she returned, but it wasn't fine. She dreaded the thought of being anywhere near Samuel's father. Just the other day, he had come by again while she was working in the garden. Her hat and gloves were on, so she tried not to panic, but he found fault with everything she did. When she could stand it no more, she made her excuses and went back in the house. The man despised her—that much was obvious. Why? She was not sure. Perhaps women in general did not measure up to his standards.

Her husband continued to watch her closely, but she didn't care. Her mood was dreadful. Having lost her appetite, yet again, she carried her plate to the slop bucket and emptied it before making her way to the work board to wash the dishes. She dragged that out as long as she dared. Then, without a word she snatched her sweater off the hook and headed for the outhouse. A cold chill ran through her that had nothing to do with the weather. She could feel it in her bones. The tranquil days she had been sharing with Samuel since her birthday were coming to an end. The tension was building. As hard as she tried to tamp it down, she was losing ground. She should have known their peaceful repose couldn't last forever.

Samuel waited on the back step. After seeing to her needs, Ruth slid out the door and didn't come toward him as he anticipated. Her swift strides took her to the barn. Since it was possible she had assumed they'd be taking Pride, he did his level best to restrain his irritation. Weary of fighting her, Samuel reached the entrance to the barn as she led his restless stallion out of the stall. Samuel stayed in the shadows while she secured the cross ties and began brushing Pride down. Her lack of fear amazed him. Not many women would even contemplate handling such a high-spirited beast. To her it was second nature. That much was evident. Apparently she had been paying close attention the other night because she knew which tack was Pride's and retrieved it. After putting his blanket and saddle in place, she secured the synch straps, bridled him, and then went back to retighten the girth before tucking the straps in with skilled precision—exactly like he would have done. He was so impressed that his anger abated. While he made no move toward her, he said, "I didn't know you were so experienced with horses, Ruth."

"You forget that Papa had no sons. I've been working with horses most of my life. Why wouldn't I be at ease with them?"

He shrugged. "Just don't try riding him alone. Pride has never been receptive to other riders."

Still in an impertinent mood, she mused, *If you could see*

my proficiency with Pride, you might reconsider giving me access to one of the other horses—possibly even allow me to help care for the animals from time to time. Desperate to gain his approval, she set his warning aside, stuck her foot in the stirrup, swung herself up into the saddle, gathered the reins and flew past her husband. She was almost to the house when she reined Pride back toward the barn. He stood on his hindquarters, protesting the short release, yet she did not so much as falter in her ability to handle him with ease.

Samuel said nothing when she rode up beside him, but his frown told her much. He mounted behind her, and cracked her leg with his leather crop. "You pull something like that again when I've told you not to, you won't sit for a week."

Her leg was stinging, her anger flaring, but more than anything her spirit was crushed. *I'll never gain your approval in anything, will I, Samuel? Your father made sure of that! I don't even know why I try.* She wanted to dismount, to get away, but knowing he would not release her kept her from a desperate attempt. Although tears filled her eyes, she refused to let them fall. Would the ache in her soul ever ease? Stewing, she sat stiff as a board and rode in silence to his parents' house, dreading their visit with everything inside her.

As Ruth suspected, Samuel and his father would not leave her and Naomi alone. Naomi's bruised hand and enflamed cheek may have added to their reluctance. Ruth could only assume that her father-in-law found it necessary to prove his dominion over Naomi and didn't want her spreading her tale of woe. As if Ruth didn't know he was at fault.

Lord, forgive me. She wasn't normally so judgmental, but

then she had never met anyone like Samuel's father. She was learning the hard way that his son was not much better.

Ruth, thinking they could both use a distraction, turned to her mother-in-law and asked, "Do you feel up to teaching me a few of those fancy embroidery stitches while I'm here?"

"I'd be glad to, Ruth Anne. Would you mind helping me gather the supplies?"

Samuel, hanging on their every word, stopped his wife as she was leaving the room. Handing her his cup, he said, "I could use some more coffee and another piece of pie."

"But ..."

Shaking his head he said, "I'll help Mom."

Ruth scowled, but the wicked look he sent her way stopped her from protesting further. Her father-in-law followed her to the kitchen. Although he made her nervous, as usual, he didn't say a word. He just watched her. *Why?* she did not know.

Ruth had finished her third cup of tea before she had a good handle on the new stitches. She looked up when Naomi said, "You're gifted with a needle, Ruth. A few more visits and you'll have mastered all of the stitches I know."

"Do you think so?"

Naomi smiled. "I do."

Ruth caught her husband grinning at his mother's remark and although she wondered what he was thinking, she didn't ask. Her needs were pressing in, and since Samuel didn't seem ready to leave, she reached for the lantern by the door and inched her way toward the outhouse. Darkness, along with her unfamiliar surroundings frightened her more than a tad, but she continued on her way. By the time she reached the outhouse, desperation shrouded her suspicions.

When Ruth slipped in the back door, Naomi was nowhere to be found. Had she gone upstairs? Samuel and his father were conversing in hushed tones in the sitting room. While she harbored no doubts, their conversation was meant to be private, curiosity got the best of her. She drew a little closer and saw what her father-in-law slid into a cloth bag before handing it to her husband. Her heart faltered. As if seeing was not enough, she overheard the advice he gave Samuel and gasped.

Samuel turned to meet her heated glower, just before she spun on her heel and ran out the door. Although she heard her husband calling, she never looked back. She swung Pride's reins over his head, mounted and took off at a full gallop.

Halfway to her parent's house, Ruth managed to calm down enough to consider the repercussions of what she was doing. As much as she wanted to go home and fall into the safety of her parents' loving arms, angering Samuel further would not help her. More than likely her desperate act would encourage him to take his father's advice—as if Samuel wasn't cruel enough without his father goading him. Why could her husband not see that his father was destroying any chance they might have of finding love in their union? More than likely, her feelings were not even a consideration?

For you, Mama, I will go back, but only for you.

As she reined Pride around and headed home, Ruth began to tremble from the cool night air, or was it raw fear of who awaited her upon her return.

Meticulously, she brushed Pride down and was putting him back in the stall when Samuel entered the barn. Ruth heard him come in, knew where he was standing, but didn't so much as glance his way when she moved passed him and headed toward the outhouse. Her stomach was a mess.

A quick peek at the full moon lighting the evening sky sent prickly shivers through her frame. Did it mean something? She hoped not. Even so, her insides were in utter turmoil. A sense of dread swept over her—as if heaven and hell were about to collide and she was in the middle.

After seeing to her needs, she entered the back door with caution, hung her sweater from the hook, removed her boots, and headed toward *their* room. Her mistake was looking up as she passed the parlor.

Samuel was sitting in the dark, waiting. "Come and take a seat, Ruth."

Too frightened to disregard him, she slithered into the first chair she came to.

He was patting the cushion beside him. "Not there ... here ...."

She cringed at the thought. "If you don't mind, I'd rather stay here ...."

If only his narrowed look could be ignored.

On shaky limbs she moved toward him. She was about to sit next to him when he pulled on her arm and she fell awkwardly into his lap—the last place on earth she wanted to be. When she remained in spite of her uncertainties, for some odd reason that pleased him.

Snuggling her close, he ignored her bristly countenance as he fingered the stray curls around her face. "Have you ever shared your struggles with your parents, Ruth?"

She hesitated, wondering where this conversation was

heading. "On occasion."

"Then I'm sure they've given you advise that you may or may not have agreed with, but you listened out of respect."

Looking back, the only advice she could recall disagreeing with them about was marrying him. Reminding him of that would not be wise. For lack of a better response, she merely shrugged.

"That's what you overheard my father giving me."

A moment of silence passed awkwardly by. "I wish I could believe you, but your actions of late tell me otherwise. Besides, I saw what your father gave you. What did you say that would prompt him to offer that kind of advice?"

"That you're fighting me at almost every turn and I'm not sure what to do about it."

She should have known. "I'm not doing it intentionally, but try putting yourself in my shoes. No matter how hard I try, you make me feel like I'll never measure up. Why must everything be your way?"

"Because I am master of this house!" Though his words were matter of fact, they came out as a growl, exposing his impatience.

Then what does that make me? There was so much she wanted to say to this man, but was it wise to expose her thoughts? She had to try. "You don't want a wife, Samuel, you want a servant."

"That's not true. Having you in my life has brought me much joy. I love you, Ruth."

She harrumphed. "I wish it were so ... really I do, but love is patient. Love builds others up, without expectations. I'm not convinced you're capable of giving anything without expecting something in return."

He drew her closer, as if to prove his point. "That's not true ...."

"My parents taught me that love is gentle and kind. It cannot be self-seeking or it isn't love at all." When he offered no response, she continued, "I suppose you wouldn't understand that, would you? Your father's example of love has been oppressive at best. In all these years your parents have never had a marriage built on mutual respect. They have never known what it is to be *one* as God intended. Perhaps you'd be wise to take notice, Samuel. Your mother is living proof of what his tyranny has availed him. She despises the man and rightly so."

"She respects him!"

Ruth's head swayed from side to side. "Perhaps you should look again. Or better yet, if you really want the truth, talk to your mother when your father's not around."

When Samuel's hand flew up, she recoiled, fully expecting to be slapped, but that was not his intent. Instead he shouted, "Enough! I won't have you tearing into my father."

"But he would have you tearing into me without thought for our fragile union. Can't you see what his cruelty has cost him? As if destroying his own marriage is not enough, you're allowing him to destroy any chance for our happiness."

Samuel could only stare. Her insight astounded him, but it annoyed him as well. When his annoyance intensified, he took the defensive. "I agree with my father in some ways. Changes must be made. I've told you that, but you don't take me seriously. Your attitude toward me is often intolerable."

"Like yours is any better! We look at life so differently, Samuel. In some ways I can see that you're trying, but in others you've made my life miserable." Her heart grew heavier with every moment that passed. Unable to bear his stern regard, she averted her gaze and tried to get up. He would not release her. "Please, let me go. I'm tired. I don't want to say something I'll regret."

"You're not going anywhere, Ruth ... we need to discuss this."

"That's just it. There's nothing to discuss. You don't care what I think. You insist that I bow to your every demand or else. Well, I'm sick of it! You don't see me as your wife. I'm nothing more than a servant who bears the effects of your wrath. A servant should have sleeping quarters of her own. I need to go and move my things."

"You're not going anywhere!" he gritted.

She faced him boldly, her eyes glistening with unshed tears, sadness filling her body and soul. "After what I heard tonight my hopes of having a real marriage are gone. I will serve you until Mama and Papa have gone to their final resting place. I owe you that much for all you have done, but you should know, I am here for their welfare alone. You don't love me and I'm not convinced you ever will. I'm moving upstairs."

"You'll do no such thing!" he spat. When he stood abruptly, she toppled to the hard floor. Yanking her to her feet, he proceeded to shove her down the hall and into their room.

When he retrieved the bag from his father, her heart faltered. Looking for a way to escape, her eyes skittered to the closed window, then back at the door.

He stood too near.

She would never get past him. "Samuel, please don't hurt me."

"You leave me no choice ...."

Holding his piercing glare, her voice trembled as she spoke, "You're wrong. You do have a choice. Everyone does. You can choose to honor your vows instead of hurting me. You promised ..."

she reminded him and started to cry, "you promised to love me before God and our parents. Were you lying then like you were about your father's advice?"

"I was a fool to disregard his counsel. I should have listened to him from the start. If I did we wouldn't be having this discussion."

Her anger suddenly matched his. "Counsel! Is that what you call it? More like the devil himself goading his evil spawn!"

"You push too far!" Samuel informed her, holding nothing back when he released his fury on the woman he claimed to love. He was angry with himself for giving into a fit of rage, but she was wrong to push him as she did. When her vulnerable anguished state suddenly overshadowed all else, he left the room.

Without thought for what he might do next, Ruth crawled beneath the covers and succumbed to her suffering. Her heart, already in shreds, faltered when Samuel came back into the room, shed his outer garments, crawled into bed and turned her to face him.

Ruth burst into tears all over again. "Samuel, please! You have to leave me be ...."

"I don't have to do anything!"

She wasn't surprised when he gently dried her tears. Although his actions were tender, his words that followed were written in stone.

"You are my wife. No matter what comes between us that will never change. I don't like hurting you, Ruth, but I refuse to put up with your defiance any longer. Are we clear on this?"

Her eyes slid shut against the weight of her circumstances. How could she survive a lifetime of *this*?

When she did not respond, Samuel grated, "I'm waiting for

an answer!"

Bringing herself to look at him was not possible. Her wrenching heart wanted to shut him out, but he would not allow that. Her voice, deepened by tears, cried out, "I'll never be the woman you want. I don't even know why I try."

He lifted her chin. Sorrowful eyes met his. Fingering several of her tear-dampened curls, he said, "You're wrong. You're the only woman for me."

She shook her head. "I'm not a bird, Samuel. You can't put me in a cage and expect me to forget the life I once had. Family and friends have always been an important part of my life. They are a part of who I am."

"You have a new life now. Let me fill that void."

How could she help him to understand? Minutes passed. "Have you ever had a friend?"

He shrugged. "I have you now. You're enough."

She looked away. *God, please help me!*

"I've been with you long enough to see that you're tender when it suits you, but for the most part you treat your animals better than you do me. How do you think that makes me feel?"

Unprepared for this, his mind stumbled over her words. *Could she be right? Do I treat my animals better than her?* Samuel, needing to silence her, kissed her with amazing tenderness, but she did not respond and that bothered him. As gentle as he was when he pressed her further, the wounds he had inflicted tortured her. Setting his need aside, he held her sodden face in his rough hands and said, "When I wake up in the morning you had better be in this bed. And there will be no more talk of you being my servant. Do I make myself clear?"

She offered a cursory nod, knowing he would not relent until she did. However, in her heart of hearts she suspected, a servant was all she would ever be. Although she sensed he wanted to say more, he did not. The moment he turned away, she did the same. How could she ever come to love and respect a man like *him*?

As she lay there listening to him breathe, the realization of what had just happened came to her. She tried to set it aside, but that still small voice whispered softly in her ear, *Tell him.* Perhaps it was trivial, but it was a step in the right direction. "Samuel ..."

"Hmm?"

"Thank you."

He paused, confused. "For what?"

"For giving me a thread of hope."

He wanted desperately to look at her, but he could not— the pain he had seen in her eyes still tormented him. Instead he admitted, "I don't understand."

She hesitated long enough to consider her words. "You put my needs above your own. That was a decision that could only come from your heart. Thank you for showing me that you care, if only in the smallest measure."

Craning his neck around and kissing her on the mouth, he said, "Thank you for telling me, Ruth. I want to love you as I should, but I'm beginning to see that I'm a lost man when it comes to matters of the heart. I have much to learn. Please don't give up on me."

"I'm trying not to." She really did want to love and honor him, but he was not making this easy.

When Samuel laid his head down and closed his eyes, her thoughts turned heavenward, *I don't know why this is happening,*

Lord, but I know You're with me or I would not know such peace. Show me what I need to learn. Help Samuel to see that instilling fear to control me is not love at all.

Unable to sleep, when she heard her husband's soft snore, she slid off the bed, slipped her robe on and moved toward the kitchen.

A nice cool swim in the river would be soothing, but her fear of dark places curbed that thought. Besides, she wouldn't chance Samuel finding out and taking his anger out on her, again. Though hurting, her wounded heart ached so much more than her battered frame.

Mechanically, Ruth took the small washtub down from the pantry wall and filled it with chilled water from the barrel. She found a bar of fragrant soap on the pantry shelf along with a length of toweling. Dropping them next to the washtub, she shed her robe, unmentionables, and stepped in. It took a moment to convince herself to submerge in the cool liquid, but was glad when she finally had. Although the invigorating fluid soothed her enflamed skin, it did nothing for her tortured soul. Her sore eyes slid shut as she raised the saturated cloth to her face, rinsing away the dried remains of tears.

Samuel, realizing that his wife was missing, crept silently through the house. Hearing trickling water, he moved toward the kitchen. Standing just out of sight, he watched his wife bathe. Her beauty held him captive. The way she was put together amazed him, but more than anything he loved her passionate spirit. Was his father right? Or would his cruelty eventually crush the very essence of the woman he adored? If his father was right, why did he feel so awful when he hurt her? He caught a glimpse of the ugly welts across her pale skin and cringed. He lost his temper yet again and she bore the effects of his cruelty.

Thinking she was alone, Ruth spoke softly to the empty room. Samuel clung to her every word.

"Oh, Papa," she admitted, "I love you in spite of what you've done. I would never tell you the extent of my suffering; you would blame yourself. I couldn't bear that. Better you go to your grave thinking you've done your best for Mama and me. No matter how hard the road ahead, with God's help, I will try to press on. I pray that I'm not a fool for believing there's more to my life than suffering at Samuel's hand. I really do want things to be different between us!

"Lord, I'm willing to change if you'll just show me what I'm doing wrong. So often I am confused. Why? I am not sure, but I ached to be loved—truly loved by this man. When he hurts me I feel inadequate, as if I'll never be good enough. Perhaps it is wrong to ask, but help him to see that he's pushing me further away.

"Papa, you said that the key to having love that stands the test of time is for that love to be built on solid ground. I'm not so sure what all that entails. If Samuel would just let me go to church, I would try my best to find out.

"I have so much to learn about You and Your ways, God. I'd love for Samuel and me to share a love that's sweet, as sweet as my parents'. My husband can be kind and even gentle when he wants to be. Right now it seems like such a far-fetched dream, but I have to believe that dreams really do come true. Even if my misery is for Mama's benefit alone, help me to endure."

Baffled by her admission, Samuel backed quietly away. As he did, his thoughts questioned, *Ruth asked that we would share a love as sweet as her parents'. Could she really mean that, even after … Why does she have to push me over the edge? I don't even know why I let her. I don't want to hurt her. I want to love her. Maybe she's right. Maybe I don't know what real love is. Maybe I never have.*

Samuel didn't know how, but if it took him the rest of his life, he would find a way to make this up to her. He headed back to their room, but he had no more reached the entrance when he turned around and called out, "Ruth!"

"I'll be there in a few minutes, Samuel." Frantic, she was trying to rinse the excess soap off when he entered the kitchen, sat down beside the tub, and offered to help. His help was the last thing she wanted. In fact, Ruth needed him to go away. She was still uncomfortable bathing in front of him. His treatment of her ran so hot and cold; how could she relax in his presence.

Samuel, ignoring his wife's deepening flush, kissed her cheek and then went to fill the empty pitcher with the tepid water from the pot on the stove.

She welcomed its warmth when he poured the water over her sudsy skin, but found his expression unsettling. After all his harshness earlier, his gentleness both surprised and pleased her. Maybe she shouldn't be so quick to expect the worst from him. His mother had a gentle way about her. Was it possible that he retained a few of her qualities? There were things he did that were kind. Perhaps if she focused more on them, she would not despise him so. She really did want to care about him—maybe someday even love him. He was, after all, her husband.

When she stood, he reached for the towel, gently dried her damp skin, and carried her back to their room. She was pleasantly surprised when he retrieved a clean gown, helped her into it, and wanted only to hold her in his arms. She drifted off to sleep praying—praying for a love that's sweet—as sweet as her parents.

Chapter Fourteen

A Determined Heart

HE MINUTES ON THE MANTEL CLOCK ticked slowly by, and so the hour hand moved ever forward. Days turned into weeks and still Ruth found only snippets of relief from Samuel's overbearing ways. She didn't understand how anyone could be so callous one minute and tender the next. The man was nearly as unpredictable as the weather. Just when she was sure she could stand no more, he would try making reparations with outbursts of kindness following his cruelty. Nothing made sense. She couldn't recall her papa ever being so unpredictable. At least not until the day he told her she would have to marry Samuel. Although there were times she wanted to leave her husband, she couldn't bring herself to abandon her mama. Unfortunately, her papa's health was failing fast. She and her mama would be counting on Samuel's support.

When Sunday arrived bright and clear, she made a decision. After Samuel went out to work in the field, she was going to church. Fully aware of the consequences of her actions, she shoved them to the back of her mind. If she didn't give Samuel a reason to hurt her, he would find one anyway. She had to do something that would bring her joy—something that would give her life purpose. Her parched soul needed quenching or she would not have the strength to go on. She may not find what she was looking for at this meeting, but she was desperate enough to go and find out.

The preacher had already begun to speak when she slipped though the barn door and took a seat toward the back. Immediately she was captivated. *Processing the Battles of Life* was the title of his sermon. *How fitting!* she thought.

Ruth sat next to a portly gentleman with a thatch of white hair and a gentle smile that eased her every apprehension about coming. When he laid his Bible on the bench between them, allowing her to follow along, she beamed with gratitude. With a deep reverence for the Holy Book, she couldn't restrain the desire to run her fingers atop the ancient words.

The elderly gentleman noting her wonder, picked up his Bible, placed it in her hands and for a time just watched her glittering eyes as they scanned the page with reverence. When the preacher asked them to turn to Second Corinthians, chapter four, uncertainty swept over her. The kind gentleman turned to the passage for her and a shared smile chased her fears away.

The preacher read the eighth verse and continued on. As he read the eighteenth verse, though it reminded her of her life with Samuel, it gave her hope.

> *"We are troubled on every side, yet not distressed;*
> *we are perplexed, but not in despair; Persecuted, but not*
> *forsaken; cast down, but not destroyed;... While we look*

*not at the things which are seen, but at the things which
are not seen: for the things which are seen are temporal;
but the things which are not seen are eternal."*

*Oh, Lord, help me to cling to this promise. No matter
how bad my circumstances, You won't allow my spirit to be
destroyed. Your love is eternal. This is good news!*

While the preacher had so much more to say, she could
hardly contain it all. She would have to bring along pencil and
paper from now on and take notes.

Folks greeted her kindly when the meeting came to a close.
Although she didn't like hurrying off, she really didn't have a
choice. Her husband would be coming in for his meal and he
would not be pleased if he found her missing.

As Ruth moved swiftly along the path, she meditated on
the things the preacher had said. She was a little confused when
he suggested that she take the things he was saying and make
them personal, but when she gave it a whirl, the reason for his
suggestion became crystal clear.

When I'm depressed, I should think about the goodness of God.

When I'm defeated, I need to think about the greatness of God.

*And, when my situation looks darkest I need to think about the
closeness of God.*

If she could remember these things long enough to write
them down, she was sure they would help her in the days and
weeks to come.

As she reached the path leading to their home, a sliver of fear
weaved its way up her spine. Although she steeled herself against
whatever awaited her, she was pleasantly surprised. This time,
Samuel was not waiting for her. Was it possible he was unaware

of her outing? *Oh, God, I know it is not right to deceive him, but please let it be so ....*

Ruth hummed the tune of the last hymn they sang in church as she tied her apron around her waist and pulled the pan of ham and creamy scalloped potatoes out of the oven. They were drying out a bit, so she added more milk and sprinkled them with slivers of cheese before putting them back in to brown. Sliding the coffee onto the burner, she was setting the table when Samuel came in the back door. Glancing his way she asked, "Hungry?"

"Starving! What smells so good?"

She grinned. "Something new," she admitted, as she pulled the pan of cooked apples off the burner and poured them into a bowl. When everything was on the table, she joined her husband, and without thought reached for his hand. He did not pull away, so she bowed her head and silently offered up thanks before serving the meal.

"Mmm!" Samuel said as he took a small bite, "This is good!"

"I'm glad you like it. Mama has been making them on Sundays for years."

"I see ...." he said without looking up.

She ached to tell him all about her morning, but knew the folly of it. *Perhaps the day will come sooner than I think, Lord.*

"Samuel, are you terribly busy today?"

His eyes met hers. Something in her tone was different when she wanted something and his decision to try and be more accommodating altered his response. She really didn't ask much of him. A little give could go a long way toward building their relationship. "Nothing that can't wait. Did you have somewhere you wanted to go?"

"Actually … two places …" she paused, a bit too long.

"To your parents and ..?"

A smile she could not restrain curved her mouth. "If we only have coffee with my parents, would you mind stopping by to check on Meg and the children?" Ruth held her breath—hoping he would say yes. When he didn't answer right off, she added, "She is looking forward to meeting you, Samuel. We don't have to stay long. Just to see that she has food and a full water barrel."

His grin taunted her, "What is it worth to you?"

Confusion furrowed her brow.

When the crook of his finger bade her to come near, she hesitated too long. He stared her down. "You've been up to no good, Ruth Anne."

Scowling, her upper lip came up in that irresistible way, and she asked, "Why would you say that?"

"The only time you shillyshally is when you've done something I won't approve of."

A wave of guilt washed over her. She should tell him, but if she did, their day would be ruined. Instead she said, "My fears are not unfounded, Samuel."

"Perhaps!"

As her uncertainties dissipated, he scooted his chair back, held out his hand and waited for her to come to him. She smiled when he pulled her into his lap, and kissed her tenderly. "You're in a funny mood."

He snuggled her close. "I suppose I am. Have a few things on my mind, is all."

"If you already have plans for the day, we could go visiting another time."

He shook his head. "No reason we can't fit everything in if we get moving."

A curious look crossed his face, but she didn't press him.

"If it can be arranged without too much effort, a picnic supper would be nice to take along."

She nodded. "I'm sure I can scrounge up something." Ruth, smelling the muffins in the oven, glanced at the stove and then back at her husband, "I don't want them to burn, Samuel. Is there anything else I should know?"

"Just that it could be late when we return, so bring along a sweater and blanket."

Excitement swirled through her and suddenly she couldn't resist steeling a few kisses of her own.

Samuel surrendered willingly to her passionate display. He loved seeing her so at ease in his presence—in his arms. "Can you be ready in a half-hour?"

Ruth nodded. Leaping off his lap, she looked back as realization dawned. *Something is changing in my heart where my husband is concerned. He is still the same man. I'm certainly not ready to let down my guard, but I can clearly see that something is different. He is trying. Have my prayers had something to do with that?* Since every good and perfect gift comes from above, she tried not to analyze Samuel's tenderness too much. Instead she whispered her thanks to God as her husband walked out the door.

Even the ride to her parents' house was different. Her enthusiasm spilled over often as she and Samuel shared memories from their past and even discussed future plans—plans that included both of them. For her this was both strange and wonderful all at the same time. How could she not be pleased? They were conversing as friends—as equals. It was as if his heart was finally as determined as hers to make this marriage work. Oh, how she prayed that it would be so.

Samuel, though pleased with the change in his wife, was clueless as to what had brought it about. He loved the way she kept touching him, running her fingers through the hairs on his arms and snuggling close as they rode along.

Her parents were tending their garden when they rode up, and quite pleased with the interruption in their day. Samuel lowered Ruth to the ground before dismounting and greeting his in-laws kindly. His eyes were stayed on Ruth as she squeezed her mama's hand and together they moved into the house. When Samuel finally turned and met Gerald's inquisitive gaze, he smiled. "She didn't cry this time. I'm hoping that's a good thing."

"I'm sure it is, Son. She looks happy."

"Today she is." His head lowered in contemplation. "Not sure what brought it on, but I'm glad for it."

Surprised and yet pleased by his honesty, Gerald offered, "Finding a wife is a good thing, wouldn't you agree?"

"Yes, but loving her as I should is where the challenges lie. Truth is, I thought I had things all figured out before we married. Boy was I wrong. She doesn't exactly fit into the mold I had pictured. Suppose I still have things to learn." After tying Pride to the post, they moved slowly toward the house.

"I've found," Gerald said, "that the physical side of love barely scratches the surface when it comes to the marriage union. Believe it or not, I can relate to what you're going through. Most of us dreamy-eyed men think we know everything there is to know about women until we marry one."

His insight made Samuel laugh out loud. "Isn't that the truth!"

"My father-in-law once told me to think of love as a gift. It must be given freely without expecting anything in return or it isn't love at all."

"You and Mom seem to have things figured out. You're so peaceful together."

Gerald's brow lifted. "Hasn't always been that way, Samuel. Remember, we've had years to get to know each other."

"So, was Mom ornery in her younger years, like Ruth? Did you find yourself having to set her straight now and again?"

Gerald took a deep breath. That Samuel would be so bold surprised him, but overreacting would not help his daughter or Samuel. *Give me wisdom, Lord.*

"In truth, my father's gentleness with my mother and her loving responses taught me much about the love that can exist between a man and a woman. I can honestly say that I have never even considered raising a hand to my wife. At times we do irritate each other, but we choose to work on our differences and honor each other regardless."

Samuel was taken aback. "Then how does that work? Are you saying she willingly submits to your will?" His fingers raked through his blonde hair. "Ruth can be so stubborn. Just when things seem to be running along smoothly, she does something to infuriate me."

"I'm sure that's true, Samuel, but love cannot be self-seeking or it isn't love at all. Marriage isn't about me and what I want or expect from my wife; it's about both of us honoring and respecting one another. Flo is my dearest friend. Our marriage union made us one in the physical sense, but becoming one as God intended didn't happen overnight, it happened over time. I can tell you from experience that loving Flo more than I love myself has had wonderful residual effects. The more I seek to please and love her, the more she wants to love and please me in return. We've been through tough times, but the love we share has stood the test of time."

Samuel's brow furrowed. "It all sounds so complicated."

"We make it harder than it is."

"This selfless love you're talking about sounds familiar. Ruth was telling me about a list you shared with her about what love is. I'd like to take a look at it, that is, if you're willing to share. You know, as a reference of sorts."

Gerald grinned, but knowing how his son-in-law felt about God, he opted not to expose the lists origin. Instead he simply said, "I'll write it down and drop it by your house real soon."

"Thanks!" he offered, his voice softening to a whisper, "Would you mind keeping this discussion between the two of us?"

"Not at all." Gerald chuckled softly as he held the door open for Samuel to precede him. His son-in-law's pride was involved in the conversation they'd had, but Gerald didn't hold it against him. His determination to love his daughter was hidden beneath that pride and the knowledge of it warmed his ailing heart. *Thank You, Lord, for allowing me to see that Samuel is searching. Lead him to the Cross and make him one with You.*

❀ ❀ ❀

Brent came running out of the house when he heard a horse ride up, but his steps slowed and his head lowered the moment a strange man dismounted. Had the man been alone, Brent would have scurried back into the house. But Ruthie was with him, so he held his ground despite his uncertainties. Cautiously, Brent watched as the tall man lifted his dear friend off his massive beast.

"Brent ..." Ruth called to him. Having noticed his deepening scowl, Ruth held her hand out to reassure him, "Come here, I want you to meet my husband."

When he didn't budge, Ruth went to Brent and lifted him in her arms. "What's wrong, Buddy?"

He leaned close and whispered in her ear. "Is he the dweaded lord?"

His memory surprised her. Ruth looked back at Samuel, who was tying Pride to the post. Fortunately, he didn't hear Brent. "He is, but I was just being silly, Honey. Samuel came with me because he wanted to meet you."

Still unsure, he clung to Ruth's neck as Samuel came near.

Samuel nodded in greeting. "You must be Brent. Mrs. White has told me so much about you."

Brent's quizzical look brought a smile to her face. "My married name is Mrs. White, but you can still call me Ruthie."

"Mr. Samuel, he comed to see Mama and Cindy too?"

"Yes. Is your mama inside?"

He nodded, leaned close, and whispered, "I can show Mr. Samuel how I butch a chicken. Maybe you could help spiff Mama."

She smiled. "He would like that." Ruth turned to Samuel, "The last time I was here I showed Brent how to butcher a chicken. He wants to show you what he's learned."

Samuel, unfamiliar with the ways of small children, was taken aback by the request. Sensing something else amiss, he played along. When he held out his hand for Brent to lead the way, the small boy took a daring step toward him, and slipped his hand in Samuel's. He relished the way the little hand felt enclosed in his.

Samuel winked at Ruth, and then smiled at Brent as they moved toward the barn.

For a moment Ruth stood and watched them, her heart warmed by the pleasure Samuel found in answering Brent's endless list of questions. As she turned and opened the door she considered her husband's interaction with Brent and realized that her uncertainties about having his children were slowly melting away.

The warm sun had a lulling effect on Ruth as they rode for what seemed like an eternity into unfamiliar territory. Samuel refused to tell her where they were heading and although she was eager to find out, she was so very sleepy. Eventually, her weighted lids would not be denied.

"Ruth," Samuel said, as he lifted her chin and brought her sweet lips to his. She had been sleeping so soundly against his chest, he hesitated waking her, but they had reached their destination.

She awoke slowly, giving way to an elongated stretch. "Where are we?" she asked, allowing her eyes to roam over the ranch they were approaching. In a nearby corral she caught a glimpse of, "Thunder!" Ruth squealed. She kissed Samuel hard on the mouth, leaping off Pride, stumbling and almost falling as she ran toward the corral. Thunder was prancing towards her when Samuel approached from behind and an elderly gentleman came out of the barn.

The older man said, "Hello, Samuel. Is this the young woman you've been telling me so much about?"

Samuel nodded.

Ruth was standing on the fence rail, leaning over, petting Thunder when Samuel reached for her waist and set her gently on the ground. She turned and smiled at the kind man.

"Dakota, I'd like you to meet my wife, Ruth Anne. You'll have to excuse her unladylike conduct; she hasn't seen Thunder in quite some time. You see, he used to be hers."

"That would explain why he came right to you, Ruth Anne. Jeremiah and Thunder have become the best of friends, but the horse tends to ignore the rest of us."

"Jeremiah?" Ruth inquired.

"Yes!" Dakota said as he pointed toward the side steps of the ranch house. A small boy was coming slowly toward them. His left leg was oddly twisted and one of his arms appeared malformed as well. "A cougar nearly took him from us when he was two, but he's a fighter. Thunder was a gift for his sixth birthday. The horse has certainly been a godsend."

Ruth met Samuel's gaze, her eyes glassing over as she asked Dakota, "Is he able to ride him?"

"Several times a day. Doc seems to think the exercise is strengthening his weak muscles."

Now Ruth was really confused. Why would Samuel bring her all the way out here to see Thunder if she couldn't have him?

"Jeremiah! You remember Mr. White. This lovely young woman is his wife."

Ruth knelt down and shook his frail hand. "You can call me Ruthie, if you'd like, Jeremiah."

He nodded. When she stood, he reached for her hand and led her toward the fence. "I was watching you from the window. The way Thunder came to you surprised me. Does he know you?"

Ruth nodded. "Very much. He was my horse before he came to live with you. I spent many years gentling him. So tell me, Jeremiah, do you like him as much as I do?"

His handsome little face lit with pleasure. "Oh, yes, Ruthie. Pappy said you must have loved him a bunch for him to turn out so good."

"I did ... I still do."

"Love, Pappy told me is a gift we offer freely."

Ruth looked up at Dakota, who now stood at the fence with Samuel. They had been listening in on their entire conversation. "Your Pappy is a wise man."

Dakota and Jeremiah went to the gate, put a lead rope on Thunder, and the two of them led the horse into the barn to saddle him, leaving Samuel and Ruth alone.

Staring blankly at the distant field, she asked, "Why, Samuel? Why would you bring me here? You know how much I love that horse. I raised him from a colt." Tears were standing in her eyes when she glanced his way.

Samuel pulled her into his arms and held her close. "I didn't know he was yours until after I had sold him. I came out here to buy him back, but when I saw him with the boy, well, I just couldn't separate them. I wanted you to see them together."

Ruth tried to pull herself together. "If I can't have him, I'm glad Thunder's with folks who will love him."

"I was hoping you would feel that way." Samuel removed his hanky from his pocket, dried her tears, and handed it to her.

After a good blow, she tucked the damp cloth in his shirt pocket and grinned when his face snarled up.

He claimed her hand and gave it a squeeze. "I have someone I'd like you to meet."

As the gentle breeze swept the dampness from her cheeks, her wavering emotions settled into a peaceful resolve. Samuel was right. She loved this horse, but she could never separate Thunder and Jeremiah, not having witnessed their special bond. "Could you give me a minute, Samuel? I'm sure my face is all red and blotchy."

His long fingers tenderly tucked her stray wisps behind her ear. "Somehow, I don't think she'll mind." Samuel grinned mischievously as he led her into the barn toward a back stall and slid the door open. "Since Thunder is unavailable, I'm hoping you might settle for this porcelain beauty."

Suddenly, Ruth's eyes were alight with pleasure. "She's a beauty to be sure, Samuel, but she can't be ridden. She's about to foal."

He nodded. "That's precisely why I didn't want to buy her without talking to you first."

"Oh?"

Caressing her cheek, Samuel said, "Her foal won't replace Thunder, but if you're up to the task, I was wondering ..."

Her heart leapt in anticipation of what he might say. When she could no longer bear the suspense, she asked, "You'll give me the foal?"

"And the mare, but they come with stipulations."

When Samuel closed the stall door and led her back outside, she cringed, imagining all sorts of things. *Here we go!*

"Porcelain is yours to ride around the farm after she foals, but if you're going further we'll need to discuss it first."

"And ..."

"We're buying her for breeding purposes. Training horses is hard work. Are you sure you're up to the task?"

Uncertainty melted away and she cackled with glee. "What do you think?"

"I was hoping you'd say *yes*!"

She jumped up and spun around. "Yes!"

When she finally settled enough to really think through what Samuel was offering, her hands slid into his and she had to know, "Can we take her home today?"

"I think that can be arranged." Dakota said as he came up behind them.

Ruth's eyes, now glittering with hope, fell back on her husband.

"I would, Ruth, but I didn't come financially prepared."

"If Pride will pull a wagon, you can borrow the one out back to transport her tack and return the wagon with the purchase price we agreed on next week."

Dakota seemed to have an answer for every glitch.

Samuel, taken aback, asked, "Are you sure?"

"It's obvious your wife has a tender spot for horses, so I'm sure Porcelain will be just as much at ease with the two of you doting over her as she would be with me."

Ruth glanced at her husband who nodded in acquiescence. Taking the lead rope Dakota handed her, Ruth shivered with excitement as she went to claim the newest addition to the White farm. Ruth led her out into the sunlight and smiled. *Porcelain* was a perfect name. A silky white angelic glow covered most of her mane and coat, all except a small black mark that kissed her face.

"Ruth, are you coming?"

Hearing her husband call from where he stood behind the wagon, she realized he was waiting for her and headed towards him with Porcelain trailing close behind.

As Samuel secured Ruth's new horse to the wagon, he lightheartedly bumped into his wife who was now standing at his side. "Your face is going to hurt if you don't quit smiling."

"Are you complaining?"

"No." His hand came up to caress her face. "No complaints here."

"I'm curious. Did you name her, Samuel?"

He grinned. "No, but I like it. Do you mind?"

"Not at all. Porcelain suits her."

Ruth was walking away when she heard Samuel say, "Now *my* porcelain beauty has one of her own." She glanced back at him and smiled. He really was full of surprises today—good ones. My, but they were nice.

Ruth, thinking the spot Samuel chose for their picnic supper was breathtaking in an eerie sort of way, allowed her eyes to scan her surroundings. Although the setting sun dimmed their vibrant shades, she spied several varieties of wild flowers blooming in a nearby field. She must have been daydreaming when they moved past here earlier in the day. Jackrabbits were out in abundance as always, feasting cautiously on their evening meals. Samuel pointed to a badger that just happened by and then scurried off, apparently they had invaded his space. Would plans for his evening meal have to wait? Surely the hawk soaring overhead had his own agenda. He would not be so quick to lay it aside. Strange noises coming from within the forest walls made Ruth shiver. "It's getting late, Samuel. Do you think it's safe to stop?"

"It's barely dusk." He said, mocking her apprehensions, studying her thoughtfully. Her arms were wrapped tightly around her frame and her eyes rarely wandered from the edge of the forest, as if something were lurking and would surely jump out. "What happened to the daring woman I married who attempted to leap out a window without thought for her welfare?"

"The woman you married was terrified of you, and now, well, she's not so daring when it's getting dark."

"You've been telling me that love requires give and take. Are you open to a compromise?"

A compromise? Gazing into the depth of his brown eyes, she caught a glimpse of something she had never seen before, longing, desire that was not only physical—it was deeper. Looking back over the day, she realized that everything he had done bespoke a determined heart, a willingness to lay self aside and touch her deeply. He had accomplished that and so much more. She did wonder if it would last, but kept her doubts to herself. All things considered, setting aside her fears to spend time with her husband would be a small price to pay. When she drew closer to him, with a gentle caress her arms slid around his neck. Resting her head on his strong shoulder, she found the comfort she sought. She had longed for a day like this, prayed that they would find love in their marriage. Could this be a new beginning? For the first time since they were joined as husband and wife she believed they had a chance—that they were possibly even meant for each other. The road ahead may still be paved with rocks and hurdles, but like his, her heart was determined to give her all.

Chapter Fifteen

Generational Curses

RUTH AWOKE SLOWLY, stretched like a lazy cat after a long nap and rolled over to see if Samuel was still in bed. He was not. As she stood and tried to get her bearings, the mantel clock chimed nine times. *Nine o'clock!* It wasn't like him to just let her laze around in bed. Why did he not wake her?

Befuddled, she crawled out of bed and went to her armoire. Her stomach rumbled as she threw on an acceptable skirt and blouse. She'd love to dress up a bit for church, but if she did Samuel might suspect she was going somewhere and stop her. How could she let that happen? The desire to learn more from God's Word was pressing her something fierce. When she reached the kitchen and Samuel wasn't there, she made herself a light breakfast. After washing up the few dishes from his morning meal, she hurried out the door. Samuel was not in the barn, so after checking on Porcelain, she went off to church.

George's message on *love's power over anger and resentment* was very enlightening. The notes she had taken would give her much to meditate on in the coming week, but time was slipping away, so she said her farewells and headed home with plans to stop by Samuel's parents' house. Growing weary of the same meals over and over again, she looked forward to trying some of the new recipe's Naomi had promised to copy for her.

Ruth's heart rejoiced over the wonderful week she'd had with Samuel. Her determination to put forth an effort where he was concerned had not waned. His tender response was such a welcome relief. Perhaps her motives were a little selfish, but deep down she longed for a marriage built on mutual trust. If mutual love were to follow, she would consider herself doubly blessed.

Ruth knocked on the front door, but when no one answered, she walked around the porch to the back of the house. Unfortunately, Samuel's father was basking in the warm sun with Naomi. As usual, he was not pleased to see her.

"What are you doing here?" he snarled.

"It's nice to see you too, Mr. White!"

"Not sure where you've been, but you'd best get home! Your husband was over here looking for you."

Holding her temper, the verse she had heard earlier that morning played over in her mind, *A fool gives full vent to his anger, but a wise man keeps himself under control.* "I left him a note so he wouldn't worry."

Naomi stood and snarled at her husband, "Oh, be still, Samuel! She came to see me, not you."

As Naomi suspected, his eyes narrowed in on her. Ignoring him, she held her hand out to Ruth, saying, "Come on, Honey. I have the recipes you asked me for all written out."

Ruth took the hand Naomi offered and they chatted on as

they moved into the house.

"Mom, Samuel will be furious when he finds out, but I went to the church service my friend told me about. The people are so friendly, and the preacher, I felt like he was speaking directly to me."

Naomi held the door open for her daughter-in-law. "Might have been."

"I can hardly wait to hear the continuation next week. You should come with me some time. It might give you something to look forward to."

Naomi shook her head. "I appreciate the invite, really I do, but I told myself a long time ago that I'd never put my faith in a god who would allow a man to treat me the way my Samuel has. You keep going though, Ruth. Don't let me discourage you. Maybe it'll cheer you up." Naomi carefully touched the blackened bruise trailing up from her daughter-in-law's wrist. "Is this my son's handiwork?"

Wary of saying, Ruth's eyes skittered about the room before falling back on Naomi. "Some days, I just can't do anything right."

Naomi walked to the small window, her gaze falling on the distant field. "Generational curse ...."

Thinking she heard her wrong, Ruth asked, "What did you say?"

Naomi turned back to face her. "Generational curses ... Until I married Samuel, I didn't believe they existed. Unfortunately, his father was just as crude as him. Can't believe I've stayed with him all these years. In my younger days I prayed that God would take him, but as you can see he's still here. When I had young Samuel it became even harder to break free. Maybe I do things to egg him on now and again, but no one deserves what he hands out. I'm sorry Samuel didn't turn out better. I really did try. He spends too much time with his father not to succumb to his influence."

When Naomi went to her room for the recipe cards, Ruth's father-in-law came in the back door with a burlap sack in his hand. Her heart faltered, imagining what was inside.

"Ruth, take this to Samuel. He was asking for it earlier today."

"What is it?" she inquired. She suspected her father-in-law was up to no good again, and she was tired of being on the receiving end of his meanness.

When he only stared, her dander rose. Recalling the contents of the last sack Samuel brought home, she felt the item. Sure enough, she was right. Where it came from she did not know, but a wave of boldness transfused her. She went to the cook stove, opened the door and threw the sack into the burning embers.

A quick glance at her father-in-law revealed his reddening complexion. She expected him to yell—even lash out, but instead he took a daring step toward her, grabbed his chest, and collapsed on the floor.

Frightened, Ruth went to where he lay on the floor and called to him, "Mr. White!" Although she held no fondness for the unpleasant man, she would never intentionally cause him harm. "Mr. White, are you all right?" she asked repeatedly with no response. Putting her cheek up to his mouth, her heart faltered. He wasn't breathing. Frantic, she yelled out, "Mom ... come quick!"

Naomi, having watched the entire scene unfold from where she stood numbly in the doorway, walked slowly into the room. Crouching down to check his pulse, she then stood and reached for Ruth's arm. "Honey, listen to me."

Ruth's eyes filled with alarm just before she burst into tears. "I think," Ruth met Naomi's gaze, "I think I killed him ...."

But Naomi shook her head as she wrapped her arms around Ruth. "No, Sweetheart, you did nothing of the sort. Samuel allowed his anger to get the best of him one too many times. He took his own life."

"But ..."

"But nothing! I saw what he put in that bag. Bout time someone stood up to him. I only wish I could have been so brave. Who knows, maybe you and Samuel will have a chance now ...." Naomi took a single step back, her eyes holding Ruth's tearful gaze. "My son may have a distorted view of love, but in his own way I truly believe he loves you, Ruth."

As much as she longed for that to be true, panic rose within her. "You don't understand. Samuel will blame me for his father's death. He'll never forgive me."

"That's why you're not going to tell him anything. Leave it to me. I will tell him."

She shook her head. "But he'll know if I'm holding back. I don't know how, but I swear your son can read my mind."

"Then we'll hope he doesn't suspect anything out of the ordinary. Go home with your new recipes. Make him a nice dinner. I'll wait a while before I come by to tell him his father is gone."

Ruth glanced down at her father-in-law and shuddered. "You would do that for me?"

"Sure I would ... trust me, Honey, I know what you're up against."

Ruth suspected she already knew the answer, but she had to ask, "Will you miss him?"

Naomi stared down at her husband, her head swaying in the negative. "Truth is, the only good that came from our marriage is our son. I've always longed for a daughter, too, and now I have you."

Ruth softly admitted, "I want to love him ... I'm trying, but he doesn't make it easy. I know what he'll do to me just for going to church, never mind this."

Naomi's stone cold features took on a deviant look Ruth did not think her capable of. "Would you like me to go home with you?"

Ruth pointed to her father-in-law. "What about him? We can't just leave him."

She shrugged. "He'll be there when I get back. Besides, I'm thinking you'll need help with dinner. Using a new recipe can be tricky."

Ruth, by no means in a jovial mood, a small smile creased her face. It pleased her to know that her mother-in-law would go out of her way to protect her. Perhaps her presence would only delay Samuel's cruelty, but it was certainly worth a try. "Are you sure you don't mind leaving your husband?"

In answer, Naomi wove her fingers through Ruth's and led her out the door.

"Would you mind if we have a cup of tea before we get started? This whole experience has been rather unsettling ... if you know what I mean."

Naomi winked. "Sounds good to me. I'm in no hurry. In fact, I have nothing pressing, quite possibly for the rest of my life."

Although Ruth was more at ease having Naomi with her,

knowing Samuel would not react favorably to her absence put her on edge. She could only hope he would not shame her in front of his mother. Fortunately, he was not in the house when they arrived.

Naomi had taken the tray of tea to the parlor and Ruth was filling a plate with cookies when the back door flew open. Samuel's rage was more than evident as he came toward her, grabbed her arm and swung her around to face him.

As hard as she tried to remain calm, her voice trembled, "Samuel ... I ... I got home from church a little while ago. Your mom ..." Oh, it was no use. His evil glare was enough to still the flow of blood through her veins. When he shoved her toward their room, her steps faltered. She would have fallen had he not had such a firm hold on her arm, but her flesh would surely bear the bruises from this tussle.

Ruth knew the very second Samuel saw his mother sitting in the parlor because he stopped abruptly. She would have given anything to have seen the look on his face, but keeping up with his forcefulness had been her only thought.

As if nothing were out of the ordinary, Naomi stood and greeted him, "Hello, Samuel. We were hoping you would join us." Nonchalantly, her gaze swung to her daughter-in-law when she asked, "I thought you were bringing a plate of cookies?"

Ruth peered up at Samuel, hoping he would release her.

He did not.

Embarrassed as she was, it took a great deal of restraint to keep from cracking a smile. The shock that registered on her husband's face was too much. Although her mother-in-law's presence had bolstered her courage, she awaited his response with maddening civility.

"Go ahead and get the plate." He leaned close before releasing her, whispering, "This isn't over. I'll deal with you later."

Meeting his fiery glare, she asked without missing a beat, "Would you like a cup for tea, Samuel?"

He scowled. "Coffee!"

"It's not fresh." She held her breath, suspecting he would insist on her making another pot, but Naomi's intervention altered everything.

"Just grab another cup, Honey. Samuel likes tea as long as I sweeten it enough. Isn't that right, Son?"

Samuel, though he wondered what had gotten into his mother, let it slide—this time. "That'll be fine." Ruth had no more taken her leave when Samuel really looked at his mother. Her presence in his home was certainly odd. "Where is Dad?"

"At home."

"Then why are you here? You know what he'll do if he finds you missing."

With a swish of her hand, she dismissed his concern. "Since when do I listen to that old coot?"

"Mom! You're real brave when he's not here to set you straight."

If I were a religious woman, I'd say amen to that! Withholding her thoughts, she merely said, "I'm here to help Ruth with a new recipe I gave her."

She hadn't answered his question, but he didn't press her. He snatched a cookie from the plate Ruth was holding and took a seat.

"So, what are you two making for dinner?"

"Your wife would like to surprise you."

Ruth was handing him a cup of tea when he asked, "Hoping I'll overlook your earlier transgression?"

"I'd hardly call going to church a transgression, Samuel," she humbly stated as she stood before him in awkward silence. "Your mother has graciously offered to help me with the meal, so I thought it would be nice if we shared it." When still he only stared, she held her ground, praying that he would not see her trembling.

"I'm not as naive as you apparently think, Ruth. My mother being here is no coincidence."

He was right, but telling him so would only give him more fuel for the fire. "You may not understand, but I need to be in church, Samuel." Feeling the intensity of his heated glare, she turned away, refusing to allow him to humiliate her further.

His annoyance still at the fore, Samuel informed her, "The only reason a woman goes to church is to meet a man!"

Her dander rose as well. "Like I need another *man* in my life! You've made it clear that you don't believe in God, and that is your choice, but I can't ignore my faith. I don't own a Bible, so how am I supposed to learn more about God if I don't attend a local gathering?"

His hand came up to forestall her. "Enough! We'll discuss this later."

Though her insides burned with repressed anger, she did not press him further. There would be no discussion later, of this she was sure. All of their disagreements ended the same way—with him losing his temper and her ... On the verge of tears, Ruth refused to allow him to suppress her spirit any more. Glancing at Naomi, she asked, "Mom, would you like sugar in your tea?"

Sending her son a heated look, Naomi stood and went to fix her own tea. Snatching a sugar cookie off the plate, she took a large bite and hummed. "These are scrumptious, Honey. Perhaps it's time we head to the kitchen. I'd be beholden if you'd allow me to take a gander at your recipes." Her eyes met her sons before adding, "That is, after dinner is underway."

A timid smile erupted on Ruth's face when Naomi finished the cookie in her hand and reached for another. Ruth understood. This particular recipe was a favorite of hers as well.

"I don't have many recipes written down, but you're welcome to look through the ones I have."

Ruth didn't so much as glance Samuel's way when she picked up the tea tray and followed her mother-in-law to the kitchen. Unfortunately, her husband followed, sat at the table, and was hanging on their every word.

Naomi, growing weary of his presence, asked, "Samuel, don't you have things to do in the barn?"

An inquiring glare swung from his wife to his mother. "That depends. Will you two be here when I return?"

Naomi snickered. He did have a point. "I have a few things to do at home before dinner, but I won't be gone long."

Meandering over to the counter where his wife stood with her back to him, it pleased him when she turned in his arms. However, her reluctance to look up told him much. Lifting her chin, Samuel held her hesitant gaze before kissing her tenderly. "I won't be long either. See that you're here when I return."

With an edge of indifference, she murmured, "If I'm not in the house, you'll find me weeding out front. Anything in particular you want for desert?"

"A cobbler of some sort would be nice. Dad likes cherry, but if we don't have cherries, peach will suffice."

She nodded, unable to release the breath she'd been holding until he turned to leave. Torn between her desire to strengthen her relationship with the Lord, and her desire to honor her husband, though his demands were often absurd, put her in a precarious state of mind. Being anxious for nothing held its challenges. She did not doubt that her relationship with God had to come before Samuel, but she had to remind herself of that truth often.

Naomi stood at the kitchen window, watching her son. "He's better looking than his father, but his personality is so much like him it scares me."

Ruth's hands came up to rub her warm cheeks. "Well, he terrifies me."

"I know, Honey. I'm so sorry. I'd change him if I could."

As Ruth's thoughts strayed, she could not restrain the giggles bubbling up.

Naomi, a bit confused, shook her head. "What's so funny?"

"Nothing ... just a silly notion, is all."

She frowned. "Surely, you don't intend to leave me in suspense!"

Although Ruth rolled her eyes at her playful remark, she sobered as she said, "Sometimes I wonder how Samuel would respond if I could trade places with him for a day or two."

Naomi's curiosity peaked. "Why, so you could have the upper hand for a change?"

"No ... I have no desire to control him, or anyone else for that matter, but I do believe his fear of losing control of me is at the center of his rage. Knowing doesn't excuse him, but it does help me to understand why he does what he does. More than anything I'd love for him to see what can exist between us when love, instead of fear, is at the core of our union."

Thoughtful, Naomi watched Ruth as she put the meat in the oven, and then took a seat across from her.

"I'm curious, Mom. Did your parents share a loving relationship?"

Naomi smiled in remembrance. "Oh, yes. They weren't perfect by any means, but I never doubted that Papa and Mama adored each other. My Samuel was good to me the first month we were married. I don't know if my son told you or not, but we're originally from Pennsylvania. I'll never forget the day my Samuel informed me that he had sold our home and we were leaving to homestead in the wilds of Michigan. Maybe I would have handled the change better if he allowed me to be a part of the decision, but that was not the case. Our relationship was all downhill from there."

"My parents are close. They have so much fun working together. I know I'm not without fault, Mom, but every time I start to feel at home with Samuel, he loses his temper and I end up ... well, you know."

"I do. I wish I could help, but being Samuel's mother puts me in an awkward place."

"I'm just glad to have someone to talk to. It's not as if I can tell my parents the extent of Samuel's abuse. They would blame themselves for arranging our marriage. I don't want that."

Naomi reached out and patted her hand. "Will you be all right when I leave?"

"I went to church when he told me not to ..." she shrugged,

"guess I've earned whatever I get."

"Ruth ... please, don't talk like that. No one deserves to be treated with so little respect."

Ruth held her mother-in-law's gaze. "At least your torment is over."

Naomi nodded, still trying to take it all in. "I'm finally free of him."

"I keep thinking about what you said earlier. You could be right. Samuel and I might have a chance now that ... well, you know."

"I do."

Tears puddled in Ruth's eyes. "I believe in miracles, don't you?"

"Not sure about that, but anything is possible when you're dealing with the human heart. I've seen love change the hardest of men and women. My Samuel chose to be cruel instead of loving me throughout our married life, but that didn't keep me from hoping for better days."

Thoughtful, Ruth fidgeted with the folds of her skirt before meeting her mother-in-law's tender gaze. "The pastor reminded us today that God's love can melt a heart of stone."

"You would know that better than me, Honey." Naomi stood and meandered toward the door. "Listen, Ruth. I hate to leave you in such a vulnerable position with my son, but I should get back and tend Samuel."

"My concern is for you, Mom. Are you sure you should go alone?"

Naomi scowled as her hand came up to swish at the air, just before she walked out the door.

Ruth could not look away as her mother-in-law's long confident strides took her across the yard. How awful it must be to come to the end of your married life, never knowing the love and respect of your mate.

Oh, Father God, she prayed, *let change begin with me. Show me how to love Samuel, as You do, so that he can see You though me.*

Chapter Sixteen

No Need to Grieve

These things have I spoken unto you, that my joy might remain in you, and that your joy might be full.

—John 15:11

RUTH, HEARING THE HINGES on the back door squeak, and the soft shuffle of feet, turned as Naomi slipped in the back door and asked, "Ruth, is my son in the barn?"

Samuel, having heard his mother's distraught voice from where he sat in the parlor, strutted into the kitchen. "Where's Dad? I thought he'd be coming with you for dinner."

Without so much as a glance in Ruth's direction, Naomi reached for his arm and led him out the door. They were almost to her house before Naomi stopped and looked up at him. "I don't know how to tell you this, Samuel ... your father ... well, his heart has been acting up for some time now."

"I know, Mom. He had a spell the other day when we were working. Is he struggling again? Should I fetch the Doctor?"

Naomi's head swayed from side to side. "I'm sorry, Son. It's

231

too late for a doctor. Your father is gone."

"What?" Dread swept over him as he ran into his parents' house and found his father lying on the kitchen floor. Samuel stooped down to check for any signs of life. Touching his father's face he swiftly pulled his hand away. *How could he be so cold already?* Baffled by his father's blue lips and the deep coloring around his mouth, he asked, "Mom, when did this happen?"

She shrugged. "Not sure ..."

His mother, though acting strange, he did not press her. His father ... he was dead. Right now nothing else mattered. "Mom, we should get him off the floor. Can you help me put him on your bed?"

"No ..." she shuttered at the thought. "I don't want him in my room. Why, I'd never sleep in that bedroom again. Just thinking about it gives me the creeps."

"He's your husband, for heaven's sake!"

She shook her head. "He was my husband. Lift his arm, Samuel. He's no longer there. "I'll help you wrap him in a blanket. We can bury him next to the big oak."

Samuel, shocked by her uncaring tone and lack of emotion, asked, "Mom ... I don't understand. Where are your tears?"

She stared at her son in disbelief. "Samuel ... you know what he was like. Trust me when I say, I have no need to grieve his passing."

Anguished by her words, he groaned. "You feel nothing for the man, even after all these years?"

Her son loved his father. She had no wish to make light of his sorrow, but she had remained silent for too long. "Let this be a wake-up call, Samuel."

He scowled. "Oh, please, Mom. Now is not the time for one

of your lectures."

Gently, she touched his shoulder. "Now is the perfect time. Think about the way you treat your wife. If you love her as you say you do, respect her, show her you love her by treating her with kindness. It's not too late for you to change—but please, I beg you, learn from your parents mistakes. Don't wait until it's too late."

"My relationship with Ruth is hardly your concern."

"You couldn't be more wrong. Your marriage made her family. That makes her my concern." For a while, an awkward silence hung between them. When Naomi covered his hand with hers, their eyes met. "I wish I could tell you otherwise, Samuel, but I won't miss him."

His eyes glassed over. "You never loved him, did you?"

"In the beginning I did, but back then our feelings were mutual. The man was so passionate when we were first married; he swept me off my feet. Unfortunately, that all changed the day he informed me that we were moving to Detroit to start a new life. He blamed me for everything that went wrong. I tried to please him, really I did, but that was impossible. His need to control me became obsessive and that obsession eventually destroyed everything that was good between us. When the beatings started, things went from bad to worse. I tried to leave, but he wouldn't let me take you. How could I leave you alone with him? He would have hurt you the way he was hurting me."

"I have my own scars that haunt me, Mom, but no matter how you feel, he was my father. He deserves a proper burial."

Her eyebrows lifted. "Are you talking about a preacher and all?"

Samuel nodded.

She tried not to grin, but couldn't refrain. "Maybe you should. It would serve him right. Why, the man would turn over in his grave if he knew what you were thinking. Won't do any good though—no god would welcome such a man in the hereafter."

His eyes fell again on his father. "That's not for you to say. I intend to do right by him." Samuel wasn't going to get any help from his mother, so he took the time to ready his father for burial before carrying him out to the barn. He laid him on the buckboard, thinking it would be easier to transport him in the morning to his final resting place.

Naomi walked with Samuel back to his place, but he didn't go in with her. Instead, he went to the barn. He needed time to think.

Ruth and Naomi were sitting at the table with another cup of tea when Samuel entered the back door. "Ruth, I want you to come with me. Mom, you can stay here if you'd like. We won't be long."

Ruth's eyes, now filled with apprehension, fell on her mother-in-law before she turned to face her husband. Did he suspect something? His blank stare sent a sliver of fear rippling through her, but Ruth did as she was told. If only she could dispel the sick feeling in the pit of her stomach.

Regardless of how she felt about her father-in-law, her husband had lost his father. When Ruth reached his side, she slid her arms around him in a warm embrace. "Samuel, I'm sorry for your loss." And, she meant every word.

He returned her hug, tucked her stray curls behind her ears and said as their sodden eyes met, "Thank you, Ruth."

They were moving out the back door, when she saw Pride

tied to the post. "Where are we going?" she asked.

Samuel lifted her onto the front of Pride's saddle, mounted behind her and they were moving away from the house before he said, "I need you to show me where the Somers place is."

She craned her neck around to look at him, worry etching her face. "Samuel ... he's a nice man. I know you didn't want me to go to church, but he doesn't know that. You won't humiliate me, will you?"

"No, Ruth. I thought I'd ask him to say words at the grave side."

"Oh!" She'd been prepared for anything but this. "He's not the regular preacher. His wife said that he only fills in when the circuit preacher isn't in town."

"He'll do fine ...."

They were nearing the turn off when Pride suddenly reared up. He lunged forward, leaping over a startled rabbit in the tall grass. A branch from a scrub tree put a gouge in Ruth's leg, but they were fine otherwise. Samuel's quick response set Pride to rights and he soon settled into an easy gate.

She pointed up the way. "Follow the road to the right where it separates. Their Farm is not far from there."

Samuel drew her closer and kissed her cheek. "You had quite a hike this morning. Were you late for church?"

She wondered where his sudden concern was coming from. Dare she hope that he had forgiven her? "Just a little. An elderly gentleman was nice enough to share his bench and Bible with me. He even showed me how to follow along."

"Is it difficult?"

She took a moment to really look at him. His interest seemed genuine enough. "Not once you figure out where the book is that the preacher is referring to."

"I've never looked through a Bible before." He shrugged. "Just curious."

"Someday... I'd like to have one of my own."

Samuel, having seen her request on the supply list several times, didn't comment as they rode up to the farm. "Who's the man sitting on the porch, Ruth?"

"George Somers. If his wife comes out, her name is Jayne. They're close to us in age."

George stood as they approached, his hand shading his eyes from the bright sun. "Hello, Ruth. Good to see you again. Is this your husband?"

She nodded.

Samuel slid off Pride and shook the hand George offered. "The name is Samuel ... Samuel White. It's nice to meet you, George. My wife enjoyed the service today."

George smiled. "We've enjoyed having her with us the last two weeks."

Samuel glanced over his shoulder at Ruth, his eyes narrowing in on her. "You don't say."

"We'd love to have you join her."

Samuel skirted George's comment by getting right to the point. "I have a favor to ask."

"What's that?"

Samuel, needing a moment to gather his thoughts, his head lowered before he peered up. "My father passed away earlier today. I'd be beholden if you'd speak words at his funeral in the morning?"

Concern etched George's brow. "I'm sorry for your loss, Samuel. Has your father been ill?"

"Weak heart."

George, noting that Samuel could not look him straight in the eye, did not wish to trouble him further, but had to ask, "Did you have anything special in mind for the service? Perhaps your father had a favorite hymn or verse?"

Samuel's head swayed from side to side. "Not that I know of. I'll leave that up to you."

When an uncomfortable pause lingered, Ruth asked, "Is Jayne home?"

Samuel, sensing the direction of Ruth's thoughts, and that she had moved back on Pride's saddle and was about to dismount, didn't wait for George to respond. He mounted behind Ruth and said, "Don't mean to be rude, but we need to be heading back. My mother's alone. You understand."

"I do. What time would you like Jayne and I to arrive?"

"Eight is fine."

George ran his hand along the stallion's thick neck. "Would it be all right if I let the neighbors know, so they can come and pay their respects?"

Samuel nodded. "Appreciate your doing so."

After saying their farewells, Samuel led Pride back to the Sauk trail, nudging him into a slow canter. They were almost home before he reined his horse in to allow him time to cool down.

The tension between Samuel and Ruth hung so thick she could have sliced it with a knife. Unnerved, her eyes jittered to and fro, searching for what she did not know. A sparrow landed in a nearby tree and took flight again. As the familiar brown bird flew out of sight, she remembered having heard that God cares about every one of them. If that was so, how much more did He care about her, His child. The thought of God's love warmed her, but it did not erase the odd feelings swirling inside her. If only she knew how to make things right with her husband.

Pride's approach startled a chubby woodchuck who was munching on a root. She watched him waddle off into the woods, but soon he disappeared behind a tree. As lovely as the wild flowers in the meadow were, she could not convince herself to ask him to stop so she could pick some for her mother-in-law. Her husband's silence, as it often did, unnerved her.

When Samuel finally spoke, the gruffness of his voice frightened her, "You stopped by my parents on your way home from church. Was my father still alive?"

Her heart skipped several beats before it sped out of control. If only Samuel hadn't turned her to face him. "Yes ..." she meekly replied, "he was resting in the sun with your mother. We spoke briefly."

"And ..."

"Why are you angry with me?"

"Things don't measure up. Besides, I know what my father was like. If he was alive my mother wouldn't have come without him."

Her head tilted. "Your mom thought he had another spell."

Samuel's temper flared. "That may be, but there's more to this. You're hiding something from me, Ruth. I won't have it!"

When she tried to deny it, he slapped her face.

"Tell me what happened. All of it!"

How could she? He would never forgive her. Instead of

answering, she leapt off Pride, a thick mixture of anger and fear swirling inside her. Her hands clenched at her sides. Finding no respite, her fingers raked through her tousled hair. Her irritation had to be soothed. An angry word would only serve to provoke him further and then she would bear the brunt of his rage. On her guard, Ruth stepped out in front of him and began to pray.

"Ruth Anne!" he berated.

Tears mingled in her eyes as she turned slowly to face him. "He was alive when I got there ...."

"And?" he prodded, his tone demanding she go on.

"Apparently, he lost his temper one to many times!"

It was the worst thing Ruth could have said. Samuel leapt off his horse and ran after her, catching her in several long legged strides.

Naomi, hearing Ruth's pain-filled screams, came running out of the house. Samuel had her pinned on the ground, and he was whipping her with his crop. Naomi hollered as she ran toward them, but it did little good. He struck Ruth several more times before releasing her. Glaring at his mother, he mounted Pride and rode off toward the barn.

There was no doubt in Naomi's mind; the beating Ruth endured was aimed at both of them. As she helped her daughter-in-law into the house, her legs kept buckling. "Oh, Honey, I'm so sorry."

Between sobs, Ruth managed to say, "It's not—it's not your fault. I should know better than to mouth off when he's so fired up."

Compassion filled Naomi for the daughter she had longed for most of her married life. Ruth had a sweetness about her that warmed this aging woman's heart. How could her son be so cruel? "Angry or not, he has no business taking it out on you."

Ruth wrapped her arms around her mother-in-law and squeezed her as tight as she could. Somehow, knowing Naomi's years of torture were finally over brought Ruth the slightest measure of joy. "I was just getting to where I could sit comfortably from the last beating." Ruth swiped at the tears blinding her, determined to chase them away. "According to Samuel and your late husband, the only wife worth having is one who knows her place. If only I knew what *that place* was."

"That's the problem. There's no pleasing them." Naomi wanted to take this poor girl home and protect her from her son. Only knowing he would come for Ruth and drag her home kept her from doing so.

Naomi led her into their bathing chamber. While Ruth removed what was left of her torn skirt, shift, and unmentionables, Naomi filled the tub with water and steadied her while she climbed in.

Ruth cringed as the cool water met her inflamed skin.

"I'd warm it, Honey, but this is best."

Ruth sat carefully on her knees, avoiding her most painful spots. The thought of sliding under the water and ending it all did cross her mind, but she couldn't bring herself to do it. The gentle voice inside her head was back, whispering hope to her tormented soul.

Naomi, after allowing Ruth a good long soak, helped her into her nightgown, brought her a light supper and tucked her into bed before turning and walking out of the house. She was angry enough to give her son a good tongue lashing, but she had no wish to make things harder on her daughter-in-law than they already were.

Ruth gathered the things she would need, climbed the steps to the second floor and slid into the open space she had found behind a temporary wall.

The hour was getting late when she awoke to the sound of her husband's stern bellow. No doubt he was angry to find her missing. Knowing she was free of his touch for a time brought her a fair amount of satisfaction. Ruth's body and spirit were aching for a reprieve—for time to heal—if only for the night. Perhaps she was wrong to abandon her husband at a time like this, but she could not summon the strength to face him. Every time he beat her, something inside her died a little more. Was it her will to press on? In truth she didn't know. *Am I really that awful, Lord? Do I deserve what he does to me?* She just couldn't face him right now. Covering her ears with her pillow, Ruth thanked God for safe shelter. For tonight she would be secure within the shroud of her latest hideout. She could only hope the mouse she saw tucked in the corner before she blew out the candle would not call his friends and put an end to her respite.

Ruth was standing at the counter making breakfast in her nightgown the next morning when Samuel came in the back door, looking stunned to see her.

For the longest moment he only stared. "Where were you all night?"

"Here ...."

"Don't lie to me! I searched the house and barn from top to bottom."

Ignoring his irritation, she peered up. "Would you like

pancakes or toast with your bacon and eggs?"

He took a firm hold on her arms. "Answer me!"

"I won't have time to get ready for the funeral if we stand around chatting, Samuel."

Noticing the bruises on her face and wrist, he wondered if he should have her stay home. "If you plan to be at my father's funeral, wear a long-sleeve dress and put a veil over your face."

Her eyes narrowed in on him. "Afraid someone will see your handiwork?"

His hold tightened. "Apparently you need another lesson."

"It takes a really big man to beat up on a woman .... But then I guess you would know that better than most. You watched your father abuse your mother for years and did nothing to help her. Tell me, Samuel, have you asked her if she'll miss him?"

"Enough!"

All too aware that her words were making matters worse, regret washed over her. "I'm sorry. I wish things were different between us. I care about you, Samuel, but I can't fight the rage inside you. Only you can. You need help."

"And I suppose you know where I can find it!" His tone oozed with sarcasm, but she ignored it.

Her soft blue gaze met his stern glare. "Wish I did. You could always try talking with someone who has a good marriage. I'm sure my father would be willing," she shrugged, "but if you don't feel comfortable with him, there are others ...."

"Like ..?" Curious as to who she might suggest, he waited.

"Do you really want to know or are you making fun of me?"

He nodded. "I'd like to know."

Her eyes lowered, and then slowly rose. "I've watched George and Jayne together. They're the best of friends. Maybe he could help us?"

He could see where all this was leading. "And the next thing I know you'll want me going with you to church. No thanks!" Samuel was still convinced that she only went to church to meet a man—perhaps James?

"If I believed God cared about what goes on here on earth, I'd think about it, but I don't! My going would only frustrate both of us."

His wife was right about one thing: his rage was becoming a problem. He didn't like the way he felt inside when he hurt her, but he didn't know how to stop. He had tried several times and failed. Although he did wonder if Ruth could be on to something, he just couldn't fathom why a higher power would want anything to do with the likes of him.

"Get breakfast on the table while I change my clothes. We shouldn't keep your new friends waiting."

Methodically Ruth poured the pancake batter into the pan and set the table. In some ways she was disappointed with the outcome of their conversation, but then again, at least he was willing to listen for a change.

God, I don't even know how to pray. I'm at such a loss. It was Your love for me that sent Your Son to the cross to pay the price for my sins. I cannot fathom that kind of love. Help me to follow in Your example and love my husband in spite of his faults. Help me to hold my tongue when I should. I want him to see You through me, like George said. I don't doubt for a second that You could change him. Look at the way You're changing me.

Ruth was trying for the life of her to recall the passage Mr.

Somers had read in Corinthians when Samuel walked into the kitchen. Although most of the passage escaped her mind, the part she remembered quite clearly came to her: *without love I am nothing.* The depth of Samuel's voice startled her, pulling her out of her reflective state.

"Quit your daydreaming girl! We need to eat."

"Oh, sure ...."As she put the food on the table, she thought about her father-in-law. He was such an odd man. In truth, she never understood him. Had his own insecurities driven him? Naomi had been quite adamant when she said she had no need to grieve her husband's passing. Although her comment should have saddened Ruth, it did not. She understood. The White men were not easy to love.

Could Mr. Somers comment at church be right? *Does God's command to love have little to do with my husband's character? Is it more about me walking in forgiveness, me seeing him as You see him? Oh, that he might see You, Jesus, in me.*

Samuel sat down at the table and was about to insist that she join him when he remembered what he had done to her. Regret burned inside of him. *Why do I hurt her?* As he was coming to expect, she stood at the counter and bowed her head in a moment of silent prayer.

While she nibbled on her food, her thoughts continued along the same vein they had been going before. *Maybe one day ... if I study Your Word, pray often, and ask enough questions, I'll find the answers I am looking for. Is it possible that even I can experience the kind of joy Mr. Somers has been talking about— the kind of joy that comes from You—the kind of joy that will fill me to overflowing as I draw closer to You?*

What I wouldn't give for a healthy dose of that kind of joy right now!

I'd give even more if Samuel and his mother could know that kind of joy, as well.

In truth, Ruth's heart ached for Naomi. She may have no need to grieve her husband's passing, but without the Lord's presence in Naomi's life, she would never find the joy she desperately longed for.

He Loves Me!

Chapter Seventeen

Enlightenment

RUTH STOOD BEFORE HER ARMOIRE, trying to decide what to wear to the funeral. She had a skirt in a respectable shade, but her only blouse with long sleeves was a bit too cheery. When Samuel strode into the room and found her standing in her unmentionables, his irritation rose. "Why aren't you dressed?"

"My long-sleeved dresses are too warm, Samuel. I don't know what to wear."

Without hesitation, he took her worn cotton calico from the hook and handed it to her. "This one will have to do."

She stared at the tattered garment in disbelief. The only reason she kept this rag is so she wouldn't ruin her good dresses when she went fishing. Did he intend to humiliate her in front of all their neighbors? At first she thought so, but his look said otherwise. She held up the worn frock, her voice faltering as she said, "I can't wear this!"

"Then choose something else. Folks will be arriving soon.

You can't greet them in your under things." Leaning close, he tenderly kissed the bruise on her face. "You pushed me too hard again and I lost my temper. I really don't like hurting you, Ruth. I hope you will forgive me?"

She, so stunned by his apology, at first said nothing. "You were upset about your father, Samuel. I really don't understand why you hurt me, but I do forgive you." Although she had so much more she wanted to say to this man, the mantel clock chimed seven times. Samuel was right. Their guests would be arriving. Another time, perhaps!

Samuel gathered her gently in his arms. The tears in her timid gaze plucked at his penitent heart. Could his mother be right? Could he change the way he treated her? If he didn't, he might never know the love he so longed to see in her eyes. As he tucked her soft curls behind her ears, he said, "I missed you last night."

No doubt in her mind, he meant every word. However, whether he was sorry enough to change was yet to be seen. What could she say? Whatever his motive, his admission did her aching heart some good.

"The wool dress lengths I bought you for your birthday will be too warm. I'll pick you up some lighter cotton when I go into town next week, that is, unless you'd like to come along and pick them out yourself."

Uncertainty washed over her. Did he really want her to go, or was he merely trying to make amends for his cruelty? Either way, if this marriage was going to work, someone had to be the one to begin breaking down the icy wall dividing them. "We could pick them out together."

He nodded and smiled. "I did some looking when I was in town last week, but wasn't sure if you'd like what I picked out. I'm sure if you asked, my mother would be glad to help you with patterns and such. If you haven't noticed, she has a real knack for sewing."

"I have noticed." Ruth's heart pranced like a frisky colt. She tried not to read too much into his offer, but couldn't help it. *Does he really want to spend more time with me? Spending more time with his mother would be wonderful as well.* She prayed it would be so, but fear of breaking the warmth between them kept her from asking as she watched him leave the room.

While his volatile personality often made her feel as though she must go through life walking on eggshells, she did hope for better days.

After donning her skirt and blouse, she looked for her veil. Unfortunately, it was nowhere to be found. More than likely it was still tucked away at her parent's house. Brushing through her hair, she left it down, hoping it would cover the worst of the bruise on her face. A quick glance in the mirror told her it would suffice.

George and Jayne Somers arrived at Samuel and Ruth's doorstep earlier than anticipated, but Ruth opened the door and welcomed them with a smile.

Their arms were filled with several baked goods and a full platter of sliced ham.

As they were setting the food on the table, Samuel walked into the room and greeted them kindly. In truth, seeing George brought him a measure of comfort. He didn't know why, but there was something about the man Samuel liked.

Jayne introduced herself to Samuel, offered her condolences and then turned back to her new friend. Softly touching Ruth's cheek, she said, "That's a nasty bruise on your face. What happened?"

Ruth caught the odd look Samuel sent her and thought carefully before opening her mouth. Although she refused to lie, leaving out a few details couldn't hurt. "I'm afraid I wasn't paying attention to where I was going. I took a tumble."

Jayne nodded, but sensed that Ruth wasn't exposing all. "My husband could tell you that 'Grace' is not my middle name either."

George met her gaze, held his hand up, and said, "I'll play it safe and keep my opinion to myself."

Jayne giggled, and so did Ruth.

"George, if you and Samuel want to head over, Ruth and I will join you in a few minutes. I'd like to freshen up a bit."

Samuel hung on their every word and although Ruth wondered what he was thinking, she didn't dare ask. Genuinely, she liked these people and so wanted Samuel to feel at ease in their presence.

George headed for the door and Ruth cringed when Samuel pulled her into the parlor. Without preamble, he asked, "Where is your veil?"

"It wasn't amongst my things, but covering it with face powder should hide the bruise from questioning eyes."

"Do the best you can." He kissed her gently and turned to leave.

The men were out the door when Ruth turned to her friend.

"I have to cover this bruise a little. If you noticed, others will. Would you like a tour of the house?"

In answer, Jayne followed Ruth down the hall and into her room. Ruth hid her discomfort when she sat at her dressing table, but when she caught Jayne's reflection in the mirror and tried to smile, she couldn't quite pull it off.

"You didn't really fall, did you Ruth?"

She couldn't turn and look at her friend face to face, but their eyes held fast to each other in the mirror. Could Ruth trust her? "I did fall, but that's not where this bruise came from."

"Did your husband give it to you?"

Ruth's eyes glassed over. "Samuel has forbidden me to leave the farm without him. Since attending church is not something he would want me to do, I didn't ask him. Needless to say, he wasn't happy when he found me missing yesterday. Then to top it off, he knew I had stopped at his parent's house on the way home because his mother came home with me. Piecing things together, he suspected I was keeping details of his father's passing from him. He insisted on knowing everything. I told him what I could."

"You said this bruise. Are there others?"

Ruth nodded. When the tears pooling in her eyes began to fall, Jayne sat down on the bench beside her. The gentleness of her hug was like a burst of warmth on a chilly day—comforting.

"I don't want to upset you more right now, Ruth, but we do need to talk about this. Would you mind if I come by another day?"

She nodded. "I'd like that."

"So would I. In the meantime, find comfort in knowing God has promised to be with those who suffer. George and I will be holding you and Samuel up before the Lord."

Ruth's eyes widened with concern. "He won't say anything to Samuel, will he?"

"I'll leave that up to him. I'm not going to assume that you're perfect, Ruth. None of us are. But no matter what Samuel's reasons are for hurting you, they're wrong. Abuse of any kind is sin. If you remember, last Sunday we learned about this very thing. The devil's will is to control us and he will go to great lengths to accomplish his will. God, on the other hand, will never force His will on us. He'll lead us though, if we put our trust in Him."

"But Samuel ... oh, Jayne ... he'll be furious ... if ... if George confronts him."

The bruises on her friend's exposed skin tore at Jayne's heart, but they did not alter the truth. "God is still God, Ruth. His love will never fail you. I understand your fear, but remember what I just told you. If you're fearful, someone is controlling you. Fear keeps you from trusting our Lord and that's exactly what satan is hoping to accomplish. Don't let him rob you of your faith—don't give in to his lies—don't play into his hand. God has promised to be with you. Stand on that knowledge. Take God's hand and allow Him to lead you through the circumstances you face, no matter how difficult they are."

A heartfelt presence wrapped her in a peaceful embrace. "I am so thankful we met, Jayne. Your words, as they usually do, bring life to me. Yes Samuel is wrong, but he can't see that yet. He doesn't understand what love is. More than anything, I need you to pray for us—often. I am weak, but God is showing me that it's in my weakness that He is made strong. Just keep in mind when you speak to George that Samuel is like most men—he's prideful. Perhaps it is selfish, but I don't want anything to get in the way of

George and Samuel becoming friends."

Jayne squeezed her friend's hands. "If they do become friends, we'll have more time to spend with each other."

Ruth smiled, admitting, "Exactly!"

Turning in her seat, Ruth glanced again at her reflection in the mirror. As she did, panic rose within. "Oh, Jayne, look at me! I'm a mess."

The giggles bubbling up could not be squelched.

"It's really not funny, Jayne! Samuel will have a cow if I show up like this."

"A cow? Really? Now that would be a spectacle to behold!"

Ruth playfully swatted her friend's arm. "I know you're merely teasing, but really, Jayne. I could use some help."

"Not to worry! We'll have your red face looking flawless in no time at all."

Rolling her eyes, Ruth said, "I'd settle for tolerable."

Jayne picked up the face powder and had been working diligently on Ruth's face for several minutes before she asked, "What do you think? Will Samuel find you tolerable?"

Relief washed over Ruth as she stared into the mirror. "You're amazing ... I can't even see the bruise."

"Good, then neither will anyone else. Are you ready to join our men?"

In answer, Ruth stood, hugged her friend and together they walked across White land to the big oak where her father-in-law would be laid to rest.

After the service and sharing a somber meal with friends and family, Naomi thanked George and Jayne, hugged her son and daughter-in-law and headed home. Ruth hated for her to be alone at a time like this, but Naomi assured her that she was simply tired and needed rest.

George and Jayne had been sitting around the table talking with Samuel and Ruth, all of them enjoying the chance to get to know each other better. Although they had mentioned leaving, Samuel asked them to stay.

Needless to say, Ruth was delighted by their presence and Samuel's feelings, if she wasn't mistaken were mutual.

While Samuel and George discussed their latest endeavors in farming, Ruth and Jayne put the kitchen back in order, chatting away about anything and everything that came to mind. They enjoyed each other immensely.

As Ruth tucked the last platter away, Jayne leaned toward her and whispered, "I'm heading out back for a minute." She turned and slipped out the door.

The men, having heard her return, were listening when she grinned at Ruth and asked, "Any chance you're up for some berry picking?"

Ruth's eyes brightened. "Always!" Suspecting her husband might not agree, she glanced at him and said, "That is, if you don't mind, Samuel."

Jayne put in, "I did a little investigating this morning before we came. The patch is ripe for the picking or I wouldn't have mentioned it."

Ruth grinned at her friend before eyes filled with hope took a gander at her husband. What would he say, she wondered, but had no way of knowing as he was too busy watching Jayne, who had just whispered something in her husband's ear.

George shook his head. "Don't you think we should be on our way? I'm sure Samuel and Ruth could use some quiet time. They just said goodbye to Samuel's father. And besides, they have a full day's work ahead of them. So do we, for that matter."

She did understand that they might need time, but she could not hold back her saucy return, "Speak for yourself, Mister. I for one have nothing pressing, and besides, we're both overdue for a little spoiling."

His eyebrow's rose into his hairline. "And I suppose you think berry pie will do the trick."

"Absolutely!"

As their playful bantering continued, Samuel scooted to the edge of his chair. He had never witnessed anything like this and fully expected George to put her in her place. When he did not, Samuel released the breath he had been holding. Crossing his arms, he sat back in his chair and waited, for what he did not know.

The narrowing of George's eyes, brought a grin to Samuel's mouth. He thought, *Ahh … haa! Now George has reached the brink of his tolerance. Now he will set her straight!*

But George merely pointed to his lips and said, "It's going to cost you!"

Surprised, Samuel chuckled. Though he might not have been as tolerant with Ruth, it was good to know he was not the only man with expectations.

Jayne kissed him sweetly. "A price I am more than willing to pay."

Pulling his wife onto his lap, George hugged her tight. "You'd best get to it if we're to have pie for supper." Glancing at Samuel, he inquired, "That is, if it's all right with you. Don't mean to intrude on your day. Jayne will understand if you'd rather the women do this at another time."

Hesitant, Samuel looked at Ruth and then at Jayne. "Where is this patch?"

"On our land," Jayne said. I'd be glad to give Ruth a ride home after we pick our fill."

When Samuel did not respond, George offered. "The women can drop me off at home and take the wagon."

"Sounds good, but I don't mind coming by to pick Ruth up."

Jayne was quick to say, "If you're coming by anyway, I have a big roast in the oven. We'd be glad to share."

A single brow lifted as Samuel met his wife's hopeful gaze. "As long as we're not imposing ...."

Ruth, beyond excitement, went to the pantry for the buckets. As she suspected, Samuel followed her, shut the door behind him, and spoke for her ears alone. "I like these people, Ruth. I want to get to know them more, but nothing has changed between us. You know what I expect." He ran his fingers through her hair, needing to touch her. "You and Jayne be extra careful. The bears get a hankering for berries just like we do. Only difference is, they're not too fond of sharing."

"I know. We'll be careful." She stood on her toes and kissed him tenderly. Are you sure you don't mind being alone? I'll understand if you don't want me to go."

"I'll be fine."

Ruth couldn't restrain a small smile. "I'd better go then."

He nodded, reached for the buckets, and opened the door.

As the four of them walked out to the wagon, Samuel said, "I'll finish my chores and come by your farm in a few hours."

George nodded. "We'll see you then!"

Samuel stood in the yard watching his new friends leave

with his wife and thought about their time together. The morning had been enlightening. Not only had the Scriptures George read over his father's grave made him wonder about his view of God, seeing George and Jayne interacting with each other gave him a different perspective on the marriage union.

Could his father have been wrong?

Was his mother right?

Did he need to rethink the way he treated his wife?

He wasn't fully convinced that his father was all wrong, but the thought of reaching the end of his life and never having experienced the kind of love Ruth spoke of did not sit well. He wanted her to care—to love him. Then he wondered, *is the desire to be loved selfish? Will loving her without expectation really bring me the greatest joy? The list from her father implied that it would. How can I really know for sure?*

Perhaps time spent with George and Jayne would be good for all of them. George and Jayne's love for each other seemed to have a reciprocal effect. With his father gone, he needed a confidant; and Ruth, well, she and Jayne were already like two peas in a pod. He could only hope the Somers would be a positive addition to their lives.

"Samuel!" George called out from where he stood at the entrance to his barn. "I've got a mare ready to foal."

"Is she struggling?"

"Has been for a while. I'm hoping she'll give birth before we head in. The women are putting the finishing touches on supper."

"I've been thinking about that promised berry pie all day. How'd they do picking?" Samuel asked as he tied Pride to a post and followed George into the barn.

"They came home with four buckets full."

Grinning, Samuel nodded. "Then they did do more than chat!"

"Yes ... but I have to admit, it does my heart good to see Jayne and Ruth laughing and talking so freely. Jayne never complains, but I know she misses her friends back East. The way our wives carry on, one would think they've been friends for years."

Since Samuel had never had a close friend, other than Ruth, he didn't know what to say. "Did you live in town?"

"No, but our family farms weren't that far out. Socials at church were a regular occurrence, so we spent much of our free time with friends. You know, sharing meals and workloads."

Samuel's brow furrowed. "My parents' property borders on mine, so we've remained close. I've had a few business acquaintances around town, but until I sought Ruth's hand, I kept pretty much to myself. Ruth keeps telling me how important friends are to her. With my father gone, I could use a friend."

"You're not alone. There are some topics Jayne doesn't enjoy discussing ... says they bore her to tears."

Samuel's soft chuckle brought George's eyes to his. "Like 'farm talk' in general?"

"You guessed it!"

As they entered her stall, the mare was giving birth to a pretty little filly. "Our timing is impeccable, George." Samuel knelt down to clear the excess afterbirth from the foal's face, but there was really no need. She was fine. Within moments she was attempting to stand and even took her first steps.

George glanced at Samuel. "God thought of everything in

creation. The instincts he put in animals to give birth and then care for their young simply amazes me. He knew us farmers would be too busy doing other things. Can't always be on hand."

Pensive, Samuel asked, "Do you really think God cares about such trivial things?"

George nodded. "Scripture tells us that He knows the number of hairs on our head. And He cares about every sparrow that falls from the sky. The more I read my Bible, the more I realize how detail oriented God is. Look at us. Each of us were created in His image, yet we're as different as night and day."

"Hmm ..." *Food for thought.* Hearing footsteps, Samuel turned to find his wife coming towards him.

"I heard you ride in."

Opening his arms for a hug, Samuel released her and pointed toward the stall. "George and Jayne have a new little filly."

Peering over the enclosure, she said, "Oh, George. She's so pretty. Jayne was hoping she'd be sorrel."

"Well, she got her wish."

Nodding, she said, "Supper is just about ready if you two want to head in and wash up."

George was moving toward the door when she said, "If you two don't mind, I'd like to watch the foal for a bit. Little ones don't come along every day. I won't stay long."

"We'll be right in," Samuel corrected.

When George left the barn, Samuel pulled his wife into his arms. "Did you have fun with your new friend?"

Peering up, she smiled. "We had a wonderful time. Jayne is like the sister I never had. We giggled and talked and picked berries till our fingers were blue." Soft endearing eyes scanned his face. "Do you mind that I left you alone?"

He shook his head. "Not if it means there will be a berry pie to top off our meal."

"We made two, and we'll have enough berries to make muffins for breakfast," she shrugged, "and who knows what else."

His long fingers ran slowly down her soft cheek, her expression exuding happiness. He loved tender moments like these. There were so many things he wanted to say to her—if only the words would come. He, so alive when she was near, if only his insecurities were not pressing in, making him fearful. His fear weakened him, causing him to listen to the voice inside his head—his father's voice—so hard to shut out. Even in tender moments like these.

"I'm glad you have a new friend, Ruth. Just remember where you belong. Nothing has changed. You know what I expect."

She swallowed hard past the lump now forming in her throat, determined not to allow anything to spoil their time with George and Jayne. Looking down at the newborn filly, she murmured, "I won't forget, Samuel." *You won't let me.*

"Good!" When an awkward silence dragged on, he added, "I might have found a friend in George as well."

This brought her hopeful gaze back to his. "If I'm the only friend you've ever had, this is a good thing ...."

Grinning, he kissed her sweetly. "And let me guess, you're hoping George and I will share a friendship as close as any brothers?"

Her eyes twinkled with glee. "Something like that."

"Perhaps we should head in. This day has been very enlightening, but if you don't mind, I'd like to take things one step at a time. For now we're only having supper with new friends, agreed?"

She tried to hide her smile and couldn't quite pull it off. Sharing a tender glance with her husband, she whispered, "Agreed!" as they moved toward the house.

He Loves Me!

Chapter Eighteen

Talking it Out

GEORGE HAD A KIND WAY ABOUT HIM and he was more peaceful than any man Samuel had ever known, but this knowledge perplexed him. With farming being their common ground, they rarely ran out of things to discuss when they were together. Oddly enough they shared many of the same goals. Trust was gradually building in their relationship. However, Samuel remained on his guard, convinced that George had to have an ulterior motive for spending time with him. With Samuel's father gone, he needed George's friendship, so he gave him the benefit of his doubt.

Several times Samuel caught himself watching George and Jayne interact when they were together. Often he was flabbergasted. Oh, he was sure they had their difficult moments. After all you can't put two humans together and expect them to always see eye to eye. Even so, the joy and laughter they shared, he longed to share with Ruth. George truly enjoyed his wife. Their devotion to each other was evident in their every response.

Even when they'd get feisty with each other, or disagree, George was never harsh—not so much as a scowl or a stern word. How George managed to hold his temper was beyond Samuel's comprehension.

George and Jayne delighted in each other's every response. They willingly looked for middle ground, submitting to each other in ways that were totally foreign to Samuel. No question about it, George was the head of their home, but not because he lorded over Jayne to keep her in her place, as his father had his mother, and as he did with Ruth. No, Jayne's reaction to George was born out of the gentle love and devotion they shared. Oh, how he wanted that for Ruth and him. If only he knew how to attain it?

Sunday held the promise of a beautiful day. After a quiet breakfast with his wife, Samuel enjoyed a second cup of coffee while she cleared the dishes and set to washing them. "Ruth," he ventured to say as he placed his empty cup in the sudsy water and wrapped his arms around her, "I'm heading out to the barn to saddle Pride. When you're ready, I'll take you to church."

Her mouth gaped as she spun in his arms and took in his unreadable features. "You're going with me?"

He shook his head. "I'm taking you. I said nothing about going with you."

"Oh ..." she said, as her eyes lowered, "Thank you, Samuel." In a bit of a muddle, she went back to the task at hand. She saw his understanding of her desire to be in church as a step in the right direction. Although she'd love to have him beside her during service, she thanked God for his progress.

Samuel, though he still believed she went to meet a man,

or someone equally as detrimental to their union, knew she'd only sneak off if he didn't take her. This knowledge prompted his decision.

After dropping Ruth off, he never did return home. Oh, he started to, but turned back before he reached the fork in the road. Edgy, he waited amongst the pines. Convinced that all those attending had arrived and were inside, he left Pride tied to the limb of an oak and ambled toward the barn door. For a while he stood just out of sight, listening to the worshipers sing. Peering through a fair sized knothole in the wood siding, he caught a glimpse of Ruth standing next to Jayne. For a second he considered joining them, but changed his mind.

When the circuit preacher stood and walked to the makeshift podium, Samuel could not turn away. It was as though an Unseen Power drew him in. Never having been to a church service, he had no expectations—only doubts—about the God they worshiped.

The preacher, a no-nonsense kind of guy, simply opened his Bible, looked out at the congregation and said, "This morning I'd like to take a closer look at what God has to say about love's power over anger and resentment. Although most of us would prefer to ignore outbursts of anger—especially our own, as God's beloved children we cannot. Anger, as most of us know, when left unchecked, can hold devastating consequences, not only for the recipient of our anger, but it can lead us to do and say things we'll later regret.

"Scripture teaches us that while each and every one of us have sinned and fallen short of God's standard, we have a choice as to how we will live. Now, here's the good news: God loved us so much that He sent His only Son into the world. He willingly took on Himself the sins of mankind, died on the cross, but He wasn't done yet. On the third day, He rose from the grave. Because of what He did, each and every one of us can choose to live for Him. We will either die in our sins and short comings, or by faith, we can accept our need for a savior, ask Christ to forgive us and invite Him into our life. From where He sits in the heavens, He keeps His promise and sends the Holy Spirit, the Comforter, to every one of His children to help us in our daily walk here on earth. That's why Paul tells us with all confidence that we can do all things through Christ who strengthens us." In Christ we can love in ways this world will not. More than that, in Christ we can love in ways this world cannot understand. And that power of love in our lives is stronger than the anger and resentment that festers within each and every one of us.

"God's Word tells us that love is not easily angered. Follow along if you will in James chapter one, verses 19-20: *Wherefore, my beloved brethren, let every man be swift to hear, slow to speak, slow to wrath: For the wrath of man worketh not the righteousness of God.*

"Each of us needs to take the time to examine our heart. If you are angry, identify the root. Ask yourself if your anger makes you feel superior to the person you are angry with. If it does, your heart follows the wisdom of the world. Take time to pray and seek God's wisdom. Then, in love, talk it over with the one to whom your anger was directed. Paul reminds us to be angry and sin not—to be kind and considerate to one another, forgiving one another, just as God forgave us for our sins through Christ."

When the words spoken had time to sink in, Samuel turned away, his anger at the fore. Was the preacher really saying what

Samuel thought? If so, then it was pure hogwash! *Of course I feel superior to my wife. A man is the head of his house. I have every right to hold her accountable when she is wrong!*

Don't I?

Frustration infiltrated his tumultuous mind. He could think of nothing but the accusatory words he had just heard. What had he been thinking? He never should have brought Ruth here. Now if he insisted on her staying home she'd want to be in church all the more. She wouldn't understand. All he needed was some do-gooder filling her mind with high and mighty thoughts. Samuel had a hard enough time keeping her in line. Oh, how he'd like to go in there and drag her out, but such a desperate act would only make him look bad.

His heart suddenly sank.

Their new friends! More than likely if he confronted George and Jayne, they would agree with this preacher man. After all, the Bible was his standard. *The Bible is their holy book—the foundation of their faith—my wife's faith?*

Samuel didn't know how much time had lapsed when he heard singing. More than likely the meeting was coming to a close. While he walked back toward his horse and stood waiting for his wife he did his best to tamp down the storm brewing inside him. He also made a decision. For now he would say nothing. Taking a stand was not an option. He needed George in his life. And besides, he could always hope that Ruth didn't hear what he heard. Anyways, why should it bother him? He had never claimed to have faith in their God. Why should he care what the man said? *I'm not accountable to anyone but myself.*

Mounting his horse, Samuel waited until most of the folks

had gone home before riding up to where his wife and Jayne stood talking. As he offered Ruth a hand up, George came out of the barn.

"Samuel! Good to see you."

Samuel nodded. "Likewise!"

"Jayne and I were wondering, that is, if you and Ruth don't have anything pressing. We'd love to have you come by for supper this afternoon."

Samuel glanced back at Ruth, who said, "Fine with me. If Samuel doesn't mind sharing, we could bring an apple pie and muffins."

George didn't wait for his friend to answer. "If you show up without them, I'll be following you home to get my due."

"Sorry!" Jayne said only half-apologetically, "The man has an incurable sweet tooth. Can you come around three o'clock?"

"Sounds good!" Samuel said, waving as he turned and rode up the path.

Samuel, so pensive on the ride home, Ruth wondered if he was angry, but she couldn't bring herself to ask. Instead she set uncertainty aside, snuggled close against his back and enjoyed the peaceful morning ride.

Porcelain had foaled a few days back, so when Samuel lowered Ruth to the barn floor, she went to check on her filly. As Ruth opened the stall door, Porcelain moved toward her, longing for Ruth's familiar touch. Ruth was glad to oblige her and the small wonder who weaved her way through her mother's long legs to reach Ruth. Were it not for the white boots on the filly's legs and white markings on her face, one would never suspect Porcelain to be the fillies mother. In truth, Ruth couldn't recall seeing a chestnut stallion on Dakota's farm. Perhaps they had taken Porcelain to another ranch for breeding. No matter, Ruth was delighted with the filly's coloring. If only Ruth could think of a name that would suit her.

"Ruth," Samuel said as he slipped his arms around her waist, "How would you feel about naming her Fancy?"

"Hmm ... I kind of like it. Her feminine markings do make her appear that way."

"That's what I thought, but take some time to think about it"

"I really don't need to, "Ruth said, with a slight shake of her head. Turning in her husband's arms, her fingers ran through his blonde hair as she pulled him close for a tender kiss. "Fancy is perfect." Her small hands caressed his prickly cheeks. "You're really good at this."

"At what?"

"Naming critters."

Samuel's head went back as he laughed out loud.

Somewhat embarrassed, Ruth mumbled, "You're making fun of me ...."

"No, Ruth ... I'm not. You surprised me, is all. It's just that I'm not used to having anyone point out the things I do well." Tucking a few wisps of hair behind her ear, he admitted, "You see the good in me and point it out, even though my less desirable traits are more prevalent. I can't tell you how much that means to me."

Her heart ached for him. What must it have been like for an innocent child growing up under such a dark cloud of oppression? To be told on a regular basis that your best efforts were never good enough would challenge the most secure adult, never mind a child who lived with it day in and day out. No wonder he struggles—no wonder his anger rules when he feels as though he is losing control. *Knowing doesn't make it okay for him to treat me the way he does, but it helps me to understand where his anger is coming from.* Although she could not turn back the hands of time and undo the damage his father had done, she could try to make a difference in his future.

Oh, Father, help me to be patient and kind, so that he might catch a glimpse of Your unfailing love. "I'll have to make a habit of pointing out more of your talents. I wouldn't want you to get a big head or anything, but so often you amaze me."

His grin mellowed and he grew serious—too serious. Splaying his hands across her flat stomach, he held her gaze. "Any chance we'll be having a little one to name in the not too distant future?"

Her cheeks warmed as eyes filled with timidity lowered and then rose slowly to meet his. "I ... I don't know, Samuel. Only God does. If we're meant to have children, then yes, someday ... I suppose we will."

"So, you don't feel any different?"

"No ... why are you asking?"

For a long moment he only stared at her. He questioned the wisdom in sharing his dreams, but if he couldn't share them with his wife, then with whom? Attaining her hand was paramount. Now that they were married, he often found himself longing for more. Children, he was reasonably sure, would unite them in ways nothing else could. "I've been watching the calendar. Your womanly time is late, isn't it?"

"No ... not really! I'm only sixteen, Samuel. It's not uncommon for my cycle to be irregular. Besides, we haven't been together very long. What's the big hurry?"

His brow furrowed. "Could you be expecting and not know?"

Shrugging, and desperately needing him to quit pressing her, she said, "If I suspect anything, I'll let you know."

"Promise?"

Hoping to lighten his intense mood, she stood on her toes, offering a quick peck on the lips. "Of course! Besides, you know my body. Do you really think you won't notice if I suddenly start getting rounder?" Rolling her eyes, she turned away. "Enough with this inquisition! I'm heading in to fix a light dinner." She had barely taken her first step when his oversized hand connected firmly with her backside. "Hey!" she complained as she spun back to face him. "What was that for?"

His eyebrows arched into his hairline. "You don't know?"

She took several distancing steps. Feeling a bit too spry for her own good, she stuck out her tongue and then took off running. By the time Ruth reached the back door, her steps had slowed considerably. For some reason, Samuel didn't come after her. Unfortunately, that did not guarantee she would not have to pay for her indiscretion. In truth, she didn't know why she taunted him so. He didn't have much of a sense of humor. One would think she'd be wiser by now, but there were times she just couldn't help retaliating in some way. Since it was too late for regrets, she set uncertainty aside and went to work on their meal.

Samuel came in the back door as Ruth was putting the meal on the table. Removing his bluchers, he went to the wash basin, his eyes dogging her every step as she moved cautiously behind him. When she reached for the handle to open the door to the cold cellar, his arm wrapped around her waist and her feet suddenly left the floor. Cradled in his strong arms, her heart fluttered unrelentingly. Big brown eyes held timid blues as he made his way toward their room.

Her stomach churned.

Sure that his intentions were anything but favorable, her heart ticked faster with every step he took. When he carried her to their bed and sat on the edge, he seemed to be thinking, so she remained perfectly still—despite the fears assailing her.

God, please don't let him hurt me.

Until his head lowered and his lips met hers, she had no way of knowing his intent. As he withdrew, his extreme look troubled her. A fresh wave of dread followed. What would he do?

Something she had heard at church came to her, easing her every care. *A spirit of fear does not come from God but from the evil one. God's children do not have to receive it, no matter what. If we give in to fear, we are not trusting God ...." Help me, God, to put my trust in You!*

"Your gesture in the barn wasn't wise, Ruth Anne."

She swallowed hard. "It was childish, I know, but sometimes ... sometimes you frustrate me, Samuel. Today I learned that venting with anger in my heart is wrong, so I resorted to playfulness. I was merely playing with you, but if I made you angry, my actions were wrong. For that I am sorry."

"Talking it out really does help, doesn't it?"

What? Did you hear the sermon? She didn't know for sure and refused to ask, but she did wonder. "Yes, it does."

"I think you know that being kind and considerate was not my first thought."

She suspected as much. "I was hoping to make you laugh, instead I made you mad."

"Yes, you did." Again he grew silent. He drew her closer and asked, "Will our meal keep for a while?"

Panic rose within. She simply had to know, "Why?

"Just answer the question."

"Yes, I haven't started cooking, but, Samuel, you're scaring me."

His gentle smile as he softly caressed her cheek eased her every concern. "In time you will learn to read me better. While I was in the barn, I came to a firm decision."

She could see the twinkle in his eyes and knew he was up to something. "Is that so ..."

"Yes! If you are going to do things that spark my temper, I think it is only fair that you make restitution."

"Restitution? But you ... Samuel, you're not exactly innocent in all of this! If I remember correctly, you're the one who started it!"

He, noticing her fierce scowl, chuckled. "I suppose I did. Then we were both in the wrong, so we both need to make restitution."

She harrumphed. "And I suppose you have something in mind?"

Grinning unremorsefully, he suggested, "I'm sure we could come to terms that would be mutually satisfying."

"Perhaps ..." Her fingers came to her mouth as sweet laughter bubbled up. His coy look was far from innocent, but how could she resist the passion that followed. Not only were his sweet kisses satisfying; the experience in its entirety had taken their union to a place they had never been.

Neither husband nor wife was very hungry when they finally made it to the table, so they shared a quick sandwich and called it good. While Samuel went to the barn to saddle Pride, Ruth tidied the kitchen before going back to their bedroom to make herself look presentable. The soapy water she had spilled on the front of her dress was soaking into her stockings, so she changed into her brown frock. Although it was plain and rather drab, her cream crocheted sweater added a bit of flair. Reaching for her dry socks, she sat on the vanity chair to pull them on.

A quick glance in the mirror told her there was more to be done. Samuel, though his kisses were wonderful, he had a gift for messing her hair. After brushing through her dark lengths, she took another quick peek. "Ugh! This will never do." Her husband would probably complain because he liked her hair down, but time was of the essence. She settled for twisting her unruly mop into a bun at the nap of her neck.

Ruth could not quit smiling as she put the pie and muffins in a basket and they headed toward the Somers place. For the first time in their marriage they had discussed their frustrations with each other and come to a peaceful resolution. True, he swatted her unnecessarily in the barn for her smart retort, but that was nothing by comparison. Her heart rejoiced over God's goodness. The things that had transpired in the last few hours were beyond coincidence. God was obviously at work in her marriage and she was richer for having experienced it.

Samuel, though he admitted to nothing, had evidently heard the sermon. Not only that, he had put into practice what he heard. Did he understand the hope that was filling her soul?

Chapter Nineteen

Fellowship

RUTH'S CRAMPED POSITION atop Pride, while balancing a large basket on her lap, and Samuel sitting close behind made the slightest movement difficult. This became an even greater challenge when the wind began to blow and something moved on her neck.

It tickled profusely!

When *it* continued to wiggle she reached for whatever *it* was, but did not succeed. Shuddering, she squealed, "Samuel! Something is crawling on my neck. Get *it* off!"

"Let me see." he droned.

Feeling his warm fingers on her slender neck, she held her breath, tried to wait, but nothing changed. "What is *it*?"

"Hold still!" he scolded.

An irrepressible shiver ran through her frame. "I'm trying."

"There!" he declared, as his fingers slid into her hair line and shook her bun loose.

Craning her neck around, she scowled. "Samuel Grady

White, *it* was only you pulling out my hair pins!"

His oh-so-innocent look did not fool her. "Whatever do you mean, My Dear?

Groaning in frustration, she whined. "Now what am I supposed to do? My hair is a mess!"

He grinned mischievously as he finger combed her long mass of waves and said, in all honesty, "Your hair looks perfect."

Glaring, she turned away mumbling, "That's your opinion!"

Samuel wrapped his arms around her waist and squeezed. "That's right, and my opinion is the only one that matters."

The man sure did have a gift for irritating her. Even in his awkward attempts to be playful he could manage to ruffle her feathers. Maybe she should be afraid of upsetting him, but for some unknown reason she felt safer—or perhaps a bit braver when the Somers were going to be a part of their day. Wiggling in his arms, she tried to break free, but he held fast to his angry wife.

"Ruth Anne," he chided, "do we need to head back home or is this settled?" When she said nothing, he added, "You know I like your hair down. Buns are fine for older ladies, but you're barely out of school."

"The waves," she reiterated, as she finger combed her unruly mop, "they're going every which way."

His silence only served to intensify her gray mood. A derisive scowl swept over her face, leaving no doubt, she was not in an agreeable mood. "If you insist on it being down, then perhaps I will ask Jayne to cut it!"

Samuel brought Pride to an abrupt halt. The basket on her lap nearly took a tumble.

She cringed, never sure of what he would do.

Samuel reached for her shoulders and gently turned her to face him. "No one is to cut your hair, Ruth."

She had no wish to fight with him, but the man was being ridiculous. If she crossed him he would show no mercy, so she asked, just to be sure, "Not even when it gets scraggily on the ends?" *Like it is now ...*

For the longest moment, his dark hooded eyes studied her features. "If you need a trim, I will gladly see to it."

Groaning in frustration, she said, "You can't cut my hair!" In barely a whisper she added, "You'll mess it up ...."

His eyes practically doubled in size. "Let me guess! As a man I am incapable of performing the task?"

"Well, yes ..."

"Well, you're wrong .... If you need a trim, I will see to it. No one else! Understood?"

You and your orders! she inwardly berated. "Alright!" Her husband was like a vulture hovering—nothing short of capitulation would induce a respite. If she did not give in, he would take her home and she didn't want that. Perhaps she should be thankful they were talking and leave it at that. Some issues were simply not worth the fight.

Gently kissing her forehead, he asked, "Is this settled?"

"Yes ..." she conceded, though a frown did flicker across her face. *Help me, Father, to lay my flesh aside and respond as You would, in love. Perhaps Jayne is right. I'm not responsible for his treatment of me, only for my response to him. More than anything, I want him to know You, the One who loves me as I am and shelters me through the storms.*

Thoughtful, he nudged Pride on. Ruth's silence troubled

him. Had his persistence taken their relationship a few steps backward? Although he wondered, he did not ask. Bringing it up again would serve no purpose.

The cool breeze nipping at Ruth's skin brought on an uncontainable shiver. As she tucked her hands deeper within the sleeves of her sweater to warm them, her husband drew her closer. "You're cold, Ruth. I have a blanket, but we're almost there."

"I'll be fine." A swirl of emotions ran through her. Samuel did have a gift for bringing out the best and worst in her. No doubt, they both had been blessed with passionate spirits. If only they did not clash so often.

Little by little she was beginning to see God's hand in placing them together. Had she married someone laid back like James, her life would have been more peaceful, but would she have been too content to see her need for Jesus? The way her marriage started out put her in a desperate state. She had felt so alone and abandoned by her parents, but God was there to comfort her when she cried out. Although God's presence did not change her circumstances, or what she must face, His presence was changing her response.

Glancing up at the sky, she sighed, contentment settling over her like a warm blanket. *I'm beginning to see You in everything, Lord. Your Grace truly is sufficient for each day and Your peace has been my source. Thank You! Without You in my life, I could not make it through a day, never mind a lifetime without Your strength and love to draw on. Because of my husband's nature, my eyes have been opened to Your great love. How could I ever regret that?*

When Ruth, seemingly out of the blue, started giggling,

Samuel's brow furrowed.

"What is so funny?"

"Us!"

He took a deep breath and let it out. "Yeah, we are quite the pair. If nothing else, we're tenacious to a fault."

"I'm curious, Samuel. Does this mean we'll have to make restitution when we get home?" As she peered up, an intuitive smile creased his handsome face.

He tweaked her chin before kissing her sweet mouth. "I suppose it does, but you're a bit too willing, might not do you much good."

Although she strongly disagreed, she ignored his comment and snuggled close to his chest. "Are we getting there, Samuel?"

"Getting where?"

"Are we falling for each other despite our struggles?"

His heart surged. "Could be ... I know I've never felt this way about anyone. I can't explain it other than to say that being with you makes me want to be a better man. I know I lose my temper far too often, but I am trying."

His admission had a deep warming effect on her. "I know you are and knowing gives me hope. My heart is changing too. Every day seems to draw us closer. Is it possible that our hearts are finally learning to beat as one?"

Strong arms encircled her. "We're learning all right, but when I look at how content George and Jayne seem to be with each other, I'm convinced we still have a long way to go." Samuel kissed the top of her silky head as they rode into the Somers' yard.

Ruth, though challenged by the tense moments in their day, was grateful for the good that had come. She gave thanks to the

Lord. Instead of seeing their relationship as broken, she chose to be thankful for the moments that were binding them as one. Looking to the Lord and believing for what is yet to come, not only gave her hope, it brought her peace.

After tying Pride to the post, the quiet couple moved up the steps. Samuel lifted his hand to knock, just as George opened the door.

"Welcome." George said, stepping aside so they could enter. "We're glad you could come. My wife is so excited; she's been singing all afternoon."

Samuel, though he found this odd, did not comment.

"Ruth, Jayne is in the kitchen if you'd like to join her."

Reaching for the basket on Samuel's arm, Ruth smiled up at him and went to greet her friend. Samuel's eyes followed her until she rounded the corner to the kitchen.

George, having witnessed his friend's interaction with his wife, wondered if the new tenderness in Samuel's eyes suggested change. Jayne had mentioned her concerns about Samuel's abusive ways, but he did not feel led to say anything. Not yet. However he was committing their struggles to prayer.

Supper could be a while. Would you like to take a walk, Samuel?"

Nodding, he followed George out the door. After removing Pride's tack, and turning him loose in the corral, they took the path leading to the river.

The leaves cresting the trees were slowly giving way to autumn's array of vibrant shades. Although Samuel looked forward to the colorful display the season would unveil, a long winter would soon follow. Along with the long winter, new challenges would arise—challenges he and Ruth had not yet faced. They would be spending long hours alone within the confines of their home. Could he trust himself to be kind—to control his temper? He so wanted to be a good husband to her—to love her, but so often he failed. If only he could replace the sadness and fear he saw in Ruth's eyes after one of his outbursts with tenderness and love.

Clearly his father's advice about many things had been wrong. Did his views stem from his own insecurities—or his twisted view of love? Like himself, his father insisted on controlling his mother, but what had that availed either of them? Why did he listen to his father when his heart told him otherwise? Erasing the things he had done was not possible, but he could certainly try to do better. Heaven knows, his father-in-law and now George's example were both turning his head.

He'd been trying to change the way he treated Ruth for some time now. Did the way he gained her hand have something to do with the way he responded to her? Did he think of her as more of a possession than a helpmate? Although he could be patient, too often he would lose his temper, hurt her, and then hate himself for it. Was he desperate enough to open up with a near stranger? Could he trust George? The man had shown a great deal of integrity. Perhaps in time Samuel would let down his guard enough to open that door. Revealing his imperfections would certainly bruise his pride. Even so, the effort might be worth it, if doing so would lead to his inner struggle being resolved.

"George," Samuel asked as they treaded down the hill toward the river bank, "I'm curious. Have you and Jayne been involved in churches most of your life?"

George studied his friend. "No. My parents stopped going to church shortly after my father's brother was hung for a crime he did not commit. Although he eventually proved his brother's innocence, for years my father blamed God for his loss."

Samuel, somewhat stunned by his confession, nodded in understanding. "My parents were never religious, so I didn't give God's existence much thought until I lost my father. I suppose your father had his reasons for blaming God for his loss."

"That could be true, but whatever his reasons were, they were wrong. God had no part in the wrong done to my uncle, but my father couldn't see that at the time. My mother did and she had a special gift for loving Dad right where he was at. No matter his struggle, she never gave up." George chuckled softly. "I'm fully convinced that God used her gentle love and prayers to draw my father back to Him. So often I'd find her on her knees praying. Even when it seemed that God was silent, she would tell me, *'I'm going to wait on Father God. He hears my prayers, but His timing is not always my own. I have to trust Him. God loves your father more than I ever could.'* I can still hear her telling my father, *'We don't live in a perfect world. God promises that He will be with us through the storms—not that He will keep us from the storms. Look at the life of Jesus, He was perfect and still men despised and abused Him. Who are we to think that we or those we love will be treated better than our Lord?'* I'll never forget the day my father turned to her, smiled, and said, *'You're right, My Love. I've been so wrong.'* I was fifteen when my father insisted on us going back to church as a family. A few years later, yellow fever swept through our town and took my parents from me."

"Were you their only child?"

"No ... I was their seventh child, but the only one who lived longer than a year."

Samuel rubbed at the back of his neck. "Man ... and I thought I had problems. How did your parents find the strength to go on? How did you after they were gone?"

George glanced out at the water and then back at his friend. "I can't speak for my parents, but I do know how grateful they were to have me in their lives. Watching them suffer and then losing them so close together was horrible. Living at the homestead kept their memory alive, but it was also holding me back. Nearly a year had passed before I realized that I had been withdrawing from everyone I knew and loved—even God."

Before pursuing Ruth's hand, Samuel had kept pretty much to himself. He had also been living alone for over a year and didn't understand. Plucking a flat rock off the ground, Samuel skipped it across the water before turning back to his friend. "I don't see the harm in being alone. Now that I have Ruth in my life, I wouldn't want to go back to being alone, but I kind of enjoyed the solitude for a time."

"I did too, but as a believer in Christ, the harm for me was in giving way to my grief. Don't get me wrong, grieving the loss of those we love is normal—healthy even, but only for a season. To forsake assembling with others in the body of Christ for too long can be detrimental to one's spiritual walk."

With a furrowed brow, Samuel raked his fingers through his hair. "Why is that?"

George smiled, pleased by his willingness to probe. "God uses fellow believers in each other's lives to encourage and build one another up. I'm sure Ruth has told you why she longs to be involved in a church."

"She mentioned needing to be there so she can learn more about God."

"That's true. Teaching helps us to understand God's Word. Meeting with and discussing the Bible with other believers is a great way to gain a clearer view of God. Without fellowship with God, and other believers who are willing to hold us accountable, it's too easy to fall back into old patterns. We tend to go our own way. The longer I know Him, the more I realize that walking close with God is a choice."

Samuel shook his head. "I'm not sure I understand what you're saying."

They were nearing George's favorite fishing hole with a couple of well-placed logs on the bank that he and Jayne used for chairs. When George took a seat on one, Samuel sat on the other. "God tells us in the Word that we were created out of fellowship, for fellowship. That simply means that God longs to have a close personal relationship with you and me, but because He is Holy, our sin separates us from God."

Frowning, Samuel asked, "I don't mean to sound disrespectful, George, but if the God you speak of is all knowing, shouldn't He be able to fix every problem that arises?"

George threw his head back and laughed out loud. Noting his friend's scowl, he was swift to reply, "I'm not laughing at you, Samuel, it's just that I asked my father that same question several years back. Apparently, we think alike."

Samuel's mouth curved into a gentle smile and his hackles dissipated. "So, what did he tell you?"

"If God simply fixed all of our problems, we'd be puppets on a string, controlled by our Creator. He said to think of God as a gentleman, one who never forces His will on others. God longs to have fellowship with us, but we must choose to walk with Him."

Samuel bent over, picked up a large rock that was on the ground beside him, and heaved it into the water. "In many ways I'm like that rock, George. I'm hard and set in my ways. In truth, I like having things my way. When I sought Ruth's hand, I convinced myself that she would come to accept my ways, and life would go on."

George's taunting grin revealed his thoughts. "She's not so predictable, is she?"

"No! In many ways she's as stubborn as I am. The woman has a penchant for trying my patience." Thoughtful, he grew quiet. Seconds passed before his ruffled brow rose. "Things are important to her that I've never even considered."

"Like?"

"God ... friends ... She makes me question the things I've been taught. Because I care and want to please her, I've been examining my ways. All too often I find them wanting."

George wondered if he was referring to his abusiveness, but didn't ask. In praying about it, he had a peace about waiting for Samuel to bring it up.

When George reached out and squeezed Samuel's shoulder in a reassuring manner, Samuel continued, "Like I was saying, in so many ways I feel like that rock since Ruth and I married. I'm beneath the surface of the water and I don't know how to get back on dry land. So much is foggy. I'm losing control of the stability I once knew and I don't know how to get it back. In truth, I'm not even sure I want to."

George leaned over, buried his face in his hands, and prayed for wisdom. "That's not really a bad thing. Remember what I said, God longs to have fellowship with you and me. Often, he uses our trials and frustrations to draw us to Him. I, too, went through a long season of unrest. Often, I wondered if I was losing my mind, but I kept searching. Nothing made sense. It wasn't until I turned to God out of desperation that I finally found the peace I had been longing for."

Samuel's silence made George wonder if he had said too much. Did his friend even hear what he was saying?

"I would like to gain a better understanding of why I am here. I'd even like to change some things I don't like about myself. It's knowing how to go about it that has me at a loss."

"Do you have a Bible?"

Samuel's head swayed in the negative. "No ... Ruth has been asking for one, but no ... we don't have one yet."

"The answers you seek are in God's Word. He says that if we seek Him with all our heart, we will find Him and so much more."

The lowering of Samuel's head and then the way his shoulders slumped, told George much. "If you're right and there really is a God, why would He want to know someone like me?"

"God's Word tells me that He knew me before I was formed in my mother's womb. That applies to you too, Samuel." George saw the ray of hope in his friend's eyes and his own glassed over. Swallowing hard, he glanced at the water, attempting to get a handle on his wavering emotions. For a moment he watched a pair of Blue Jays that fluttered by, seemingly uninhibited by their presence before looking back at his friend.

"That may be ..." Samuel admitted, with fervency in his tone, "but sin ... what about the sin that separates me from God?"

Grinning, George said, "Fortunately, there's more ... God's plan to restore fellowship."

"Does it begin with the Christmas Story?"

"Yes!"

As relief washed over him, Samuel's eyes brightened. "Good! Something I'm familiar with. My family never attended church, but I do know several stories from the Bible."

"Oh?"

"Yes! I had teachers who drummed them into my head. Only one problem, I never have been able to see how they apply to me personally." He shrugged, "I did find them interesting though."

"So, you know that God sent His Son, Jesus, to Earth. That He was born of a virgin and lived a sinless life."

"If I remember correctly, Jesus was God in the flesh."

George nodded. "In obedience to His Father, Jesus laid down His life to pay the price for our sins. In so doing He made a way for us to enter into fellowship with God."

"The Easter story ...."

"Yes! But that's not all .... Victoriously, He conquered death and the grave."

Samuel couldn't help but grin; he had retained more than he thought. "When He rose from the dead on the third day?"

"Yes! And although He had to leave this earthly home for heaven, He sent the Holy Spirit to comfort His children in His absence."

Samuel's head lowered and George wondered what he was thinking. "Have you ever had a longing—an empty space deep inside that no one has been able to fill, Samuel?"

"I suppose I have. To tell you the truth, I assumed that Ruth would fill that void, but that hasn't been the case. Don't get me wrong. She has been a welcome presence in my life. As much as I love her, I still feel like something is missing."

George reached out and laid his hand on Samuel's shoulder. "You're not alone. I've been there myself. In fact, all men and women have that same longing that only God can fill. Unfortunately, many turn away instead of seeking the One who gives life."

"I'll be honest, George, I've never really understood how anyone can put their faith in a god they cannot see."

"You can't see the air that you breathe, yet you trust that it will be there so you can take your next breath. Am I right?"

Samuel's brow furrowed. "I suppose you are ..."

"Look around, Samuel. There is evidence of God's presence everywhere in creation. It wasn't until I asked Christ to forgive me of my sins and come into my heart that I was able to see things clearly. The Holy Spirit, who now resides within me, opened my eyes to a world I never knew existed. Now I look around and see God in all of His creation. The plant and animal kingdoms are amazing enough. Then I look at men and women who were created in God's image and know their potential is endless, but there is a catch: each of us must choose to put our trust in God— each of us must choose to believe that Jesus is the Christ, the Son of the Living God.

"Choose?"

"Yes, Samuel. God, well, He never forces us to do anything. The choice is ours to believe—to follow Him. God's love sustained me through my horrible time of grief. He never said that He would keep me from hardship in this life, but He did promise to be with me. Like I told you before, we were created out of fellowship for fellowship. My loss was great, but through my struggle I've learned to put my trust in God. To know Him more has become my greatest desire."

"So what did you do?"

"After my parents died, I needed a fresh start. Praying about it, I knew God was leading me away from my comfortable surroundings. I understood the importance of fellowshipping with other believers. That was at the forefront of my mind when I started looking for a new place to call home. After selling the homestead, I moved from town to town. For a while I felt like a lost pup looking for a place to belong. Eventually God led me to the small farming village where Jayne grew up. Her family had never attended church gatherings, not because they didn't believe or long for fellowship, there were simply no churches in their rural area. That all changed soon after my arrival. I started asking around and sparked an interest. A group of believers began meeting in Jayne's uncle's barn and news spread fast."

"So that's where you two met?"

"Yes. A few months later we were married. I'll always be thankful that I took that leap of faith and left when God prompted me to. Had I not, I wouldn't have Jayne in my life. When we told her parents that we would be settling in Detroit, they were hesitant. To appease them, Jayne and I stayed with them for a few months before heading west."

George, hearing Jayne calling from the top of the crest, turned to his friend and said, "I suppose we'll have to finish this conversation another time."

Samuel nodded, a heaviness furrowing his brow. "You've

given me much to think about."

"So what do you say, should we join the women for some sweet fellowship?"

Both men stood before Samuel responded. "I'm sure those two will serve up a healthy portion of sweet fellowship, but you can also count on a delightful portion of pluck on the side."

George chuckled, saying, "If we don't get a move on, that side of pluck will end up being the main course."

Samuel's head swayed as they moved up the path. As much as he enjoyed this man's company, his mind would not rest. So much was still a mystery. And besides, how did a man who thrived on being in control of everything in his life, ever come to terms with a God who asked him to give up that control and to trust Him with everything?

Chapter Twenty

Shared Burdens

THE TANTALIZING AROMA of roast chicken made his belly growl as Samuel entered the Somers' home. Glancing back at his friend, he groaned, saying, "My stomach would be in a fix if you and Jayne weren't willing to share this meal."

"If the smell is any indication, there won't be many leftovers for the hogs tonight," George told him, as he claimed his seat at the table and rubbed his hands together. As soon as his wife and Ruth joined them, George held one hand out for Samuel to take and the other for his wife.

Samuel hesitated only seconds before taking the offered hand. As he met Ruth's tentative gaze, he sent her a reassuring wink, reached for her hand and squeezed it. Jayne completed the open circle and together they bowed their heads while George led in prayer.

Ruth, still in a bit of a fog over what had just transpired, didn't hear Samuel talking until he said her name for the second time, "Ruth, over the winter months, George has offered to help me do some finishing work upstairs."

Smiling, she responded, "That would be great. Jayne and I have quilts we'd really like to work on together. She could come with George ... that is if I can talk your mother into giving us a hand."

Samuel reached for a biscuit and chuckled softly as he slipped one on his wife's plate and passed the basket to George. "I'm sure she'd be delighted to help."

George turned to his wife and said, "In exchange, Samuel offered to give me a hand with the armoires I started last winter."

With a heckling grin, she said, "That is good news. To be honest, I kind of gave up on you ever finishing them."

He scowled something fierce. "As if you have any room to talk, Jayne, dear! Perhaps I've been waiting for you to finish the sweater you started knitting for me the week after we married."

Her cheeks turned a deep shade of cherry. "You would bring that up! You know very well that I lost the instructions in the move."

"Excuses! Excuses!"

"Ruth," Samuel said, as he leaned close and met her jovial look, "They're awfully competitive, don't you think?"

"I do, but at least they're attempting to talk things out. However, if things get much hotter in here ..."

Giggling, Jayne interrupted Ruth's comment, "We'd better be good, George. We're distressing our guests."

"Can't have that! They might take off with the apple pie. That would never do. I'm counting on a nice big slice."

"Now there's a surprise!" The rolling of Jayne's eyes brought ripples of laughter into the room, setting the tone for the remainder of their meal.

❀ ❀ ❀

"Jayne," Ruth asked as she dried the dish Jayne handed her and set it back on the shelf, "I don't mean to put a damper on this wonderful day, but I am curious, did you have a chance to speak with George about ... well, you know?" Although the men had gone out to the barn, Ruth eyes fell on the closed door. In a way, voicing her struggles with her husband felt too much like a betrayal.

"I did. I'm not sure why, but telling him about your suffering made me angry. Sad too, I suppose. I couldn't fathom why you would stay with Samuel when he hurts you the way he does. George reminded me that the marriage vows that joined you and Samuel as husband and wife, were the same vows we took. That doesn't give him the right to hurt you, but I will say, for better or worse took on a whole new meaning. "

"The day we were married I did leave him, what good it did me."

Surprise registered on Jayne's face. "Where did you go?"

"Home. I had to at least try to convince my father to have our marriage annulled, but he refused. He wouldn't let me stay. I was Samuel's wife, he said, and I should be thankful he chose me."

Jayne's brow furrowed. "But you weren't, were you?"

"No! I was angry. In so many ways, I felt betrayed. When I left my parents' house, I was heading over to stay with my friend. Out of desperation I cried out to the Lord. I couldn't face another day on my own. Like never before, I needed God's presence in my life. As I cried out, His peace filled me. It was the most amazing thing. Samuel was still the same man I thought he was when he found me and took me home, but the way I looked at everything started to change. Surrendering my shattered life to the Lord was only a beginning. Oh, don't get me wrong, I still struggle when Samuel hurts me. I don't understand why it happens or how to make it stop, but I am committed to this covenant relationship."

"As you should be …. We've been praying, Ruth. You're not alone in this. Neither is Samuel. We're here for both of you, in whatever capacity you need us."

Jayne, a friend in the truest sense of the word, was not sitting in judgment of either of them. Instead, her words were filled with love and promise that warmed Ruth's entire being. "I keep reminding myself that God loves Samuel as much as He loves me. I can't do this for Samuel, but I can pray that God will help us through this difficult time."

"You're so right, Ruth. The choice is his."

"Loving others as God commands isn't always easy, is it?"

Her head swayed back and forth. "No. It's easy to love those who are sweet and kind, but God doesn't say we should love only those who treat us the way they should—He expects us to love as He does—without preference."

"Fortunately, Christ has promised to be our strength."

Concern etched Jayne's face. "You don't have to tell me if you don't want to, but I am curious. Did you know what your husband was like before you married him?"

"I had heard rumors. The first time he and his father came to the house confirmed what I heard, but Samuel was careful not to show my father his true nature. I was led to believe they were there that day to buy a team of horses, but that was not the case. Apparently, Samuel wanted to spend some time with me before signing the marriage contract. I didn't even know he sought my hand until the day we were married. Some surprise that turned out to be!"

Jayne sighed. "I had several friends whose marriages were arranged by their fathers, but most of them knew their fiancés in advance. Samuel is a handsome man. Anyone can see that, but I wonder, are you attracted to him in other ways?"

Ruth's eyes brightened and a silly smirk creased her face. "That's what's so crazy. I'm terribly attracted to him. The man ignites a passion in me that no one else ever has. At first I found the power he had over me frightening. Now, I find comfort in knowing our feelings for each other are mutual. In some ways I feel blessed. As long as I don't cross him, he really can be quite wonderful."

Jayne stopped scrubbing at the crusty pan, turned to her friend, her expression distorted. "So, your problems arise because you're less than perfect."

Ruth rolled her eyes, but her tone grew serious, "So it would seem ...."

After drying the last dish, Ruth hung the damp towel from a hook and sat down at the table. Jayne poured them both a cup of tea and took the seat opposite her. "I don't think it would have helped me to know about our marriage ahead of time. You see, I had my heart set on becoming a teacher, but Papa's failing health gave Samuel the open door he needed to gain my hand. Unfortunately, my parents kept me in the dark about both my coming marriage and Papa's health."

Jayne reached across the table and held her friend's hand. "So often the trials of this life take us by storm. Without warning we're thrust in the midst, but how we respond is up to us."

"I'm learning that the hard way. The day we were married, I wanted to reject Samuel as my husband in the worst way. After I called out to God I was at peace with being with him. As odd as it was, I really believed that we were meant to be together. What I didn't count on was my worst fears were being realized. I was aware of Samuel's controlling nature, but I didn't know to what extreme he would go. Now I do. His outburst may not happen as much as they did in the beginning, but his rage is escalating. That terrifies me."

Patting Ruth's arm, Jayne said, "Exposing his abuse is a huge step in the right directions. You know that, don't you?"

Ruth's eyes filled with unshed tears. "Then why do I feel as though I'm betraying him to talk about it?"

"You're not. The bruises he gave you exposed his sin, not your words." Jayne's head lowered as she asked God to give her the words that would bring healing, not condemnation. "So many believe that abuse is something women as the weaker vessel must live with. That it falls under the covering of godly submission, but that isn't true. God is our rock, our refuge, a strong support and shield against violence of any kind."

"Then why does He allow it to happen? So often I wonder if He's punishing me for something I've done."

"Oh, Honey, no ...." The pain etched on Ruth's face was too much for Jayne. She stood, claimed the chair beside her friend and wrapped her arms around her. For a time, she just held Ruth.

When Jayne reached for her hanky to dry her own tears, Ruth

did the same. Looking at her friend, Jayne said, "God compares the relationship between a husband and wife, with Christ and His church. Husbands are instructed to love their wives as Christ loves the church and gave Himself for it. Please hear me well, Ruth, the way Samuel hurts you is not a problem in your marriage—it's sin. Samuel's thinking is twisted. When he hurts you, he is choosing to do so. His abuse is evidence of his sinfulness, not yours."

Ruth blew her nose and did her best to sure up her wavering emotions. It would never due to have the men walk in and find her such a mess. "Samuel came by his distorted thinking honestly. His father abused my mother-in-law. As if that wasn't enough, he encouraged Samuel to do the same with me."

"If you were able to go back a few generations, you'd probably find more men who did the same."

"His mother called it a generational curse."

"But Ruth, you have to know that there is nothing that is beyond God's reach. Talk to Him about it ... pray without ceasing."

The lowering of her eyes did not hide the tears welling up. "I have been."

"I'm so glad Samuel and George are becoming friends. God brought us together, Ruth, I don't doubt that for a minute."

"What would I do without you?"

Jayne squeezed her hands. "God is using us to encourage one another, and that's a good thing."

Ruth nodded, stirred a bit of sugar into her tea and took a sip. The room grew suddenly darker, not unlike her thoughts. Ruth glanced at the window with a faraway look in her eyes, listening as the wind whistled through the trees. Begrudgingly, she turned back to Jayne and said, "I wish I understood where

God is when Samuel's hurting me. I feel so alone. Do you think He's just sitting up there watching me suffer?"

"No ... oh, Ruth, no. Don't think that for a minute. God is always right there with you when you're suffering, just as He was with Jesus when He suffered at the hands of man. Scripture reminds us that He is close to the brokenhearted. When the deepest part of you calls His name, He will respond with great love and compassion."

"Like He did when I called out to Him the day we were married?"

Jayne nodded. "Yes ..."

Tears trailed down Ruth's face, burning her tender flesh. "I can't fathom the pain God endured the day He watched His Son suffer, knowing that only His Son's death could pay the price for our sins."

"That's how much God loves us."

"I don't doubt God's love, Jayne—I doubt Samuel's when his temper flares. Until he chooses to lay aside his anger and respond in love, I'll continue to suffer, won't I?"

Jayne's shoulders drooped as her heart sank. "Oh, Ruth, I wish I could make this all go away, but if you want to fight for your marriage, there are bold steps you are going to have to take. If you continue to tolerate his abuse—if you do nothing, it will only get worse. I wish I could tell you otherwise, but unfortunately, history has a way of repeating itself. Promise me that if you sense you're in danger you'll come to us. Remember, there is safety in numbers."

Wary of what Samuel would do if he knew their friends were aware of his abuse, her thoughts stumbled. Could she really follow through? Would Samuel continue to support her mother if she left him? More than likely not, but something had to be done. Was it selfish to want to feel safe? Oh, how she longed for a marriage built on mutual trust. Was that too much to ask? The hardest thing to accept was that no matter how much she wanted him to change, he had to want that for himself.

What if she were to get pregnant and his actions hurt their baby? She couldn't live with that. Realizing that her friend was waiting for a response, she looked up and said, "If I can, I will. I don't usually see it coming though, Jayne. I mean, I can sense the tension building, but it doesn't always mean he will hurt me. There are times when we come to a peaceful resolution."

"And that's good. Maybe in his own way he is trying."

"I've wondered that myself."

"Listen, Ruth. George has already agreed to intervene if you come to us. Our door is always open if you need a safe haven."

"I appreciate that more than you know. I'll try, but when it's over, he usually stays close. I'm not sure if it's because he feels guilty or if he's sorry for what he has done. In his own twisted way, he really does try to make amends."

"Whatever you face, Ruth, promise me you won't doubt God's love. His purpose for your suffering may seem clouded right now, but even when you can't see God's hand in your circumstances, you can always trust His heart. He loves you. His love will never fail."

"Keep praying for us. Samuel is trying to talk things out more, but he's still torn. I can see it in his eyes. The influence his father had on him is strong. The chains that bind him won't easily be broken."

"Talking is a good start, Ruth. Now, as for those chains, we both know the only Master who can set captives free."

"Yes, we do." Ruth's eyes closed for a moment, hope swirling inside as she thought of the day Christ set her spirit free. Oh, how she prayed that Samuel might know such peace. *Lord, please let it be soon, I pray.*

Hearing the men's voices outside, Ruth hugged her friend, stood and then went to the counter to wash her cup. She had a feeling Samuel would be ready to head home soon. As much as she'd like to stay and talk some more, her friend had given her much to consider. And she fully intended to bring her every concern to the Lord.

Jayne watched Ruth move quietly toward the counter and thanked the Lord for their time together. She did not doubt that because of what Jesus did on the cross, the supernatural miracle of God's grace could put Samuel in right standing with God. Even so, she was glad Ruth understood. No matter how much she wanted her husband to know Jesus, she could not do it for him. He alone must choose to walk out of darkness into God's marvelous light.

Chapter Twenty-one

A Time for Everything

A word fitly spoken
is like apples of gold in pictures of silver.
—Proverbs 25:11

RUTH TUCKED THE LAST of the breakfast dishes away, hung her apron from the hook, and glanced out the window. As lifeless as her surroundings appeared, she was hopeful a walk in the cool dank air would do her some good. A spirit of heaviness had been weighing her down for days. Although she did not understand why, she was hopeful that lifting her voice in worship as she spent some time alone with the Lord would give her a fresh outlook. She longed for nothing more than the peace that only He could bring.

Slipping into her boots, she buttoned her coat as she moved out of the house and down the stairs. Heading toward the pasture, she expected to see some signs of life, a few feathery friends fluttering about, a rabbit nibbling on clover, but nothing—even the trees were motionless. While the gray sky accented the dreary haze, her eyes rose to the heavens in defiance of its influence. No matter how gloomy her surroundings, she could choose joy. This was a day that the Lord had made and she was determined to rejoice and be glad in it.

Oh, Father, You are my hiding place. No matter what's going on in my life I can rest, knowing you hold my future in the palm of Your hands. Thank You for showing me Your ways. I don't always understand them, but I know in my heart that I can rest because even in my darkest moments You are there.

Sensing His presence, she began to sing.

As she reached the pasture, her hopeful heart soared. Samuel had apparently turned Porcelain and her filly loose to graze before he went off to work. Even so, Fancy had other ideas. As Ruth stepped up on the lowest rail of the fence, she leaned over and watched Fancy frolic in circles around her mother. She couldn't help but laugh. Porcelain grazed contentedly as if she had not a care in the world, seemingly unaware of her filly's antics. The playful scene brought to the fore memories of her childhood. Her own mama would be working her fingers to the bone while she danced merrily with a favorite doll. Although her mama often seemed oblivious to her antics, she could recall her tender glances and suspected that her mama delighted in her lively spirit as much as Ruth did Fancy's.

In the moments that followed, Ruth pondered what it would be like to have her own little gift from God. Would she be much like her own mama, delighting in her child at every turn? Would Samuel's heart be warmed as well, or would he be intolerant, always correcting—always controlling? Afraid of what she might do if he ever hurt their child, she brought her concerns to the Lord. Seeing Samuel as who he could become gave her hope for the future. In truth, she found it comforting. God could change the heart of any man, of that she was sure. She would have to trust that God would lead her if and when the time came for her to be with child. She didn't care for the idea of being on her own, but she would do what she had to in order to keep her child safe. As much as she wanted Samuel to change, she could not do it for him. He would have to turn to God and find forgiveness.

Hearing a horse galloping, she turned to find James riding towards her, a frantic look on his face. "What is it, James?"

"Your father, Ruth ... He's in a bad way. Your mother asked me to come for you."

"Okay! I'll look for Samuel. We'll come right away, but you had better leave. He won't be happy if he finds you here alone with me."

James nodded and turned to leave. Glancing back, he said, "Hurry, Ruth! I'll stay with your mother until you arrive."

"Thanks, James!"

Ruth looked everywhere, but Samuel was nowhere to be found, so she went to the kitchen and left him a note.

Samuel,

I couldn't find you. My father is not doing well. I've gone to my parents. Come when you can.

Yours,
Ruth

Ruth saddled Sandy, their extra riding horse. Although a bit skittish from lack of exercise, he didn't hesitate to do her bidding when she nudged him forward. He took off at a full gallop and Ruth did nothing to deter him until she rode into her parents' yard. Tying him to the post in front, she ran up the steps and into her parents' home. As promised, James was still with her mother who appeared to have been crying for hours. Ruth's heart sank as she glanced down at her father's still form. She had never seen him so pale, drawn.

When her mother stood, Ruth sat carefully next to her father on the bed. "Oh, Papa," Ruth softly cried.

In response, his eyelids opened and met her tearful gaze. "No tears, My Sweet Girl. God is calling me home ... that's a good thing."

She shook her head, denying his words, but she knew in her heart that he didn't have long. "I love you, Papa."

"Mama ..?" was all he could manage, but she knew what he was asking.

"We will take care of her."

His mouth turned up in a weak smile, and then he was gone.

Kissing him, she heard her mother sobbing behind her and turned. Standing, Ruth wrapped her arms around her mama and held her tight. For a time James remained silent, unwilling to invade their terrible grief. Minutes had passed and still they stood wrapped in each other's arms, so he went to the kitchen and filled the kettle with water.

When he returned to the room, he embraced both women and said, "Come and have some tea while I go for my parents."

Florence glanced back at her husband and said, "I need to ..."

Not waiting for her to finish, he said, "My parents will help you prepare the body for burial."

Florence shook her head, not wanting to leave her husband, but Ruth encouraged her, "Mama, you know Papa is with the Lord now. Let me make you some tea. Papa would want you to take care of yourself."

Numb from the long stressful night, Florence allowed Ruth to lead her out of the room and into the parlor. Florence sat in her favorite chair and Ruth laid an afghan on her lap.

"You rest, Mama, and I'll bring you some tea. Have you eaten anything today?"

"No, Honey, but I'm not really hungry."

James followed Ruth to the kitchen. When they were alone, he reached for her hand and turned her to face him. "Ruth, I don't want things to be awkward for you when Samuel arrives, so I'll send my parents over to see to your father. I'll be here in the morning for the funeral. Is there anything you need me to do?"

"The Somers home, do you know where it is?"

He nodded. "Would you like me to go for them?"

"Yes. We've become close friends. I'd like George to speak words at the funeral tomorrow morning."

"Then I won't bother the preacher in town."

An irrepressible shiver caught her unaware, but thankfully James didn't seem to notice. Even thinking about the man who married her and Samuel gave Ruth the chills. "Would you mind letting the neighbors and Constance know as well?"

"That's fine." He reached out and caressed her cheek. "I'm sorry for your loss, Ruth Anne. Your father was a good man. He'll be greatly missed."

When tears flooded her eyes, he pulled her into his arms and held on tight.

Hearing a rider come in, James released her and said, "I'll go for my parents before I make the rounds."

She nodded. "Thanks for everything, James. You're a dear friend."

As he opened the back door to leave, Samuel greeted him, "James ..." Although Samuel wondered why he was here, he didn't ask.

"Samuel ..." James returned, "I'm glad you're here. Your wife and mother-in-law need you."

When James moved beyond him, Samuel caught a glimpse of Ruth's shattered countenance and moved swiftly to gather her to him. "Oh, Honey, what is it?"

She collapsed in his embrace and sobbed. "Papa ... Samuel, he's gone."

Lifting her in his arms, Samuel held her close as he sat in the nearest chair, stroking her silky head, allowing her time to release her grief. When she began to calm, he asked, "Where is your mother? Shouldn't we be with her?"

Ruth sat up. Determined to pull herself together, she took the hanky Samuel offered, dried her face and blew her nose. "She's in the parlor. I'm supposed to be making her tea."

Never having known anyone who cared for others so deeply, his wife's grief—her anguish tore at his heart. If only he thought to offer a helping hand. "Can you manage alone?"

In answer, she stood and moved toward the pantry to collect the pot and the tea her mama preferred, while Samuel joined Florence in the parlor.

The three of them were sipping tea and eating cookies when Jame's parents, Peter and Gwendolyn Collins, arrived to offer their condolences and bring a meal. Florence, exhausted emotionally and physically, deeply appreciated their thoughtfulness and told them as much. Their willingness to help her prepare Gerald's body for burial had eased her mind considerably. Although Ruth would be willing to do anything for her beloved papa, Florence preferred to shelter her from this task. Losing her father was difficult enough.

Samuel stayed close to Ruth. Though uncomfortable with these particular neighbors, he understood that Florence depended on them. They were, after all, her friends.

George and Jayne arrived as the Collins wagon pulled away and Ruth could see from where she stood at the parlor window that Samuel was relieved by their presence. Her heart rejoiced. The Somers were the only friends he had ever known. Their willingness to lay aside their own responsibilities to be there for them in their time of need blessed her beyond measure.

Seeing Jayne move toward the house, she opened the door. The embrace she received from her friend was like a warm fire on a chilly day—comforting.

"Ruth, I'm so sorry for your loss." Ruth took a plate of baked goods from her and placed it on the table. "How is your mother?"

"She's in the parlor having a cup of tea. I think she's still in shock."

"This seems so sudden."

"I know. He was doing so good the last time we were together. Mama said he was fine yesterday until around noon. He told her he wasn't feeling well and went to lie down. She didn't think much of it, but when he didn't feel up to eating supper, she grew concerned. Hoping a good night's rest would do him some good, she didn't come for me. Unfortunately, he took a turn for the worse during the night. My friend James came by this morning to bring them some milk and Mama sent him for me." Ruth's eyes filled with tears, her voice crackling as she tried to go on, "I think Papa was waiting for me to arrive. He died soon after I got here."

"Oh, Honey, I am so sorry!"

Ruth pulled a hanky out of her sleeve and took a moment to get a handle on her strained emotions. "Papa was such a wonderful father. I can hardly believe he's gone."

Jayne wrapped her arms around her and held her close. "He's not gone forever, Ruth. He lives on in your heart. You have so many wonderful memories of your childhood. And you know you'll see him again in heaven."

She drew in a rasping breath and said, "I know ... you're right, but it might take my heart a while to comprehend that even in this, God's grace can abound."

Ruth and Jayne waited for the men to come in the back door before joining her mama in the parlor.

Trapped in a shroud of unreality, Ruth moved mechanically through the days following her papa's funeral. Her inability to sleep and lack of appetite were robbing her of energy, and she was beginning to wonder if she would ever stop crying. Just the thought of her mama being all alone in their house brought her tears back in full force. She was so confused. Samuel's heartlessness had exacerbated at a time when she desperately needed his support. How could anyone be so heartless—so cruel?

George and Jayne had been wonderful the day her papa died, helping them plan the funeral when their minds could not focus. However, following their evening meal they had to be on their way.

While she helped her mama put the house in order for the day of the funeral, Samuel disappeared outside, but that was nothing out of the ordinary, so she didn't give it a second thought. Her mama had picked up her Bible to read after she readied for bed, so Ruth ran up to her old room, gathered an old set of night clothes and had just stepped into a warm bath in the pantry when Samuel came in the back door.

"Ruth," he called out, "are you ready to go?"

"No ..." she responded from within the small pantry.

Samuel opened the door and scowled miserably. "What are you doing?"

Finding his question absurd, she shook her head, unwilling to state the obvious. Dipping the washcloth in the warm water, she held it over her sore eyes, effectively shielding her view of his angry stare.

"Ruth Anne, answer me."

Lowering the cloth, her eyes met his. "Samuel, I won't have time to bathe in the morning. Besides, this has been a difficult day. A warm bath always helps me sleep. You know that!"

"That may be, but I still have chores at home to attend. You can have a good soak after we get home."

But ... she had assumed ... "Samuel, I'm not leaving Mama here alone after all she has been through."

His deep eyes narrowed. "She'll be fine, just like my mother was when my father died. Life stops for no one, Ruth. Your place is with me."

In her present state his cold-heartedness did not bode well. Pain and defiance mingled as one. As her eyelids slid shut, she prayed that he would have a change of heart, but it was not to be.

She caught a glimpse of him as her fingers slid around the handle on the pitcher of warm water. Pouring it over her hair, she reached for the soap, and cringed when she heard his steps coming toward her on the wooden floor. Without warning, his rough hands slid under her arms and he plucked her out of the tub. When he picked up the toweling and slung it at her, he said, "Get dressed! I'll expect you outside in five minutes."

Standing by the small tub, trembling from head to foot, she heard the backdoor shut. He was gone. In an odd state of unbelief, Ruth wanted to resist him, but how could she? Both she and her mama depended on him for their survival. Besides, the thought of her mama witnessing one of his cruel outbursts would only add to her terrible grief. Unwilling to put her through more, Ruth dried off, wrapped her hair in the towel, slipped the clean nightgown over her head, wiggled into her tattered robe and secured the ties. After tidying things up the best she could, Ruth found her mama half asleep on the couch. Ruth nudged her and told her that Samuel would not allow her to stay. Although her mama said she understood, the pain in her eyes said otherwise. Unfortunately, there was nothing Ruth could do. "I'll be here early in the morning, Mama."

"Don't fret over me, Ruth Anne. I'll have to get used to being alone. Perhaps Samuel is right. There is no time like the present."

Ruth hugged her tight. "Come and bar the door, Mama."

Florence tried to put on a brave front, but if truth could be told, she was afraid. Never having lived alone, she didn't care for the thought. Even so, some things couldn't be helped. She would have to look to the Lord for comfort as she faced her fears head on. "I will. You get along, Honey. No sense upsetting him further."

When Ruth appeared outside in her nightclothes, Samuel came close to lashing out, but one look at the tears glistening in her eyes, snuffed out the fire in his own. He would be mortified if anyone came across their path. Even so, he would have to deal with it. His wife was in a delicate state having just lost her father. Holding her close, unbound in her soft pink gown and wrapper would be payment enough for her willfulness.

As he mounted Pride and offered her a hand up, she asked, "Where is Sandy?"

"In the barn ... we'll take him home tomorrow, after the funeral."

Distancing herself would have been preferable, but as usual, her husband had other ideas. He held her too close, kissing her temple softly. Did he think tenderness would erase his harshness? Why did his kisses have to be so sweet? Would she ever understand him? He could be so nice when it suited him.

Even so, her frustrations remained at the fore. Although the tension that hung between them was deafening, Ruth thanked God for the silence. Her emotions were held together by a tattered thread that would surely break if he said a word.

As they moved slowly along, the stressful day caught up to her. Evening shadows fell fast and night creepers offered their various songs as Pride's hooves clomped out a steady beat on the beaten trail.

Lord, I look around me and listen to the sounds of night

and cannot deny that Your Word is true. To everything there really is a time. Isn't there? Even the sun and moon know when and where to appear. Your timing keeps things in order, ever moving forward. All of creation knows this, so why have I never understood the importance of time—Your timing—until now? Perhaps to a degree I did, but Papa's death has touched me deeply—not only because I love him, and will miss him terribly, but his passing is showing me the importance of every moment You give us.

Time should not be wasted. It is a gift to be treasured. Death feels so final right now. In a way it is, but not really ... Papa loved You ... he surrendered his life to You. Your promise that I will see him again is so comforting.

Yes, Papa's time here is over. You've called him home to his eternal reward. Help me to accept what I cannot change. And please, Lord, help Mama through this time of mourning. Thank You that this is only a season. Joy will come to us again.

If only her terrible grief was more predictable, like the slice of moon, now hanging in the velvety heavens. As hard as she tried to get a handle on her emotions, they had a will of their own. Memories of her papa flooded her mind—the sound of his voice—his playful heart—his amazing smile—and his wonderful hugs that could ease her every care. Unable or willing to shut them out, she buried her face in her husband's chest. His arms enveloped her, holding her close as she gave into the tears threatening to choke her. How long she cried, she did not know, for she awoke to the familiar rooster crowing and the soft morning sun winking through the crack in the curtains as she had so many times before.

Time ... it really doesn't stop for anyone. Does it Lord?

Chapter Twenty-two

A Light in the Darkness

... Oh that I had wings like a dove!
for then would I fly away, and be at rest.
Lo, then would I wander far off,
and remain in the widerness. Selah.
I would hasten my escape
from the windy sorm and tempest.

—Psalm 55:6-8

THREE DAYS HAD COME AND GONE since her papa's funeral. Though she pleaded with Samuel every morning to allow her to go and check on her mama, his dreadful scowl and penetrating glare had a way of silencing her.

Even so, her inward turmoil would not be silenced. Could he not understand? Her mama had never lived alone before, and besides, Samuel had a buyer for the farm. Ruth was her only living relative. She should be there to help her pack—to help her work through her terrible grief.

At breakfast she said nothing to Samuel about her mama.

He would have suspected something if she brandished him with silence, so she broached a less volatile subject. "Samuel, how long do you think it will be before we can start separating Fancy and Porcelain?"

His brow furrowed. "Why do you ask?"

"Well, Porcelain seems like a fine horse, but I won't really know how much work she'll need until I've had a chance to ride her."

"You're welcome to saddle her and start working with her in the corral. Fancy won't bother you, but I'd just as soon you wait until I'm around to help."

"Why? You've watched me with your spirited stallion. You know I can handle him. Porcelain has given no indication that she'll be anything less than congenial, so why should I need your help?"

"Up till now she hasn't been a problem, but we have no way of knowing for sure."

"We have Dakota's word."

He shook his head. "I'm not taking the word of a man I hardly know when it comes to your safety, Ruth Anne."

"So my word means nothing!"

"Leave it alone. Ruth ...."

So, let me see if I have this straight! It's okay for you to beat me black and blue, but heaven forbid I chance getting hurt doing something I love! Her thoughts were not helping her to get a handle on her rising irritation, so she stood, went to the cook stove and made another cup of tea. Now was not the time to aggravate him. Taking a deep breath to soothe her enflamed nerves, she added two cubes of sugar to the strong tea and rejoined her husband at the table. She couldn't trust herself to look at him, so when he laid his fork aside, she began clearing the table.

He stood, came up behind her at the counter, and turned her to face him. "Ruth," he said, his tone barely a whisper, "We'll work with her soon." Lifting her chin with his long fingers, he kissed her with amazing tenderness and walked out the door.

The man was a walking contradiction. Even so, she refused to allow his unpredictability to ruin her day.

She stacked the dirty dishes in the drying rack and covered them with a towel. When she returned to make dinner she'd have to do double duty, but she didn't care. Standing at the window, she watched Samuel move into the barn. When he headed toward the fields with the workhorse trailing close behind, her mind raced with excitement. He should be gone for quite a while.

Though a slice of uncertainty wedged its way into her hopeful mind, she ignored it. She could not wait another day to tell her mama the good news. Naomi had come by the previous morning, revealing her desire to have Florence come and live with her instead of renting a place in town. While Ruth suspected they would get along famously and ached to tell Samuel, Naomi had insisted on her silence. With Samuel's controlling nature, Naomi refused to let her son think he had a choice in the matter. She preferred her independence and was certain Florence would agree.

The prospect of having her mama so close thrilled Ruth's soul. And Naomi's excitement gave Ruth the courage she needed to defy Samuel's ridiculous orders once again. However, for reasons of self-preservation, she prayed that he would not find out.

After saddling Sandy, Ruth walked cautiously out of the barn and didn't mount until they were a ways down the trail. A quick glance over her shoulder told her no one was following, so she nudged Sandy into a canter and did not slow until she took the turn off for her parents farm.

Her mama, hearing her ride in, came out on the porch. "Oh, Honey!" Florence exclaimed as Ruth slid off the horse and came into her outstretched arms. "I was beginning to think you'd never come."

Ruth squeezed her tight. "I'm sorry. I tried to get away sooner, but you know what Samuel is like."

Florence smiled as her hands slid over Ruth's soft hair. But you're here now. Be sure to thank him for me." Ruth's sheepish grin told Florence something was amiss. "He doesn't know you're here. Does he?"

Ruth reached for her mama's hand and led her into the house. "I'm praying he won't find out, but I have something to tell you that cannot wait."

Florence went to the cupboard and reached for another cup before joining her daughter at the table.

Pouring tea from her mama's hand-painted pot, Ruth said, "I can't stay long, but Naomi came by yesterday and put hope back into my dark days. She'd like you to come and live with her instead of renting a place in town."

Her eyes brightened. Squeezing her daughter's hands, Florence said, "I would love being so close, but, Samuel, is he in agreement?"

Her head swayed from side to side. "Naomi has no intentions of asking him. She's asking you. Apparently the house is debt free.

The sewing she takes in will more than cover the other expenses the two of you would incur. As long as you don't mind helping her with the garden, chickens, and other chores, you two would be self-sufficient. Naomi's husband was such a controlling man, she prefers to maintain her independence as long as possible. So, what do you think?"

Florence grinned. "Samuel would have one less thing to hold over your head if I did."

Ruth's fingers came to her lips. "That's true, Mama. So what should I tell her?"

"I'll need a few days to pack up. When would she like me to move in?"

Ruth rolled her eyes. "She told me I should bring you home with me, but I thought you might need a few days."

"Are we on our own or is Samuel going to help?"

She shrugged. "I'll have to wait and find out."

Florence, feeling a bit rebellious, said with a twinkle in her eyes, "If he won't help, I could always ask James."

"Mama!" Ruth scolded, "I do believe you're more ornery than me."

Her head tilted as an impish grin rose on her face. "Could be."

Glancing around the kitchen, Ruth admitted, "I have a hankering for something sweet. Do you have anything made?"

"Oh, just a little something under the tin on the counter."

Ruth opened the lid and found two big pieces of chocolate cake. "Yum! Are you having a piece?"

Florence nodded. "Just bring a couple of forks and we'll eat off the plate."

Ruth placed the plate between them and they savored every

bite. Feeling more than satisfied, she took her last swig of tea, sent her mama an apologetic look and stood. "I hate to leave so soon, but you know what he's like."

"Don't give it another thought. If you don't return for me in three days, I'll find someone with a wagon and see to the task myself."

Ruth hugged her tight. "Sounds good!"

Meticulously, Ruth brushed Sandy down, eliminating the indentions from the saddle and bridle before returning Sandy to the stall. She cleaned the tack, then hung everything in its place. Ruth even swept the dirt floor to be sure Samuel would not detect evidence of her outing. Before leaving, she scanned the barn one more time to be sure everything was as she found it before heading for the outhouse. That big piece of chocolate cake she ate, though irresistibly delicious, was making her stomach churn. Perhaps fear of being found out added to her internal unrest. Oh, how she hated subterfuge, but her husband's controlling nature made avoiding it impossible.

After seeing to her needs, she walked over to the garden, picked a few ripe tomatoes and moved toward the house. Bacon and tomato sandwiches sounded good to her. She was pretty sure Samuel would agree.

Off in the distance she could hear a horse and buggy. George and Jayne, if they were coming over would travel that way. Since they had never come by without an invitation, she didn't give it a second thought.

Sliding in the back door, Ruth set the tomatoes on the bench, removed her boots, hung her sweater from the hook, and reached for her apron. Slipping the loop over her neck, she tied it around her waist and moved into the pantry. As she reached for the handle on the root cellar the room suddenly darkened. Turning, she found Samuel standing in the frame of the door.

If only his evil glare could be ignored.

Out of guilt, shame emerged like an unwelcome guest, playing havoc with her emotions. If only she could go back .... When he continued to stare, her heart skipped a few beats before taking flight.

"There's no need to ask where you've been, is there, Ruth?" he stated in an outraged snarl.

Too frightened to speak, she tried to ignore him, and reached again for the handle on the root cellar.

But Samuel was not finished. "You know what I expect!" he grated. His hand flew out and stuck her cheek with enough force to throw her off balance. When she tumbled back, pain shot through her arm and head as they hit the wood shelf behind her—just before she rolled over onto the hard floor. She tried to get up, but the intense throbbing in her arm paralyzed her. In Samuel's overweening rage, he did not falter. Scarcely, she caught a glimpse of the leather strap wrapped around his hand, just before it connected with her back in a punishing blow. Her screams permeated the air as he struck her repeatedly, reminding her, "You brought this on yourself!"

As he lifted his arm to strike her again, a stern male voice, combined with a sudden yank on the strap, drew his attention, "Samuel!"

In stunned fury, Samuel glared at the man who dared enter

his home without invitation. "Get out, George!"

"Not without Ruth!" he firmly avowed, holding his ground with unyielding civility.

"This has nothing to do with you!" Samuel growled, his face purple with a jumble of anger and mortification.

George, noting the extent of his friend's wrath, silently cried out, *Lord, help me!* Determined, George moved past Samuel and offered Ruth his hand. "Can you walk?"

Still in a bit of a fog, she wavered but managed a nod. George helped her stand and then said, "Go to Jayne. The two of you wait for me in the wagon."

Her features were a mixture of anguish and fear as she looked up at her husband.

In no uncertain terms, he told her, "You're not going anywhere!"

George's response made his intent quite clear, "She leaves with me or I go for the sheriff." When Samuel remained silent, George said, "After Jayne and I see to your wife's injuries, I'll be back. We have much to talk about, Samuel."

Letting her go went against Samuel's better judgment. She belonged with him, but now was not the time to set his friend straight. Or, maybe … Samuel wondered as he met Ruth's pain-filled eyes, one of them swelling shut, before looking down at her arm, now hanging unnaturally … he should let her go for now. As she moved to walk beyond him, he reached to caress the tender skin of her cheek.

She recoiled.

Little wonder.

As she and George moved cautiously past him and out the

door, he really looked at his wife in her weakened state and asked himself, "What have I done?" Moving to the window, he watched the wagon pull away. Ruth glanced back, her eyes brimming with grief and confusion. Suddenly, as if a bolt of lightning had struck him, he saw his transgressions against her for what they were, cruel beyond measure—twisted—anything but loving. The realization bore a hole in his soul, tore at his heart, as if part of him was being ripped away.

It was.

How could he have done this to his dear sweet wife—the woman he claimed to love? As regret washed over him, he covered his face with his hands and sobbed.

✿ ✿ ✿

George helped the women into the house before going for the doctor.

Fortunately, George had the chance to apprise Dr. Williams of Ruth's condition before they reached the house. Ruth had been through enough and the good doctor's first reaction was one of cold fury over learning about the abuse she had suffered.

George agreed with the man. Her torment was inexcusable, but when Doctor Williams insisted on George bringing the sheriff into this, George convinced him otherwise. He preferred to handle this with a measure of grace and civility. Though Samuel's actions were wrong, George suspected that approaching him as a caring friend could alter the outcome. George had no delusions of this being an easy task. He had witnessed the fury in his friend's eyes, but he also saw regret.

Ruth admitted that she had hopes for restoration with her

husband. While that depended entirely on Samuel's response to counsel, George would give it his all and leave the outcome in the Lord's hands. He believed that men could change their evil ways. If change was not possible then God never would have said to get rid of all bitterness, anger, and rage.

George would do all that he could to see that Ruth was not hurt again. However, he would call the sheriff as a last result. Besides, he was all too aware, the law rarely intervened in domestic issues, so he saw no reason to give the gossips fuel for their fires. Though barbaric, most believed it was not only a man's right, but his obligation to keep his wife in line. More than likely, the sheriff would return Ruth to her husband and recommend that George and Jayne mind their own business.

Well, George and Jayne knew otherwise. Their friends needed this intervention if their marriage was going to survive.

The Bible was clear. As believers in Christ we are bound to say no to ungodliness and worldly passions and live self-controlled lives. His friend may not be a believer, but he was dead wrong. Because George cared, he would do everything he could to show Samuel through kindness a better way.

Jayne was sitting with Ruth in their guest room when she heard Doc and George come in. "Would you like me to stay with you, Ruth?"

"No, I'll be fine, but thanks for offering, Jayne."

As Jayne walked out of the room, Doctor Williams entered, closed the door, and settled into the chair Jayne had just vacated. "I am so sorry for all you have been through, Mrs. White."

Her eyes filled with fresh tears, imagining what he must be thinking. Having seen her reflection in the mirror, she knew she looked horrible. "Samuel is a good husband in many ways, Doctor Williams, but he has a fierce temper."

"I can see that." Setting his bag on the bed, Doc's gentle hands touched the enflamed skin around her eye. After careful examination, he said, "You'll have a terrible bruise, but this should heal without any permanent damage."

Drying her tears with the hanky Jayne had given her, for a moment her good eyelid slid shut. When she opened it, the compassion in this doctor's eyes gave her the courage to ask, "I haven't said anything to Samuel, and I wouldn't want anyone else to know if I am, but I've missed my monthly."

He nodded. "So you think you might be with child?"

She shrugged. "Not really sure." Growing suddenly nervous, her words came out in a rush, "If I am ... well, you know ... pregnant, is the baby going to be all right? I mean, most of my body is bruised .... I didn't hurt my stomach, but Samuel is very strong .... I couldn't bear to think my baby is suffering because of me ...."

His gentle fingers came to her mouth, putting an end to her frantic plea. "To begin with, you need to understand that no matter why Samuel hurts you, it is not your fault. His inability to control his temper brought this on you. If you made him mad, he should talk to you. Never is it okay to take our anger out on others." When she offered no response, he asked, "Did you know that God hates abuse of any kind?"

She dried the tears burning the tender skin around her eyes admitting, "That's what Jayne told me."

As Doctor Williams continued with his examination, he said, "George and Jayne mentioned that you're welcome to stay here with them. They won't hold you here against your will, but now that Samuel's abuse has been exposed, this would be a good time for you to take a stand."

"What do you mean?"

The fear in her eyes was almost his undoing. "Ruth, I wish I could tell you this is going to be easy, but it's not. As hard as it might be, Samuel has to know that you are not going to put up with his abuse any longer."

She harrumphed. "Like I can stop him ...."

"You might be surprised, but a man who resorts to abuse is usually very insecure. I'm sure he has his reason for thinking it's okay to hurt you, but he's wrong."

Her eyes lowered. "That may be, but I'm not sure you understand ... his father was just like him. He never changed."

The desperation in her voice caught his attention. Yes, her body needed medical attention, but her deepest wounds were not flesh and blood. He reclaimed the seat beside her and gently squeezed her good hand. "Someone has to care enough to let Samuel know that what he thinks is acceptable, *is not*."

She shuddered at the thought of another confrontation with Samuel. More than anything she longed for a marriage built on love and mutual trust, but she was beginning to wonder if that was a realistic goal. "I have tried to stand up to him in the past, but my efforts ... all they ever got me was another beating."

"No one is going to ask you to face Samuel alone—not for a while anyway. I think you know this could take time."

"I'm afraid, Doctor Williams."

His gentleness brought her wary eyes to his. "I understand, but this isn't just about you anymore. Your baby needs to be safe and so does his mama."

Breathlessly, she asked, "Oh, Doctor Williams, am I?"

He nodded. "Yes. Everything seems to be normal, but I'm going to ask you to take things slow for a few days. I'd insist on total bed rest, but those welts across your back won't heal if you lay on them too much."

"I don't think I could anyway. They hurt too much."

"Just promise me that if you have any cramping, you'll stay in bed and have George come for me. God has your baby well protected, but you've been traumatized, Ruth. Remember, this baby needs nourishment and plenty of water. No moping over what you've been through, okay? Just give your cares to God and let George deal with your husband."

"Yes, Sir." Ruth had no wish to trouble the kind doctor, but her greatest challenges were by no means over.

"Now tell me, how did you injure your arm?"

"When Samuel slapped me, I was thrown off balance and hit both my arm and head when I fell against the wooden shelves in the pantry."

"Does it hurt much?"

"Worse than anything. And I can't seem to get my hand to work right." She held it up to show him.

"Then don't try, Ruth Anne."

His head swayed from side to side as he gradually examined each bone in her arm and wrist. Tenderly, like a father would a cherished daughter, he touched the slender bone that trailed up the outside of her arm. "The break is right here, close to your wrist, but you're fortunate. The bone lined back up nicely." He pulled a few items out of his bag. "This splint will hold it steady until the bones have time to heal."

Scowling, she asked, "How long will that take?"

"Five, maybe six weeks."

She grew thoughtful. "I can live with that, but I'm not so sure about Samuel. Who will do my chores?"

"He'll have to do them himself. Besides, I thought we agreed that you would be staying here."

"I'd wear out my welcome if I stayed that long, Doctor Williams."

He smiled. "I doubt that. Jayne will take good care of you. I'm leaving so you can rest, but I'll come by in a few days to see how you are doing. Your bone needs time to set, so no buggy or horseback riding for at least two weeks. Agreed?"

"Yes ..." she said, though she suspected that her husband would demand otherwise. He wouldn't let her stay the night with her mama when her papa died. Why would this be any different?

Ruth's eyes slid shut with the closing of the door, although her spirit and flesh were weak, her heart rejoiced over God's goodness. *You've brought such wonderful hope in the midst of this storm, Lord. Thank You for this precious little one growing inside me. Although my body is hurting, this news has filled me with a joy that could only come from You. Be with my husband, Father. There are so many things about him that I am coming to love, but then there are those things that terrify me. Doc's words were hard to hear, but I believe he's right. Help me to take a stand with the hopes of a permanent change in our marriage. I saw the way Samuel looked at me as we were leaving the farm. No doubt, he's in turmoil over what he has done. Even so, this is not the first time I've witnessed his remorse. I forgive* him, Lord, but my willingness to forgive does not change my circumstances. As much as I long for us to be together as a family, this isn't just about me anymore. Help me to be patient, to trust You, Lord, and lean not on my own understanding. Use what You will. I want nothing more than to see Samuel walking with You, but just like I had to, he must choose to receive Your free gift of love—a love so pure, so freeing that if he will walk toward You, Jesus, a whole new world will open up to him.

He Loves Me!

Chapter Twenty-three

My Truth or God's

"HOW IS MY WIFE?" Samuel asked George, as he came in the back door.

"Doctor Williams was out to the house. Her arm is broken close to the wrist, so she's in a splint. One eye is swollen shut, but he doesn't believe her vision has been affected. The welts and bruises will make resting difficult. Given time, her physical wounds will heal, Samuel, it's her spirit that concerns us the most."

The extent of her injuries only intensified Samuel's resolve to ask this man for help. If only his pride—his shame had not kept him from asking sooner. Unable to look at his friend, Samuel retrieved the coffee pot, poured himself a full tankard and asked, "Would you like some?"

"Sounds good." For a time George stood watching Samuel. The droop in his stature bespoke of regret—the puffiness around his eyes indicated remorse, along with his downcast mood. Silently asking God for wisdom, George thought about this man's character. He came across as being dignified and confident, but George suspected that inside that hard outer shell, dwelt a man who had known great heartache. Unfortunately, the walls Samuel had erected to protect himself, also shut others out. George couldn't help wondering what his childhood must have been like. Was he abused? More than likely he had witnessed his father's repeated abuse toward his mother. Did he see abuse as normal? Well, it wasn't normal. And George cared too much about Samuel and Ruth to make light of what he had done. He would confront him in love, and with God's help, hold him accountable for his actions from this day forward. Change could occur, George believed that with all of his heart, but it would come at a cost.

Samuel handed George a cup filled with hot brew and said, "The chairs are more comfortable in the parlor. If you don't mind, we can talk in there."

As he entered the room, George set his Bible on the small end table and took a seat. Lifting the cup of coffee to his lips, he blew on the steaming liquid before taking a small sip. As of yet, Samuel had not been able to look George in the eye, but George didn't see that as a bad thing. The absence of guilt, however, would be cause for concern. While guilt could ravage the soul if allowed to fester, God could use anything to convict hearts. Fortunately, this was God's department, not his. He would do his part and leave all else in God's hands. *Father,* he prayed, *use what You will.*

"Samuel," George began the moment he was seated, "Before we discuss what happened today, I'd like to ask you a few questions."

"Okay ..."

"Do you realize that I care about you and Ruth ... that I want

God's best for both of you?"

Samuel's brow wrinkled. When he cleared his throat, his tentative gaze rose. "If you didn't care, you'd have sent the sheriff instead of coming yourself."

"Doc didn't think it was wise not to, but after we talked, he agreed to give me time."

Samuel's eyes slid shut before he looked up at George and said, "I value your input. If I didn't, I never would have let you take Ruth home—my pride wouldn't have allowed it."

George saw his admission as a good thing. "You do understand that I had no choice."

Samuel nodded.

"You need time ... and so does she."

"I understand." Samuel glanced over at the window and then back at him. "Your willingness to stick your neck out for me ... I've never had anyone ..." All choked up, he took a moment to regain his composure. "Your example makes me want to be a better man, but where Ruth is concerned, so often I fall short."

George's head dipped, the warmth in his eyes unwavering. "Then you need to figure out why this happens, My Friend. The abuse has to stop."

"Friend? We were on our way to becoming friends, but with all of this ... how can ..."

George's hand came up to forestall him. "I can see why you would wonder, but there's no need. I can tell you in all honesty that if our friendship is based on merit, both of us are going to fail. It will never last. I don't know about you, but I would like our friendship to last. Besides, only God is capable of perfection."

"So ... what are you telling me, George?"

How could he make this clearer? "My hope is that the joys and struggles we share in this life will bind us closer than any brothers."

Samuel's cheek twitch as his eyes glassed over. What manner of man was this sitting across from him? His father would have spurned George for meddling in his life. Samuel knew he was in the wrong. He was also coming to realize that his father cared little for anyone but himself. Samuel wanted more. George's friendship mattered. He was different—kinder than any man he had ever known. And he was peaceful. All too often Samuel found himself longing for that same peace.

Ruth had been telling him about her new-found relationship with God. George had been sharing God's intervention in his life as well. Could God really make that much of a difference in his life—in his marriage?

In some ways he believed Ruth was coming to love him. Even so, her fear of him continued to escalate. His rage was out of control. The way she looked back at him from the wagon as they pulled away was tearing him apart. He could only hope that he could change—and that she would give him the chance to make things right between them.

George lifted his tankard to his mouth and sipped slowly at the steaming coffee. His friend looked as though he could use a moment to sure up his unsteady emotions.

Feeling suddenly awkward, Samuel looked up at George. When he spoke his words came out coarser than intended, "I can appreciate what you're saying, George, but let's not fool ourselves, you didn't come to build on our friendship, you came to confront me about what I did to my wife!"

"You're partly right."

His brow lifted. "Am I?"

"Yes ... You don't need me to tell you that what you did was horribly wrong. You know that. I can't change what has already happened, but I'd like to have the chance to help you work through your anger."

Samuel's head lowered. "If only you could .... How can I expect a man like you to understand what I go through?"

George shook his head. "I too am fallible, Samuel. Since the day I surrendered my life to Jesus Christ, I strive to honor Him, but make no mistake, I am only a sinner being transformed by God's Grace."

"Then tell me why ... why you would even try to help a man who beats his wife?" When George did not readily respond, he confessed. "This isn't the first time, you know."

George stared at his friend. His admission, though not boastful in any way, surprised George nonetheless. Ruth had mentioned Samuel's prior abusiveness, even so, George did not let on. She needed to have someone to confide in. "That may be, Samuel, but it can be the last time. The choice is yours. Besides, God wants me to look at you and see who you can become." Intervening would not be easy for George, but God works through His children. In so many ways he felt inadequate. However, God would guide him in his weakness. Of this he was confident.

He really doesn't understand, Samuel thought.

Noting Samuel's furrowed brow, he asked, "You're not convinced that change is possible, are you?"

His insightfulness astounded him. "I'd like to believe that it is, but my father's influence was strong. When Ruth openly defies me, I try to control my temper, but it seems the harder I try, the more I lash out."

George suspected as much. "If I'm not mistaken, earlier today I saw remorse in your eyes. Be honest with me, as one friend to another, are you really ready to love your wife as God intended?" When he offered no response, George added, "With God's help, I can show you a better way of dealing with your anger, but ultimately the choice is yours. As much as I'd like to, I cannot do this for you."

"I know ... but *how* is where the problem lies."

"The problem is a matter of the heart. God never would have told us to get rid of all wrath, along with every form of anger, if it were not possible."

Surprise registered on Samuel's face. "Do you really believe there's hope for someone like me?"

His incredulity eased George's heavy heart. "Yes, there is hope, and so much more ...."

Samuel leaned back, taking all this in.

Several moments passed before George, looking for a lighter topic, asked, "Would you mind telling me how you and Ruth came to be man and wife? I'm curious, did you know her very well before you were wed?"

Thoughtful, his fingers came up to rest on his mouth. His pride was still severely bruised from when George walked in on him that morning. Could he chance exposing all? This wasn't really anyone else's business. Then again, the man was willing to help him. He should be somewhat cooperative. Although he couldn't see what George's inquiry had to do with change, he let down his guard. "I know it sounds cold, but at the time I didn't see it that way. I'd been looking for a wife for some time when Ruth happened to catch my eye. She was shopping in town with her parents. I didn't know where they lived, so when they left town a few hours later, I followed them. After seeing her several times, there was no question in my mind I wanted her for my wife. So without her knowledge, I started working on her father. At first he wouldn't give me the time of day, but when he found out he was dying, that all changed. He couldn't stomach the thought of leaving Florence and Ruth destitute, so we eventually came to a financial arrangement both of us could live with."

"So, you didn't know her as a person, you only knew what she looked like before your marriage took place?"

"Yes on both counts. The day I signed the final papers we spent a few hours together, but she didn't know that I had come to meet my bride. Her father only told her that I was there to look over a team of horses they were selling. I wanted to tell her, but her father would not allow me to court her or tell her."

"Did he ... tell her?"

Samuel shook his head. "No ... not until just before I arrived at their house with my parents and the preacher."

George took a moment to digest this. Ruth's father must have been desperate. He could not imagine a loving father putting his daughter through such an ordeal otherwise. "Wow! I've heard of arranged marriages, but most of the couples knew each other or they were told ahead of time. Would you say Ruth was accepting of the marriage?"

He harrumphed. "Hardly! When I arrived, her father said she had just run upstairs. I heard her slam her bedroom door. He asked me to try and to talk to her, so I did. When she didn't answer her door, I went in and caught her just before she let go of the window ledge. It took her a while to realize that I was not going to change my mind about making her my wife. Although we were married, we had a rough first day. It wasn't until that evening, when I told her about her father's illness that she became more accepting."

"I'm sure that day was hard for both of you."

"You're right. I can see that we're growing closer in some ways. We have our good times, but I still struggle with the way I acquired her hand."

He wasn't sure what Samuel was trying to say. "Can you talk about it?"

Samuel uncrossed his legs and leaned forward, his elbows resting on his knees. "She wanted nothing to do with becoming my wife."

"How did that make you feel?"

Samuel struggled a bit before admitting, "Insecure. I mean, at first our relationship was so one-sided. Don't get me wrong, George, she has given of herself freely, but I often wonder if she does so out of obligation. I ask myself, if she had an out, would she leave me?"

"Has hurting her made either of you feel more secure in your relationship?"

"No ... but a man should be master of his own home. Even you can understand that. Submission ... well, she struggles with it. If I'm not mistaken, the Bible backs up my belief—wives are supposed to submit to their husbands. If she would just obey me, I wouldn't have to put her in her place."

George swallowed that earful, doing his best not to react.

Telling Samuel right off that his interpretation of Scripture was twisted might raise his hackles and he didn't want that. George intended to show him God's truth on the matter, but first things first. He picked up the throw pillow sitting beside him, his fingers outlining the embroidered horse frolicking in a field of grass. "When you think of your wife, Samuel, tell me, how do you view her?"

His furrowed brow was almost a scowl. "I'm not sure what you're asking."

Understanding the underlying cause of his abuse was key to Samuel and Ruth moving forward in healing. Otherwise they would be stuck in a vicious cycle.

"When I purchase a horse, I tend to buy the best looking one I can find in my price range. I see a horse as a possession—as something I own. When you sought Ruth's hand, how did you view her? You mentioned that you were attracted to her, but did you see her as a woman, an individual complete with needs and desires of her own, or did you see her as a possession?"

"No! Well, maybe ... I didn't know her ... not really, so maybe in some ways I did see her as a possession ... who knows, maybe in some ways I still do." When George did not respond, Samuel watched him.

George handed Samuel a piece of paper and a pencil with a line drawn down the middle. On one side at the top of the page it said: *my truth*, on the other it said: *God's truth*. "Samuel, we've had other discussions about the Bible, but you have never said, do you believe the Bible is God's Word—a manual of sorts to guide us in this life?"

Samuel grimaced a bit, but said, "I can't rightly say that I've ever had much of a desire to read it, but I've never doubted that the Bible is God's Word."

"Then you won't object to my sharing a few verses that would show you God's truth?"

He shrugged. "No ... not at all."

"Then go ahead and write down the truths you've already mentioned. After we read the passages together you can write God's truths across from your truths. I find it helpful to see the comparison on paper. If there is contradiction, you have to decide whose truth you are going to believe: the truth you've believed up till now or God's truth."

Samuel's frown deepened. "You want me to write down that I see Ruth as a possession?" He didn't care for the idea of having this in writing, but he could always burn it before Ruth came home. For now he'd play along and see where George was headed with this.

"Yes ... that's one. You also mentioned that she struggles with submission ..." he gave Samuel time to write that down before going on, "... you believe it's okay to beat her when she's in the wrong ... you're insecure in your relationship ... and the last one you mentioned, you're afraid she will leave if given the chance."

Samuel stared at his friend for the longest moment. Had he acted superior in any way, this conversation would have been over and he'd be on his way to reclaim his wife. Since that was not the case, he finished writing.

George set the pillow aside and plucked his Bible off the table. "Can you think of anything else you'd like to add?"

Samuel's head swayed in the negative as he looked down at the list. "No ... that about covers it."

"Well, if something else comes to mind, you can add it later. "

George had Samuel join him on the sofa before he opened his Bible, explained how it was laid out and then turned to Genesis, chapter two. "You might enjoy reading the entire creation story, but for the sake of time, I'd like us to start reading in the middle of verse twenty:

> *"but for Adam there was not found an help meet for him. And the LORD God caused a deep sleep to fall upon Adam, and he slept: and he took one of his ribs, and closed up the flesh instead thereof; And the rib, which the LORD God had taken from man, made he a woman, and brought her unto the man. And Adam said, This is now bone of my bones, and flesh of my flesh: she shall be called Woman, because she was taken out of Man. Therefore shall a man leave his father and his mother, and shall cleave unto his wife: and they shall be one flesh."*

"Would you like to take a stab at personalizing the passage?"

Looking down at the written page, Samuel said, "God gave Ruth to me for a help meet?"

"Yes, so that you would have a companion, a partner in this life."

"*One flesh*, is that talking about the physical union between husband and wife?"

"Yes ... that's part of it. If you turn back to chapter one, verses twenty-six through twenty-seven, we're given another account of the creation story that clarifies the oneness God intended for husband and wife. Read along:

> *"And God said, Let us make man in our image, after*

our likeness: and let them have dominion over the fish of the sea, and over the fowl of the air, and over the cattle, and over all the earth, and over every creeping thing that creepeth upon the earth. So God created man in his own image, in the image of God created he him; male and female created he them."

"God is saying to Jesus and the Holy Spirit, 'Let us make man in our image, after our likeness,' here he's talking about the Godhead—or the trinity as we know it. There are three distinct persons in the trinity: God the Father, God the Son, and God the Holy Spirit, but they are one God. Do you understand?"

His brow furrowed. "It's a little confusing. Is the trinity one of those things I may never completely understand, but by faith I can believe it because God's Word is truth?"

"Yes. He cannot lie."

George turned to the book of John and said, "here in chapter seventeen, verse twenty, Jesus is praying for all those who have chosen to follow Him—believers. He talks about believers being one with each other and the Godhead:

"Neither pray I for these alone, but for them also which shall believe on me through their word; That they all may be one; as thou, Father, art in me, and I in thee, that they also may be one in us: that the world may believe that thou hast sent me. And the glory which thou gavest me I have given them; that they may be one, even as we are one: I in them, and thou in me, that they may be made perfect in one; and that the world may know that thou hast sent me, and hast loved them, as thou hast loved me."

The same is true of the marriage union. God created man and woman in the image of the Godhead and like them, a husband and wife become one in marriage. Not just in the intimate physical union, but in the spiritual sense as well."

"Are you saying that men and women were created as equals?"

"Yes, Samuel, I am, but in God's order, a man is to be the head of his home. Ephesians five, twenty-three says:

"For the husband is the head of the wife, even as Christ is the head of the church: and he is the saviour of the body."

"A wife should submit to her husband out of respect for his position, but not because she is inferior—or so he can lord over her. Trust me, much more is required of husbands. Let me read on in verses twenty-eight and twenty-nine:

"So ought men to love their wives as their own bodies. He that loveth his wife loveth himself. For no man ever yet hated his own flesh; but nourisheth and cherisheth it, even as the Lord the church:"

"Wow!" Samuel murmured, more to himself than anyone, "so, if this is true ..." Stunned by this realization, he could not go on.

"I know you're overwhelmed, Samuel. There's so much more that I want to share with you, but you need time. I'd like you to consider what we've talked about. See how many of God's truths you can pull out of these passages that coincide with your truths. If your truths are not in line with God's truths, ask yourself what you are going to do about it. We've talked before about the void in our hearts that only God can fill. His purpose for you is clear—

He wants to be your Savior, to cleanse you from all your sin, to fellowship with you, but that is a choice that only you can make. If you are searching, John chapter three, verses sixteen and seventeen, and chapter ten, verse ten will help you to see this more clearly."

Samuel took a moment to write the passages down on the back of his paper, but he was still too numb to speak.

"I know you haven't walked with God, Samuel, but that doesn't matter to Him. He longs for you to come to Him, but you must open that door. Talk to Him. Read His Word and allow Him to lead you. I have found Him to be my most faithful friend."

Samuel nodded. "Thanks for coming, George. I appreciate all that you've said and done. I will take it all into consideration."

George closed his Bible and held it out. "Would you like me to leave this with you?"

Samuel shook his head. "No ... I think it's past time for me to have one of my own. If it's alright with you, I'll come by to see Ruth on my way back from town."

"That's fine, as long as you understand that she won't be coming home for a while."

Samuel's eyes narrowed. "Have you forgotten that she's my wife?"

"No, Samuel, I haven't. She is your wife, but God's plan is that you two become one. Do you love her as your own body? Like all of us, Ruth has a need to feel safe and secure. She does care, but she told me that until she is convinced that she will be safe, she won't be coming back. She's not saying no to you, Samuel. But she is saying that if you want her here, change is necessary. You both need time to work this through. I'll leave you with this

Scripture to consider: James chapter one, verse nineteen says:

"Wherefore, my beloved brethren, let every man be swift to hear, slow to speak, slow to wrath:"

"Take the time to examine your heart .... Identify the source of your anger. Ask yourself if your anger makes you feel superior to Ruth. If it does, your heart is following the wisdom the world has to offer. Take time to pray about it. Seek God's wisdom. Then, in love, talk it over with Ruth. We're reminded to be angry and sin not. God wants us to be kind and considerate to one another, forgiving one another, just as God forgave us for our sins through Christ."

"As I said, you've given me much to think about." When Samuel stood, George did as well. Samuel reached for his friend's hand to shake it, but instead, George wrapped his arms around him and hugged him tight. Samuel hugged him back and George found himself fighting tears.

"Plan to have an early supper with us, Samuel."

"Are you sure? Jayne won't mind?"

"I am sure. Jayne is the one who asked me to extend the invitation. Every couple has struggles, Samuel. She too is praying that God will not only restore your marriage, but that it will be sweeter than it has ever been."

"I would like that."

"If I'm not mistaken, Ruth asked Jayne to make a pot of chicken soup."

"Sounds good ...."

He Loves Me!

Chapter Twenty-four

Love Without Partiality

A NIGGLING UNCERTAINTY crept up Samuel's spine as he took the path leading to the Somers home. As much as he ached to see his wife, he wondered if he should give her more time. Would she refuse to see him? He wouldn't blame her if she did, but could he handle her rejection? He would have to.

George's words swept through his tumultuous mind. The passages on God's view of abuse plagued him. Even so, they did not surprise him. The way he felt after his outbursts should have sent up red flags, but he ignored the warnings, listening instead to the counsel of his father. Even so, his sin could not be laid at his father's feet. His heart sank, knowing he alone was responsible for his responses to Ruth, reprehensible as they were.

Her parents had entrusted him with her care. Though he had failed miserably, he had no one to blame but himself for the vulnerable state he was in—that and the unwelcome feebleness that prevailed.

Yes, he yearned to be alone with Ruth, but he would not ask her to come home. George was right. They both needed time. His desire for restoration forced him to look at his relationship with Ruth more rationally. Though she would find his counsel odd, he intended to encourage her to read God's Word and follow His lead.

Passages on oneness had given him much to think about. The oneness of the Godhead, this he understood. He and Ruth were created in God's image. They were meant to be one as God the Father, God the Son, and God the Holy Spirit were one. Knowing this still boggled his mind.

God's truths were so foreign to him. Before George had enlightened him, he was completely unaware of God's plan for them as husband and wife. His lack of knowledge hacked at his pride. He had so much to learn. Would he ever get this right?

Samuel was a man who preferred order. Even his father, a man whose compliments were sparse, had commended him for the way he prepared before taking a wife.

True enough, Ruth appreciated their fine home, but so often her sodden eyes revealed her heart. Things were not important to her. Their relationship needed work. *Why did I not listened to my wife? If only I had* ....

Ruth was wise in ways he was not. A stranger to spiritual matters, he could not comprehend why God would want anything to do with the likes of him. Even so, he was determined to approach George's counsel with an open heart and mind.

He wanted to change. Although he had failed in the past, perhaps accountability was key.

Only time would tell.

Dismounting, Samuel tied Pride's reins to the post, retrieved the package he had purchased for Ruth, and moved with caution toward the porch. George must have heard him ride in because the door opened as Samuel reached the door.

"Come on in, Samuel."

Without so much as a frown or hint of judgment, George greeted him. His acceptance of Samuel was obviously not based on merit. Oh, how this baffled him. Realizing that his friend was talking, Samuel wiped his bluchers on the rag rug and looked up at him.

"Ruth is resting in the guest room at the end of the hall, but she has been asking for you. She'd like to join us at the table for our meal."

Samuel nodded. Raking his fingers through his disheveled blonde hair, he lumbered toward the door at the end of the hall. Tapping his fingers on the frame, he didn't wait for a response. Ruth's eyes were closed when he entered the room and shut the door behind him.

Sitting gingerly on the edge of the bed, an irrepressible desire to touch her prevailed. Caressing her soft brown hair, he sighed. Her eye was dark and swollen from where she hit the shelf, but he didn't know how badly until her good eye fluttered open and the other one remained shut. "Oh, Honey. What have I done to you?"

This time he did not even try to place the blame on her. Stunned, speech evaded her as he gently held her sweet face in his hands. "You may not be ready to believe me, Ruth, but I really am sorry."

Recalling Doc's words, she attempted to sure up her wavering emotions. Normally putty in his hands, she could not give in to

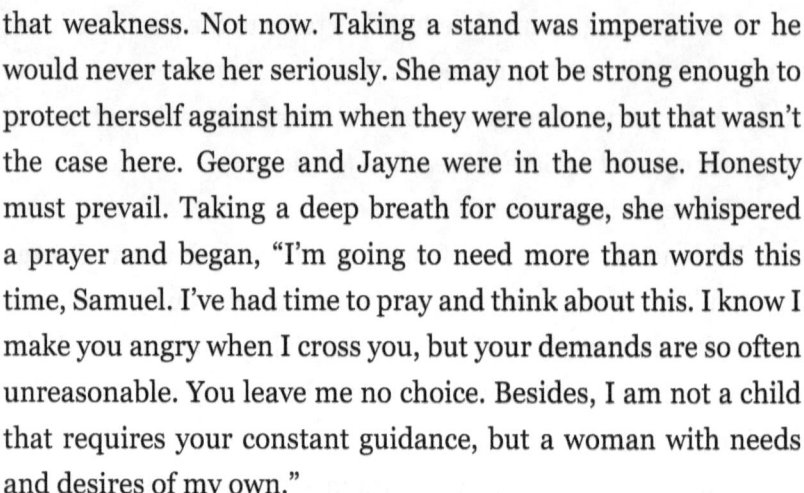

that weakness. Not now. Taking a stand was imperative or he would never take her seriously. She may not be strong enough to protect herself against him when they were alone, but that wasn't the case here. George and Jayne were in the house. Honesty must prevail. Taking a deep breath for courage, she whispered a prayer and began, "I'm going to need more than words this time, Samuel. I've had time to pray and think about this. I know I make you angry when I cross you, but your demands are so often unreasonable. You leave me no choice. Besides, I am not a child that requires your constant guidance, but a woman with needs and desires of my own."

His head lowered. "I know that now."

Her frown deepened into a scowl. "Do you?"

A single nod was his only response. He appeared overwhelmed. She had so much more to say to him, but it didn't all have to be said now. She settled for one more plea, "I deserve your respect, Samuel, no matter if we agree or not."

Concern furrowed his brow. "Ruth," he gently entreated, "you've been through so much. We don't have to figure everything out right now. George and Jayne are fine with you staying here. You need time."

"And what about you, Samuel? Are you open to George's counsel?" For a moment he withdrew, appearing thoughtful. She waited.

Holding his strained emotions in check, he said, "I am." Annoyance at the fore, he added, "In truth, the man's not giving me a choice, but maybe that's what I need. Your wounds say otherwise, but I do love you, Ruth. I want my wife back."

The tears trailing down her cheeks were his undoing.

"Do you?" her vulnerability tore him apart.

Appearing confused, he asked, "Want you back?"

Fighting tears, she nodded.

He reached out and caressed her soft cheek. "More than anything in the world," Samuel admitted, pulling his hanky out of his pocket and gently drying her tears. "But before you can come home, I have much to learn. George has shown me a few passages about God's view on abuse. You were so right. My truths and God's don't come close to lining up."

Lining up? She wasn't really sure what he was alluding to, but his passion could be mistaken for nothing else—a desire to change, and the knowledge of it warmed her aching heart.

"He also spoke of the oneness God has in mind for us. Do you remember trying to tell me that?"

Still too close to tears, she managed another nod.

"I wasn't ready to listen then, but I am going to from now on. You know how stubborn both of us can be. I can't say that we'll always agree, but I will hear you out, Ruth. My wife is wise in areas I am not."

For a while an awkward silence dragged on, but the bright sun streaming through the window reminded her of the One who had changed her life. Perhaps in time Samuel would know His love and the changes only God could make in him. For now she would take things one day at a time. "I can appreciate what you're saying, Samuel, but like I said, I'm going to need more than words. My life is not the only one you put in jeopardy today."

This statement drew his undivided attention. "What are you saying?" he insisted on knowing.

With a look of endearment, her hand slid reverently over her flat stomach. "Our baby and his mama need to feel safe ...."

The tears flooding Samuel's eyes were a vast contradiction to his first response. "Oh, Ruth. A baby? Are both of you all right?"

"Doctor Williams seems to think so, but I'm to stay in bed and send for him if any problems arise."

Feeling awkward, he reeled in all traces of highhandedness, and asked, "You will follow his recommendations, won't you?"

The corners of her mouth rose. She could see it in his eyes, he wanted to lay down the law, but didn't. His tentative words told her just how much he was trying. "Don't worry, Samuel. If necessary, I will stay in bed the whole nine months if that's what it takes to keep our child safe."

"I'm glad."

"When I mentioned my concerns to Jayne, she reminded me that God has not forsaken me. If our baby is meant to be here, he will be. I have to trust in His perfect will."

"I'm sure you're both right."

Samuel grew quiet again and while she wondered what he was thinking, she did not have to wait long to find out.

"Will you ... I mean ... can I ... kiss you?"

The odd feelings his defenseless look stirred plucked at her aching heart. How could she resist him? "You are my husband, Samuel. You have some hard choices to make if you want us to come home, but I do love you. As long as you understand that no matter how sweet your kisses, and I do find them sweet, I cannot live with you until I feel safe."

"I agree." Samuel sighed as his lips caressed hers.

His fear of losing her had been great. Still was. The control he had sought did nothing to bring them closer. Divide them was more like it. And yet here she was, his dear sweet wife, surrendering to his kisses. If he lived to be a hundred, he would never forget this day—the day Ruth not only told him that she was carrying their child, she admitted her love for him, and then showed him that she did by her willingness to stand up to him when he was wrong.

Suddenly his desperate need to control her seemed foolish. How could he have believed such lies? He determined then and there that he would take himself by the scruff of the neck and seek God's truths.

The desire to have this woman walk beside him in this life took on a whole new meaning. Oneness, maybe there really was something to it. The Godhead had oneness in mind when creating the family unit. Perhaps the day really would come when Samuel and Ruth would be one as intended.

Samuel, realizing that his mind had been wandering, looked at his wife and caught her watching him. "George is convinced that God is waiting for me to come to Him, but why would He want anything to do with the likes of me?"

Hope leapt within. "I know from personal experience that George is right, Samuel, but you'll have to see that for yourself. If you had a Bible, you could search it out for yourself, but ..."

"That reminds me," he interrupted. "I went into town before I came here and picked something up for us."

Her curiosity peaked. "Oh?"

"Yes ..." he laid the package on her stomach, waiting for her to loosen the tie and open it. As he suspected, she was in awe, but then she started to cry. "Honey, don't do that ...."

"I can't help it. I've wanted one for so long. What made you..?"

He handed her his hanky again and waited for her to blow her nose. In truth, he needed a moment too. Confessing his faults never came easy. "Selfishness, pure and simple! I had myself convinced that if you did get closer to God, He'd be one more wedge between us. George set me straight. The man told me that was a bold face lie from the pit of hell." Samuel shook his head and grinned. "That friend of mine, he doesn't mince words."

Ruth grinned. Who was this man sitting beside her?

"I'm pretty sure it sent the devil to blustering when I bought myself the same Bible. The way I see it, I need it more than you."

Her good eye widened as she stared up at him in shock.

Noting her odd expression, he tried to explain, "George seems to think God's truths are the only ones that matter in this life. I'm kind of wondering if he could be right. I just thought it would be nice if the two of us could, well you know …"

She shook her head. "I'm afraid I don't, Samuel."

"Study the passages George has been showing me, and then discuss them when we're together."

Her full-blown smile warmed his heart. "I would like that very much."

"Good … I haven't had a chance to make you a list of the ones he gave me earlier, but I could bring them by tomorrow."

She smoothed out the wrinkles in her blanket and said, "That would be fine."

Treading on unfamiliar ground, he asked himself, *does she sense my dreadful awkwardness in her presence. Then he wondered, Is this how young couples feel when they're courting? Did my underhanded way of attaining her hand keep me from experiencing the insecurities that now hover. My arrogance offered me a false sense of security. Now my need for control has to be relinquished. In truth, I'm hoping to offer her something more—something that will last a lifetime. Could that something be genuine love? In truth, I don't really know. Her trust is something I will have to earn. God's truths must be key. How to find them in that big black book will be a challenge, but I am determined to take on that challenge, no matter the cost.*

Realizing that his thoughts were wandering, he glanced at his wife and said, "There's paper and a pencil in the bottom of that package. You know, something to take notes on, in case you think of any of those, what are they called ..."

"Verses?"

"Yes. If you have any you'd like me to read, write them down."

"I will ...." She couldn't say more. Her mind was so full of wonder over this change in her husband, she wanted to shout with joy. Thinking she might frighten him, she rejoiced inwardly, her heart and soul alight with gladness, thankful for this new beginning.

Samuel spoke his thoughts out loud, bringing Ruth's back to the present. "I'd like to read the whole Bible from cover to cover, but some of it is kind of confusing. It might take me a while to get through it."

"I know what you mean. My parents read to me from the Bible as a young girl, but I didn't understand much of it until I surrendered my life to Christ. Now I'm understanding more. I can't seem to get enough. When I asked Papa about my hunger for God's Word, he said that my sin was like a wall between me and God. Until I believed that Jesus died to pay the price for my sin and I saw my need for a Savior, Scripture was obscure.

I couldn't understand the things of God because His Spirit, the One who gives understanding was not living in me."

"So, are you saying that His Spirit lives in you now?"

"Yes ... I was missing out on all that God had for me—His comfort—His joy. I was oblivious to it all." For several seconds she remained quiet, measuring how much she should say. "Nothing would bring me greater joy than to have you accept Jesus as your Savior, too, but I cannot do it for you. It would never work. Your relationship with God is personal."

Not really understanding, but wanting to please her, he offered, "I'll think about what you've said, Ruth."

That's all I can ask. Samuel?"

"Hmm ..."

"Thank you!"

His brow furrowed. "For what?"

"The Bible. For approaching God's Word with an open heart and mind. For being willing to counsel with George with the hopes of our marriage being restored."

"I told you, Ruth ... he isn't giving me a choice."

"You have a choice. Everyone does."

His shoulders slumped a little more and his hands came up in complete surrender. "And look at what I have done to you. The choices I've been making have to be a thing of the past. You deserve better. I'm so sorry for all I've put you through."

"I forgive you, Samuel, but never forget that only God can cleanse you from sin. Only He can make you new—only He can help you to start over again."

Thoughts of having a relationship with God was so foreign to him, but a better relationship with his wife, that was conceivable.

"I want to love you the way I should, Ruth. I thought I did, but I'm finding out the hard way that my view of love is skewed. I'm determined to see that change."

"I'm so glad."

"George mentioned that you'd like to join us at the table for dinner. Are you sure you're up to it? How is your arm?"

If she told him it was throbbing, he might insist that she stay in bed, so she kept that bit of information to herself. "I'm supposed to keep it stable, so I'll need some help getting up."

With care, Samuel lifted her in his arms. For a while he just stood there taking in the essence of her femininity before once again sampling her soft pink lips. Though he would love to hold her for hours, he reminded himself that good things come to those who wait. Before they were wed, waiting for her seemed endless. Now he must wait again, but it couldn't be helped. If he was going to survive this time without her at his beck and call, he would have to take each day in stride. Stealing one more kiss, he stood her on her feet and steadied her with his strong hands when she swayed a bit. "Dizzy?"

"A little. I'm not used to being in bed for so many hours during the day."

"Your eye could be making the dizziness worse."

Her hand came up to her swollen skin. "Am I too frightening to look at, Samuel? Should I stay hidden away until the swelling is down?"

"No, Ruth. Only the Somers are here and they've proven that they care no matter what …."

"Do they warm your heart as much as they do mine?" When he nodded, she said, "Like Christ, the love they've shown us is without partiality. I am so blessed to call them friends."

Samuel smiled as he opened the bedroom door. "That goes for both of us."

❧ ❧ ❧

The air had cooled considerably before Samuel headed home. Though huddling inside his saddle blanket shielded him to a degree, he was not nearly as warm and cozy as he would have been if Ruth were in his arms. Unfortunately, that couldn't be helped. This time of healing would be good for both of them. The spiritual realm held so many mysteries to explore and with George's offer, he would also get a good start on the finishing work upstairs. He would love to have it done before the baby came.

The baby!

As he wrapped his mind around this thought, tears came to his eyes. He couldn't remember who, but someone had once told him that children were a blessing from the Lord.

A Blessing?

Gazing up at a darkened sky, he wondered, *God, are You really up there? The people I care so much about insist that You are.*

On the off chance they were right, he could no longer ignore his budding desire to find out. Feeling a bit odd, he spoke again to the star-covered heaven, "Why God? Don't take me wrong, I'm thrilled that we have a child on the way, but I really don't understand why You would bless me in this way? You know what I'm like. Ruth's another story. Her gentleness and kindness would put many to shame. She loves You, but me, I've done nothing to deserve Your blessings, let alone my wife's love. What I deserve is your wrath for what I've done to her—for what I've been doing to her since the day we married." A wave of sadness swept over him—or was it remorse? In truth, he did not know. His attempts to discharge the terrible ache inside seemed to weaken him even more.

As he relinquished his pride, tears filled his eyes and flowed down his face. Although he faltered, it was only for a time. He had so much to confess. "God, I'm so sorry ... I vowed to love Ruth, but I've failed her in so many ways. Please help me. I don't mean to tell You how to do your job, but I'm so confused. Why would you bless a man like me? This kind of love—this love so freely given could take me years to grasp."

He Loves Me!

Chapter Twenty-five

Accountability

MORNINGS AND EVENINGS without Ruth were difficult. Samuel missed her something fierce, but deep down he knew this time apart would be good for both of them.

George's commitment to help him through this time of amendment could not be faulted. Every morning for the last week, when chores were barely out of the way, George would appear on his doorstep with baked goods in one arm and his tool chest hanging from his other hand. Today was no different. Hearing the knock, Samuel went to the door and welcomed him.

"I hear you have a few rooms that need finishing. Mind if I help?"

"Not a bit, but you don't have to come every day." Concern etched Samuel's brow.

George only grinned and said, "Oh, yes I do!" he declared and Samuel knew without asking what he would say next. "Jayne is counting on the armoires being on our to-do list for the afternoon shift."

Samuel's eyes sparkled with glee. "Well, as long as it means I can spend some time with my wife, I'm all for it."

"That, and you won't have to cook!"

Rubbing his belly, he admitted, "Always a bonus."

Samuel, though he did not let on, looked forward to their times together that involved so much more than woodworking. With his Bible, pencil, and ongoing list of his truths verses God's truths close at hand, Samuel often found himself laying aside his work to add to that list.

George didn't miss an opportunity to discuss pertinent Scriptures with his friend, and Samuel, longing to have his wife and growing child back home with him, listened intently. One thing was perfectly clear: although the things he had been taught were not all wrong, when it came to his relationship with his wife and others, God's Word showed him repeatedly that his views were not only twisted, they required change. Ruth was not his possession, but his wife—a gift from God—someone to walk beside him in this life.

George's counsel made so much sense. In fact, he held nothing back and Samuel could appreciate his frankness. Samuel had no right to lash out when Ruth did not meet his expectations. Instead of allowing his anger to control him, he could use it as a motivation to do things God's way. The right way!

Samuel now realized that his anger had little to do with Ruth. The years of watching his father abuse his mother should have been enough to turn his stomach. Instead he allowed his father to convince him that a good beating was the only thing a stubborn woman would understand. He bought into that lie and his wife had paid for it dearly. *What a fool I have been.*

In his desire to relinquish control—the driving force behind his anger, he read several passages over and over again, committing them to memory. Proverbs chapter twenty-two, verses twenty-four and twenty-five frightened him, as if he were seeing himself through God's eyes for the first time.

The warning was clear.

Too clear to ignore!

"Make no friendship with an angry man; and with a furious man thou shalt not go: Lest thou learn his ways, and get a snare to thy soul."

No wonder Ruth had to leave with George and Jayne. Even so, he was thankful George did not abandon him as well. He would have every right. Perhaps George would be wise to be on his guard. Samuel didn't plan to, but anger was a demanding taskmaster—one not easily suppressed.

Proverbs twenty-one, the second verse, had him pegged to a tee:

"Every way of a man is right in his own eyes:
but the LORD pondereth the hearts."

Self-righteous! Oh, he had been quite sure of himself. As if that were not enough, like his father, he was a master at covering his sins against his wife. But if George was right—if Scripture was right, and he was coming to believe that it was, nothing could be hidden from God. Although asking God for help was not within his rights, not after all he had done, he would do his best not to fall prey to this sin again.

Though the Scriptures he read were not always clear, the

truths he did comprehend were wondrous to behold. The longing to know more drove Samuel to his Bible. He simply couldn't get enough. George encouraged him to hide God's truths in his heart. In so doing, he stumbled often. Grace was not something he could earn, it was a gift freely given through the shed blood of God's Son. But how could this be?

Could his sins really be forgiven? He thought not, so he worked hard at memorization, hoping his efforts would evoke change?

George's willingness to try and clarify the passages that confounded him helped. Samuel's determination to change was opening his heart and mind to the things of God as never before.

To think, had George not been willing to confront him that day, he might have gone on hurting Ruth for years. How sad that would have been. His wife would have continued to suffer for what? For nothing. Their relationship would be in more tatters than it already was. Like his parents, they might have learned to exist together out of obligation, but they never would have known the love—the oneness God intended for them.

Samuel and George were riding towards the Somers farm before he summoned the courage to ask, "George, do you think Ruth would be willing to go for a walk with me today?"

His friend was taking great strides. George could see that, but he still challenged him at every turn. "I want you to think of the most trying thing she has ever said or done. Ask yourself if you would be able to lay aside your anger if she did it again?"

The path was clear in front of them, so Samuel closed his eyes and didn't readily respond. "My hope is that the things you've been showing me are firmly planted in my mind, but until I spend time alone with Ruth, I won't really know how deeply rooted they are." He glanced at his friend. "I want to do right by her. I hate knowing how much I've hurt her, both physically and emotionally. She deserves better."

"Do you respect her enough to break the chains you've used to bind her?"

He scowled. "What do you mean?"

"Your greatest fear is losing her, but until you're willing to relinquish control, she'll never be free to be herself with you."

"You obviously have something specific in mind. Give over."

"The list of chores you insist on her following is one example. It makes her feel like a servant in your house. She should be free to do things her own way, even if her ways fall short of your expectations. Can you accept her ways without criticizing her?"

He harrumphed. "And what else has she told you?"

Samuel was annoyed, but he would have to get over it. Their future happiness could depend on George's honesty. "Ruth goes out of her way to defend your finer qualities, but until you're willing to relinquish control, nothing is going to change. Does your fear of losing her keep you from letting her come and go as she pleases?"

He scowled. "Her responsibilities are at home!"

"No, Samuel. Her main responsibilities are at home, but that doesn't mean she cannot be a vital part of this community. If you let go of this hold you have on her, I think she might surprise you. I don't doubt that she loves you, but your need to control her will destroy that love if you're not careful."

He frowned something fierce, but he also saw the truth in George's words. "My mother has been telling me the same thing."

Samuel's flat response held no conviction and George

suspected his ego was involved. "Perhaps you should start a new list," he lightheartedly chided.

Samuel rolled his eyes. "Let me guess, you want me to write down every way I try to control my wife and then the date I relinquish that control."

George shrugged, grinning just a tad. "Not a bad idea. Just keep in mind that once you relinquish control, you cannot take it back up. You might have to keep reminding yourself to let it go, but that is part of the healing process."

Taking a deep breath, Samuel asked, "Do you really think that's possible?"

He nodded. "I do."

"You may find this odd, George, but I find your willingness to hold me accountable comforting. Old habits are difficult to break. Seeing how happy you and Jayne are helps me to keep things in perspective. I want that with Ruth. Besides, my pride took a beating when you walked in on me hurting her that day. I don't care to repeat the experience."

"I hope you mean that. Be sure that what you're doing and saying lines up with God's Word. Intimacy with your wife excluded, if you're doing something you'd be embarrassed for others to know about, more than likely you're walking outside of the boundaries God intends for you to live within."

"Hmm ... I suppose that makes sense."

"Then we're in agreement. I don't have a problem with you spending time alone with your wife, provided she feels safe. Are you willing to accept her decision?"

He nodded. "If she says no, I won't press her."

Grinning, George said, "You've come a long way in a week,

Samuel. God wants to help you with all this, but ..."

Samuel held his hand up to forestall his comment. "I know I have to be the one to open that door. I'm not ready, George. Not sure that I ever will be."

"You'll have to forgive me, but I intend to keep praying for you. I know from personal experience that if God gets a hold of your heart, you'll never be the same."

Samuel could appreciate what he was saying, but George had lived a sheltered life. His sins could not begin to compare with Samuel's. He was sure of that. In his heart and mind, the forgiveness of God was incomprehensible.

❦ ❦ ❦

Samuel slid his arm around his wife's waist and moved at a turtles pace toward the river. "George and Jayne have a couple of logs down by the river that we can sit on. I don't want you pushing yourself, but ..."

"It's okay, Samuel. I'm not in as much pain and besides, we need time alone together."

He kissed the top of her silky head. "I miss you every minute of the day, Ruth, but the mornings and evenings are the worst."

"I'm struggling too, but we have to take this slow. Besides, Doc doesn't want me riding in a wagon or on a horse for another week or so. Something about my bones needing time to set up."

"Are you planning to go to church in the morning?"

She nodded. Looking up at him she smiled. "I'm excited to have my own Bible to follow along in."

Samuel grew quiet, feeling awkward even asking, "Would you mind if I come early so we can walk together?"

"To church?" In her surprise, the words barely squeaked out.

"Yes ... thought I'd join my lovely wife inside, instead of trying to listen through the holes in the barn wood."

Her eyes twinkled with glee. "I wondered ...."

Grinning, he drew her a bit closer so he could kiss her cheek. "I can be mean and ornery, Ruth, but curiosity is an attribute most of us possess."

Giggling, she reached for his hand, her thumb caressing his palm. "I'm not exempt when it comes to meanness, after all I did kick you in the shin the day we were married."

He finger combed a few of her stray wisps while gazing into her lovely face. His brow furrowed and he chuckled as he said, "Yeah! I'd almost forgotten about that. And if memory serves me, you tried to stomp on my foot!"

Her head tilted as she shrugged. "Could you blame me?"

"No ... your father should have told you sooner about our arranged marriage."

"Perhaps, but we can't go back. I know I can be spiteful when pushed too far, but ornery ... I'm never that."

He rolled his eyes playfully. "I beg to differ with you, Dear."

She giggled, admitting, "We both have our faults. I don't expect perfection, but I shouldn't have to live in fear."

"I hate the way I feel when I hurt you, but my father ..."

She reached out and touched his arm. "You're open to learning a better way."

"Oh, Ruth. I want nothing more than for you to feel safe and secure with me. I've made so many mistakes in the short time we've been together. My heart aches for you. Sometimes I feel so overwhelmed with all George is showing me, but I really am trying. The passages George has me reading are enlightening. So often they contradict the things my father taught me. As much as I want immediate change, I'm learning that these kinds of changes take time. Knowing what I should do is good. Doing it is where the challenge lies. So often my normal and God's don't measure up."

A branch swaying in the cool breeze got caught in the loose weave of her shawl. Samuel forestalled her attempt to right it and soon had her bundled back up. "We're all in process. That's why it's so important to stay in the Word. I'm learning new things every day. Sounds like you are too."

"I am."

She leaned into him and peered up. "Do you feel as I do, that we're being given the chance to start all over again? Perhaps it's nothing but a dream, but that dream gives me hope and right now I need something to cling to. I want our baby to be raised by both of his or her parents."

"Between George's willingness to hold me accountable and my determination to have you back in our home, I have to believe that our hopes will become reality."

She withdrew for a time, her expression laden with concern. "We have to learn from our mistakes, Samuel, but we can't let them keep us from all that God has for us. Jayne reminded me just this morning that Jesus came to set us free of those constraints, but the choice is ours. To remain in the past and walk in unforgiveness will only destroy us."

Samuel, noting her sudden lack of strength, supported Ruth and led her to the stumps he and George often sat on to fish and converse. When she claimed one, he took the other.

The gentle breeze added to the peacefulness of the setting and for a time his eyes fell on the moving river. Covering her good hand with both of his, he rested his elbows on his knees as he looked at her and asked, "Do you really think we have a chance, Ruth Anne?"

Her head dipped several times, but his agonizing expression exposed his doubt. She was about to question him when he humbly stated.

"I don't understand how you can forgive me."

Her gentle smile was like healing oil to cracked skin. "My forgiveness will never erase what you've done to me, Samuel. I'll always remember. My physical wounds are a reminder of what I have suffered at your hand, but forgiving you has nothing to do with merit. No one can earn forgiveness. Like love, it is a gift. As a child of God I am to follow in the example Christ set. My sins would send me to hell if not for what Jesus did for me. He forgave me and so I must forgive you. If I deny you forgiveness, Jesus won't forgive me. So you see, Samuel, I'd be the one hurting if I chose to walk in unforgiveness. Unforgiveness separates us from God."

Relief washed over him. "Whatever your reasons, I am thankful, Ruth. Just knowing you're willing to give me another chance keeps me going through the lonely days and nights. "

His avoidance of discussing what Christ had accomplished on their behalf did not go unnoticed, but he heard her out. For him this was a huge step in the right direction. "I'll continue to pray for you. God is willing to do a work in you, just like He is doing in me, but ..."

His hand came up to forestall her. "I know ... George told

me ... I have to be the one to open that door."

She nodded. With a tenderness born of desire—a desire to show him that she cared and longed for their marriage to be healed, she reached up to caress his cheek. "You are my husband, Samuel. Yes, we are struggling, but I have to believe God has things to teach us through this time that we couldn't have learned any other way. His Word reminds me that He has not abandoned us. You might find this hard to believe, but my commitment to you is stronger than I ever thought possible. I long for us to be truly one, but that won't happen unless we're both willing to die to self. There are so many things about you that I've come to love. Nothing would bring me greater joy than for us to be reunited as a family, but rest assured, your actions will continue to speak so much louder than words. If you want us to have a future together, it is up to you. I won't take your abuse any longer. God says that husbands should love their wives as they do their own bodies—as Christ loves the church. I won't settle for anything less."

He could see it in her eyes. She meant every word. Rubbing his jean clad legs, he said, "My love for you is changing Ruth. I want us to be together, but so much of what you and George are showing me in the Word is contrary to what I've been taught. I feel like a new kid at school who doesn't know the alphabet, but is determined to learn how to read. Needless to say, I'm struggling."

"I pray you'll find a way to deal gently with us soon. Without you by my side, I find it difficult to sleep, so I've been memorizing Scriptures." Her cheeks warmed as she looked away.

Surprised, he asked, "Do you know any by heart?"

A small smile escaped, relaxing her brow. "I have James one, verses nineteen through twenty down pretty good ....

"Wherefore, my beloved brethren, let every man be swift to hear, slow to speak, slow to wrath: For the wrath of man worketh not the righteousness of God."

She couldn't let him think that only he was at fault. "My smart mouth doesn't help when you're angry, does it, Samuel?"

He nodded. "That may be true, but it's no excuse. I have to learn to control my temper."

Her sodden eyes met his. "Pastor said that each of us should take the time to examine our heart .... If our anger makes us feel superior to the person we're angry with, our heart is following worldly wisdom. He recommends that we pray about the situation and seek God's wisdom. Then in love, we can calmly discuss the things that upset us. Paul reminds us to *be angry and sin not*. I need to listen to you and withhold my cutting retorts, but only you can change the way you respond to me."

Samuel swished away a fly that had landed on her broken arm and then asked, "Who is Paul?"

"The author of the book of Ephesians and many others. He's the one who said we're to *be kind and considerate to one another, forgiving one another, just as God forgave us for our sins through Christ.*"

Feeling his light touch on her hand, Ruth looked at Samuel's profile. He was scowling at her broken arm.

"Your whole hand is swollen, Ruth. Should we head back? Maybe you should lie down?"

"I'd like to say I'm fine because I'm enjoying our visit, but Doc did say that it would swell if I have it hanging down too long."

Samuel made an attempt to be stern, but the sparkle in his eyes defied his piercing stare. "Apparently I'm not the only one who needs to be held accountable!"

"I have things to work on too."

"Both of us do." Leaning close to his wife, he kissed her with amazing tenderness. At that moment he knew he would lay down his life, if that's what it took to keep her safe from harm. Knowing he was the cause of her current injuries, guilt or was it shame washed over him anew. *What possessed me to hurt her, God? I'm not convinced You care about me, but I'd be beholden if You would show me how to be the loving husband she needs.*

He Loves Me!

Chapter Twenty-six

Reaching Out

FEELING STRANGER than a man riding side saddle, Samuel sat next to his wife on a bench in the makeshift church.

Ruth glanced over at her husband and smiled at the picture he presented. She had never seen him look more insecure. Was he aware of the way he held his Bible against his chest as if it were a shield? Metaphorically speaking, God was often referred to as a shield in Scripture, but she suspected Samuel didn't know that. She could only hope he would relax enough to hear God's Word presented.

Samuel, all too aware that this was not the typical little church building, complete with steeple and bell, even so, it was having the same effect on him. A swift exit would alleviate the odd feelings swirling inside him, but knowing his wife's disappointment would be great held him in his seat.

Folks came up to greet Ruth and she introduced him with a smile. They inquired about her injuries, but she merely said that she had taken a spill and thanked them for their concern. He marveled at her willingness to protect his honor, even though his abuse proved otherwise.

Although the woman confounded him, he recalled the humble list her father had shared with him about love. For the most part, his wife was a walking testament of the kind of love described—the same love he aspired to show her but often failed. The love her father spoke of was not only patient, it was kind, it was not envious or boastful. As if those attributes were not enough to expose his lack, he reminded himself that pride and rudeness could not exist in love.

Ruth had told him often that love could not be self-seeking or it wasn't love at all. If only he had listened.

He struggled the most with anger, and as it turns out, even that must be snuffed out for love to be genuine.

If only he could display some of the other characteristics on that list. Letting go of the wrongs done to him was a bit of a stretch. Forgiveness challenged him, except where Ruth was concerned. He could see why he should not delight in evil, and even why he should delight in the truth. Oh, that he would seek to protect her and their children in the future—and that mutual trust could build between them. He would continue to cling to the knowledge that in love there is always hope, and, oh, how he longed for the strength to persevere.

The hymn being sung pulled him back to the present and he gladly followed along, but he did not even try to join in. Melodious rhythms were too much of a leap for a man who had grown up without frivolities.

Some of the things the preacher spoke of were familiar,

but hearing new concepts were swiftly becoming the norm for Samuel. The things he did not understand, he scrambled to jot down. Unfortunately, the brunt of his concentration had been on flipping from passage to passage. Thankfully, his wife had already learned and was a patient teacher.

※ ※ ※

Another week had passed before Doctor Williams deemed it safe for Ruth to return home with several stipulations. She was only to do light housework. Her husband had to agree to helping in the kitchen, and most of her day should be spent resting, allowing her body to continue healing. Doc also made it clear that he would not stand by and allow his patient to fall prey to Samuel's temper again. Had George not promised to check in on Samuel and Ruth every day, Doctor Williams would not have given in, and didn't mind saying so.

George had his own reservations, but after discussing them with Ruth and spending time in prayer, he had a peace about letting her go. The time had come for Samuel to be put to the test.

Their wagon would have given Ruth more room to spread out, but the ride would have been too bumpy. Pride offered the smoothest ride and holding her close as they moved away from the Somers home suited Samuel just fine.

"Our mothers came by early this morning, Ruth. They were cooking and cleaning when I left the house. From what they tell me, you won't be cooking or cleaning for weeks to come."

She looked up at him and smiled. "Did you tell them about the baby? Is that why?"

He shook his head. "No, but I did tell them about your

injures. I thought you'd like to be there when we tell them about the baby."

For several seconds she remained silent, but then she remembered their agreement to talk things out. "I'm not so good with secrets, Samuel. Perhaps we should tell them right off."

Chuckling softly, he said, "That's fine with me."

She was contemplating how to tell them when Samuel's hand splayed possessively across her flat stomach.

"When did you plan to tell me ...?"

Peering up, she asked, "Tell you what?" At first she thought he was referring to the baby, but that didn't make sense.

"That our mothers are now living together."

"Oh, that ..."

"Yes, that!"

She stiffened at his gruff tone, and her thumping heart did little to ease her disquieted mind. "Samuel, please. It was your mother's idea, not mine. Don't be angry with me."

"Angry? Why would I be angry. I only wish I had thought of it first. No doubt, they'll be good for each other."

Wide eyes met his. "Oh ... you sounded angry and that makes me feel vulnerable ... I don't like feeling vulnerable, Samuel."

He reached out and caressed her face, his eyes exposing his tender heart. When he could think of no other way to reassure her, he leaned forward, his mouth covered hers and she savored his amazing kisses. "Then I'd best work on the way I say things from now on. I want you to feel secure, but I'm sure we still have much to work on. Keep telling me if I do something that frightens you."

"I'll try."

❦ ❦ ❦

Samuel, Ruth, Naomi, and Florence were sitting around the table with cups of tea and a tray of warm cookies when Samuel glanced at Ruth and smiled. "Would you like to tell them or shall I?"

She nodded, delighted by the joy radiating from his eyes. "You do the honors."

Florence and Naomi glanced at each other, then leaned forward in anticipation.

Samuel, enjoying their suspense a bit too much, sat back and asked, "So tell me, how would the two of you feel about someone calling you, Grandma?"

"Grandma!" they echoed as they looked to Ruth for conformation. Her gentle nod, glistening eyes and exuberant smile said it all.

"What wonderful news. Do you know when?" Naomi asked.

Ruth said, "In about seven months, give or take a few weeks."

Florence sighed. *If only Gerald had lived long enough to see their first grandchild.* Determined not to overshadow this delightful moment with regret, she smiled and said, "That should give us plenty of time to be ready. Oh, but, Ruth, did you see the doctor? Is everything alright?

She didn't know what Samuel had told them about her injures, so unless they inquired, she would not offer details. "Doc says I'm fine and everything appears to be progressing normally. Our little one is in God's hands."

When the new grandmas began telling about their own pregnancies, Samuel took his cue and stood. Kissing Ruth's warm cheek, he left her and their unborn child in their mother's capable hands.

Ruth, looking forward to a quiet evening with her husband, stirred the dry noodles into the small pot of chicken and broth her mothers had left simmering on the stove. Adding the bowl of sliced carrots, she thanked the Lord for Naomi and Florence and the joy they were finding in their new life together. The thought of having them close at hand to help raise this child gave her peace of mind. She could only hope the baby would not be too spoiled, but then looking back at her own childhood, she realized that it wasn't possible to be loved too much.

Hearing Samuel come in the back door, Ruth set the table while he washed up. As he came into the kitchen she was standing on her toes reaching for the plates when he said, "Let me get those!"

Surprised, but relieved, she stepped aside. "Would you mind grabbing your coffee cup too?"

As he set them on the table, he glanced around the room and asked, "You're not overdoing it, are you?"

Smiling, she looked up at him. "That's not possible. Our mothers cleaned while I was napping and although they allowed me to cut the noodles, they forbid me to help with the other meal preparations. Those two are not only bossy, they're a couple of chatter boxes. You should hear them together, Samuel. I could barely get a word in edgewise."

Samuel chuckled at the way her upper lip had come up. And the pout that followed was so adorable, he couldn't resist kissing her. "I stopped by to check on them the other day. They didn't even know I was there for several minutes. I'm beginning to wonder if I should find them a good watch dog."

Her eyes met his. "Them? What about me. Oh, Samuel, I've always wanted one. *Grungy critters to have in the house,* Mama would say, *riddled with ticks and fleas.*"

"Is that so? Well, on the off chance she's right, I certainly don't want one in the house with a baby on the way."

As quickly as her hopes had risen, they were dashed away. *I should have kept mama's appraisal to myself.*

Samuel put the water over to heat for their evening bath, saw to the dishes, tidied the kitchen, and when everything was put to rights, he swept his wife off her feet and carried her to their bathing chamber.

The way he doted on her seemed so out of character for her husband, but she wasn't about to question him. This kind of caring a woman could get used to.

❁ ❁ ❁

The sound of a wagon traveling too fast, hoofs pounding the hard ground, and someone screaming off in the distance drew Ruth's attention as she came out of the barn. Her eyes narrowed. She strained to catch a glimpse of the driver, to no avail.

Who could it be?

With Samuel out clearing another field, she took every precaution. Returning to the barn, she reached for the gun, slid around the corner, and watched from a hidden corner. No sense asking for trouble.

The second her friend Meg came into view she breathed a little easier, put the gun out of harm's way, and waited for her to bring the wagon to a halt.

Meg jumped down. Wide eyes brimming with fear, met Ruth's before Meg pulled her to the back of the wagon.

Ruth stood there in shock. Her hand came to her mouth to squelch the emotions threatening to escape. However, the frightened child needing her help put her mind to rights.

Her little buddy lay motionless on his back. A blood-soaked bandage was wrapped around his small leg, and his baby sister tucked in the crook of his arm. His big brown eyes, though pleading, lacked their usual zeal.

Propelled into action, she glanced at her friend and said, "Meg! Run to the back field and fetch Samuel."

Meg took off running in the direction Ruth had pointed and never looked back. With her husband away, Meg depended on the kindness of neighbors—them, and the good Lord.

Naomi and Florence had apparently heard Meg's screams because they were headed Ruth's way as she climbed into the wagon. With her good hand, Ruth reached for Brent's small fingers, and said, "Hang in there, Buddy. We'll go for the doctor. He'll fix you up good as new."

Ruth, wanting to get her little friends inside, accepted the hand Naomi offered to steady her as she stepped down from the wagon. With tender care, Florence lifted the small baby that was tucked in the crook of her brother's arm and handed her to Ruth. Cautiously gathering Brent in her arms, Naomi glanced up at Florence, who informed her and Ruth that she would take the wagon and go for the doctor.

Naomi, after laying the small boy on a quilt that Ruth had spread out on the kitchen table, went to look at the damages. She had just started removing the bandage when Samuel and Meg flew in the back door.

"We saw Florence heading for Doctor Williams," Samuel said, as he came toward Brent and ran the crook of his finger along his tear-dampened cheek. "You hang in there, little man.

We'll have you fixed up in no time."

Ruth reentered the kitchen, her hand filled with clean bandages. Noting Meg's frantic expression, she said, "Cynthia is sound asleep on my bed. Pray, Meg. We'll do everything we can to help him, but you know Brent is safest in the Lord's hands."

Meg swished the tears from her eyes with the back of her hands and said, "I will. Thank you, Ruth."

Naomi and Samuel removed the bandage, took one look at the four inch gaping wound in Brent's leg, and knew stitches would be unavoidable.

"Ruth," Samuel said, having noticed her weakening stance. "Honey, maybe you should sit down and hold Brent's hand while we work on his leg." She willingly complied, but the boy's mother didn't look much better, so he pulled up another chair and said, "Meg, can you hold his other hand? He'll need his mama close."

Samuel hated to be the cause of more tears spilling down the boy's face, but there was nothing he could do. The wound would have to be cleaned before Doc could stitch it up or infection could set in.

Naomi retrieved a basin of warm water while Samuel went to their bathing chamber for towels. As Samuel cleansed the boys wound, Naomi marveled at her son's gentle care of the small child. The way he kept checking Brent's face for signs of distress, warmed her heart. Perhaps her hopes of him being a good father could be realized.

Confident he had done his best, Samuel applied a thick bandage, hoping the boy would not bleed out while waiting for the doctor to arrive.

When Brent slipped into a sound sleep, Ruth released his

small hand, caressed his sweet cheek, and went to make a pot of coffee. This could be a long day, and they would all need refreshing.

Doctor Williams's concern was understandable. Brent had lost a lot of blood, but they were all thankful he slept through Doc stitching him up.

Meg was in the parlor feeding Cynthia when Ruth brought her in a cup of freshly brewed coffee and said, "Samuel and I were talking. We would like you and the children to stay for a few days. At least until Brent is up and around."

Glancing at Ruth's arm, Meg's head swayed from side to side. "You're in no shape to have company, Ruth. You never did say how you broke your arm."

"I hit it on the shelf in the pantry when I fell, but it's healing fine. Doctor Williams won't allow me to do much, so your being here would really be a help, not a hindrance." Ruth was thankful Meg didn't press her further. Although Samuel was in the wrong for doing what he did, the struggles in their marriage were a matter for prayer, not public ridicule. She would not put up with his abuse any longer, but George and Jayne were aware and they too would hold him accountable. She was determined to honor her husband, despite his faults, and trust God with all else.

"As long as you're sure."

"I am."

"Ruth, thank you for everything. With Paul gone, I didn't know who else to turn to."

"You're like family, Meg. Please don't ever hesitate to come to us."

Meg had a faraway look in her eyes as she focused on the beam of light streaming in through the window. Suddenly the room grew darker, a fitting depiction of the uneasiness pressing in. Her head lowered as she said, "The doctor, Ruth, he will expect payment ... but I have nothing to give him."

"I've spoken to Samuel. He already covered it."

Tears flooded Meg's eyes, "With our financial constraints, being my friend can be costly. I hate it, Ruth, but wanting things to be different changes nothing. I talk to the Lord about it ... so often He is silent."

Ruth touched her friend's hand in a reassuring manner, effectively bringing Meg's gaze back to hers. "In more ways than I can count, you've been there for me. You always give of yourself, Meg, so please don't start measuring your worth by the worlds standards—your giving heart is a gift I treasure. Wealth is just another tool God uses to help His children—a gift as well. If you ask me, God says yes more often than we realize. This time His provision came through us. Aren't you the one who has been telling me for years that God provides the things we need, when we have need of them?"

The irrepressible grin that brightened Meg's face told Ruth she had gotten through. Besides, if Ruth truly believed that God was her provider, and she did, who was she to withhold His bounty from a friend in need? Thankfully, her husband agreed.

Meg tucked her sleeping daughter in the crook of Ruth's good arm so she could button her dress before the two of them went to check on Brent. When they found him sleeping in Samuel and Ruth's bed, they tucked Cynthia in beside him and went to start supper.

Samuel was coming in the back door with a cradle he had confiscated from his mother's attic when Ruth and Meg entered the kitchen. Samuel, after taking the cradle upstairs, a bedframe and tick for Meg soon followed, along with a cot for Brent and a small lamp table. Ruth and Meg were only too happy to collect the blankets and coverings needed for the beds.

The change in Samuel was miraculous. Why, not so much as a scowl had crossed his face when he paid the doctor or when she suggested that Meg stay with the children until Brent was back on his feet. The first time she had tried to reach out to Meg and her young family came to mind. Her efforts had been rewarded with a sound thrashing. As odd as it was to see him going out of his way to see them settled in before the evening shadows began to fall, she thanked the Lord for His goodness. She wasn't ready to lay uncertainty aside completely, but his actions were living proof that God's Word was true. Change was possible. Only time would tell if this new kindness in Samuel was here to stay.

Chapter Twenty-seven

Humility

*R*UTH AWOKE to the sound of a baby crying. Pushing her covers aside, she yawned as she tried to get up, but Samuel's arms slid around her and he drew her close.

"Meg will see to Cynthia, Ruth. You need your rest."

Although he was right, his stern tone set her on edge. "Are you angry?"

"No, not angry, but I am concerned about you and our little one. You haven't been resting enough with guests in the house."

Reaching out in the darkness, she caressed his earlobe, marveling at its softness. The intimate gesture, as it often did, had a soothing effect on both of them. "Meg will be heading home after church in the morning. I'll have plenty of time to rest, unless of course you have a new list of chores forming."

Her downcast tone reminded him of George's suggestion. Old habits had to go ... relinquishing control would not be easy, but it was necessary if he and Ruth were going to move forward. A sense of ownership is what he long for her to feel. She was not his servant, as his obtrusive ways implied. This was not only his home, it was her home as well. Taking in a deep breath and releasing it, he admitted, "You're more than capable of caring for our home without my input, Ruth."

Her brow furrowed. "What? No more lists?" Her words could be construed as mocking, but then his demands were often ridiculous. She watched him closely. While his features did tense a bit, he told her with a slight grin in place.

"No more lists ...."

"Are you serious?" Excitement exuded from her.

He chuckled softly. "Yes!"

As quickly as her excitement spilled forth, she grew quiet .... Peering up at him she asked, "Will you still be critiquing my work?"

He kissed the tip of her nose. "Nope! Not even if I see dust bunnies in every corner and webs streaming down the walls. The house is your domain. Do with it as you see fit."

Sweet giggles bubbled up as the image of webs flowing from the ceiling transfused her mind. "I would never let our home fall into such a shambles, Samuel. Surely you know that."

"I do ... just so you keep in mind that Doc wants you resting more. The work will get done eventually, even if we have to work together at it."

Did he just offer to help in the house? Her mouth had to be gaping open. Needing a moment to gather her wits, her head lowered and she merely said, "I won't forget." Did he know how much his concession meant? Caring for their home would be such a pleasure, now that ... now that she could do things her own way without criticism. My, but the thought alone freed her.

Samuel, drawn to her warm lips, twirled her long brown hair

around his finger and said, "I've enjoyed having our friends here, Ruth, but I have to be honest, I'm looking forward to having you all to myself."

In response, she tried to snuggle closer, but her broken arm got in the way.

Samuel remedied the problem by crawling over her and laying on her side of the bed. "That's better," he declared, and as she turned to face him he drew her closer and kissed her sweet mouth.

His irresistible kisses had a way of relaxing her every care, but it wasn't long before Samuel drifted off. Unfortunately, her new position in their bed did not have the same calming effect. For what seemed like an eternity, she tried to find her rest, but nothing helped.

Her husband, unaware of her struggle, also had her trapped. Closing her eyes, she talked to the Lord about the coming day. When she ran out of things to pray about, she began reciting passages from memory. By the time Samuel relinquished his hold, the rising sun was trickling in through the crack in the curtain. She slid out from under the covers, reached for her robe, and stuck her feet into her warm slippers. The door creaked when she slipped out, but her snoring husband was undisturbed.

After filling the kettle and placing it on the cook stove, she stoked up the flames and went out on the porch to take in the morning's heavenly display.

"Can't sleep?" Samuel asked as he joined his wife.

"No ... but I really don't mind. This view is spectacular in the morning."

In truth, he had never given it much thought, but one look

at the rising sun exposed the source of her enchantment. "The variations in color really are something!"

Her arm slid around his waist. Snuggling close, she said, "I'm in awe of the creativity of our God. I don't know about you, Samuel, but all I have to do is look around at His handwork and no matter what I am going through, I know how much I am loved."

His brow furrowed. "By God?"

"Yes ..." her arms spread wide, "He didn't forget a thing when he created all of this for us to enjoy. He knows us inside and out and cares about the things that matter to us in great detail. His love never ceases to amaze me."

Samuel, considering what his wife had said, remained silent as he took in their surroundings. Did God really care—about everything? Could his wife be right? If so, would God extend forgiveness to someone like him? He thought not, but perhaps when he met with George the next time, George would shed some light on his disparaging thoughts. For now he led his wife back inside to prepare for their day.

Wanting their last morning with Meg and her children to be special, with Ruth close at hand, Samuel began frying up bacon and eggs. Apparently their mothers had the same idea and had been up early baking. They arrived at the back door with the results of their efforts—a basket full of warm cinnamon rolls. Samuel put the coffee over to boil and made his wife a pot of tea. With their growing child unsettling her stomach, tea was quickly becoming her brew of choice.

The aroma of cinnamon filling the air summoned Meg and Brent from their slumber. Mother and son trudged down the stairs and were greeted with smiles as they entered the kitchen.

Brent wasted no time inquiring, "What is that smell?"

Naomi and Florence glanced at each other and grinned as Florence said, "Maybe you should peek in the basket and find out!"

❀ ❀ ❀

Her eyes were on her infant, tucked in the crook of her arm when Meg accepted the hand offered to her as she stepped down from the wagon outside of the George and Jayne's barn. Looking up to thank the kind gentleman who had offered her aid, her heart faltered. Tears spilled from her eyes as a mixture of joy and relief filled her. Though she fought to regain her composure, she was a lost cause when her husband drew her into his arms. Moments passed before she managed to say, "Paul … you're home!"

The Whites, thinking this family would appreciate some privacy, walked into the barn and took a seat.

When a man Ruth did not recognize stepped up to the podium, panic rose within her. *Who is he?* she wondered as a sudden concern for her husband's fragile state ebbed into her anxious mind. Having heard a few over-the-top preachers in her days, fear raised its ugly head …. However, a quick peek at Jayne, who was seated beside her, calmed her. Jayne squeezed her hand, leaned over, and whispered in her ear, "God has not given you a spirit of fear, My Friend. Trust in His timing."

Was she that transparent? Perhaps, but she didn't give it another thought. Her fears were not coming from the Lord. That much was obvious. Nodding, Ruth picked up her Bible, took in a soothing breath and turned to the passage being read in James the fourth chapter.

"But he giveth more grace. Wherefore he saith, God resisteth the proud, but giveth grace unto the humble. Submit yourselves therefore to God. Resist the devil, and he will flee from you. Draw nigh to God, and he will draw nigh to you. Cleanse your hands, ye sinners; and purify your hearts, ye double minded."

"My name is Travis Drake. A few months back I wrote to brother Somers, a former school mate of mine, and asked if he would allow me the opportunity to come and share my testimony with you. Not only because I long for others to know my Jesus, the One who can set men free, but also to raise an awareness of the degradation and abuse that continues to destroy marriages and families across our great country. You see, God's plan for our lives is to prosper us, to give us hope and a future. But never forget that the devil has a plan for our lives as well. If he can keep marriages in turmoil and children defeated, he will succeed in his plan of destruction.

"I am here to tell you that the love of Jesus has changed me from the inside out. I believe that a large part of God's call on my life is to expose the devil for the liar he is and to share with you the amazing grace that is available to those who will simply believe in the One who has sent me, Jesus Christ, the innocent Son of God who paid the price for my sins and yours."

Ruth had goose bumps to the point of shivering. Travis's words hit so close to home, she chanced a peek at Samuel. His eyes were so stayed on the man speaking, as if no one else in the room existed.

Sensing the presence of God's Spirit permeating the room, she began to pray for her husband as Travis continued.

"If you're sitting there thinking it's really none of my business how you deal with your children, your wife, or others you come in contact with, then this message is for you. If you have suffered at the hands of someone whose need to control you has left you with a broken heart, I am here to remind you that God is close to the brokenhearted. He is willing to save those who are crushed in spirit. If you are guilty of abuse, this message is for you. There is no sin so great that it is not covered by the blood of our Savior, Jesus Christ.

"All I ask is that you hear me out ... give me a chance to expose the devil for who he is: a liar bent on destruction.

"Although the way I was brought up is not uncommon, God has shown me through my failures how wrong—how dysfunctional—if you will, my thinking had become.

"Like many, I grew up believing my father was the only higher power I need concern myself with. He ruled with an iron thumb. To say that he was a cruel, self-centered man would be an understatement. I honored him because of his position, but the way he treated others was wrong, and to this day no one will convince me otherwise.

"Although my mother suffered at my father's hand on a regular basis, my brothers, sisters and I were no strangers to his harsh words or his cruel punishments.

"Anxious to leave home, I took a job at the livery in town. The job paid for my room and board, so I saved almost every penny placed in my hands. On occasion I would see my father when he'd come to town, but his message remained the same, I would never amount to anything. Out of a sure determination to prove him wrong, I saved up enough money to buy a farm that was fairly well-established. Soon afterwards I married the sweet young woman I had fallen deeply in love with.

"Joan and I were happy and getting along just fine until her mother took sick. Joan would stay with her mother for days on end and although I understood, her absence put a huge strain on our relationship.

"I could have sworn that I would never turn out like my father—that I would never lay a hand on another person in anger, but I was wrong.

"Joan came home when her mother passed away, but I was not the same man she left. Loneliness had been a cruel taskmaster. My insecurities and fears plagued me. Anger became my constant companion as my father's words tumbled around in my mind.

"If only I had known then that a wise man keeps himself under control—only a fool gives full vent to his anger.

"Like my father, my abusive ways escalated, taking its toll on our marriage. At first the abuse was verbal. Then it moved on to an occasional slap to emphasize my point. I convinced myself that I was superior to her. That she would obey me or else. When my anger continued to intensify, the beatings began. I blamed her for everything and made sure she knew it.

"You see, allowing my anger to rule me was a choice, but I didn't know that at the time. I hated who I had become, but I didn't know how to change. The pain in Joan's eyes when I would lash out tore me apart.

"Sin, if you haven't figured it out, takes us further than we want to go and keeps us longer than we care to stay. Sin also costs so much more than we are willing to pay.

"Joan was carrying our first son. In her sixth month, I lost my temper over something she said. I beat her, and both of us paid the ultimate price for my sin. God spared my wife's life, but our child was born too early. To this day I can still see our innocent baby boy lying lifeless next to my sobbing wife. As far as I was concerned, my father's proclamation that I would never amount to anything came true that day.

"My father was right! At least that's the lie I believed at the time.

"Out of desperation, Joan began going to a little church in town with a friend. By the third week the change in her was amazing. Her joyful spirit had returned, but me, I was still a defeated man. In truth I was jealous. I was also terrified of losing her.

"Standing at our son's grave, she told me in no uncertain terms that if I ever raised my voice or hand to her in anger again, she would leave.

"I believed her.

"Joan was wise, she didn't try to shove her faith down my throat, she just lived her faith before me. When I asked her questions, she answered me to the best of her ability. Recently she informed me that I was too bull-headed for her to preach to me. If I was going to find God, it would have to be on my own terms—not hers.

"She was right.

"I was a proud man, but I was also very insecure. I could not fathom how God could love someone like me.

"Winter arrived early that year. Under a protective guise, I insisted on taking her to church in the sleigh. I told her I wouldn't take a chance on her being caught out in a storm. Sounded like a good excuse to me. You see, my curiosity had gotten the best of me. Her joyful countenance held a powerful draw and I was determined to find out where it came from.

"What I heard that day blew everything I had been taught right out of the water. I thought I loved my wife, but I really didn't have a clue.

"Love," the preacher had said, "is an action word. Genuine love isn't about me and what I stand to gain. It isn't about what others can do for me. Love reaches out and does for others. Since love is the greatest gift we can offer, I'd like you to listen as I read from the Bible about what God has to say about love or charity.

"Charity suffereth long, and is kind; charity envieth not; charity vaunteth not itself, is not puffed up.

Doth not behave itself unseemly, seeketh not her own, is not easily provoked, thinketh no evil;

Rejoiceth not in iniquity, but rejoiceth in the truth;

Beareth all things, believeth all things, hopeth all things, endureth all things.

Charity never faileth."

"Needless to say, I was shocked by his words.

"I was even more shocked to learn that God loves me so much that He sent His only Son to pay the penalty for my sin.

"My sin! Was that possible?

"He went on to say that putting myself down and not believing God was capable of forgiving my sin, no matter how heinous, was a form of pride.

"Yes, the things I had done to my wife and child were unforgivable in my mind, but when the preacher said there were no sins that the shed blood of Jesus could not cover. My heart was overwhelmed.

"I burst into tears, not caring who saw them. I longed for the peace and joy my wife had.

"You see, there's no earthly love that can do what the shed blood of Jesus can do for a sinner in need of God's Grace. He can cleanse you today, just like He did for me on that glorious day when I surrendered my pride, my fears, my shortcomings, my failures, to the only One who could make me a new man. The One whose selfless love paid the ultimate price and took my sin upon Himself so that I could have life and have it more abundantly.

"You might not be able to understand how this can happen to you, but the Bible reminds us to lean not on our own understanding. In all our ways acknowledge Him and He will direct our path. You are not alone. Lay your sin at the cross. Ask Jesus to forgive you for all your sins and invite Him into your heart. I'm not promising you an easy life—but Jesus does promise to be with you every step of the way. While we sing the closing hymn, if anyone would like to come forward, I would love to pray with you."

Samuel reached for his wife's hand. Bringing her fingers to his mouth, he kissed them gently while attempting to get a handle on his strained emotions. Could he really be forgiven? Giving her hand a squeeze, his big brown eyes, now filled with tears, met hers. Leaning close, he whispered, "What do you think, Ruth? Are my sins against you and God covered by the blood of Jesus?"

He Loves Me!

Chapter Twenty-eight

A Heart Set Free

Search me, O God, and know my heart:
try me, and know my thoughts:
And see if there be any wicked way in me,
and lead me in the way everlasting.

—Psalm 139:23-24

RUTH THOUGHT back on a conversation she had with George a few weeks back. He said that it was okay to hate Samuel's sin, but no matter if they were together or not, God required her to love the sinner. She couldn't do that in her own strength. After many weeks of praying for her husband, her mind was on firmer ground. In her weakness, God truly was stronger. As she surrendered her cares, His Spirit's response overwhelmed her, flowing freely in and through her.

The realization was life-changing.

Tears spilled down Ruth's face as she clung to Samuel's strong arm and spoke from her heart, "Every last one of them, My Love."

Her words were his undoing. God's love flowing through Ruth exposed the truth of it all. She had not only forgiven him, she loved him, even honored him as her husband despite his failures. He couldn't understand why God or his wife would want anything to do with him, but God's Word said otherwise. His truths were the only ones that mattered.

Samuel was a desperate man. Was he desperate enough to surrender all? The yearning to take God at His Word was welling up inside him. George had said that leaning not on his own understanding was key. His friend had to be right because none of this made sense. Although his flesh still longed to make amends for his wrongs, he suspected that was not possible. Accepting this free gift being offered was the only way to find the peace he longed for.

Total surrender to the One who gave His all—God's one and only Son.

As the congregation stood and began singing the closing hymn, he could no longer deny his need. Glancing again at his wife, he released her hand and made his way to the front.

George joined Samuel who willingly accepted the hug he offered. "Is it time, Samuel?"

Overwhelmed with emotions, Samuel said, "Yes ..."

When Travis came over and laid hands on Samuel, he asked, "How can I pray with you, Brother?"

"Hearing your testimony has given me hope. So many of the things George and my wife have been sharing with me are starting to make sense. I don't know why God would love me so much that He would send His Son into this world to die for me, but I believe that He did. I've sinned. I need God's forgiveness." After taking a moment to blow his nose and gain a semblance of control, Samuel continued to share what was on his heart, "Nothing would bring me greater joy than to know Jesus in a personal way."

"Then let us bow our heads together and pray. Father God, You've heard the confession of Samuel's heart. Your Word reminds us that whoever believes in You, they will have eternal life. Samuel, are you prepared to surrender your life? Are you asking God's Spirit to come into your heart and make you a new creation in Christ Jesus?"

"Yes."

"Father God, Your Word says that by his confession he is a new creation in Christ. Spirit of God, come into his heart. Comfort him and make him new. Thank You for all that was accomplished for us on the cross and for opening the door so Samuel can begin anew. Be with him, Lord. In the name of Jesus Christ we pray, Amen!"

An unfathomable joy flooded Samuel's soul. In that moment, he felt different, like a heavy weight had been lifted from his shoulders. "I cannot thank you enough for your willingness to expose your inward struggle." Samuel glanced at his friend and said, "George has been planting many seeds, but hearing your story—so close to my own—has helped me to see that just maybe, with God's help, there is hope for me too."

Travis smiled and hugged him. "Thanks for telling me, Samuel. The day will come when God's still small voice will encourage you to share your story with others. When He does, remember this day. Don't allow pride to keep you from sharing God's intervention in your life. He wants to use you too, Samuel."

"I won't forget. How could I?" He leaned forward and whispered, "I feel like shouting from the rooftops!" Glancing over at George, Samuel said, "Thanks for being there for me, Friend. I wouldn't be standing here if you hadn't been willing to reach out in love when I was at my worst."

George hugged him tight, admitting as they turned to leave, "I'm rejoicing with you, Samuel. I'm here, should you be tempted. Keep your eyes on the Lord and He will direct your path."

"Wow! What a day!" Samuel shouted to the inhabitants of the barn. While they did not respond, he was fairly certain God was aware of his thankful, exuberant heart—of Samuel's new awareness of God's Spirit, now alive in him.

An onlooker would think him crazy. Even so, he didn't give it a second thought. Surrendering his life to Christ had started a chain of internal events he never wanted to forget. In surrender, he found forgiveness. The heavy burden of sin had been lifted from his shoulders. Oh, he suspected he still had much to work on. Although he held no hopes of this being an easy transition, he knew without a doubt that he was different—lighter—free of the chains that had him bound for as long as he could remember.

The lens he saw things though had changed so drastically it both boggled and delighted his mind. Wondering if his wife would notice the changes, he finished his chores in lightning speed and ran toward the house.

Seeing that Ruth had supper on the table, he washed up and decided not to say a thing about it. If she noticed, she would share her thoughts on the matter. There was nothing shy about his wife. True, she had learned to hold her tongue to assuage his bursts of temper, but he prayed that would all change soon. He wanted her to be at ease. She should be able to speak her mind—to be herself around him. In truth, he welcomed the challenge. What was that passage George had him memorize? *"I can do all things through Christ who strengthens me." Even control my temper!*

Of course, George had said that if his life was truly surrendered, his need to control others could be denied as well. *Oh, Father God! I sure could use your help! Please, I so want to walk in obedience to You.*

Lifting the coffee pot off the stove, he poured their coffee and retrieved the cream and sugar without thought.

Ruth caught herself ogling the man collecting odds and ends they would need to complete their meal. He placed them on the table and then proceeded to hold her chair out and waited for her to take a seat before sitting across from her.

Samuel managed not to smile, but it wasn't easy since her mouth was hanging open. Oh, how he wanted to kiss those rosy lips, but he resisted the urge. Reaching for her hands, he bowed his head and for the first time since they were married, he returned thanks for God's provision.

She waited until Samuel stood to dish up the meal before saying, "I don't suppose I need to ask if God is changing you, do I, Samuel?"

His brow furrowed. "What do you mean?"

"Papa always said that actions speak so much louder than words. Don't get me wrong. You have been more helpful since I came back from George and Jayne's, but that was out of necessity, possibly even obligation. There are things I simply cannot do yet, but this ... this is different."

He smiled. "How so?"

"You brought things to the table without my asking. You held my chair out for me. And, Samuel," she looked up at him with tears spilling down her sweet face, "you prayed over our meal."

Setting down the plate he held in his hand, he went to her. Lifting her out of her chair, he sat back down and held her close. As understandable as her confusion was, his heart was breaking for her. She had put up with so much from him since the day they had married. He gave her no choices—things had to be done his way or else. She laid aside her dreams, desires, opinions, and so much more to make a life with him, so that her mother would be cared for when her father died. The realization of how much she had truly given up for him hit him hard and fast.

"Oh, Honey. If we could go back and start over again today, I would, but we both know that isn't possible. I hate the way I treated you in the past—like you were nothing more than a possession. I can see my sins against you so clearly now. You were right, I didn't understand what love entailed, but I do now—I'm beginning to anyway." Seeking the right words, he took a deep breath and sighed. "Oh, My Sweet Porcelain Beauty, I do love you—so very much. The day we married, I really believed that I was simply getting what I deserved. I had so much to offer you and I assumed you would feel blessed that I had chosen you. What an arrogant man I was. Can you ever forgive me? I don't even like that selfish man. Is there a chance that we can begin anew?"

She burst into tears, clinging to him, and for a while he just let her cry. As he was praying that God would give her peace, she said, "I'm sorry, Samuel."

"For what?"

Taking the hanky he was offering, she blew her nose, determined to find a semblance of control. "For crying when I should be rejoicing. I am so happy for you ... for us ... for our baby. Now he or she will have two parents who love God."

His hand came up to caress her cheek. "And each other."

Gazing into her lovely face he could see so clearly the love that shone in her eyes for him. "I honestly don't know how or why you've put up with me for so long, but I am so blessed to call you my wife, Ruth Anne. I pray that this day will mark a new beginning for us," his eyes fell on her gently rounding stomach and his hand splayed over their little one before he added, "and our gift from God."

"Anything is possible, if we believe, Samuel."

His calloused fingers came up to gently touch her rosy lips. Caressing the soft skin around her mouth, he smiled. "It may take me a lifetime to make up for all the wrongs I've done to you, but I fully intend to have fun trying, My Love."

Her twinkling eyes held a touch of mischief as she coyly said, "Fun ... hmm ... A lifetime, you say? A heart set free by God is an amazing thing. Perhaps the journey will be fun for both of us." Melting into his strong arms, her whispered words said it all, "With God at the fore, nothing is impossible, My Love."

And now he knew that she was right.

He Loves Me!

Epilogue

 AMUEL STOOD AT THE KITCHEN WINDOW
 washing breakfast dishes, smiling as he watched his
wife waddle toward the barn. Fortunately, the bone-chilling
winter winds had given way to spring's milder temperatures. The
snow that had fallen only days before was a good reminder of
the unpredictability of Michigan weather. Thoughts of putting
his hand to the plow had crossed his mind, but he had more
important things to consider. He wouldn't dream of leaving his
wife in her strained condition.

Earlier in the week, Doctor Williams had come by and
said that the baby could arrive any time now. Though Samuel
suspected that Doc was right, nothing seemed to slow her down.
Most days she had more energy than he. Oh, he teased her about
her huge belly something awful, but she didn't seem to mind. In
truth, their days alone during the long winter months had given
them the time they needed to really get to know one another. His
wife was an amazing woman. She appreciated and responded to

his attention, no matter how she was feeling.

His heart rejoiced over the wife God had given him. Had it not been for her, he never would have known the hope that now filled his soul. Sure, he had his moments. The temptation to fall back into his old ways did creep in. Even so, caving in to those temptations was not an option. His relationship with Jesus Christ had drastically altered the way he looked at everything in his life, including his wife and coming child.

On occasion he'd find himself daydreaming about what it would be like to have a little girl, one as happy and beautiful as her mama. Often he would get caught up in the wonderment of what she would be like. Somehow or another, his thoughts would stumble upon the day they were married. He knew, without a shadow of doubt, that if God blessed him with a daughter, she would be choosing her own husband, if and when she decided to marry. No man would ever do to his daughter what he had done to Ruth. He was appalled by his choices—and they were his choices. Scheming for her hand and then treating her like she was nothing more than a piece of merchandise. No sir! If a man wanted to marry his daughter, he would have to prove himself, not only to their daughter, but to him, his wife, and any other siblings she might have at the time.

Even with all the mistakes he had made, God's hand was on his marriage. He could rejoice knowing God had shown him the error of his ways. No woman should ever be put in such a vulnerable place ....

Samuel, seeing movement out the window, looked up and saw his lumpy wife trying to mount Porcelain. His heart stopped and then sped out of control when she made it up and then came close to going over the other side.

What in the world!

Flying out the door, his steps slowed as he neared Ruth's horse. He had no desire to spook the noble creature or his wife. "Now where would you be going in such a big hurry, My Daring Porcelain Beauty? Our child should arrive any time now and it wouldn't do to have my very pregnant wife running off now would it?"

Ruth burst into a fit of giggles. "Do you remember saying something similar the day we were married when you caught me trying to jump out the window?"

He grinned. "I suppose I do. But then it had to do with my bride trying to run off. So tell me, Ruth Anne. Where are you heading? Anywhere special or just taking a turn about the farm?"

"I was planning to head over and see Jayne, but something happened when I almost fell off Porcelain."

His brow rose. "Oh! Anything I should know about?" Reaching up to lay his hand on her hard belly, he noticed a trail of fluid dripping from the saddle. "Did you have a bit of an accident, My Dear?"

She clouted him a good one. "No!"

Accustomed to these playful outbursts of hers, he ignored her reaction, but his thoughts scrambled. The only other explanation would be ... "The baby! Do you think it's time?"

When she nodded, he took off in the direction of their mothers' farmhouse. But before he was out of the yard he realized that he had forgotten something—something important. Strutting back toward his grinning wife, he said, "Sorry, Ruth. Guess I'm excited about greeting our little one."

"You're not alone, but I could use some help. My belly seems to be stuck in a hard knot."

Lifting her off her horse, he set her gently on her feet, then led her into the house. After insisting that she stay put in the chair at the table until he returned, he darted out the door to retrieve their mothers.

Ruth couldn't help but smile as she watched him leave. Although she'd like to obey his frantic order, she could not remain in her wet clothes any longer—she would freeze. Waddling into her room, she cleaned herself up, donned a comfy nightgown, secured her robe, and then went back to the kitchen to fix a cup of tea.

As of yet her pains had not started. Suspecting she still had hours to spare, she wasn't about to miss out on her favorite brew, or the yummy dinner she had in the oven. After time spent in the chilly air, she needed something to warm her insides.

Samuel, having reached the farmhouse in record time, opened the back door and yelled out, "Hey, you two ... it's time!"

Nothing!

A quick run through the empty house left him dumbfounded. Where would they go?

Time was a wasting, so he didn't give it another thought. Finding a piece of paper and pencil, he left a note on the table and went back to check on Ruth before heading out for the Doctor.

"Honey," he asked as he moved in the back door. "do you think that's wise?"

"What?" she innocently inquired, while chewing on a forkful of cheesy potatoes with ham. Glancing down at the large pile still on her plate, she shrugged. "If the baby is coming, I'll need my strength."

Samuel had no wish to order her about, so he approached the topic with care. Stooping down beside her, he said, "Do you remember what Doctor Williams said about eating when you're in labor?"

Her eyes puddled with tears, effectively shattering his heart. "Oh, Honey, come here."

The warmth of his arms about her did not help. She cried all the harder.

Emotional as she had been over the last few weeks, he refused to press her. "Ruth, you do what you think is best."

Reaching for the hanky in his pocket, she dried her tears, blew her nose, and was pushing her plate aside when Naomi and Florence burst in the back door.

Samuel, thinking this was a good time to take his leave, gently slid his fingers under her chin. When her eyes met his, he kissed her tenderly and said, "I'll be back as soon as I find Doc."

Desperate, her slender fingers grasped the front of his shirt. Pulling him close, she whispered, "Please don't be gone long. I need you with me, Samuel."

If he read her correctly, she was frightened. He nodded and then kissed her again. Sharing a concerned glance with their mothers, Samuel headed for the barn to saddle his horse, trying to understand what had just transpired. A fog of confusion swept over him. *I thought women preferred to have babies without their men around.*

Perhaps he was wrong.

Having recognized the niggling of fear in Ruth's eyes, Samuel nudged Pride into a canter. He had to get back to his wife and child as quickly as possible.

❀ ❀ ❀

With the dawn of the new day, Samuel and Ruth greeted their son, who now lay staring up at them. Yes, his delivery had been touch and go for a while, but Samuel never left her side. Their love for each other deepened in the process.

Tucked in the quilted warmth of their bed, Ruth smiled up at her husband. "Our little Kaleb is handsome, just like his papa."

Samuel couldn't resist asking, "Hmm, so you think I'm handsome, do you?"

Ruth grinned but offered no response, she was too busy examining his miniature features. "Look at the size of his hands, Samuel."

"They'll be big like mine, but you can rest assured, there are things I intend to teach him about his hands that I've learned from our Heavenly Father."

Curious, she pressed him, "Like what?"

Samuel caressed her cheek before looking down at his own hands—strong calloused hands. "I haven't always used these hands the way God intended. He gave me these hands for many things: to clear the ground, to plant, to harvest, and to take care of the farm and our animals. And then there is you, Ruth. God blessed me with a beautiful wife who needs and wants me by her side despite my imperfections. I am so thankful you didn't give up on me. I've watched the way you draw on God's strength and mine as well. God never intended for me to use these hands to bring you harm, but to help you—to support you—to walk beside you in this life—and to love you most of all."

"Yes, love ... little wonder God's Word reminds us that love is the greatest gift either of us can offer."

Samuel nodded, kissing her sweet mouth and then his son's small brow. The long night with no sleep was catching up with all of them. As he watched his wife and son drift off, God's truth about love trickled through his mind and penetrated his heart: *Charity suffereth long, and is kind; charity envieth not; charity vaunteth not itself, is not puffed up, doth not behave itself unseemly, seeketh not her own, is not easily provoked, thinketh no evil; Rejoiceth not in iniquity, but rejoiceth in the truth; beareth all things, believeth all things, hopeth all things, endureth all things. Charity never faileth.*

He whispered a prayer before drifting off that he would keep this ever before him, for only God's truth mattered when it came to loving his precious family and others who graced his life.

Daisytales

He Loves Me!

The
Michigan Chronicles

Donna's signature series, *The Michigan Chronicles*, is fiction at its best, with purpose.

As one reader tells us:

> *"Donna Rhine has a gift for writing stories that entertain and warm your heart, while teaching moral and Biblical principles. Her works may be fictional, but she has a real relationship with the Lord, as evidenced in every book she writes."*
>
> K. MacDonald

Book 1

A Decision of the Heart

He said her heart was a gift that only she could give ... *Could she?*

Not just a moving story of faith rising above suffering, slander, and life's circumstances, it's about a tender love that begins with a decision -

A Decision of the Heart

www.amazon.com/dp/0615455336
6x9 Paperback: 478 pages
Kindle Book

The Michigan Chronicles

Book 2

A Heart of Joy

When her impending loss plunges her into an uncertain future, her faith will be tested as never before ....

A moving saga of overcoming faith, it's also a heatwarming romance filled with adventure that ultimately leads to:
A Heart of Joy!

www.amazon.com/dp/0615466060
6x9 Paperback: 450 pages
Kindle Book

Book 3

A Heart Takes Flight

Will exposing the truth send her back to jail or into the arms of love?

A life changing story of God's abounding Grace and love's powerful influence - filled with intrigue, romance, and so much more ....

www.amazon.com/dp/0615486665
6x9 Paperback: 464 pages

The Michigan Chronicles

Book 4

A Heart Set Free

Her trials led to surrender. Could they also lead to her greatest blessings?

An an intriguing love story that evokes the heart's greatest passions, exposing the degradation of abuse in the light of God's Word — the power of God's redeeming love.

www.amazon.com/dp/0692021906
6x9 Paperback: 411 pages

Quick Note from Donna,

Thank you for all your continued support.

If this book has blessed you please let me know. Your comments and insights are both encouraging and enlightening. So often your input comes at a much needed time.

My hope and prayer is that my books have helped you get a little closer to the awsome God we serve.

My email: **donna@daisytales.com**

Other Works by Donna Rhine

In addition to Donna's popular series, *The Michigan Chronicles,* she has co-authored other books. Some of these titles include:

- *Still Dancing* - Gabriel Ford's autobiography shares the inspirational details of her life as a way of encouraging others yo move beyond their struggles and know that anything is possible.

- *Silent Tears, Loud Victory* - This heart wrenching story of one little girl's survival of abuse and her jourrney to become a woman of God. Edith Eddins reminds us that with God in our hearts, not only can we overcome horrific tragedy, we can forgive even the most deplorable sin and shine in the world as an example of His all-encompassing love.

You can find these and other works by Donna Rhine on Amazon.com by typing her name (Donna Rhine) in the search bar. Additional titles are in development, soon to be released.

Armoury House Publishing

Armoury House Publishing is dedicated to equipping of the saints through the printed word and other electronic media. Our mission is to draw all people one step closer in their personal relationship with Jesus Christ

Other Titles published by Armoury House Publishing:

Old Paths Series by John Charles Ryle

JC Ryle's conversational style of writing is easy to grasp and understand. Deep enough for the oldest of saints to find healthy portions of meat but lean enough to feed the new born Christian.

INSPIRATION of the Bible

How was the Bible written? Where did it come from ... Heaven? or of man? To what extent is God's word really God's Word? What do we mean when we say the Bible is inspired by God? How do the answers to these questions impact the way we live?

www.amazon.com/dp/1497476283
5x8 Paperback: 64 pages

OUR HOPE - The 5 Marks of a Good Hope

How do you distinguish a good hope from a mistaken hope that ultimately ends in a lie? Bishop Ryle gives us five characteristics of a good hope to follow.

www.amazon.com/dp/1499229798
5x8 Paperback: 48 pages

Old Paths Series (continued)

PERSEVERANCE

One of the most misunderstood topics of God's Word.

www.amazon.com/dp/1497590728
5x8 Paperback: 87 pages

KNOWING GOD THE HOLY GHOST

What place has God the Holy Ghost in your religion? What do you know of His office, His work, His indwelling, His fellowship, and His power?

www.amazon.com/dp/1499317018
5x8 Paperback: 76 pages

ALIVE OR DEAD?

By far one of JC Ryle's best talks. A topic deserving our full attention. What does God say?

This is a great read for every Christian. A good book to pass on to those who are searching for an answer to life's biggest question, are you among the living, or among the dead?

www.amazon.com/dp/1497554136
5x8 Paperback: 54 pages

C.H. Spurgeon Works

PLAIN ADVISE FOR PLAIN PEOPLE

The wit and wisdom of one of the greatest men of the 19th century. Formerly published as "John Ploughman's Talk."

Spurgeon spans the denominational lines. His focus being that *"good wisdom is that which will turn out to be wise in the end; seek it, friends, and seek it at the hands of the wisest of all teachers, the Lord Jesus."*

John Ploughman

www.amazon.com/dp/1796309044
6x9 Paperback: 165 pages

These and other Armoury House Publishing books are available on Amazon.com and other on-line book distributors.

Thank you.

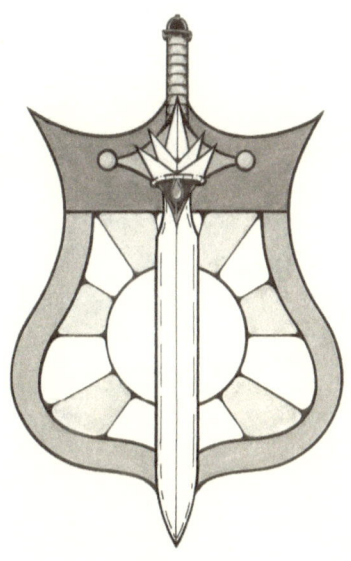

Armoury House Publishing
P.O. Box 60
Carleton, MI 48117   USA

No god is like you, O Lord.
No one can do what you do.

Psalm 86:8

GOD'S WORD Translation

www.ingramcontent.com/pod-product-compliance
Lightning Source LLC
Chambersburg PA
CBHW020832030726
47496CB00001B/196